# FORTUNE FAVOURS THE GRAVE

E. S. Drake grew up in Bedford, initially aspiring to train as a doctor but unfortunately fate intervened. She instead worked through various low-paid jobs, finally joining the police and building a varied career in criminal justice. Outside of this, she owns and runs a busy archery and survival business whilst pursuing her greatest love, writing. The darker aspects of her past have been her main motivation for creating flawed and complex characters to encapsulate the pitfalls of humanity, attempting to navigate our vulnerabilities with humour and compassion.

*Also by E. S. Drake*

The Afterlife Agency Series
*Acts of Cupidity*

# FORTUNE FAVOURS THE GRAVE

E S DRAKE

ZAFFRE

First published in the UK in 2026 by
ZAFFRE
An imprint of Bonnier Books UK
5th Floor, HYLO, 105 Bunhill Row,
London, EC1Y 8LZ



A CIP catalogue record for this book is
available from the British Library.

Hardback ISBN: 978-1-80418-623-7
Trade paperback ISBN: 978-1-80617-012-8

*Also available as an ebook and an audiobook*

1 3 5 7 9 10 8 6 4 2

Typeset by IDSUK (Data Connection) Ltd
Printed and bound in Great Britain by CPI (UK) Ltd, Croydon CR0 4YY

MIX
Paper | Supporting responsible forestry
FSC® C013604
FSC www.fsc.org

The authorised representative in the EEA is
Bonnier Books UK (Ireland) Limited.
Registered office address: Block B, The Crescent Building
Northwood, Santry, Dublin 9
D09 C6X8, Ireland
compliance@bonnierbooks.ie
www.bonnierbooks.co.uk

*For Shadow, you saved me in every way.*

*For Dad, it's high time you made me that train now,*
*I've written two books and you've had thirty-seven years to*
*get started on it. Wzm, wzm, wzm. Love Middle.*

# 1

# *Gold*

SAM RIVERA WAS SQUASHED UP on a foul-smelling train on the eastbound District Line. The man beside him, a pasty-looking student with a shaved head, was busy talking at him about his theory on escaping destiny. The student's tartan shirt was covered in pin badges, and he smelled like pickled onion flavour Monster Munch.

'Mate, it's all written out for us. But we can change it, y'know? All you gotta do is be able to see these gods that walk among us.' The man clenched his jaw as he spoke. 'There are these guys called Oracles. They have the gift. They can see the gods, they have the power to change their fate, and ours, if we follow them.'

Sam had mostly zoned out, not all that interested in mindless conspiracy theories, but he offered the occasional nod to seem polite. He adjusted his red paisley bandana so his long dark hair would provide a subtle shield between himself and Monster-Munch Man.

'You hearin' what I'm saying, fella?' the man spat, rudely waving his hand in front of Sam's face.

'I can hear you. But there's not much I can do about changing my fate, is there?'

Sam wasn't new to crazies on the train; more often than not he would get some odd looks and hurtful comments for his most distinctive feature – a milky-blue eye that had been blind since the age of five. He'd learnt at a young age when to ignore people, and that included the inane ramblings of the wandering senseless.

'Well, one day we will all open our eyes to them. There are green ones, golds and reds . . . and dark grey ones, stay well away from them,' the man rambled on, his bulging eyes scanning the carriage as if he were surrounded by enemies.

Sam's ears pricked up. 'Sorry, what?'

'The gods!' the man hissed in a low voice. 'They have glowing auras, some of the Oracles say they look like wings. We call 'em Fireflies.'

'Do you see them?' Sam queried. 'You're one of these Oracles?'

'Nah, man, I don't have the gift. But there's a website of people who do. It all happened since the Goosening.' The man tilted his phone screen towards Sam, his hand jittery as he scrolled the web page. It was on the dark web and mostly seemed to be a forum of bizarre conversations between anonymous usernames.

The train abruptly pulled into Victoria Station and the man thrust his phone back in his pocket. 'Gotta go, man. Look up the site,' he stated, handing Sam a grubby scrap of paper with the website name before exiting the train among a throng of other commuters.

Sam breathed a sigh of relief as the doors closed with their usual hiss and clatter. He had heard the term 'Goosening' more than a few times, all in relation to the strange incidents that had plagued London in recent weeks, everything from a huge sinkhole collapsing the Tower of London to the DFS sale ending. Though the city was quickly returning to normality, the Great Goosening was the hottest topic of conversation almost anywhere you went.

Sam would normally pay no mind to wild ramblings on public transport, but something the student said had turned his blood cold. He knew exactly what the Oracles could see, as he had been detecting faint colourful auras around certain people ever since the Goosening. Curiosity rose in him as the train sped through the dark tunnels of the Underground.

He finally reached his stop, exiting the station into bright February sunshine, enjoying the last leg of his journey on foot. A short while later, he arrived outside a shabby little shopfront in Pennyfields, pulling a key from his pocket and unlocking the drab red door.

The soft hum of the neon 'Open' sign seemed enough to keep evil at bay from the spiritual shop that he now owned. A sun-bleached list of services was hung in the window, everything from tarot readings to dream work. The shop sign, Path of Destiny, had been hand-painted by his father and hadn't seen a coat of varnish in years. Sam had had to run a few errands that morning so pulled a note off the door explaining his absence and started tidying the shelves, hoping to encourage some afternoon trade.

He'd been left the shop a few months prior after his mother had passed away from illness and his father had been killed in a violent altercation not long after. Running the place was a steep learning curve for a man in his mid-twenties, but he'd thrown himself into the challenge.

A few customers came and went, mostly browsers who purchased the odd knick-knack. As the afternoon wore on, Sam found himself thinking over the one-sided conversation he'd had on the Tube. It nagged at him, making him wonder if it was actually destiny of sorts that had put him in the path of the raving pickled-onion student, to learn more about his so-called ability to see something others could not. He'd consulted opticians about the auras, but several tests later, no cause was found, and follow-ups had been scheduled in three months.

Curiosity got the best of him, and he made his way to the back of the shop and down a dark stairway into the room below, fishing out the scrap of paper he'd been given from his pocket. He'd moved into the basement a few weeks before, owing to the fact his previous flat-share had ended due to 'goose-related complications', according to the landlord. Sam relished the freedom of his own place, despite the fact it smelled of mildew and had previously been used as a butcher's storage kitchen before his father had bought the building. His parents hadn't ever used the basement, so it still had some of the old steel tables and tools from its previous owners. The cold tiled floor was easy enough to mop, and Sam had set up a small metal-framed bed in the corner opposite his desk, which held his prized MSI gaming computer.

Safe in the knowledge he would hear the shop bell ring if a customer turned up, he flicked the light on, the dim bulb giving off just enough illumination to help him navigate to his computer. Locating the mysterious website took him longer than expected, despite having some knowledge of the dark web from having messed around on there as a teenager. Finally, he was granted access and began scrolling through the stories on the Oracles' website, with their claims that gods walked among the living, controlling the course of events or even killing people off, depending on their aura. Some argued they were angels, or aliens, or any other number of wild theories, but all reached the consensus that they were meddling in human lives. Normally, Sam would have scoffed at the idea, but the more he read, the more he was convinced. Undisturbed by any customers, he was absorbed for over an hour, the people on the forums claiming that some veil had been lifted, allowing a glimpse of a completely hidden world, but only for some who'd once been denied the gift of full sight. Each self-proclaimed Oracle had damaged vision in one or both eyes, setting them apart from the forum members who were unable to detect the auras but were fully invested in the lore.

Sam thought back to when he first saw one of the so-called Fireflies. It was very hazy at first, subtle tints of emerald green that emanated from a man in Covent Garden, three weeks prior. He hadn't paid much attention at the time and had put it down to tiredness.

Reluctantly, he switched the computer off and climbed the stairs to the shop, intent on cleaning the window display. As he polished the trinket display shelf, he glanced out the window, the breath catching in his throat.

A man in a long black coat was standing across the street, seemingly minding his own business; a golden aura glowed and rippled around him, pulsing like a heartbeat and extending like wings from his back. It had been a week or so since Sam had seen a gold one, but this time he paid attention. He pulled out his mobile and snapped a quick photo just as the man answered his phone, turned on his heel and walked in the direction of the Chinese restaurant around the corner.

Sam fumbled for his keys to lock the door of the shop before taking off in the direction of the man. He was bursting with curiosity, and very much convinced the morning's events were starting to line up in a strange twist of fate.

* * *

'Yeah, I'm really not feeling up to that.' Erron Grover chewed his thumbnail as he spoke on the phone in his distinct Cockney twang. The person on the other end was clearly negotiating with him. 'Honestly, I'd rather just go without a fuss. Anyway, I'm near the park. Are you here?' He changed the subject. The cool wind ruffled through his unkempt dark hair, bringing a slight glow to his pale skin.

As the call ended, he glanced over his shoulder. A thin man with long dark hair and a paisley bandana was following him, one of his eyes a milky blue. Erron thought nothing of it and headed towards Pennyfields Park, where he found a place to sit, pulling a flat lollipop from his pocket, the type dentists would give out to kids in the nineties before sugar was overly frowned upon. Erron had a stash of them in his inside pocket since giving up cigarettes, the sugar hit only just taking the edge off.

Sam watched from a distance, partially hidden by the bushes. He couldn't take his eyes off the man's golden aura; the closer he had got, the more it seemed to sparkle and burn with the intensity of starlight. Aside from a slight luminescence to his skin, the man looked every bit human, with a scar on his cheek, rough stubble and faint bruising around one eye. A tall, well-dressed woman joined him. To Sam's surprise, she shared the same aura. She glowed with more intensity, a captivating vibrance to her dark complexion, the glimmer of gold eyeshadow highlighting sparkling eyes of deep brown. The two Golds struck up conversation, with Sam straining to hear them through the rustle of leaves in the wind.

'If it isn't the new boss of Apollo,' Erron said with a smile as Freya Carthage settled next to him.

'Hey, Grover,' she said warmly, giving him a one-armed hug. 'I'm a little disappointed you didn't want a leaving party, but I guess I can understand.'

'Is it too late to cancel everything?'

'Oh, I'm not cancelling thirteen pizzas and a whole lot of alcohol just because you won't be there. We'll just have a great time without you,' she teased.

'That's good to know.' He faked a smile and stuck the lollipop on the roof of his mouth.

Freya leant forward to look him in the eye. 'How have you been anyway?'

Erron hadn't seen Freya much since she dropped him back to his flat after his long stint in hospital. She'd checked in with him via text, but having been recently promoted to run the Apollo Division, she'd had far too much on her plate, fixing all the issues her predecessor had left behind.

'I'm fine,' he lied.

'Well, Casey said he's barely seen you. We're all really worried.'

Erron's mind drifted. It had been a few weeks since the almost-end of the world. Life had quickly returned to mostly normal, the afterlife not quite as easily. Everyone at the agency had been on edge, suspicion and mistrust had hung in the air like a dense fog following the revelation that the Apollo Division boss Kendra Eckhart and her Hades accomplice, Izobella Cain, had tried to bring about the apocalypse. Apollo agents Erron Grover and Casey Hart had been caught up in the eye of the storm, both of them nearly sacrificed to open portals for the Chaos demons to travel through and run amok. But nothing was worse than the personal hell Izzy Cain had put Erron through.

Freya waited for Erron to offer any more, but he awkwardly stared off into space while tapping the lolly against his teeth.

'OK,' she finally said and pulled an envelope of documents from her inside pocket. 'Here's your official transfer letter to Hades Division and instructions for the relevant procedure at the Raphael Sanctuary. There's also your leaving card; we were hoping to give you that this evening. Casey's got the gift we arranged so I'm sure he'll pass it on.'

Erron took the envelope but didn't open it in front of her. 'Thank you. You shouldn't have gone to such trouble.'

She squeezed his arm. 'You'll be missed, Erron. There's always a space for you at Apollo.'

Erron almost regretted his decision to leave, knowing that he was going to miss out on how much better Apollo would become under Freya's command. She hadn't long been in post, but she'd already made so many positive changes. He knew it would be a culture shock going from nearly forty years of being a Cupid, undertaking the Apollo assignments making mortals fall in love, to joining the Hades Division and becoming a certified Grim Reaper. But he had to follow his heart, and Hades were expecting him to start first thing Monday morning.

'Do you know that guy?' Freya interrupted his train of thought.

He glanced up, catching sight of Sam peering from behind a bush.

'No, but he followed me here and he seems to be looking right at us.' Erron was confused, as agents were mostly imperceptible due to their natural cloaking abilities. The man scurried off once he'd been spotted.

'Strange, well, he's gone now.' Freya shrugged and stood, brushing down the wrinkles in her smart white suit. 'You know you're going to have to show your face at some point to clear your desk.'

'Casey can do that.' Erron rubbed the back of his neck.

'Don't, Erron. Don't make him do that. You're breaking his heart enough by avoiding him.' Her voice was stern. 'At some point you're going to have to face whatever it is that's driving you two apart. You're best friends, for Fates' sake.'

Erron hated himself for allowing the abuse by Izzy to cloud his relationship with Casey, having confessed his feelings to him in secret two weeks prior. Since then, he'd barely been in touch for fear of the unknown.

'OK, I'll clear my desk,' he finally agreed, a knot forming in his stomach.

'Damn right.' Freya fixed him with a formidable look. 'Anyway, I have to get back to the office. I hope you change your mind about tonight.'

He pursed his lips in a polite smile and nodded, having no intention of attending his own leaving do. He sat alone for some time, thinking about everything and nothing, the flat lolly dissolving slowly against his tongue, the first hints of spring blowing on the breeze.

* * *

Sam had rushed back to his shop, adrenaline coursing through his veins. He took the stairs to the basement two at a time, eager to upload the picture he'd taken of the man onto the Oracles website. Though the aura didn't show up on the photo, he was keen to see if anyone could identify the mysterious Gold. He settled in to read more about the so-called gods that walked among them and whether he'd inadvertently stumbled across the keys to destiny itself.

# 2

## *Hell on Me*

THE NIGHT HAD PASSED SLOWLY, the black sky fading to a deep Prussian blue as the early hours crept into the city. Standing in a pool of moonlight, Erron stared at the bed that hadn't been slept in since the day Freya had brought him home from hospital. The covers were a dull grey in the darkness, bleak and unwelcoming. Once more, he turned his back and returned to his sofa, a cold shiver running down his spine.

Perching on the sofa's edge, he chased two painkillers down with a glass of lukewarm lemonade, listening to the faint bustling of Canary Wharf outside his apartment building. His hands trembled and his left leg bounced uncontrollably on the hard wood floor. It had been over a month since he'd come home from the agency hospital, the Raphael Sanctuary, but it still didn't feel like home to him. Despite everything, all he could see in that room was *her*. He glanced down at the jagged scar on his stomach, still remembering the feeling of the blade that had left it there. The staples had all been removed, but the pain lingered. Instinctively, he hunched over, averting his gaze to the floor.

He reached for the envelope that Freya had given him, noting his appointment for the hospital was the next day, citing his Apollo wing removal and skill transfer to Hades procedure. The leaving card slipped out from the paperwork and landed by his bare feet. Tentatively, he picked it up and opened it. Dozens of messages were scrawled inside, wishing him well and saying he will be missed; the usual sentiments. But his eyes automatically sought out Casey's neat cursive and a lump formed in his throat as he read the short but sweet message.

*To my best friend. I taught you how to make people fall in love. You taught me the meaning of love. I owe you the world, Casey xxx*

He stood the card on the coffee table and reached across for his personal phone, flicking through random news sites, anything that might distract him. After a few minutes his thumb hovered over an unopened message from Casey. He tapped it.

*Is everything OK? Are we OK? Please talk to me xx*

He exhaled slowly. Casey had done much better at trying to move past the events that had nearly ended both their lives, and the world. Erron didn't seem to have the same level of resilience; he hadn't been sleeping well for weeks. It wasn't the brutal stabbing with the ceremonial dagger or the painstaking recovery following it that kept him up at night. It was the horrific memories he didn't have from the violation he suffered at the hands of Izobella Cain. He was haunted from seeing photos of his abused body, only being able to piece together the events of that night from twisted nightmares that arose from his subconscious.

It had been a closed trial for Izzy, with no public gallery. Despite that, there were more than enough people there that he knew, and the photos had been shared as evidence, making Erron endure the humiliation of being accused of being a consenting party. He'd witnessed Casey's face at seeing the pictures again, as well as having to give his own perspective on the events that unfolded in front of a room of people judging his every word, including Izzy, who had stared blankly through him the entire time. He'd wanted her to face Obliteration, a sentence that would have seen her chewed up into an atomic mass of eternal suffering, but they'd only settled on sending her to Hell, a weak punishment by comparison.

He took another long sip of the lemonade and scrolled back through his message chain. He'd not responded in three days since Casey had suggested making him dinner one evening. He tapped out a reply and nervously clicked 'send'.

*I'm sorry, everything's OK. I'm just not having a good time right now.*

The phone buzzed within three minutes.

*Want me to come over? Just to talk? xx*

*Why are you awake, Case?*

*I'm worried about you xx*

*Go to sleep, you absolute lamp. I'm fine. I just got to figure something out.*

*OK . . . Try and sleep if you can xx*

He sat poised with the phone, feeling waves of different emotions crashing into him. Tears stung his eyes, and he angrily wiped them away before sending one last goodnight message and curling back up on the sofa, a thin blanket wrapped round him.

* * *

Several streets away, in the lamplit basement in Pennyfields, Sam Rivera was still up, the glow of the computer highlighting his tired eyes. His research on the Oracles website had taken him deeper into the rabbit hole that was the 'Firefly People' phenomenon. Most people offered ideas that were generally peaceful, spiritual in nature, and believed that the Fireflies were simply angels or guardian beings. A darker thread on the forum suggested that those with charcoal auras, nicknamed the Greys, had been spotted in places where people had died, insinuating that they may have been the cause. Sam had seen a lot of the dark grey ones before but had never stuck around long enough to witness a death.

He chewed at his nails, thinking about his own mother, who had died of a congenital heart defect while waiting for a transplant. He didn't remember seeing a Grey near her, but he'd not been at her bedside when she'd passed.

His dad had been tragically killed when an unstable teenager had gone on a stabbing rampage at their local bus stop one evening, incensed by rage and online radicalisation. The boy, having been rejected by a sixteen-year-old girl waiting for the bus, took out a bowie knife and attacked five teenage girls, when Sam's dad had stepped in to intervene. He'd suffered a fatal injury to his abdomen but was hailed a hero by the media when the CCTV had shown him use his body as a shield.

The more he had read about the Greys, the more Sam was convinced they were responsible for his death. His fingers hovered hesitantly over the keyboard. He had to know. Trembling, he brought up the footage of the Pennyfields Bus Stop Massacre, which had been published online since it happened. Some of the gory bits had been redacted carefully, but the general affray was exceptionally clear for a city camera.

He saw his beloved father standing a few metres from the group of girls, the killer lingering nearby, eight minutes before the attack. Sam, having seen the footage a couple of times, had never watched it so intently. An unknown woman entered the frame and briefly spoke with Sam's dad, seemingly laughing at something he'd said, touching his elbow before making her way down the road out of shot. Sam watched it again. Just as the woman appeared on screen, there was a brief flickering, a smudge of fuzzy shadow that seemed to envelop her. Initially, it had looked like static on the lens. But it faded after she made contact with his dad. Sam watched it again. And again. Each time, the blurring and the flickering was there.

The grief in his stomach made room for a hot anger. His father's death appeared to have been orchestrated by one of the Greys, and he wanted answers. He went back to the Oracles site and joined a thread talking about the Greys, furiously stabbing at the keys as he typed up his own experience. Other users had already commented on his picture of the Gold, asking him for more information and proof of the things he could see. He welled up with excitement at the prospect of being another confirmed Oracle, and able to see beyond the veil of mortality, convinced his vision loss was a hidden blessing from some higher power, for a much greater purpose.

He daydreamed about what it could mean for him: the admiration that other Oracles received was the kind of attention he'd never had in his life, and to be valued in such a way gave him butterflies in his stomach. He eagerly replied to several comments, making promises to collect more photos of other Fireflies he saw out and about.

The digital clock display on his laptop blinked at 4.04 a.m., and he realised if he didn't get any sleep, he wouldn't be able to function at all when he opened the shop. Reluctantly, he switched the computer off and curled up on his narrow bed, drifting off to grand ideas of fame and recognition.

# 3

## *Nothing Breaks Like a Heart*

CASEY HART WAS STOOD OUTSIDE of the Raphael Sanctuary in Weston Rise, central London, just as Erron was making his way to his skill transfer appointment. A cold breeze was building from the east, the skies threatening rain. Shivering, Casey buttoned his old Chesterfield coat and adjusted his grey trilby, his long sandy hair tangling in the wind. The hospital building itself appeared grey and uninviting, with drab outer walls and a gated front entrance, despite its top-of-the-range interior and modern architecture. It was completely cloaked from the mortal world, set within one of the agency liminal zones which could only be seen by those in the afterlife. To anyone else, it took on the appearance of a private multi-storey building with nothing outstanding to catch the eye. Medical staff came and went through the doors, briefly adding a glow to the drab morning with their warm wings of bright light, which earnt them the name Archangels.

Erron cautiously approached him, wringing his hands together and wearing a pained expression. 'Hey, Case. I assume you're here to see me.'

'I knew you'd be here. Sorry, is that creepy?' Casey greeted him with an anxious grin.

'Super creepy. Not quite *watching me sleep* creepy, but it's up there.' Erron shook his head and smiled.

'Well, I always watch you sleep, but you don't know that,' Casey joked.

'Liar. I don't sleep. Not anymore anyhow.' Erron pushed his hands into the pockets of his black overcoat and looked at the floor.

'Well, maybe if you did I might watch you more.' Casey rolled his eyes emphatically.

'Sorry for the interruption in service.'

A short pause hung between them, Casey's expression softening. 'Joking aside, I brought your farewell gift from Apollo.' He lifted a carrier bag that was hung on his wrist.

'You didn't need to go to any effort coming here.' Erron awkwardly shifted his feet on the concrete as a few drops of rain began to fall.

'It's no effort. Look, I know you need space, and I'm not here to talk about anything heavy. But I don't think you should go through this alone. I'm coming in with you, and I will just be there if you need me, that's all ... If you want, of course,' Casey blurted out, his hands raised in a pacifying manner, the carrier bag swinging against his side. 'It's just ... I've been through the skills transfer process and it's no walk in the park.'

Casey had once upon a time belonged to the Nemesis Division, agents responsible for dishing out justice and vengeance, but had transferred to Apollo when he realised he wasn't cut out for seeing people suffer, no matter how much they deserved it. He'd more than settled in as a Cupid, delighting in the gentle orchestration of mortals falling in love, and had long outstayed his contractual requirements of two hundred years service.

Erron nodded, grateful for the support, and nervously went through the main door with Casey in tow. He had a rough idea of what needed to happen, but he wasn't looking forward to any of it. Agents who transferred to other departments had to have a full skill flush, involving an entire body blood transfusion, which took anywhere between ten and twenty-four hours, and the removal of their existing wings. It would take a while for his Hades wings to grow in their place, and he wasn't looking forward to being flightless for the first time in decades.

Once inside, the hospital smell assaulted Erron with a myriad of bad memories and Casey gently guided him towards the reception area. They were greeted by Dr Carroway, the soul replication specialist and overall most unenthusiastic man they had ever met. He was tall, with a broad nose, deep blue eyes and wore the expression of a man who had only just sat down before being asked to take the bins out.

'Some of our transferees experience strange dreams during the process. It's not unlike having a bad trip on psychedelic mushrooms or maybe getting the ice-cream van portal to the moon six times in a row at double speed,' the doctor explained as he filled out the relevant paperwork. 'I'm sure you've probably tried both.' He looked Erron up and down with sheer disdain.

'No, actually—' Erron protested.

'Seven times in a row,' Casey mumbled, stifling a laugh.

'Yeah … maybe … but not the mushrooms.' Erron gave Casey a sideways glance.

'I thought as much,' the doctor muttered. 'You'll be sedated through the wing removal, naturally. From your notes you have significant scar tissue on your back. We will be careful not to interrupt the healing on that, however you do understand we can't guarantee that it won't be somewhat worsened?'

Erron nodded, trying to forget the crudely carved runes that ran down his spine.

'If you sign here, and here. The procedure requires us to momentarily stop your Photoplasmiacelestioral Infusion, but this is standard. It gets reset pretty quickly.' Dr Carroway was referring to what was commonly known as the cosmic satsuma, the pulsing sphere of pure celestial energy that powered agents' hearts and kept their replicated souls functioning as their old heart would have. He pushed a consent form over. 'We can get you prepped straightaway. Any questions?'

Erron's face grew pale. 'You've got to stop my heart?'

Casey reached over and squeezed his hand. 'It's fine, they'll bring you right back. It's much more reliable than a human heart. I've had mine done.'

'Like your friend says, we know what we're doing.' Dr Carroway nodded towards the consent form, clearly growing impatient.

'OK. So what happens to my Apollo blood?' Erron asked, curious.

'Bit of a weird question.' The doctor seemed nonplussed. 'We all toast to your health and drink it following the surgery.'

Erron raised an eyebrow.

'Of course, that's illegal. So, it gets disposed of like any medical waste. Any sensible questions?' Dr Carroway stood up before Erron could think of anything the man might consider sensible.

The doctor introduced the newest member of the Archangel hospital team, Dr Jared Enleigh, as he stepped into the room with a chart. He had a warm smile, a slight gap between his teeth and reddish hair. By the overall weathering of his young face and scruffy facial hair, he looked more like he belonged on a survival show than in a surgical theatre. He shook Erron's hand and greeted Casey with a polite nod.

'Dr Enleigh will be leading your procedure today, Agent Grover,' Dr Carroway explained. 'He's new to the agency but his experience is extensive from his mortal life as a trauma surgeon and will be specialising in Afterlife Procedures. You're his first patient in this department.'

'That's not overly encouraging, no offence. There, uh, aren't many wings on normal people.' Erron laughed nervously, concerned he was being used as a guinea pig.

'There won't be any on you shortly either,' Dr Carroway chided. 'But Dr Enleigh will be completely proficient in cutting bits off of you, so best to just trust that he knows what he's doing.'

Erron was led away into a room full of daunting equipment, where he was asked to change into a surgical gown and lie on a gurney as more medical staff surrounded him, going through the details of each procedure before he was sedated. The room gradually faded from vision, and he was transported into a world of hazy dreams and timelessness.

* * *

It was the early hours of the next morning when he eventually awoke, groggy and nauseous in an unfamiliar part of the hospital. Casey's hand was resting on his, though he was fast asleep in the chair next to his bed. He had been placed on his side to recover from the wing removal surgery and he instantly felt they were missing, the comforting weight of them no longer hanging on his shoulders. It would be a while before he grew his Hades wings, though at least his new ones would not be marred by the damage caused by Izzy, or stained in his own blood from Elzifur's blade. Despite how long it had been since he'd grown his first set of wings, he could easily recall the dull growing pains and wasn't looking forward to the discomfort of the gene activation injections he needed to start off his new ones. Not to mention having to be extra careful not to lie on his back until they were strong enough to support his weight.

He watched Casey as he slept, the gentle glow of his Apollo Flush adding radiance to the dark corner of the hospital room. Erron would sorely miss having the Flush, and the ability to charm his way in or out of anything when using it. He watched Casey for some time – he looked so peaceful and angelic in the dim light, his long sandy hair loose around his shoulders – until he stirred, his eyes blinking away sleep.

'Hey, you made it.' Casey smiled softly, his hand tightening around Erron's. 'How are you feeling?'

'Like death warmed up,' he answered croakily. 'Well, I guess that was the objective. I had some weird dreams. I was back in Bedford, on the town bridge following that bloke, Gunther Hoffmann.' Erron furrowed his brow as he painfully remembered the real Gunther, who had jumped to his death into the river instead of falling in love as he was meant to. 'But this time, he was beckoning me to follow, so I did. I felt the cold of the water, dragging me under. But he was talking to me, saying something . . . something about bad energy.'

'It just sounds like a nightmare from seeing him jump,' Casey reasoned. 'Dr Carroway said you'd have bad dreams.'

'Yeah, you're right. But he was so insistent. Repeating it over and over.' Erron shook the thought away and glanced down at his hands, no longer having the radiant glow of a Cupid. 'Do I still . . . look like me?' Erron was conscious that he would now have the gaze-averting aura of death, the *Umbra Noctis* power coursing through his new blood that all Reapers possessed.

Casey leant forward, his expression sincere. 'Of course you do. You always will to me. You feel colder to the touch though. I don't know if that comes with the Hades territory or the anaesthetic.'

'Who knows. But I regret agreeing to attend my Hades induction tomorrow.' Erron groaned at the thought of it, but the medical staff had assured him he would be fine after a good night's sleep.

'Just keep on top of the painkillers and you'll manage. You're tough.'

'If you say so. But you need to go home, get some proper rest.' Erron slowly withdrew his hand.

'You don't want me to stay?' Casey looked hurt. 'I could get you some food and we can chat?'

'It's probably for the best if you go home.'

Casey's expression fell. He nodded, resigned to the fact he was being dismissed. 'OK. As you wish.'

'I'll see you soon?'

Casey sighed and stood up. 'Yeah, OK, sure.' He set down the gift from the Apollo team on his chair and didn't look back as he left the ward, hurt and confused that Erron had turned so cold towards him. He understood but couldn't help the feeling that he was being punished for something he didn't do.

* * *

Later that evening, Casey was regretting folding to the persistent requests by his enthusiastic trainee, Nikita Wolf, to join her at their favourite hangout spot, Nightjar in Shoreditch.

He was moping at a small round table when she set down an enticing milkshake in front of him, announcing its flavour as cinnamon, chocolate and toffee.

Nightjar, with its medley of jazz and vibrant cocktails, was a popular spot for agents of all divisions to while away the hours incognito among mortals. Its cosy decor and good music made it the perfect place for quiet conversation and a great atmosphere, whether you were living your best life or socialising after death.

Casey couldn't help but notice the absence of a cocktail umbrella beside the monolithic milkshake and was trying his best to raise his spirits. Nikita was a great person, he enjoyed working with her and couldn't deny that her involvement in saving his and Erron's lives had strengthened their friendship tenfold, but it wasn't the same as working with Erron. Nothing was the same anymore.

'That was well over a tenner so don't just stare at it.' Nikita nodded towards his drink. She smiled widely at him. Her red hair, tied up in a halo of braids, perfectly contrasted against her green sparkly jumper. She sipped on a tangy pineapple cocktail, wrinkling her nose at the strength of the alcohol. 'Now I've got to take shifts in that goddamn call centre, I am spending my money wisely.'

'You'll get used to it.' Casey gave her a wan smile and took a sip from his drink, not entirely convinced the flavours complemented each other. 'No one enjoys the side hustles for mortal money.'

'I wish the agency would pay us in pounds and not bloody novas. It's great spending money on the moon but it hardly foots the bill for a decent Burger King,' Nikita scoffed, having only just got to grips with the two currencies. 'And I hate dealing with complaints for a dating site, it's mind-numbing and painfully ironic.'

'There are much better restaurants in Elysion than Burger King,' Casey chided, his head snapping round when a cheerful voice called his name over the crowd.

It belonged to Ember Songfire, who he'd known for years. She was an agent of the Fortuna Division, responsible for dishing out luck, and was joy personified. She leant down to give him a warm hug, standing out like a sore thumb in her neon pink tie-dye dungarees and long blonde plaits. The light shimmered off her colourful and iridescent butterfly wings, a unique Fortuna trait, perfectly complementing her usual luminous attire. 'Can we join you?' She had company.

Dion Laszlo from Nemesis gave Casey a warm smile. They had met a few times but never at length. He was usually fairly quiet; a sturdy man with a deep voice and an unspoken authority, common among the Nemesis agents. Behind him stood a familiar-looking man who reached over to shake Casey's hand.

'Jared, Jared Enleigh, you remember me from yesterday? I did the surgery on your Hades friend at the Raph.' The young Archangel smiled.

'Yes, of course, sorry. How's he doing?' Casey took another sip of his strange milkshake.

'Oh, just fine, he was discharged a few hours ago with a ton of pain relief. There were no complications.' Jared took up a seat at the table, followed by Ember and Dion.

'Good to hear.'

'Nice to meet you.' Nikita shook the doctor's hand. 'I love your tattoo, that's really intricate.' She noted the complex mandala design on his forearm.

'Oh, thank you. It's one of those so-called magic ones from Arcane Ink,' Jared answered, showing the tattoo around the table. 'It's on Elysion. There's a new artist there, apparently the artwork gives you some kind of magical boost, but nothing's changed for me.'

'What was it meant to do?' Nikita asked.

'Supposedly give me more energy, but I reckon they're just a gimmick.'

'You'll have to introduce me to the artist,' Ember replied. 'I've been thinking of getting some more ink.'

'I'm sure I've got his card here somewhere.' Jared fished around in his pocket as Dion changed the subject.

'Osato sends her regards, Casey, Nikita,' Dion said in his low timbre. He referred to his boss, Osato M'Raya at Nemesis division, who was still cleaning up the loose ends of the Great Goosening, but ever grateful for the efforts of the two Cupids for their help in restoring the natural order. 'She's been singing your praises for some time now.'

'Are we due any medals?' Nikita teased.

'Well, you'll have to take that up with her.' Dion gave her a hearty smile.

'I best get us some drinks,' Ember announced, pocketing the tattoo artist's business card before heading to the bar.

Two hours passed, and the conversation naturally leant towards work. Nikita was describing one of her latest assignments in great detail, particularly focusing on the distinct improvement of her marksmanship.

'Nikita, I bet you're having a great time now the world isn't ending.' The cheerful Fortuna agent sipped on her strawberry and kiwi cocktail with a mischievous grin.

'I have to say I am thoroughly enjoying my new life, or death, or whatever this is. Now things are settled, anyhow,' she agreed.

'Oh, I will have to add you to our social media.' Ember pulled her phone out of her bag.

Nikita hadn't realised there was such a thing in the afterlife. She'd gone cold turkey from scrolling aimlessly through feeds and it had been almost as much a shock to the system as being cold-baked in a tank of celestial water. 'I take it I can't add all my old friends.' She laughed at the thought.

'Unfortunately not.' Ember grinned and opened an app called Fatesbook.

Nikita snorted at the name. 'They really went there.'

'The agency love a terrible play on words at times.' Dion chuckled. 'At least you are settling in quickly. Casey must be a great teacher, Nikita.'

'He is, yes. He's exceptionally patient with all my questions still, annoying as I am.' Nikita smiled at her mentor, who was still nursing his milkshake.

'You're no trouble,' Casey replied quietly, with a half-smile.

'Still adjusting to a new crewmate?' Jared asked, sensing Casey was far from his cheerful self. 'What was it, thirty-odd years with your last one? That's a huge change. Still, at least the replacement is young and beautiful. What more could you want?' Jared winked at Nikita.

Casey gave them a weak grin.

'That's quite enough of that.' Nikita laughed it off. 'Of course it's a big adjustment. Trust me, I am still getting used to the afterlife.'

'How long has it been now?' Ember asked.

'About six and a half weeks, but no point looking back really, not when the afterlife is so much livelier.' Nikita beamed.

'Oh wow, you are basically a baby then!' Ember clapped excitedly. 'I am coming up to my . . .' she went quiet while totting up the years in her head then resorting to counting on her fingers '. . . around fifty-three years, I think.'

'Don't worry, Nikita, I am only seven months in,' the young surgeon added. 'It's all new for me too.'

Jared and Ember went to the bar for another round of drinks, and Dion took his cue to leave; he rarely stayed out past ten. Nikita leant towards Casey as he checked his phone for the umpteenth time that evening.

'What's going on, Casey? You're still on your first Mega Milky Mocha Moo or whatever it's called.' She frowned at the half-full milkshake. 'That's got to be warm by now.'

He sighed. 'It's nothing.'

'No, it's not.'

'It's Erron,' Casey caved.

'What's he doing? Or not doing? Or doing wrong?' Nikita prodded.

'He had his wing surgery and transfusion last night. I stayed with him till he woke up, but then he pretty much dismissed me. Since he stayed over on my birthday, he's barely spoken to me. I don't know what I've done wrong.'

'Oh, he stayed over?' Nikita asked. 'As in, just as friends, or . . .' She tried to wink subtly but it looked anything but.

'He confessed he's in love with me.' Casey smiled shyly at the memory.

Nikita grinned widely. 'So, a double dose of Apollo Flush in one bed, eh?' she teased. 'Must have been electric.'

'No, nothing happened. Erron wasn't even fit to be flying let alone … anything else. And I'm really not the type to jump into things. Call me old-fashioned.'

'That's understandable, there's no rushing these things. I take it he wasn't hoping for more and felt like you weren't interested?'

'No, not at all. If anything, he was nervous about staying in the first place. It took a long time for him to be comfortable with the idea of sleeping next to me fully dressed.' Casey took his hat off and scratched the top of his head. 'I don't know if I did something wrong to upset him, as he's completely shut me out now.'

Nikita thought for a moment. 'I don't think it's anything you've done, Casey. He's been through a lot. You both have, but Izzy's trial was harrowing. Those photos, everything he's suffered because of her, it must have been pretty traumatic.'

'But why has he changed after that night?' Casey looked morose.

Nikita softened her voice and gripped his arm gently. 'Trauma like that can manifest at any point. Maybe the realisation that physical intimacy is now on the table has triggered it. You haven't done anything wrong; I think maybe we need to try and give him space.'

'I suppose you're right.' Casey squashed the sides of his hat to his temples in exasperation.

'He just needs time; when someone's gone through something like that, they take a while to distinguish between healthy affection and assault.' Nikita sat back and sucked the straw of her cocktail. 'You've waited all these years for each other, it will happen, just give him time.'

Casey nodded reluctantly. 'I guess we have plenty of that now.'

# 4

## *Bulletproof*

AFTER CLOSING UP THE SHOP on Sunday night, Sam slunk down to his computer and buried himself in research, reading everything there was on the Oracles website. He was seeing into a dark world of mystery and magic that his parents had only dreamt of finding. It spurred him on to know more.

*Take control of your destiny!* the chat thread had screamed at the top of the Oracles forum; it hadn't taken Sam long to get absorbed into the rage posts of other members that were convinced the Fireflies were responsible for killing people or changing their destiny for the worse. The thread had become its own echo chamber of negative experiences and opinions, and Sam was lapping it up. He'd quickly connected with another user of the forum, who shared a similar anger towards the Greys. They bonded over a common interest in racing and the fact they both lived in London.

It wasn't long before he had a private message blink up on his screen, asking him if he was willing to prove himself as an Oracle. He was determined to become recognised for his unique abilities, even if the request felt wildly uncomfortable to him. Despite his concerns, Sam craved the attention of the verified Oracles, as they had a growing and dedicated fanbase, and he was willing to do whatever it took to be recognised as one. They were revered, treated like celebrities among the forum users without the gift, and he desperately wanted to be their next icon.

He was on his third energy drink before overwhelming exhaustion finally persuaded him to switch the computer off and get some sleep. His special task for the Oracles was the next morning, and he wasn't about to let them down. He clambered into the small metal bed, the springs creaking under his weight.

He slept fitfully, his conscience at war with him all night, until the swelling sound of morning traffic slowly roused him from his bed. When leaving the shop, he paused briefly, wondering if he was doing the right thing and whether he ought to open up the shop as normal instead, before finally convincing himself he wanted to be more than just a shopkeeper. His journey took him towards Kensington, where he took up a seat outside a place that was renowned for its profiteroles.

Coffee and mini binoculars in hand, he waited.

* * *

A few miles away, Erron had woken himself up by strangling a sofa cushion, his unconscious mind having conjured hideous nightmares of his attack. He sat up, his heart racing and cold sweat glistening on his skin. It took a few moments for him to recognise the dark shapes in his living room and the fact that he was alone. His phone screen showed 5.32 a.m., and he was due to start his first day at Hades at 7.30. He breathed deeply for several minutes, chasing the mental images from his consciousness.

It was still dark, the blinds partially open, allowing the glow of city lights to highlight the vague shapes of his open-plan living area. The floor-to-ceiling fish tank he'd dedicated hours to maintaining bubbled quietly, its colourful residents swirling and flitting through the various nooks and crannies of the rocks and wavering aquatic plants, completely oblivious to life outside their glass walls.

Erron's eyes traced the room in the darkness, falling on the carrier bag he'd brought home containing his Apollo leaving gift. It had sat unopened since Casey had left it with him at the hospital, but he knew he couldn't ignore it for much longer. Reluctantly, he leant over and dragged it towards him, then carefully rested it on his lap.

Inside, there was a small box neatly wrapped in gold paper. Within it was a velvet case that contained a very expensive watch in gunmetal and black. He turned the watch over in his hands, noticing a distinct and familiar inscription on the back: *Evil is powerless when the good are unafraid.* A lump formed in his throat; he knew Casey must have had it engraved with the same phrase that was on the lighter his brother had given him, since he'd lost it at the scene of one of the failed assignments that had led up to the Great Goosening. He slid the watch onto his left wrist and fastened the metal clasp.

Two buses and over an hour and a half later, Erron shuffled through the entrance of Highgate Cemetery as flocks of dawn birds finished off their repertoire among the spring branches. His back was still sore from the wing removal, but he'd been given the all-clear to start work and also a hefty prescription of morphine-based painkillers. He clasped a coffee in one hand and was nursing a headache from his sleepless night, his mind struggling to switch off from the images it had created in his nightmares.

Deeper within the confines of the cemetery, surrounded by the eternally peaceful, where the birdsong grew quiet and the air carried the unheard whispers of the dead, Erron descended the stone steps that led to the Hades headquarters.

Set into a grey stone wall was the door of an unassuming mausoleum draped with old ivy and wisteria. Above the heavy door was a carved inscription of *Morior Invictus* in lichen-rich copperplate. The memorial plaque read 'Ed Les Orsman, 1866–1934' and was positioned above a wrought-iron knocker. In all the years the door had been in place, not one passing person had questioned there being a knocker on the entrance to a crypt, and it was wise not to wonder who might have answered. Incidentally, Erron had an access card that he swiped under the plaque which caused the creaking door to swing inward and allow him entry to the inner vestibule of the Hades Division. A wide spiral stairway led deep into the offices where the Reapers went about their daily admin tasks, far below the lowest crypt of the cemetery. Remarkably, it was not a grim or dingy workspace. Great care had been taken in sculpting the lofty ceiling spaces into well-lit vaulted areas, where sunlight-simulation bulbs bounced soft but cheerful lighting around the stonework. The offices were edged with modern water features, including an artificially created stream which separated workspaces, softened by multiple exotic plants. The rooms were echoey and clean, rich with sandstone tones and decorated with contemporary adaptations of artwork from ancient civilisations, ranging from Roman columns, Greek statues and Egyptian papyrus paintings. Erron had initially thought it looked like a luxurious version of the Aztec Zone in *The Crystal Maze*.

A further set of steps led downwards to a café known as The Casket. The stream above formed a waterfall into a vast koi pond in the centre of the seating area, where plush sofas and armchairs were dotted around coffee tables.

He approached his new boss's office and tentatively knocked on the glass-paned door. The name 'Merletta Crawford' was painted in gold lettering on the glass, but everyone knew her as Lettie. In life she'd been a formidable prosecution barrister, and in death she had climbed the ranks to be a specialist in reaping the souls of the criminal underworld.

'Enter!' her cold voice called through the door.

The office was small and adorned with neatly shelved files and an exceptionally large elephant-shaped lamp in the middle of the floor. It added character to what would be a very bland space. Lettie never explained why it was there, and no one ever mentioned it.

She motioned for him to sit in one of the black swivel chairs opposite her desk. He inched his way around the huge elephant lamp and awkwardly settled into the chair.

Lettie's gaze was stern; her eyes, hawk-like. Two silver stripes on her dark hair framed her face, and her age was near impossible to place. She was well aware of his involvement in the recent events nicknamed the Great Goosening, as she had been on the panel during the trial of Izobella Cain. Erron could barely make eye contact with her, knowing she'd seen the photos of his abuse.

'How are you coping, Grover?'

'With the transfer?'

'Not with the transfer.'

He paused, conscious of his leg bouncing with built-up anxiety. 'I'm not doing so great,' he finally admitted.

'Have you had any counselling yet?' she asked, leaning back in her chair.

He shook his head.

'Well, we have two options here: you can head over to the Raphael Sanctuary and get booked in for some regular counselling and we grant you extended leave, or you can take your first assignment today to get you into the swing of things. It might be a welcome distraction.'

'I'll take the job.'

'OK. But I want you to look at support options. I need my staff at their best.'

He nodded reluctantly, conscious that she'd politely told him she wouldn't put up with anyone that wasn't pulling their weight.

'Like the initial day of the Apollo Flush, you'll likely experience the "Day of Sorrow", an unbearable weight of grief as you get used to your *Umbra Noctis*.' Lettie looked him up and down. 'But you look miserable enough as it is, so I can't imagine you'll notice when it starts to kick in.'

'Oh.'

She handed him a card with a name, location and time of death. 'You'll be shadowing Theodore Roscoe; I know you know each other. Might do you good to start off with a familiar face.'

'Thank you.' He pocketed the card and stood to leave.

'And, Grover,' she said firmly. 'If you find this isn't the right place for you, let me know sooner rather than later and I'll fast-track your return to Apollo.'

He left her office, feeling remarkably unwelcome, but determined to prove her wrong.

Roscoe, the resident friendly Reaper with a retro rock-star look, was delighting a few colleagues with stories of his youth around the water cooler in the main open-plan office when Erron approached him. His gold tooth and various piercings glinted in the light as his animated expressions brought forth laughs from the other Reapers.

'Ah, here he is: man of the hour, young Grover,' Roscoe greeted him warmly and placed one ring-bedecked hand on his shoulder. 'How're you settling in, son? Ready to be a certified Ghoster?' he asked, referring to the unofficial term for Reapers with an enthusiastic tone.

'As ready as I can be.' Erron quickly noticed the lights had started flickering within a five-metre radius of where he stood.

'You'll be fine. Nice area we're heading to, near Fortuna HQ for your first reap, we might even be lucky enough to see our butterfly-winged friends milling around.'

'Kensington, could be worse,' Erron agreed.

'Yep. We'll set off when you're ready. This one is your job, the rest today you can just observe. We need to figure out how you react to taking a soul before giving you too many in a day.' Roscoe nodded towards the ceiling. 'Oh, and for future reference, once you get on a live job you need to leave via the south tunnel, as everyone gets pissy with the lights going berserk.'

'Noted.' It was only then Erron saw a crudely written sign on a nearby wall stating *NO FLICKERS YOU FUCKERS* over a row of desks, their occupants throwing him scornful glances as their laptop screens crazed with distortion.

# 5

## *Over the Rainbow*

THE STREETS OF KENSINGTON WERE busy with spring term school trips visiting various areas of interest, the newest an urban goose-petting farm that had just opened its doors to visitors near Holland Park, which everyone had concluded was an awful idea, but they opened it anyway. Roscoe sauntered along, hands in the pockets of his suede drainpipe trousers, the slight heels of his faux-snakeskin boots tapping gently as he walked. Erron had dressed in plain suit trousers that morning, black tie and crisp white shirt, his usual mid-length overcoat flapping in the breeze in time with Roscoe's footsteps.

The assignment card wobbled slightly in Erron's trembling hand. The name read Hannah Hallington, and she would lose her life on the corner of Exhibition and Cromwell roads and was due to arrive in half an hour. He had no idea what she looked like, but her date of birth made him doubt why he had made the transfer to Hades Division. Roscoe had kindly checked her file before they left so he could point her out, firmly reminding Erron that it was his job to do that with every assignment in future.

Roscoe made small talk as Erron occasionally checked the time on his phone. There'd been no message from Casey all day, which was most unusual. He paced back and forth, dying for a cigarette, his nerves on edge.

A swell of schoolchildren was approaching the Natural History Museum to their left, their excitable chatter filling the air and their brightly coloured backpacks bobbing along behind them. They must have only been around seven or eight years old.

'Look lively, kid, you're up.' Roscoe gently nudged Erron who had zoned out from his surroundings and was lost in his thoughts.

A group of schoolboys was chasing a young girl out of the gates of the museum, hurling taunts at her. Her eyes streamed with tears and there were scuff marks on her bare knees.

'Hannah, Hannah's got a stammer, beat her with a big old hammer!' the boys taunted her.

The young girl was ten feet from Erron when one boy caught her by the backpack and pulled it from her shoulders. He removed a soft unicorn toy from her bag and threw it as far as he could into the road, laughing in her tear-stained face, just as a teacher was jogging out of the museum gates screaming their names.

Erron closed his eyes, took a deep breath and brushed his hand against the arm of the child as she sprinted past him into traffic to fetch her unicorn. He didn't open his eyes until after the squeal of brakes and sickening thud. The stuffed toy vaulted into the gutter, a spatter of blood across its rainbow tail.

Erron clenched his jaw as he faced the boys. Roscoe had to hold him back.

'This isn't our fight, kid,' Roscoe said softly and led him away before the screaming started. The driver of the BMW was already calling an ambulance; the teacher had just got to the roadside and was shouting orders to the other children who had started to gather.

Around the corner, with a shaking hand, Erron dutifully recorded Hannah's final thoughts. It was just one word: *Starlight.*

Roscoe allowed Erron to do what came naturally to most Reapers on their first assignment. He stayed near the scene, unspeaking. Erron understood the impact of taking a soul was part of the process, and he was not new to being at grisly scenes of accidents from his previous life as a detective, but this one had clawed the last of his humanity from the pit of his stomach. First responders had tried to resuscitate the girl, but she died of internal bleeding at the roadside. There was a brief flutter and twinkle of multicoloured lights across her body that only the Reapers could see.

'Beautiful, when a soul goes straight to Arcadia. Instant, the innocent never have to wait for their paradise,' Roscoe said quietly, leading Erron far enough so they could observe the scene from a distance. 'It reminds me of Christmas lights on a foggy night. A glimmer of colour against the bleakness.'

After the ambulance had taken her away and the police were on scene, the older Hades agent tapped Erron's arm.

'Time to move on. You know she's in a good place.' Roscoe walked off round the corner, humming a steady tune.

'I'll be there in a sec,' Erron called after him, jogging back over to the road where Hannah Hallington had fallen.

When Erron caught up to his mentor again, the senior Reaper explained their next move. 'We're heading south of the river. We've got forty minutes. Are you up to walking there? Lettie said you've got to go easy after your injuries and the wing surgery, of course.'

'I can manage.' Erron didn't want to say that he'd suffered a half-hour flight in stormy weather, still held together with surgical staples, in order to profess his love to the man that he was currently avoiding for no good reason. He was confident he could manage a leisurely stroll.

They had only been walking for ten minutes when Roscoe had an urgent phone call. His face dropped its usual cheery demeanour into one of deep concern as the voice on the other end explained the situation. He ended the call and pulled a card from his pocket.

'We've got a blind card. You know the ones . . . when there's an unexpected death,' Roscoe said solemnly. Words slowly crawled across the card, forming a name and time of death.

Erron was well aware of them. It wasn't long ago that his own name had appeared on one, the night he'd almost died for the second time.

'I really hope this isn't another apocalypse in the making.' Erron went pale, all the anxiety of the disastrous Apollo assignments flooding back to him. Roscoe grabbed his shoulder as if to steady him.

'No, no, nothing like that. It's an agent, not a mortal. One of the Archangels is already on scene; they must have been nearby. I'm the nearest senior agent, so I've got to attend, you won't need to do anything.'

'Oh, right, OK.' Erron swayed a little as his heart rate went back to normal. 'Who is it?'

'Willow Madison.' Roscoe read off the assignment card before folding it and putting it in his top pocket. 'I just don't understand though. She's a Fortuna agent, they're damn near indestructible with all their luck, and Lettie said this sounds like foul play. In all my years I've never once heard of one turning up dead like this, though there's been mutterings around the office that the Goosening messed up a few things that haven't yet been ironed out.'

'Like what?' Erron looked at him, perplexed, the surge of worry once again bubbling to the surface.

'I overheard Lettie speaking on a conference call with the other bosses that there are some lasting effects of the veil being thinned. Mostly around the portals or something. I wonder if this is linked?' Roscoe pondered. 'But don't worry, agent deaths don't impact destiny, there won't be any rubber duck storms or rivers of lemonade again.'

'I hope not,' Erron answered quietly, shaking off the memories.

Roscoe scratched his chin in thought. 'Hey, kid, didn't you used to be a detective?'

'Once upon a time.'

They turned a corner by a café that Erron recognised as somewhere Casey had invited him to before, known for their profiteroles. Beyond that was a narrow alleyway, used mostly for commercial bins as it led to a dead end. They were met just outside the alley by a wide-eyed Dr Jared Enleigh.

'Luckily members of public haven't stumbled across her,' the Archangel said quietly. 'I only came down here to take a look as some shifty-looking guy was running from the scene. He had blood on his shirt, but I don't know where he went.'

'Was he mortal, or an agent?' Roscoe asked.

'I couldn't tell. He was fast, I didn't get a good look,' Dr Enleigh explained.

'What do you remember?' Erron pried.

'I honestly couldn't tell you anything useful. He was fairly tall, thin. All I really saw was the blood on his shirt, I was looking down at my phone when he ran past. I only glanced up briefly.' Dr Enleigh shook his head apologetically. 'Anyway, I have checked her for any signs of life but there's no chance of bringing her back from this.'

The Archangel moved aside so the two Reapers could access the alley. Behind a council bin, Willow was slumped against a metal gate, her head lolled forward and her auburn hair wildly tousled as though she'd put up a fight. Erron knelt down beside her and gently placed the back of his hand against her cheek.

'She's still warm,' he muttered almost to himself.

A pool of blood was forming around her left wrist, which was twisted upwards in her lap. Her left hand was missing, a clean cut severing it from the joint. Erron used a pen to carefully brush the hair back from her face on one side. A deep ligature mark ran the circumference of her neck, fresh blood was only beginning to clot around the wound.

Erron looked up at the others, a grim expression on his face.

'What do you think, kid?' Roscoe asked quietly.

Erron exhaled audibly. He glanced around the scene and back over the body for a few moments before he answered. 'It's just a theory, but I would say he snatched her from the street using a piano wire or some other type of garotte around her neck, pulling her into this alley.' He stood up and retraced his steps back towards the road. 'She couldn't scream or breathe. It wouldn't have taken long to get her to pass out. At that point he tightened it enough to make sure she wouldn't wake up.' He went back to where Willow was slumped. 'What worries me is that it looks like he took a trophy.' He pointed at her left wrist.

'You don't think that would have been injured in the struggle?' Roscoe asked.

'Her hand wouldn't have just fallen off. She's not exactly made of bloody Lego.' Erron rolled his eyes. 'Even if it did, where is it? And why is it such a clean cut?'

'We really ought to make her disappear. Her cloaking ability would have died with her.' Dr Enleigh glanced warily out at the street. They were mostly hidden from view, but it was best not to get discovered.

'Don't you think we should look into this? Roscoe, you said Fortuna agents are pretty much indestructible. Doesn't this ring major alarm bells? What about forensics?' Erron challenged. 'Don't we have some kind of crime investigation people?'

'Not really. Nemesis usually mop up misconduct issues and stuff. We don't usually have any incidents like this.' Roscoe rubbed the back of his neck. 'Instead, we have to do our job now. What we were sent here to do.'

'How do we reap her?' Erron queried.

'Well, agents are already a baked soul, so there's no soul to release like a mortal . . . We have to dissolve her,' Roscoe explained gently.

'Dissolve her? What? Like with acid or something?' Erron took a step back.

'No, no. We use the Ferryman's Touch. We place a thumb over each eyelid and hold it until the body fades to dust, then the energy of her soul goes back to the stars. But only senior agents can do it, hence why I'm here.'

'So, no chance of finding her killer then?'

Roscoe considered the dilemma. 'You have a good point. This really is unprecedented and probably needs some investigation. I suppose we could complete her reaping at the hospital and just explain this all to Lettie. She might be able to link it to whatever issues the Goosening left behind.'

'Urgh, this is . . .' Erron paced, frustratedly muttering. 'Bloody hell, why on my first day?' He clapped his hands together decisively. 'Right, yes. We need an Archangel team to take her to the Raphael Sanctuary, but they need to bring a body bag and we need to wait on scene to make sure nothing important gets disturbed. She deserves to have her murder investigated to the best of our abilities. The least we could do is preserve any forensic evidence before you go turning her into ashes without a cremation.'

Dr Enleigh had already called for a team who were en route. 'I don't know how preserved the scene is. I checked her over when I got here, so I could have my hair or fingerprints anywhere.' He sounded panicked.

'We'll note that down,' Erron reassured him.

They waited in silence, the body of Willow Madison sitting like an exhausted angel in the gloom of the alley, her delicate Fortuna wings torn and tattered behind her, her dress covered in the dirt and grime of the bins. Neither Reaper had known her personally, but both felt the weight of her loss.

Erron checked his phone again. It was approaching lunchtime and there was still no message from Casey. Just then, the Archangels swooped down from the rooftops behind him and settled down next to Willow, with a stretcher and the requested body bag. Their wings of pure light lit up the dim alleyway, adding a warmth to the grim scene.

'I guess we have to make our own way to the hospital,' Roscoe stated. 'Owing to my flightless bird here.' He nudged Erron playfully.

'Yeah, sorry to hold you back,' Erron replied with a smile. His back ached for his missing wings. 'I'm a regular dodo at the moment.'

'As long as it's not a bastard goose.' Roscoe laughed. 'I'll get us a cab, my treat.'

# 6

## *My Immortal*

CASEY STARED ACROSS AT THE empty desk, oblivious to anything around him. The Apollo office was buzzing with agents going to and fro, collecting assignments, handing their cards in, typing up their daily reports and chatting round the coffee machine. But he may as well have been completely alone: Erron's chair sat vacant in front of him, and he hadn't yet got used to seeing the desk without papers strewn everywhere, or rings of coffee stains all over it. Erron had cleared his desk out overnight, once again avoiding everyone in the office. He had, however, left the figure of the marshmallow man from *Ghostbusters* on Casey's desk.

It was approaching lunchtime, and his new crew mate, Nikita, was in Freya's office going through recruitment formalities that Kendra should have cleared up on her first week at Apollo. She'd been in the office for well over an hour, and Casey's gaze drifted towards the window, where a pigeon was bobbing back and forth on the windowsill outside.

A pair of arms wrapped themselves around his neck from behind, and for the briefest moment he closed his eyes and hoped it might be Erron.

'Hey, Case.' Nikita planted a light kiss on his cheek and released him from the hug. 'Sorry that took so long. It's amazing how much Kendra didn't bother telling me when I started. You OK?'

He extracted himself from his thoughts and raised a half-smile. 'Yeah, not bad.' He had more than a couple of days of stubble, his eyes were tired and his usual Apollo glow was faded. He hadn't bothered to put on one of his signature pinstripe suits, instead he was slumped in a pair of worn tan corduroys and a white shirt.

Nikita perched on the edge of his desk. 'You look like you need some high-end, serious croissants, mister.'

Casey's smile widened. 'You know what, that sounds like an amazing idea.'

'How about we go get some from Phillipe Conticini's? But first, Freya said you need to show me how to fill in some timesheet.' Nikita slumped down in Erron's old chair and wheeled it next to Casey's desk. 'You know, if I'd have known I needed to fill in timesheets all over again, I should have let the world turn to Marmite and rubber ducks.'

Casey laughed and opened his laptop. 'Yep. Apparently even death is not a good enough excuse for escaping the European Working Time Directive.'

It was well known in the afterlife that there were certain things that were inescapable legacies from the mortal world. Contrary to popular belief, it wasn't death and taxes that were certain, but death and timesheets. For some reason, the time regs were carried forward and no one entirely knew why, but there was a hefty penalty for not completing them on time.

As they were going through the dull process of completing tick boxes, Nikita's phone buzzed across the desk with an incoming call.

'Oh, it's Emrys.' She grinned as she saw his name on the screen. It had only been a matter of weeks into her relationship with the shy Fortuna Division boss, but she was thoroughly enjoying the fact he was a true romantic at heart. Her cheery tone gradually faded as he spoke until she hung up the phone, her expression sombre.

'Everything OK?' Casey asked, concerned.

She rolled her chair closer to his and spoke quietly out of earshot of other agents. 'One of his agents was murdered a few hours ago. He's quite shaken up about it, and was checking I was safe. Obviously, it's not common knowledge so don't say anything.'

'Who's been murdered?' Casey's stomach sank, as he had close friends in the division.

'A woman named Willow Madison.'

'I don't think I know her. But that's awful. How would a Fortuna agent run into that kind of bad luck? It's unheard of.'

'I honestly didn't think of that. But yes, that's a very good point.' Nikita pulled out her trusty notebook and wrote it down. Before her indoctrination into her new role at Apollo, she'd been a keen journalist and had a knack for rooting out the truth of a situation. It was something she'd not given up after death, though the direction of her investigation skills had changed dramatically from scandals in the local news to researching ritualistic blood magic in the afterlife. It was a leap, but ridding the world of marauding Chaos demons was much more interesting than running a story about some bloke called Greg who was secretly going dogging on Hampstead Heath every Friday night.

'Are you already collecting clues?' Casey raised an eyebrow. As much as he wanted to make fun of her, it was largely thanks to Nikita's investigation skills that the world didn't end with the Lord of Chaos collapsing the natural order, and him and Erron getting turned into a Cupid smoothie via Obliteration.

'You know me, I live for this kind of thing. Anyway, you never know, it might come in useful. Emrys said Roscoe and Erron were on scene and ordered her body to be taken to the hospital for investigation, instead of processing the usual way. They sound like they are keen to find out who killed her,' Nikita explained.

'Sounds like a very Erron thing to do.' Casey gave her a wan smile.

'Right, we are getting those croissants. You've moped around enough.' She picked up the marshmallow man and put it away in Casey's desk drawer. 'First step, stop staring at the things that remind you of Erron. He's not dead – well, OK he is, kind of. But the point I'm making is he loves you and things will be fine. Get your sappy arse up and fetch your bow.'

He exhaled and slapped the top of his thighs before standing. 'Right, yes. You're right.'

Nikita turned to pick up her kitbag and Casey subtly placed the marshmallow man back on his desk before following her to the door.

* * *

Just over a mile from the Apollo Division headquarters on the Isle of Dogs, Sam Rivera was sitting in the darkness of his parents' shop, the blinds rolled down. His hands trembled slightly; he'd managed to clean the blood off them easily enough, but his shirt had to be binned or burnt. The adrenaline was still coursing through his veins following his quick retreat from Kensington, avoiding all the main streets and sprinting through the alleyways. Sweat trickled down his back as he toyed with the idea of logging on to the Oracles website, but ultimately decided it wouldn't be wise to write anything on the forums too soon. Instead, he double-checked the lock on the door and went out to the courtyard at the back, dragging a large metal bin behind him to throw his bloodstained clothing in. Standing in just tracksuit bottoms, he doused the clothes with his father's old single malt whisky and struck a match, pausing briefly to wonder if he had done the right thing.

Thick smoke curled into the overcast sky, the low flames reflecting in his good eye. His heart rate slowed, and the fear was slowly replaced with a strange exhilaration. The blood on his clothes had glimmered as though filled with thousands of tiny flecks of greenish glitter, giving him more than enough reason to suspect the Fireflies were not human at all. He had no idea what ramifications would come from the woman's death, but he couldn't imagine the police would be knocking on his door anytime soon.

Once the fire had receded into a smouldering heap, Sam re-entered through the back door, bolting it behind him. He couldn't resist logging back into the Oracles website but decided to keep a low profile. More than anything, he was keen to learn about the creatures with sparkly blood that walked among them. The topic of the Fireflies was quickly becoming an all-consuming addiction.

# 7

## *Resurrect Me*

WILLOW MADISON LAY UNDER A white sheet on a steel table in the reanimation department of the Raphael Sanctuary. There was no need for a morgue at the hospital, as the unexpected deaths of agents were incredibly rare and were usually processed by Hades in the standard manner. Instead, Dr Carroway had made room in one of the unoccupied labs, adjusting the temperature as low as they could to keep the body chilled.

Emrys Taliesin, the softly spoken boss of the Fortuna Division, stood across the table from Erron and Theodore Roscoe, letting out an exasperated sigh at the sight of his fallen agent. He ran a hand through his scruffy, silver-blond hair before breaking the silence in the room.

'Do you think we can trace her killer?' he asked quietly in his gentle Welsh timbre.

There was a long pause before Erron spoke. 'I don't really know. I noticed one camera outside the alley so we could get an Apollo agent to charm their way into getting the footage maybe. We know agents appear on CCTV, which at least works in our favour. There's not likely to be any witnesses who saw anything in person, however, due to agency cloaking. She wouldn't have been able to scream with the garotte, so I expect it was swift and silent. We aren't exactly equipped for forensics here, not really.'

'I'll get Nikita on the CCTV. What exactly can we do here?' Emrys was trying to remain hopeful.

Erron rested his hands on his hips and exhaled slowly. 'Well, we can try to check her over for any fibres or hairs, anything that seems out of place. But we have no way of testing for things like DNA. My career in the police ended in the eighties; I'm not exactly up to code with modern forensics even if we had all the right stuff, but I'll do what I can. But even if we found the killer, and they turned out to be mortal, we don't really have any powers in that respect. It's not like we can send them to prison.'

'Osato could authorise *Caedes Justificatum*,' Emrys stated quietly, referring to the Nemesis arrow of justified death, used only in extreme circumstances.

'It's an option, I guess.' Erron fidgeted, feeling his exhaustion catching up with him in the unbearably cold room. The stitched wounds on his back from his wing-removal surgery ached and stung under their dressings, reminding him he was well overdue some pain relief. He shifted his weight from one foot to the other to distract himself from the ever-increasing discomfort.

'Unfortunately, there's not much else we can do; the agency isn't equipped for such things. Maybe after all the disruption of late, we really ought to rethink a few things as an organisation.' Erron folded his arms across his chest.

'Osato has been working hard to arrange some kind of team for dealing with things outside the norm that threaten the agency. And a murder of one of our own definitely falls into that category.' Emrys was close with the Nemesis boss and knew she would do anything within her power to help investigate any wrongdoing to an agent. 'I'll have to see where she is with that. Things have been a bit messed-up since the near-apocalypse.'

'That's a good call, boss, the sooner the better really,' Roscoe concurred. 'We need to head back and speak with Lettie about this one and explain why we haven't reaped her just yet.'

Dr Jared Enleigh entered the room, back in his Archangel scrubs and holding a clipboard. 'I can take it from here, gentlemen.'

'I'd like to stay. With all due respect, no one else here has dealt with crime scenes or victims in this capacity,' Erron insisted. 'I can try and isolate any evidence before it gets any more contaminated.'

Roscoe placed a firm hand on Erron's shoulder. 'I'd love to let you, kid, but I can't leave you here on your first day, and we are expected back. You can come back in your own time.' Roscoe's assertive tone suggested Hades were much stricter about their rules and regulations than Apollo ever was.

'Don't worry, I'll be careful not to disturb anything,' Dr Enleigh reassured them.

Erron reluctantly left instructions for the doctor.

On the way back to Highgate, he tried multiple times to convince Roscoe to let him return to the alley before any other evidence was lost. Rain clouds were building on the horizon, and he desperately wanted to take photos of the scene before anything important was washed away.

'Listen, Grover, I know it's a fellow agent and we have a duty of care as Reapers, but death is death and all we are paid to do is make sure it happens,' Roscoe explained gently. 'I know it's your first day and you've had a howler of a morning, but agents *do* die unfortunately, and we just have to follow the right procedures. It's a terrible loss, I know, and I understand that this sort of thing is far from the norm, but that's no excuse for us to go off on side quests for the afternoon.'

'How many agents get murdered though?' Erron asked belligerently.

'Well, we haven't had a murder in decades, not in this district at least. But that's not the point. Lettie sent us there to reap her. She didn't send us there to solve a mystery. You're not Scooby Doo and I'm certainly not Velma.'

'Well, bloody jinkies, you sure?' Erron rolled his eyes. 'Surely you can't be comfortable with just adding Willow to your list of successfully deleted people for the day?'

Roscoe stopped walking and fixed Erron with a stern look. 'I know it's a culture shock, kid. But if we actually start using that mindset with everything, we will be trying to solve all the world's problems. Kids dying from diseases. People trapped in train wrecks. An old man that drowns trying to save a dog. The dog too, for that matter. You see, good people die all the time, no one would say it was justified or right. But they all get to where they are supposed to be in the afterlife, death is just a stepping stone. You of all people should know that.'

'But she won't. She gets no afterlife, no paradise, no ice cream. Nothing,' Erron retaliated.

Roscoe softened his expression into a fatherly look of concern. 'No. And no one wants that for an agent, but we can't undo what's been done. Look, I admire your sense of justice. But you're a Reaper now, and you have to be as cold as the grave sometimes.'

Erron reluctantly conceded, letting out a defeated sigh.

Back at Hades headquarters, Lettie gave him the rest of the day off and told him to get home and try to sleep. She worded it delicately, but the message came through that she was less than impressed, hinting that he should adjust his attitude.

He left the headquarters, utterly crestfallen, a simmering anger in his gut. He pulled a pack of the morphine tablets he'd been prescribed from his pocket and took two as he stalked through the gravestones in the dimming light of the afternoon. His skin was crawling with the need for a cigarette, but he was desperately pushing through the pledge he made to Casey that he would quit smoking.

Thick grey clouds were building overhead, and with his new place of work being a three-hour flightless walk from his flat in Canary Wharf, he was forced to rely on public transport.

He considered returning to the alleyway, but by that time, the rain was sluicing down the sides of the tombs at Highgate, washing away any hope of gathering evidence. Reluctantly, he headed to the nearest bus stop, his hair plastered to his face and rivulets of water seeping down the back of his coat collar, soaking his shirt.

The first bus had a distinct smell of vomit towards the back and at least three screaming children on board. Erron closed his eyes and stood near the front, holding loosely to the hand-rail as the motion of the bus swayed him in a jolting, bounding fashion over the wet streets of London. The morphine kicked in on the second bus, which smelled better, but was slow enough that Erron wondered if it was more efficient to walk. He was grateful for the wave of pain relief seeping into his blood, drowning out the pulsing in his ears and the sound of someone's tinny iPhone speaker on full volume.

He stepped off the second bus into a deep puddle, cursing under his breath at the cold slop of water that entered his boot. Without the distraction of physical pain, his mind became restless, recounting the events of the day, gradually decaying into the memory of his nightmares. Only the persistent rain kept his mind from spiralling, and he wasn't ready to face the silence that waited for him at home.

Instead, he dawdled in the streets around Canary Wharf, the rain drenching his hair, running into his eyes and dripping off his nose. Where other people scattered to find shelter, he wandered through the puddles, not perturbed by the persisting sogginess of his clothes. Somewhere east of Jubilee Park, he felt indescribably, unbearably lonely. He perched on a wall, watching the rain dance over the surface of Middle Dock.

He reached into his inside coat pocket and pulled out the small bloodstained cuddly unicorn that had belonged to Hannah Hallington. *Starlight*. That was her last word. The same word he found scrawled on the toy's label in purple crayon. Hot tears stung his eyes and mixed with the rain on his cheeks as he crushed the unicorn to his chest, unable to hold back the wracking sobs that drained the last of the breath from his lungs.

An hour passed, the rain eased, and Erron carefully squashed the unicorn back in his pocket, knowing he had no right to have picked it up from the road. He checked his phone; it was nearing sundown and there were still no notifications. Part of him needed the loneliness, craved the silence with just the beat of his cosmic heart in his ears. But the rest of him needed someone. Needed Casey.

His thumb hovered over Casey's contact on his phone. He wanted nothing more than to share a drink with him and fling around their usual harmless insults over a game of chess. But he couldn't summon the power to press the call button, and after a few minutes, he put the phone away.

* * *

Casey was finishing his shift with Nikita, having had a full day of assignments around the city, each of which had gradually brought him out of his shell and into a far better mood. With every arrow he fired, he felt the tiny cracks in his heart heal over, knowing he was bringing joy to the people he had in his sights. Nikita had stood by her word and bought him a decadent croissant, and he was almost feeling his usual cheerful self by the end of the shift. It was only when Nikita was putting her kit away in the locker room that he checked his phone, feeling a distinct slump when he realised his only notification was an agency email advertising a new Weetabix restaurant on Elysion.

'You're not getting another fancy croissant each time you look like a sad, lost puppy, Casey.' Nikita nudged him playfully, having returned from the locker room.

'I don't think I could manage another one.' Casey forced a smile.

'Liar.'

'You got me.'

'You got a spare umbrella?' Nikita asked, looking out at the rain sliding down the windows of the Apollo office.

'Of course.' He pulled an umbrella from a stand beside his desk. 'Going out this evening?'

'I'm meeting up with Emrys. He's taking me to a new noodle bar on the moon.' She grinned widely. 'Moonoodles it's called. Apparently, it's really popular.'

'It doesn't rain on the moon.' He looked confused.

'Duh, but I still have to get home on foot. I'm not mad enough to go out in this without a brolly,' she teased him, taking the umbrella. 'What about you? You got any plans?'

He stretched his arms and yawned. 'I think I might put in a few hours at the call centre, keep my mind off things and top up my mortal money.'

'Don't overdo it, that place is mentally draining.' Though new, Nikita had already done her fair share of shifts in the complaints call centre. She pulled on her jacket and kissed him on the top of his head. 'Have a break first. I'll see you tomorrow.'

# 8

## *Slow Hands*

THE RAIN HAD EASED SOMEWHAT by the time Nikita approached the ice-cream van in Greenwich. She'd made the effort to dress up for her date with the Fortuna boss and had built up an appetite for Moonoodles.

'What'll it be?' The ice-cream man looked down on her, his deadpan expression matching the disinterest in his voice.

Nikita momentarily forgot the order she was meant to say to get access to the agency portal behind the Mr Whippy machine. 'Oh. God. Umm, a ninety-nine Flake please with, umm, sprinkles?'

The man shook his head and went about dispensing ice cream into a cone and adding sprinkles. He handed it to her and asked for £4.50.

'I got the order wrong.' Nikita blushed. 'I'm trying to get into the machine.'

'Love, this ain't *The Matrix*. And there's no refunds.'

Panicking, she resorted to the Apollo Flush to turn on her best charm. 'Can a girl get a one-way ticket to the moon maybe?' She winked and plastered on her warmest smile.

The ice-cream man leant forward on his counter and lowered his voice. 'Love, I'm not interested in whatever euphemism that's meant to be, no offence. You seem like a nice lady but I'm not looking for a fun time.'

Nikita's face turned a deeper shade of crimson. 'No, you've got me all wrong there.'

The man's face broke into a dull grin. 'You should know better than to try using the Flush against me, miss. It's a ninety-nine Flake, hold the cone.' He nodded for her to climb aboard.

'Of course.' Nikita buried her embarrassment as she clambered into the back of the van, almost tripping on the long green dress she was wearing.

The man opened the Mr Whippy machine, revealing the swirling vortex that would take her to the city of Elysion, and just as she was about to step through, he grabbed her arm.

'You've still got to pay for that.' He nodded to the ice cream in her hand.

'Serious?'

'I'm not running a charity here.'

'Jeez,' Nikita muttered as she rummaged in her purse for some coins to cover the ice cream.

The sensation of being flung through the portal to Elysion was not dissimilar from the drop of the highest roller coaster on earth while simultaneously feeling like a pair of socks in a tumble dryer. By sheer design, agents didn't look like they had been tumbled when they arrived, it was just their stomach that felt it. Nikita arrived in the celestial lagoon still hanging onto the ice cream which looked a little worse for wear after the roll through space, but she licked it cautiously, realising just how hungry she was.

'You look beautiful, Rocket.' Emrys approached her from the nearby steps where he'd arranged to meet her. He couldn't help himself using the daft nickname he'd given her on their first meeting, after an Elton John song, when Nikita had explained she disliked the real one she was named after.

Emrys handed her a single lunar rose, which glowed with ethereal translucence. She smiled and offered him the half-eaten ice cream in exchange.

'Novel,' he said, bemused, but he took it anyway.

Nikita had insisted earlier that they could postpone the date, owing to the unexpected death of a Fortuna Agent, but Emrys was hoping to talk about the incident and escape the office for the evening.

Being on Elysion was still a novelty for Nikita, as she'd only visited a couple of times. The beauty of the city overlooking the glow of Earth still caught her off guard, the glimmering lights of the waterways and luminescent willow trees were a spectacle far removed from the grime of central London. It always felt like a balmy summer evening in Elysion, unless the artificial atmosphere was changed for special events, and Nikita loved the gentle warm breeze on her skin mingled with the sights and smells of a summer night in the bustling streets. There were so many zones she'd yet to explore, some with dedicated themes and others with spectacular experiences that gave agents just a small taste of what to expect when they finally retired to Arcadia, the cosmic heaven that awaited them.

Before their dinner reservation, they took a swan-shaped pedalo past the Hall of Unconscious Stories, a place Nikita was desperate to visit. It was where you could pay to relive some of your favourite dreams, all preserved in the great cosmic web of memories. The gentle flow of the waterways took them to an infinity lake at the far side of the city, overlooking the stars.

'This is the most beautiful thing I have ever seen.' Nikita leant into Emrys, enjoying the feeling of safety in his arms, and the chance to rest her legs from pedalling.

'Across that lake is the entrance to the real afterlife. The Oblivion Fields that lead to Arcadia.' Emrys rested his head on hers. 'There's only one way across, and you have to summon the Ferryman.'

'I didn't realise that heaven was on the moon,' Nikita marvelled.

'It's not, but the portal to get there is.' Emrys kissed her cheek.

'You missed the perfect opportunity to say that it is, because you're in heaven right now,' Nikita teased, nuzzling into his neck.

'I stand corrected.' He blushed. 'Though I could argue that being with you is better than heaven, and by default, my initial statement is accurate.'

'Smooth,' Nikita conceded.

She checked the time. 'When's our table booked for?'

'Umm, honestly don't even try and figure out the time zones up here. I get a fifteen-minute warning on my phone when our table is ready.' He pulled his phone out and his eyes widened when he realised the notification had come in six minutes previously. 'Oops . . . Swift needs to be the swan that wants noodles!' he exclaimed as they hurriedly turned the boat around and pedalled manically back the way they had come.

'And there's me thinking the phrase was "the early bird gets the worm".' Nikita rolled her eyes and laughed.

'Same thing. More elegant.' He puffed as they turned another corner at a dangerous speed for a swan boat.

The noodle restaurant was a far cry from the ones found on earth, with a cascading waterfall of Szechuan noodles that ran through the centre of the neatly arranged tables, floating trays of prawn crackers in the shape of clouds and a strikingly realistic hologram of a Chinese dragon which seemed to meander effortlessly through the air and under the chairs of visitors.

Over dinner, having only just got there in time, Emrys broached the subject of Willow's murder in a quiet tone.

'Casey said it was strange that a Fortuna agent would have such bad luck to end up in that situation,' Nikita stated between mouthfuls of teriyaki noodles.

Emrys paused mid-dumpling. 'I'll be honest, that was my first thought. We don't tend to find ourselves in those kinds of circumstances and even if we did, it wouldn't take much to miraculously luck our way out of them. Like your Apollo Flush, we have a much higher resonating luck aura.'

'So is it possible statistically, or is this a zero-chance kind of thing without there being some sort of outside influence?'

Emrys finished the dumpling and sat back in thought. 'The closest we have to anything you would deem bad luck is what we call "red-light luck". Nothing to do with some dodgy district in Amsterdam, mind.'

Nikita raised a questioning eyebrow.

'Red-light luck is what people have when they think they are having a pretty bad day, when all the traffic lights turn red and there's loads of roadworks, or you drop your keys or forget your bag, that kind of thing. But it is actually luck working in your favour, slowing you down, holding you up, etc. In such a way that you avoid a much worse situation, like getting hit by a bus,' he explained.

'I could have done with some of that a few weeks back,' Nikita huffed, remembering her death.

Emrys covered his mouth, horrified he'd used that example. 'I'm so sorry, I forgot about that.'

'It's quite all right.' Nikita waved off the comment. 'So how would that relate to Willow?'

'Well, all Fortuna agents are given a hefty dose of green-light luck, which is our Fortuna Diaboli, where everything just seems to fall our way in a generally positive way. But we also have a good measure of red-light luck, which means we can evade or escape dangerous situations through inconvenience. So, for Willow, something should have held her up passing that alley like having a drink spilled on her. But for there to be no intervention, either the killer knew how to disable her luck, or something had upset her natural skills.' He picked up another dumpling and dipped it in sweet chilli sauce. 'There have been some knock-on effects from the Goosening, and I'm starting to wonder if this loss of luck is linked. My biggest concern is that there's a fine balance of luck in each district, and losing an agent could start to tip the scales into the negative.'

'Oh, that sounds serious.'

'Yes, Osato strongly believes the veil between the mortal world and the Chaos realm hasn't resolidified as well as hoped. She's had a meeting with the Demons of the Balance and they confirmed that multiple portals have been cropping up.'

'That's even worse.' Nikita lowered her chopsticks. She'd had some dealings with one of the Demons of the Balance, Dantalion, who was one of several entities that guarded the agency libraries and acted as a liaison between the realms. He was as old as time itself, neither good nor evil, and could only be summoned with a tribute of cosmic blood.

'Quite, but Osato is looking into things.'

'So this goes far deeper than I initially thought,' Nikita said.

'The loss of luck is deeply concerning. Had it been another division, I could see it being possible. Even with your charms, you likely couldn't flutter your eyelashes out of a garotte. If anything, if this guy is a straight-up psychopath, the Apollo Flush would probably translate as bloodlust to him, as opposed to . . . you know . . . normal lust.' His face dropped into a grave expression, and he placed his chopsticks down. 'Promise me you will be extra vigilant.'

'I promise.' She reached across the table and squeezed his hand. 'But let's worry about how we can find the guy before he has the chance to hurt anyone else.'

The hologram of the dragon weaved its way over their table, it's vibrant scales almost tangible in the air between them. Nikita instinctively reached out to touch it, smiling with fascination as her fingers passed right through, leaving swirls of rainbow smoke in its wake.

'Yes, that's the main thing. Do you think you could get hold of the CCTV for the alleyway? Erron will do what he can in regard to forensics, but he says it's going to be near impossible to gather evidence when we don't have dedicated equipment for it. Our best bet is seeing if this guy is on camera.'

'Sure, I can certainly try. Which building is it on?' Nikita asked.

Emrys pulled up mapping on his phone and found a street view of the alleyway. 'It was this one.' He zoomed in on a building which was occupied by a bakery.

A text popped up on his phone from the Nemesis boss, Osato M'Raya, inviting him to a meeting the following day.

'Osato's provisionally sorting a team to oversee things that are a risk to the agency,' he explained before she could ask.

'Like murders? And maybe psychotic demon-summoning human disco balls that try to speed up the goose-laden apocalypse?' Nikita asked with a wry grin.

'Yes, in short. I put your name forward for the team. You spot things that others don't. I think the agency would be stupid to let that go to waste.'

'I'd love to, obviously.' She wiggled in her seat with excitement.

Emrys broke into a warm smile. 'I was hoping you might say that. Let me get the bill and we can talk more about it at my place ... if you'd like?'

'Smooth, Mr Taliesin. I thought you'd never ask. But before we go, do we have time to go the Hall of Unconscious Stories? I have been absolutely dying to go there.'

Emrys took her hand and kissed the back of it, before fixing her with a gaze of pure adoration. 'Anything for you, Rocket.'

'Wait, do we need to get back in a pedalo to get there? My thighs are still aching from reaching Mach 10 in a giant swan, I don't think I can handle it.' Nikita winced.

'No, not at all.' Emrys patted his stomach. 'I need to walk off this meal anyhow.'

They were handed two fortune cookies as they left, and Nikita was excited to open hers straightaway. The tiny slip of paper inside read, 'You're going to get lucky this evening.'

'Oh, that's certainly a bold statement.' She blushed and asked Emrys to open his cookie.

'Well, this feels a little presumptuous.' He showed her his paper which simply said, 'You're lucky.'

'Guess that works out well then.' Nikita winked mischievously.

The walk took them through some of the back streets of Elysion, places Nikita had never seen before, with so many sights and sounds catching her attention. She was particularly drawn to a glowing neon storefront called The Late Night Jelly Bean Shop, which unsurprisingly did exactly what it said on the tin and sold an overwhelming array of jelly beans between the hours of 8 p.m. and four in the morning.

A smaller shop nearby sparked Nikita's curiosity; it had a low sign hanging over the door saying 'Grendal's Gizmos, Gadgets and Goose-down' in bright red writing, with a window full of curiosities. Sensing her intrigue, Emrys led Nikita into the shop and watched her eyes light up as she browsed.

'We have to get one of these!' she exclaimed, holding up a small metal contraption which claimed to perfectly separate the layers of bourbon biscuits.

'I'm an expert at pulling apart a bourbon without one of those,' Emrys said confidently.

She giggled and moved on to another shelf, which contained bunion paint, nose-hair beads and eyebrow curlers.

'Looking for anything special?' rasped a voice from behind the counter.

A wheezing, thin man with long white hair stood up slowly and gave them a toothy smile.

Nikita was already in front of a display of paranormal paraphernalia. 'Just browsing, thank you. Though, what is this?' She lifted up an odd pair of headphones, with a row of LED lights going over the headband and two antennae either side. Both earpieces had several dials attached.

'They're Poltergeist Podcast headphones,' the shopkeeper replied. 'You set the antennae and dials to the right frequency for your location to hear what the ghosts are chatting about.'

Emrys raised an eyebrow, just as intrigued as Nikita was.

'You can have them for forty novas.'

'Thirty-eight,' Emrys haggled, after seeing Nikita's expression of excitement.

'Sold.'

Emrys stepped forward to pay, waving off Nikita's attempts to cover the cost. The shopkeeper scanned the agency ear cuff he wore, which stored all his banking details, and took the payment.

Outside, Nikita was fascinated by the device, fiddling with the controls the first chance she got.

'You know it's just one of those things that picks up white noise and makes you think you're getting something useful,' Emrys said sceptically. 'It's just a novelty.'

'Well, I plan to test it on the ghosts at the Eligos Library.'

'You'll have to let me know what they say then, I've never made any sense of their inane chatter.' Emrys wasn't denying the existence of ghosts, but they were well known to be the lost souls of mortals who had escaped the clutches of a Hades agent in the short time frame for reaping them successfully. Very little progress had been made in getting the lost souls back from their existence in the shadows, and it seemed they were content enough creating blurs in photographs and whispering in the halls of haunted places. Some had even progressed their skills to create a slight chill in the air.

Ten minutes later, they stood outside two conjoined buildings, one being the Hall of Unconscious Stories, and the other being the Nostalgia Rooms. They were both run by the same people and had the same price for a thirty-minute experience.

'So which is it then, do you want to tap into your dreams or revisit a childhood memory? Or both? My treat.' Emrys gestured for her to enter through the large brass revolving door.

'I don't expect you to pay. You've spoiled me enough,' Nikita replied.

'I know you don't, but I've got to make use of my pay grade sometimes.' He flashed her a charming smile.

Knowing arguing about it was futile, Nikita opted for the dream experience when they reached the friendly female attendant at the main counter. The lobby was plush, decorated like an old cinema from the late nineties, with red and gold carpets, colourful lights and a traditional stand of overpriced Pick 'n' Mix.

'Mr Taliesin, it's an honour to have you.' The attendant beamed, having instantly recognised the head of the UK Fortuna Division.

'Thank you. Thirty minutes in the Hall of Unconscious Stories for Agent Wolf here, please.' Emrys gestured to his date with a warm smile.

'Of course. Follow me,' the attendant beckoned.

'Have fun, I'm going to remortgage my apartment for a bag of the gummy worms.' Emrys watched Nikita be led away before heading to the Pick 'n' Mix counter.

Within the Hall of Unconscious Stories, Nikita was asked to settle in a luxurious recliner chair as the attendant fitted her with a headset and a pair of technologically sophisticated gloves. She was advised there would be a slight sharp sensation in her temples, as the headset would need to access her unconscious through two tiny needles that went into her mind.

'Is it safe?' Nikita asked, horrified at the idea.

'Perfectly safe. You won't notice a thing once you're immersed.' The attendant continued to explain the instructions.

Reluctantly, Nikita agreed, and within moments she was waking up in a strange room, wearing plain grey pyjamas and looking at a huge screen full of thumbnails of dreams. She was able to scroll through them by a swift wave of her hand, and when she found one that she liked, she selected it with a firm push.

The room melted away, gradually loading into a dream Nikita had recently had, where she'd envisioned her own funeral, an event she never got to experience. Rows of her friends and family sat from her previous life, and she paused the dream to study their faces, feeling emotions welling up as hot tears sprang from her eyes.

The images shuddered to a halt and a tumble of eerie voices pierced the silence, sounding urgent and terrifying. Nikita recoiled as the voices amassed around her, swirling and prodding at her unconscious mind with a vicious persistence. The words gradually coagulated, becoming a multifaceted but singular voice, murmuring the words: *Hear us! Bad energy!*

Nikita instinctively cowered, covering her ears, just as the headset was hastily removed and the attendant seemed flustered.

'What happened?' Nikita asked, feeling cold sweat on her brow.

'There was some interference. I'm so sorry, I'll have to refund you.' The attendant hastily ushered her out of the chair and back to the lobby where Emrys was waiting.

'Everything OK?' Emrys asked, a gummy worm poised, half eaten, in his hand. The attendant apologised profusely again and began hurriedly closing up shop without much of an explanation. As they were leaving, they overheard the attendant speaking in hushed tones to the manager.

'It's the ghosts again. They are getting more persistent since the veil thinned. I don't know how to block them.'

Nikita shot a concerned look at Emrys before explaining what she'd heard in the simulation.

'It's probably nothing to worry about,' Emrys reasoned. 'Those simulators aren't always perfect. Let's head back to mine.'

His apartment building was in the Western District of Elysion, overlooking the sparkling lake grounds. It was a compact two-storey structure with an ornate balcony and airy open spaces indoors. His love for art from his former life was evident with all the paintings tastefully hung on the walls, a good mix of bright colour and muted tones. Nikita meandered around the carefully arranged furniture, admiring paintings and enjoying the small pockets of chaotic lived-in spaces. Her favourite room, however, was a tiny library room unlike the rest of the house, with an extensive collection of fossils and books on archaeology, as well as displaying a distinct interest in the occult and paranormal with various volumes and artefacts. Shelves full of interesting books and knick-knacks, with a bright tapestry rug and signs of life strewn everywhere, from discarded slippers and scarves slung over a chair to dirty mugs and a mess of paperwork.

'Oh, yes, sorry I haven't had a chance to clean in there yet.' He ushered her out of the library room and closed the door, a cacophony of books crashing down behind them.

'I like it. I had a few of those books.' She smiled fondly at the memory of their first real encounter on the plane to the Oriax, the agency reference building in Edinburgh, when they talked a whole lot about the paranormal.

'Let me get you a drink. How about a crisp home-made lemonade with a twist.' He fetched two cups and set them on the black marble kitchen counter.

'Ooh, what's the twist?'

'It's lime. I didn't have any lemons. But I did add vodka.' He started to pour her a glass. 'I could do with a proper drink after today.'

'I don't blame you.'

Her gaze was drawn to the balcony where he had an easel set up and a whole array of paints and brushes. The canvas was half finished, a beautiful portrait of a woman with red hair. 'Did you paint that?' she asked in amazement.

'Oh, yes. It's not finished yet obviously.' He hurried around the kitchen island and went to draw the blinds to the balcony, but Nikita stopped him.

'No, I want to look.' She wriggled past him and went to admire the painting. 'This is amazing.'

His face turned crimson as he held out the drink to her. 'It's supposed to be you,' he admitted quietly. 'It was meant to be a surprise.'

'Really? She's so beautiful.' Overwhelmed by the gesture, she flung her arms around his neck and kissed him, almost spilling both drinks. He fumbled for a surface to set the glasses down on so he could take her in his arms. His heart started to pound against his chest as she kissed his neck, her hands finding their way down his shirt buttons, opening them as she went.

'I'm glad you like the picture,' he said through shallow breaths, quickly forgetting the horrors of the day.

'I love it.' She smiled mischievously and pulled him towards the bedroom, fully intending to fulfil the prophecy of her fortune cookie.

# 9

## *Leave Out All the Rest*

CASEY HAD MUDDLED THROUGH THE week filling his time with assignments and overtime, slowly growing more comfortable with the gaping hole in his life that Erron had left behind. It could never be filled, but he was taking Nikita's advice and focusing on the things that made him happy, while refraining from reaching out. He knew it was important not to push the issue, and give Erron the space he needed, despite the emptiness he felt with every day that passed without any contact.

Instead, he'd wandered the shops of Westfield in Kensington, eaten at his favourite cafés and spent lonely evenings revisiting his love for playing the piano in his cosy town house in Craven Street. He didn't even feel guilty about getting to the letter R in a family-sized Toblerone in just one sitting to soothe his misery. Despite all his distractions, he couldn't help but wish things had gone much better.

It was one o'clock on Saturday morning, and he'd decided to take a night stroll after his late shift. He wasn't tired, and the cool spring night kissed his skin as he enjoyed the glimmering lights of London. The usual nightlife spilled from noisy doorways where pubs and clubs dominated the streets, the smell of alcohol and cigarettes lingering around gatherings on the pavement. Casey moved effortlessly through the throng of people, absorbing the upbeat atmosphere. His natural cloaking ability made it easy for him to blend into the crowd; he wasn't completely invisible, but all agents were immediately forgettable the moment they were out of sight and generally ignored so long as they kept a low profile.

He dodged a group of rowdy men just as a visibly distressed young woman in a black cocktail dress crashed into him, blinded by her own tears and shaking uncontrollably. Casey steadied her, giving her a moment to get her balance.

'Help, please,' she mouthed, clutching Casey's arm in a death grip. 'There's a man following me.'

He glanced behind her, catching a glimpse of a man with long dark hair and one milky blue eye skulking in the shadows of a side street. The man backed away out of view and Casey instinctively used his full height to shield her from view.

'Are you OK?' he asked her softly.

She smoothed her hair down and fixed her dress. 'I can't find my friends and I just want to go home.' She wiped at the streaks of mascara from her cheeks with the back of her hand.

'How long was that man following you for?'

'Only for a bit, but he was creeping me out. He kept getting closer.' She peered around the side of Casey to see if he was still there. 'He was hanging around this patch of wasteland not far from here and when I passed by, he got up and followed.'

Casey placed an arm around her protectively, the warm and soothing influence of the Apollo Flush working instantly on her. She relaxed against him and smiled.

'Where did you last see your friends?' he questioned.

The woman pointed back down the alley. 'We got separated in a club a couple of streets back. They said they were going to head to Bonanza so I walked this way to see if I could find them.'

Casey glanced up at the name of the club they were stood near; in neon lights the word 'Bonanza' flashed against the night sky. He knew it as one of the places that was often frequented by agents and was generally known to be a safe and popular night-time spot. 'Right, here's what you need to do. Go into the club and speak to the bouncer, tell them you've been followed and ask if your friends are inside. If not, get them to call you a taxi and I will wait here until I know you are safe.'

The woman beamed up at him. 'You're really beautiful.'

'Thank you.' Casey loosened his arm from around her shoulder. 'Did you hear what I said?'

She nodded, her eyes glazed in an infatuated stare. 'I'll go in there now. Will you come with me? We could get in a cab back to my place if you want?'

'Best not.' Casey guided her gently to the door of the club.

'God, you're so *hot*,' she whispered, stroking his arm. 'What's your name?'

He eased away from her, conscious the alcohol in her system was just amplifying the effects of the Apollo Flush. 'Just go find your friends, please.'

She pouted, disappointed. 'Are you single? Just tell me your naaame,' she whined.

'Yes and no. You need to get going.' Casey tried to use the Flush to his advantage, convincing her to do as he asked with a charming smile.

Reluctantly, she did as instructed, quickly reuniting with her friend group. Casey watched her tell her story enthusiastically about being followed and being saved by a tall, handsome stranger, though she instantly forgot what Casey looked like when her friends asked to point him out. She looked around confused, eventually shaking her head and thinking she'd imagined it, the memory of the Cupid fading faster than a December sunset.

A light rain began to fall, giving Casey every reason to take his walk homeward bound.

* * *

Erron had been on the night shift when the blind card came in for Leo Romano, a Fortuna agent that had been brutally killed not far from the Bonanza club in central Kensington. Another Hades agent had initially responded, though alerted Theodore Roscoe when the circumstances of the death had become apparent.

'You ever seen anything like it, kid?' Roscoe shook his head slowly in disbelief.

Leo was displayed on an old sofa dumped in a patch of wasteland, missing both his feet, hands and eyeballs. The two Reapers surveyed the scene before approaching the body, the third Hades operative keeping watch to divert any mortals that might wander by. The area was a discontinued section of a construction site, which had been loosely fenced off.

'I've seen plenty of crime scenes, but you don't get many like this.' Erron folded his arms and leant over the body, scanning for any details that may be useful. 'The missing pieces look surgically removed, but in a hurry.' He pointed out the jagged cuts on the victim's wrists. 'The victim was likely killed right here, the blood patterns on the sofa near his neck suggest he was being strangled and thrashing about.'

'Interesting.' The senior Reaper glanced around the surrounding buildings. 'I can't see any cameras.'

Leo was a tall, well-built man, conventionally handsome with dark wavy hair. His facial hair was trimmed to a neat goatee and he still smelled heavily of beer.

'He was intoxicated, but I can't see him being easy to subdue. I think we are looking for someone who is either pretty strong or exceptionally dextrous.' Erron pulled his phone out from his pocket and took multiple pictures of the scene. Dr Enleigh and another Archangel named Dr Rufus had turned up, ready to transport Leo to the temporary morgue.

'There's something odd here.' Erron knelt down by the man's severed ankles, with Roscoe leaning closely over his shoulder.

'His feet are missing?' the old Reaper observed.

Erron slowly turned to Roscoe, one eyebrow raised. 'No ... surely not?'

Roscoe pursed his lips in a dry smile and playfully slapped his protégé over the head. 'Go on, what were you about to say?'

Erron rubbed the back of his head, pretending to be gravely injured. 'Well, now I can't remember a damn thing as you've given me a concussion,' he stated drily, as he pressed his hands to the uneven stone and peered under the sofa. 'It started raining in the early hours, and all this area is mostly non-porous rock. Blood mixed with water expands significantly, so for these kinds of amputations we would expect to see a significant volume of blood. Even with the rain it wouldn't have washed this area as clean as this.' He used a pen to lift the cuff of Leo's jeans. 'No ligature or marks, no tourniquet was used.'

'What are you saying, this fella had no blood?' Roscoe carefully adjusted where he was stood, noticing his suede boots were being scuffed by the rubble.

'No, I think the killer drained the bulk of the initial blood flow and somehow took it with him.' Erron stood up and brushed off his knees.

'Oh ... damn.' Roscoe rubbed his chin, deep in thought. 'So this is some *Twilight* kind of shit?'

'*Twilight*? What? Oh, Christ no, we aren't talking vampires, you absolute lantern.' Erron gave his mentor an incredulous look. 'More than likely he bagged up the feet before hacking them off and collecting the blood.'

Roscoe just shrugged.

'Either he's trying to keep the scene from getting too messy, or he's got another use for the blood.' Erron watched the Archangels carefully manoeuvre Leo Romano onto a stretcher. 'No doubt the pieces of victims being removed are trophies of some sort.'

'He could be eating them,' Roscoe suggested.

'So we're jumping from vampires to, what, cannibals now? But I guess, as horrid as it sounds, it may be possible. Though most cannibals take less bony bits – the thighs, calves, sides, that kind of thing.' Erron shook the rain out of his hair.

'You ever tried people-meat?' the old Reaper asked bluntly.

'*What?!*'

'How do you know the feet aren't the best bit?'

'I'll try it sometime and let you know.' Erron rolled his eyes and took a few more photos of the empty sofa, where the blood spatters were slowly diffusing with the rain.

Roscoe chuckled. He was really warming to his new apprentice. 'Well, kid, our shift ended two hours ago, so how's about we wrap this up and get home?'

'You can do just that, but I am going to follow Leo to the Raphael.'

'Sure. You go do your thing. But Lettie won't authorise any overtime.' Roscoe winked and flew off into the grey dawn.

* * *

Frustrated by public transport and itching to get his new wings, Erron trudged into the hospital nearly an hour later, his overcoat soaked through. He grabbed a lukewarm vending-machine coffee before making his way to the makeshift morgue, his back aching from having been on his feet for nearly twelve hours straight. Hades was far busier than any other division, as only death was a fixed point for everyone, unlike other division assignments, which were only issued if they had a specific impact on destiny. He was starting to miss having a few hours' downtime between assignments at Apollo. Instead, he was going from job to job for most of his shift, with only the odd chance to grab food on the go. He caught himself daydreaming about lounging in a café somewhere chatting to Casey between tasks and rarely ever having to do a night shift.

The hospital smell summoned psychosomatic pain, tangled memories of recent injuries made manifest with bitter antiseptic. He threw back another dose of the tiny morphine tablets and shook out the tired aching in his arms.

His phone rang, and though he didn't recognise the number, he automatically assumed there was an emergency for someone to phone him so early in the morning, his stomach knotting in anticipation of bad news.

'Agent Grover, it's Osato. How are you?' the Nemesis boss asked, her voice much more mellow than usual. It was a welcome change from the curt comments made by his new boss, Lettie.

'Tired, mostly,' he replied warily.

'Merletta Crawford has just informed me you were called to the scene of another murder, is that correct?'

'Yes, honestly, nothing to do with me.' He panicked.

'No, of course not. Please relax. I know you just finished a night shift, but would you be able to attend a meeting at Nemesis by 9 a.m.? It's purely to discuss the effective investigation of these murders, nobody is making any accusations. We're setting up a team and I want you to be part of it.'

He shook the sleeve off his new watch and checked the time. He had less than two hours. 'I'll try and be there.'

'Thank you.'

Erron hung up and went in search of Dr Enleigh. Leo Romano was laid out on a gurney next to Willow Madison, with the Archangel taking notes.

'Hey, I've got to be at a meeting shortly. Do you mind if we just go through this quick and return to it later?' Erron asked.

'Oh, at Nemesis? Yeah, I have to be there too. If you want I can give you a ride over when we're done. I've got a car out back.' Dr Enleigh smiled.

'Great.' Erron peeled his overcoat off and hung it up before pulling a pair of blue latex gloves and a plastic apron on.

# 10

## *Leave a Light On (Talk Away the Dark)*

'HEY, STRANGER,' NIKITA GREETED ERRON warmly in the lobby of the Nemesis Division headquarters near Southwark Crown Court.

'Hey,' Erron replied, subdued. He was stood awkwardly, making himself as small as possible in the corner of the room. A shadow of his former self, the usual cocky confidence evaporated into a remnant of who he once was. It was the first time she'd seen him since he'd started at Hades, and his aura of death was a stark difference from his former Apollo radiance. He looked exhausted, twitchy and uncomfortable.

'Settling in OK?' She gave him a gentle smile.

'Not too bad so far. Busy. I've just finished one hell of a night shift.'

'How dare people not die during office hours.' Nikita rolled her eyes and smiled.

'I know, right? Anyway . . . how's Case?' he asked cautiously.

'He's holding up OK.' Nikita was glad he asked. She could see he wanted to say more, but before he could speak, a heavy wooden door was flung open and the formidable presence of Osato M'Raya cast a long shadow.

The Nemesis boss looked impeccable in a sleek black suit and shaved head, a row of exquisite hand-crafted beads of her homeland adorning her neck, perfectly preserved from when she'd enjoyed the prestige of being a warrior in the once-named Kingdom of Dahomey. Her voice was no less commanding than her physical stature, and she led them into the lift and up to the top floor, walking into her office with the presence of a woman about to deliver a life sentence to a hardened criminal. Already sat at the vast conference table was Dr Carroway from the Raphael Sanctuary.

Nikita hadn't sat in that office since she was first summoned by Osato to discuss any information she had about Erron and Casey's involvement in recent apocalyptic events. Her eyes traced the clean lines of the furniture, once again taking in the minimalist decor and clinical organisation of the room. She shivered, the coldness of the room emphasised by the lofty ceiling and full-length windows that let in the grey morning light.

Erron cautiously sat next to Nikita, slouching down and folding his arms around his chest, his dark hair flopping over his tired brow. A few minutes passed before Emrys arrived, a bundle of paperwork under his arm. He perched on the empty seat between Nikita and Dr Enleigh.

Osato closed the door behind him and stood at the head of the table.

'I will get straight into it.' She spoke solemnly. 'Another Fortuna agent was killed just before five o'clock this morning. Hades Division arrived around half an hour after the time of death to dissolve the body, but as instructed, it has been transported to the Raphael Sanctuary instead. Unfortunately, the agency does not have the luxury to leave a body at the crime scene for long as it's just too risky.'

Emrys was clearly distressed, having only heard the news of Leo Romano's murder an hour before the meeting. He stared at the wall in thought as Nikita threw a concerned look his way. He was wearing a beige linen shirt with enough creases to match the worry lines on his brow, paired with a wine-red jacket, hastily buttoned up wrong.

Osato continued, 'It's clear we have a serious problem on our hands. Following recent events with Elzifur, I submitted a proposal to create a mini division to tackle the sort of situations that threaten the existence of the agency or the running of fate. It may be a surprise to no one, but the veil has not returned to its original strength as anticipated, and we need to be thinking ahead to protect the future of the agency and the mortal realm. Anyway, it took some persuasion, but I have finally received approval and funding. This team will remain small for now. We will be known as the Medusa Division, and I have handpicked you all to join, if you agree to this. I'll open the floor for discussion.'

Nikita raised her hand. 'I am chasing CCTV from the first murder; it should be with me in the next day or two. It could be our first lead.'

Osato nodded approvingly.

Erron half raised a hand. 'What is it we'd be doing exactly?'

'Primarily, your only focus as a Medusa Division member will be to investigate these murders. Once the situation is resolved, the team will become largely dormant, only responding to threats if they arise again in the future, which hopefully they won't.'

'And how will this impact our normal jobs?' Erron asked.

'For standard agents you will be granted set time aside for this work and this has been agreed with your division leads already, as no more than fifty per cent of your usual shifts. However, you can choose to work overtime at a rate of time and a half, paid in novas. Emrys will need to maintain his normal working shifts aside from being the Fortuna point of contact,' Osato explained.

'That suits me fine,' Emrys replied. 'But do you think just having the Medusa Division is enough? Shouldn't we really be thinking national, even global to tackle these things before it gets to the stage where it's an emergency?'

'I appreciate your concern, Emrys, but we aren't dealing with anywhere near the scale of threat that we did with the Lord of Chaos. Two murders are incredibly tragic, yes, but not a global threat. It's unlikely to affect anyone outside of our district.'

Osato passed out an official-looking document pack, with a signature sheet on the reverse and a bundle of pens. The emblem at the top was an infinity snake surrounding the sun and the moon, simple enough but eye-catching. 'If you're happy to proceed, please read and sign this document, it should answer any questions you can't think of right away.'

Nikita glanced through the pages, a hastily thrown-together contract and role profile as well as an FAQ sheet of pay, shifts and expectations.

'You will each be assigned your own tablet. Please use it to store any evidence, research or anything of value for the Medusa Division. You can contact one another on these and I have taken the liberty of creating a group chat system as well to keep everyone in the loop of developments.' Osato pushed a stack of slim boxes over to Dr Carroway, who began distributing them. 'Dr Enleigh has volunteered to be our medical liaison for the Raphael Sanctuary. Dr Carroway is giving him free rein to use the funding to get the forensics suite equipped.'

'Well, I don't know how much value I can add, but count me in.' Emrys was the first to put pen to paper, signing his name in a sequence of sophisticated swirls.

'I'm always happy to help,' Nikita chimed in, already excited at the prospect of diving into the investigation.

The two Archangels followed suit, leaving only Erron staring at the paperwork, twiddling his pen between his fingers.

'Agent Grover, I'm keen to have you on board. You've been at both scenes so far and have a good insight into investigations. Will you join us?' Osato's gaze felt as hot as a sunbeam through a magnifying glass. Erron shrank further into his seat as the eyes in the room fell on him. He wanted to help the investigation but had so much on his plate with learning a new job and trying to get past everything he'd been through; he wasn't sure if he wanted to be at the forefront of yet another unprecedented event. Picking up on his hesitance, Nikita reached over and slid the document away from him. 'I'm sure Erron is more than happy to assist, but I think it's unfair to ask him to sign this without letting him get some sleep first.'

'Surely there are newer ex-detectives in the agency?' Erron asked quietly. 'People with relevant skills, I'm practically archaic.'

'Skills can be learnt. I want people I trust, and I know you well enough now that you're someone I can count on to do the right thing,' Osato replied, her face sincere. 'Let me know by tomorrow if you'll join us. I hope you will.'

Erron nodded dutifully.

'I'd like to help with setting up the lab,' Nikita offered. 'I'm no expert but I've watched enough true-crime documentaries to have a fairly good idea of forensic techniques, even if I have to learn how to use them.'

'It wouldn't hurt.' Dr Enleigh shrugged. 'I'm fairly new in service so I have up-to-date understanding of processes in medical evidence, samples and whatnot. I'm sure between us we will be up to speed in no time.'

'Right, well, time is a popular flavour,' Emrys announced, quickly noticing the confused looks. 'As in, it's always running out. Shall we set some actions?'

'Yes, agreed. With the news of the second victim, I think it's pertinent to obtain whatever evidence we can. Agent Wolf, you are released from duty for your next couple of shifts if you can make a start with enquiries?' Osato requested, scooping up the signed papers and piling them neatly on her desk.

'Of course,' Nikita replied.

Emrys slid across a folder to Nikita. 'This is Leo's file. You'll find some relevant details: fingerprints, known associates, crewmates, etc. I've got Willow's here too.' He placed another thick folder on top. 'See if there's a particular link beyond their division.'

'Right, here are your badges. These give you direct authority to carry out your duties by upper management. Now you may encounter some resistance, until we put out an agency-wide notification of their official purpose today.' Osato handed out leather wallets, complete with a metal Medusa symbol as the badge and an ID card. 'We will reconvene when there is relevant progress. I have secured us a side room at the Eligos Library where we can have full confidentiality, the location and passcode is in your welcome pack. For anyone that hasn't been there, it's located in Hampstead Grove on the crossroads, but I believe most of you know where it is. From now on that will be our meeting place,' the Nemesis boss concluded.

* * *

The new Medusa Division team found their way back to the lobby, leaving Osato to conduct her usual daily business. Nikita gave Emrys a farewell hug and instructed him to call her later. She turned to Erron who was haunting the doorway.

'Erron, honey, you look like you need a week of sleep. You heading home?'

'I can't. I don't know which way to turn, or if I'm going to be any use if I join this team.' He pressed his palms to his forehead in exasperation. 'Even if I did, I can't sleep. I just can't fucking sleep.'

'Walk with me, let's get a cup of tea.' Nikita wrapped her arm around his and guided him out into the city streets. The rain had eased, rays of sunlight sparkled in the recent puddles as they headed for the nearest café, finally settling on an independent business with a penchant for cat-shaped teapots.

Nikita ordered for both of them as they squeezed into a tiny booth in the corner. The café was fairly busy, with enough ambient noise that they wouldn't be overheard. Erron opened his mouth to speak several times before biting back the words and glancing out the window.

'I'm going to be blunt, Erron,' Nikita began, just as a large tabby teapot was placed between them by a waiter. They were each given a mismatched cup and an excessively large jug of milk. Once alone again, Nikita continued, 'What you're going through is acute trauma from a very brutal assault. Of course you can't sleep. Are you having nightmares or flashbacks, stuff like that?'

He poured his tea, holding the ceramic tail of the cat with both hands to steady himself, adding just a splash of milk and three sugars. He stirred the spoon robotically, staring at the cheerful lemon-print tablecloth. 'The nightmares are awful. They're not always the same, but it's always her. My brain is filling in the gaps I don't remember, and I don't know if it's imagined or real,' he finished with a heavy sigh, his whole body slumping as he spoke.

Nikita gave him space to continue, just lightly touching his hand that held the cup. He could tell her Apollo influence was working its magic, as he could feel his walls crumble in her presence. It was a strange feeling, being on the receiving end, and Nikita wasn't even trying. Somchow he felt comfortable enough to begin blurting out his inner thoughts.

'I can't stand going home and seeing the bed,' he uttered. 'I want to burn it, throw it out the window. But part of me is so bloody angry that it was *my* bed, *my* space. Why have I got to lose even more of myself?' He dropped the spoon with a clatter on the saucer. 'I know I have to get rid of the bed, but I can't even bring myself to touch it. I'm sleeping on the sofa or at least trying to. But I can't shut off and all I can do is go over and over *and goddamn over* everything that's happened. And what good will it be once I've thrown out the bed? I can't exactly throw out the memory.'

Nikita held his gaze, nodding softly to encourage him to continue.

He tried, choking up when a silent teardrop slid down his cheek, followed by three more before he aggressively wiped them away with his sleeve.

Nikita passed him a serviette. 'It takes a long time before you'll feel whole again. And even then, that stone of grief still rattles around on your bad days. But I'm here for you,' she said softly.

Erron lost his words among the folds of the tissue he held scrunched against his face, desperately trying to hide the shame of his tears. Nikita gave him a few moments of silence, just holding his arm before she spoke again.

'This is a weird-ass teapot.' She focused her attention on the detail of the cat's bizarre grin.

'Yeah, it's bloody awful. And I like cats . . . but this . . . this is something else.' Erron managed a half-hearted laugh as he steadied his breathing.

'Don't lie, you want it in your kitchen,' Nikita teased.

'Yeah, you got me. You think it'll fit in your bag?'

'God, no.'

'Oh, what a terrible shame. We'll have to steal it another day.' His face broke into a weak smile.

'Terrible shame.' Nikita faked a sincere look of disappointment.

There was a pause as they slowly drank their tea. Nikita made small talk as Erron listened, easing into his feelings more. Nikita made a conscious effort to exude just enough Apollo charm that Erron would keep his guard down and get things off his chest. Twenty minutes went by before he spoke, giving his side of the story about his night spent at Casey's.

'Do you think he'll still want me?' he asked quietly, pushing his empty cup to one side.

'Are you an ugly ceramic teapot that looks like roadkill?' she replied.

He shook his head.

'Then Casey still wants you. Hell, knowing Casey, he'd want you *and* this goddamn monstrosity on the table.' She turned the teapot round the inspect all of it.

'He'd love that sort of thing.' Erron laughed. 'He'd feel sorry for it and be compelled to give it a home.'

'Give me one good reason why he wouldn't do the same for you then. And between you, me and the teapot, I know for a fact he loves you more than anything. He doesn't even have to say it. I could tell on my first day just by the way he looks at you.'

'He's too good for me, always has been. I can't even bring myself to touch anyone right now, not in *that* way. I just . . . I can't . . .' He trailed off, his expression twisting with anguish.

'It's OK. That's totally normal for what you've been through, Casey will understand. Take your time, Erron, and be kind to yourself. But for now, you're coming to my place to get some sleep while I make a start on this Medusa assignment.' She stood up and pulled on her jacket.

He wasn't afforded any time to protest as she led him out of the café and hailed a cab to take them back to her apartment block. Once there, she made him a valerian herbal tea and handed him fresh blankets.

'You can have the bed,' she stated.

'I can't let you do that.'

'It's my flat, so do as you're told.' She folded her arms. 'You can lock the bedroom door, if it makes you feel safer.'

'I really need to get my shit together. I can't carry on like this,' Erron muttered angrily.

'It takes time. You can't do anything productive when you're sleep-deprived.'

She tugged at his overcoat until he relented, allowing her to hang it up behind the door. 'Have a think about joining the Medusa team. You'll be working with me for a few days and then you've got forever after to go back to Hades. It might be good for you to spend time with a friend. Look, I'll be out for a little while, give you a bit of space. I will leave you a spare key by the door, hang onto it.'

'Thank you. I hate feeling like this. I'm supposed to be the strong one,' Erron muttered as Nikita busied around him, closing the blinds and fluffing the pillows.

She turned to face him with a stern look. 'I saw you impale yourself on a dagger to save Casey. If that's not strength, I don't know what is.' She perched next to him on the edge of the bed. 'Sometimes, Erron, you have to let Casey be strong for you instead. You can't carry every burden on your own.'

He nodded in acceptance and reached for the valerian tea, taking a tentative sip. 'Nikita . . .' he started and paused. 'I really appreciate this.'

'I've got you.' She ruffled his hair and smiled. 'You've got this.'

When Nikita had left the apartment, Erron slid his shoes off and loosened his black tie, eventually falling back onto the bed and into a deep, dreamless sleep.

* * *

The mood on the Oracles forum was electric. Word had spread that two of the Firefly people had been killed, and there was significant discussion around whether they were human or something entirely else. One thread was less than sympathetic.

Comments echoed back and forth encouraging violence and feeding off the resentment in the group.

> *If you ask me, they deserve it. It's about time someone meddles with their lives when all they do is meddle with ours. I'm pretty sure they are out there right now taking revenge somehow. Stay frosty and don't let any of them touch you. Weird shit happens when they touch you, especially the Greys.*

Sam massaged his face, easing the tension that had developed across his forehead. He had been staring at his screen all morning, reading all the replies eagerly and watching the flames of anger against the Fireflies spread. Previous ambivalence was turning into rage, and Sam was glad he was not alone in his anger. He felt like he was at the forefront of something major, a huge reveal that would soon shock the world and make everyone realise how their lives were being coordinated by outside forces. He opened a private message chain between himself and another oracle.

> TruthHunter11: *Did you see the dead Green near the club?*
> AlphaKingGetYou9: *Oh yes, I put him there. I think I have proved my worth.*
> TruthHunter11: *It was you???*
> AlphaKingGetYou9: *Stupid question. I took his eyes, two good eyes that can no longer look down at people like me with my bad eye.*
> TruthHunter11: *What did you do with them??*
> AlphaKingGetYou9: *Gonna sell 'em. I've got some interested buyers already. These things have some kind of magical power.*

TruthHunter11: *That's risky. What kind of power??*
AlphaKingGetYou9: *Not when you know the right people. I don't know yet but if you touch them, it feels like something good is about to happen.*
TruthHunter11: *Weird! Where will you be looking to go next?*
AlphaKingGetYou9: *Give me a week or so, I've got to pick the next one. I want to be able to take my time. I'll be in touch.*
*AlphaKingGetYou9 has gone offline.*

Sam switched off the computer and stretched. He reluctantly opened the shop door and put out his sign. It was long gone midday, but the customers would wander in to buy candles or knick-knacks more often after having lunch at one of the nearby restaurants. He had hastily learnt the art of vague tarot card readings sufficiently enough to blindside people with things they wanted to hear. He didn't have the true gift that his mother had had; she could pull deep messages from some spiritual nether-where and astound people with her readings. Sam had a group of women booked in for a reading at 4 p.m. so he busied himself setting up a table and the right ambient lighting. He figured with enough of the right aesthetic, he could forego the accuracy of his words.

He needed a few days to focus on running the shop to keep it going, before he could go on his next Firefly tracking mission. Deep down, he hoped his father would have been proud of him and everything he had achieved.

# 11

## *It Is What It Is*

OVER IN KENSINGTON, EMRYS TALIESIN was staring blankly at a glass case in his office. Inside, a set of ornate scales rested, each side had a glowing ball of cosmic energy levitating over the gleaming gold plates, one red, one green. They measured the balance of good and bad luck in the district, and since the death of two of his agents, the bad luck ball had gotten fractionally heavier, tilting the scales for the first time in decades. He swivelled around and picked up the receiver of his vintage rotary phone, dialling Osato's number with several spins of the interface. She answered promptly, but was barely able to get a word in before Emrys blurted out his concerns.

'We're losing good luck. This district is going to have serious issues if this continues. The scales have dropped massively.'

'How much have they dropped by?' Osato asked.

'Nearly two millimetres.'

'For Fate's sake, Emrys. How can you even tell? That's nothing to be worried about,' the Nemesis boss chided.

'We didn't take the apocalypse seriously enough the first time round, I don't want another one,' Emrys rebutted. 'I can't stand Marmite for a start.'

'This isn't another apocalypse. Besides, we have the best people looking into it now, Nikita will be all over it,' Osato said calmly. 'Let's have some perspective here, it's a tragic loss of two agents. You'd need to lose half your district before the luck balance becomes critical.'

'I'm still not convinced.' Emrys glanced back at the scales. 'But I suppose they say shit's always warmer than your hand, don't they?'

'I'm guessing *they* is just you, Emrys.' Osato had a unique way of communicating her eye roll over the phone. 'But I assume that's a roundabout way of saying look on the bright side.'

'Of course, no one likes holding shit that's gone cold,' Emrys mused.

'I'm hanging up now.'

* * *

Stepping through the gates of the majestic Eligos Library in Hampstead Grove, Nikita breathed in the earthy scent of the gardens, enjoying the deep silence that surrounded the ornate building. Ancient magic coursed through the stonework, one of London's oldest agency liminal zones, hidden from the mortal world and steeped in history. She walked along the gravel path towards the entrance, glancing up at the gargoyles on their sentinel posts around the gothic roof, eventually passing between the two iconic statues of winged knights on horses, each holding a book in one hand and sword in the other.

The last time she'd been at the library the world was ending, and she'd made quite a scene summoning Dantalion, one of the Demons of the Balance, with an offering of her cosmic blood. Inside the heavy oak doors, she felt back at home among the myriad of candles and the heady smell of old books.

Her breath caught in her throat when she spotted a familiar figure haunting the far corner of the ground floor, leafing through a weighty book on philosophy. The senior Ghoster, Darren Oliver-Alliott, known less affectionately as D-O-A from the common medical acronym meaning Dead on Arrival, glanced up briefly, as if alerted to her presence, before returning his gaze to the pages of his tome. His usual smart black attire and striking black wings were in stark contrast to his shock of white hair and deathly pale face. Had it not been for the ice blue of his eyes, he could easily have blended in with a monochromatic photograph.

Nikita would never forget how he'd helped her with preventing the apocalypse, or how he'd taken care of her when she'd fainted after summoning Dantalion. She could still remember the look of conflict on his face when he'd been given the blind card to reap Erron the night he lay bleeding out on the floor of the Sky Pod Bar. For a Reaper that inspired nothing but fear, he had a heart that Nikita was starting to wonder if only she could see.

She paused on the ground floor long enough to dig out some books on forensic investigations before making her way to the new Medusa Division meeting room.

* * *

It had taken her ten minutes to find the room, as it was cleverly tucked away adjacent to the stairway to the vault, where confidential and rare books were kept, covering the agency history, and titles that were ancient and irreplaceable. The room itself was small; the walls were a deep blue with an entire swirling galaxy painted on them, as if revolving around the large image of a sun carved into the wooden ceiling boards and stained a deep gold. Nikita was instantly drawn to the circular window, beautifully leaded with a spiral design, tiny crystals embedded in the glass, each casting a scatter of rainbows across the floor.

There was a round desk in the centre, with twelve chairs crammed in around it, all made from antique wood and varnished to a shine. Osato had gone as far as including their own tea urn and selection of mismatched mugs.

Nikita set down her armful of books and unloaded her bag. She'd brought her new Medusa tablet, her own laptop and the files of the victims that Emrys had given her, along with her trusty notebook and pen. The tablet pinged with an agency-wide email from Osato introducing the new team and stating cooperation with them was expected, as well as an alert for agents to be careful out and about.

She got to work poring over the information in front of her. Hours slipped by as she compiled what little evidence she had, compared the victim files and made a list of modern forensic processes that she was confident the agency could adopt.

Her eyes were tiring and eventually she decided to stretch her legs, hoping to try out her new Poltergeist Podcast headphones on the lower floor to see if they were just a gimmick, or if they actually held the potential to decipher the whisperings of the Eligos ghosts that were known to haunt to hallways of the ancient library.

She pulled them from the bottom of her bag before packing everything else away and exiting the cosy room. A handful of agents were scattered around the vast space on the ground floor, but many were already leaving as the evening closed in. Nikita fiddled with the dials on the headphones, placing them over her ears and wandering aimlessly between the shelves, waiting to pick up the hushed voices of the lost dead.

She gave D-O-A a nervous smile as he watched her go by, an incredulous look on his face at the strobing LEDs on her headband, the antennae sticking out at odd angles. She felt his gaze follow her long after she's passed him, the weight of his *Umbra Noctis* raising the hairs on the back of her neck.

She only started to hear some faint whispers as she approached the stairs to the lower floor, where the pool was situated. Ever curious, she descended.

The pool room, with its vaulted ceilings and gentle echo of the lapping water, was a perfect place for lost souls to gather, deep in the belly of the Eligos, where the ambience of peace might encourage them to gossip.

Nikita pulled off her shoes and socks, rolling up her jeans and plunging her legs in the warm water, just as a low murmur crackled through her headphones. She tweaked the dials slowly until the murmuring gained clarity, separating into several overlapping voices, much like what she'd heard in the Hall of Unconscious Stories. She picked out odd words, snippets of conversations that held little relevance. After ten minutes of trying to sift through the chatter, she went to pull the headphones off, conceding the point that they were nothing more than a novelty.

A single, urgent word came through as if right next to her ear, drawn out, each letter perfectly enunciated. *Wolf.*

Her hands remained frozen to the earpieces, her cosmic satsuma beating at a rate of knots.

'Yes?' Nikita found herself saying to the empty room.

Through the static, the same voice whispered, *Hear us.*

Unnerved, Nikita regretted trying the headphones in such an eerie room, just as the voice spoke up again. *Wolf can hear us.*

'How do you know my name?' Nikita asked shakily, trying to remind herself that she, herself, was also a member of the afterlife, albeit a more solid one.

*Web*, came the answer.

'Stuff this,' Nikita whispered to herself and began to withdraw her feet from the water.

*Stay, Wolf.* The voice was fainter, filled with more static.

The room took on a sudden aura of darkness, the air heavy with a sense of dread. Nikita's heart nearly stopped when she saw D-O-A appear to her left, his immense black wings filling the archway of the stairwell.

'They're getting clearer, aren't they?' the senior Reaper said in his cool tone.

'I haven't exactly spent much time listening.' Nikita pulled the headphones off and stuffed them in her bag. 'You've got some headphones too?'

'No, but in the last few weeks I've picked out actual words. You need to be in the water to hear them properly,' D-O-A explained.

'Why in the last few weeks?'

'One can only assume it's another symptom of the veil thinning,' D-O-A said, matter-of-fact. 'Water is like the cosmic web: it flows and envelops everything it touches. It is more powerful than light; it has the ability to give life and take it away. It's why the ghosts are using it to communicate. I've heard rumours that any reflective surface is becoming a conduit to other cosmic realms now, including water.'

'That's terrifying.' Nikita absent-mindedly dragged her socks over her wet feet. 'So Chaos agents could start leaping out of the pool if I cut my foot in there. I don't want to go summoning a demon by accident. Once was enough.'

'I don't think the veil is quite that thin.' D-O-A folded his arms. 'We're quite safe. Besides, the ghosts live in our realm, sort of. *Live* being a generous term.'

Nikita realised the Reaper must have spent centuries haunting the library himself and was likely older than most of the spirits in the building. 'Do they talk to you a lot?'

A slight smile crawled the edges of the Reaper's mouth. 'Let's just say they know when I'm in the mood to communicate. Otherwise, they wouldn't shut up. But this is the first time they've started to make sense, usually it's just formless whispers.'

'I'll have to practise that. I don't suppose a Ouija board would be easier,' Nikita said, letting out a nervous laugh. She pulled her shoes on and stood up.

'I wouldn't. You won't be connecting with lost souls; those things will only entice agents of Chaos to play with you.' The smile had quickly left D-O-A's face.

'Noted. I better get home.' Nikita edged towards the stairwell, the Reaper graciously moving out of the way.

'My lady.' He bowed slightly as she passed, stopping himself before completing the gesture, grimacing when he realised he'd slipped back into his medieval ways.

Nikita smiled and turned back to him, attempting her best curtsey. 'My lord.'

For the first time since she'd met him, his face melted into a broad smile that reached his eyes and brought a tinge of warmth to his deathly pale cheeks. At the top of the stairs, she checked the time. It was nearing the end of her usual shift, and she hadn't called Erron, hoping he was still fast asleep. Instead, she made her way home, picking up a takeaway curry en route and a bagful of essentials from the nearest department store.

Her flat was silent. She carefully emptied her bags on the kitchen side and went to peek into her room. Erron was passed out on the bed, still wearing his shirt and suit trousers, though barefoot and scruffy-haired. Nikita sat down quietly on the edge of the bed and gently shook his arm. 'Ready to rejoin the land of the afterliving?' she asked as he turned his head and blinked up at her. 'Dinner's in the kitchen,' she added.

'Dinner?' he mumbled as Nikita got up and left the room, gesturing for him to follow.

A couple of minutes later, Erron appeared, bleary-eyed, his feet cold on the tiled floor.

'Chicken tikka, garlic naan and a veggie samosa.' Nikita finished plating up two dishes and handed him one.

'What time is it?' he asked, his voice croaky.

'Half six. Get that down you.' She guided him to the living room.

'Fuck.' He blinked several times in astonishment. 'I've slept so long. What have I missed regarding the investigation?'

'Sounds like you're considering joining the team,' Nikita said hopefully. 'Anyway, you've missed nothing. Jared is at the hospital, and I have been at the library all day. How do you feel? Any nightmares?' Nikita was already digging into the curry.

Erron relaxed into the cushions on the sofa. 'No nightmares, thankfully. I feel a lot better, bloody starving though. Thank you for this. How much do I owe you?'

'Oh, just your eternal gratitude, or do the dishes,' Nikita teased. 'But you're welcome. I picked you up a few bits so you can stay here for a week or so.' Nikita nodded towards the other bags she'd brought in. 'Some clean clothes, bathroom stuff, etc. It's only basic but you need to get out of your flat for a bit.' She wolfed down some naan.

He paused, fork midway in the air. 'You sure?'

She rolled her eyes. 'Yes, dumbass. What are friends for if not looking out for one another. Besides, I hate doing the dishes.'

'Thank you. Consider me your personal dishwasher then,' he conceded. 'I might even cook for you, if you like instant noodles.'

'Sounds exquisite, Chef Grover.'

* * *

Early the next morning, Nikita rushed into the Apollo headquarters to grab a few things from her desk. Casey was mid-croissant as she turned up. He had tidied himself up and was wearing a sharp fifties suit complete with gold cufflinks and matching sleeve garters. Nikita, on the other hand, had overslept, her hair was bundled in a messy plait, complementing her thrown-together outfit of jeans and baggy blue jumper.

'Mormumm, Makiya,' Casey mumbled through a mouthful of pastry. He swallowed and tried again. 'Morning, Nikita, was what I meant to say.'

'I guessed that. How're you doing? You look great today.' She paused from stuffing her bag with books. 'I wish I had time to nab one of those.' She looked hungrily at the bag of fresh raisin croissants.

'I'm good actually! I've been keeping busy. Learning all about beekeeping.' He smiled broadly, passing her the remaining bag of pastries. 'You can have the rest of these. I have already eaten four.'

'Sorry, what? Beekeeping? You aren't setting up a hive in central London?' Nikita set her bag down.

'You don't think it's a good idea?' He tried to hide his disappointment. 'The world needs bees. Plus, I do love honey on toast.'

'I know the world needs bees, and that's a very noble idea, but, and don't take this wrong, you sound like you are having a mid-death crisis,' she said softly, trying not to giggle at the mental image of Casey stumbling around in a beekeeper suit on his rooftop terrace. 'I mean, do you even have enough room for all the kit? Not to mention you don't exactly have fields of flowers anywhere nearby for them to go and sit.'

Casey sighed and scratched his head. 'Yeah, I see your point there. I'm just trying to keep busy, you know. Anyway, how is the investigation going into that murder?'

Nikita checked her watch before pulling up a seat next to him, keeping her voice as quiet as possible. 'Just between us, there's two murders now. Another Fortuna agent was killed in the early hours of yesterday morning behind the Bonanza club.'

'Wait, another one? Who?' he whispered.

'Leo Romano, he had about sixteen years' service with the agency. The poor guy had bits of him chopped off and his eyes gouged out.'

Casey's face grew pale. 'I was passing by Bonanza that night when a young woman came up to me and said she was being followed by a strange guy. She was really scared. I didn't think anything of it at the time as there are a lot of strange men out at night, but do you think it might be connected?'

'It could well be.' Nikita glanced at the time. 'I really have to get going, Case, but can you jot down any details you remember and we'll get a statement from you as soon as possible?'

'No problem, I'll be glad to help.'

'That's great. If I can get any footage from that area I can compare it to the CCTV from Willow's death . . .' She hadn't yet had a response from the first CCTV enquiry. 'I need to chase that up. But if the same guy appears on both, it might be our first solid lead.' She got ready to leave.

'Before you go, how's Erron getting on? I haven't heard from him,' he asked cautiously.

Nikita shifted the weight of her bag on her shoulder. 'Not so great. He's staying at mine to get some sleep. He says he can't stand the sight of his bed, because of Izzy. Long story short, I had planned to go round later and see how I might be able to get him a new bed set up without him knowing. I just need to find the time.' She checked her watch again.

'Do you have the key with you?' Casey asked.

She nodded, pulling them from her jeans pocket.

'Leave it to me.' He held out his hand. 'It's the least I can do, and I have most of the day free. Sundays are usually quiet round here, most people are too tired or lazy to fall in love on a Sunday.'

She dropped the key in his open palm, seeing in his face that he already had a plan formed. 'You're a lifesaver.'

'No problem, you go do your thing and save the day.' He smiled, the Apollo glow gradually returning to his face.

Nikita was halfway out the door when she called back to him, commanding him not to get any bees.

* * *

She got to the makeshift morgue at the hospital an hour later than she'd wanted to and was pleasantly surprised to see Erron there. He was looking much better, having slept the whole night through again after his curry. He had thrown a lab coat over one of the white T-shirts that Nikita had bought him, instead of his usual shirt and tie. The lab coat slightly drowned his five foot five frame but he seemed to pull off the look, and it was a refreshing change from his usual darker attire. He was hunched over, examining Leo Romano's neck with intense focus.

'I take it you're joining the investigation then?' Nikita asked.

'I thought I better had. I can't leave this to amateurs, can I?' He flashed a cheeky grin in her direction. 'I told Osato I'd drop the contract off later.'

'Oh, I could hug you right now.' Nikita beamed. 'It's so good to have you on board.'

'Well, like you said, it probably wouldn't hurt for me to delay being at Hades for a few days. Anyway, I've put in a request for a chromatography kit, DNA analysis and full evidence collection kits for on scene. We need a decent camera too, but I haven't the faintest clue about photography so wouldn't know what's best,' Erron replied, not looking up from where he was carefully pressing on the neck vertebrae of the second victim. 'The hospital has already given us use of their high-spec microscopes and toxicology suite.'

'You're on it, then. I can help with the camera; I've done plenty of photography.' Nikita pulled on a pair of blue latex gloves. 'Have you found anything helpful yet?' She joined him next to table and watched him work.

After a short pause he stood up straight again and pointed to Leo's neck. 'Something isn't sitting right with me here. The bones feel almost too far apart; I mean, I am no medical expert, but they definitely don't feel right.'

Curious, Nikita felt around below Leo's skull. 'I see what you mean,' she said after a few moments. 'But then, how do we know that's not what his neck was always like? Cause of death was likely the garrotting and the pieces removed afterwards, would you say? Has Jared examined him yet?'

'He's just finishing up the post-mortem on Willow. He took her down to one of the surgical theatres as it was better equipped. He's going to process Leo later today. But I would make that assumption about the cause of Leo's death. If he was conscious while his feet were being sawn off, they wouldn't nearly be as clean cuts.' Erron rolled his gloves off and binned them. 'Dr Enleigh said he took a toxicology screening as soon as both of them were admitted, and apparently there was no trace of anything that would have been used to sedate them. But the curious thing is, Willow's neck felt similar. It doesn't seem to fit the cause of death.'

'So they weren't drugged and both of them have abnormalities to their neck ...' Nikita repeated out loud to herself. 'A bit like a hanging, would you say?'

'I couldn't say with one hundred per cent certainty, but it looks that way. The big question here is, who would be targeting Fortuna agents?' Erron looked perplexed. 'I'm wondering what else links the two of them because I can't see how else they would be singled out.'

'Well, we aren't in possession of the full facts yet. We need to establish connections first, rather than making assumptions.' Nikita was already trying to think of possible scenarios but was coming up short.

At that point, Dr Enleigh walked in, pushing the gurney that held Willow's covered body. 'I haven't found any fibres, latent prints or unusual bloodwork on either victim. There's next to nothing forensically and we can't go on using our current equipment. Willow's cause of death was from the garrotting; her hand was removed after death.' He shook his head, dismayed. 'And even though it's as cold as we can get it in here, it's not cold enough. The bodies will begin decomposing soon.'

'We've got limited time then and the new equipment will take a few days to get here,' Erron grumbled. 'Doc, can you run an X-ray on these victims' necks?'

'Why?' Dr Enleigh asked.

'You might have already noticed, but both victims have distorted neck bones. I just wanted to compare it to neck injuries associated with hangings. Would that be possible?'

'I've already confirmed the cause of death is the garrotting; I'm sure the neck injuries would have been from them struggling from what I've observed.' The young doctor folded his arms.

'I'm not doubting your expert opinion, but it would be good to have a visual representation for evidential purposes.' Erron leant back against the counter, tucking his hands into the pocket of the baggy lab coat.

'Fine, I'm not an X-ray tech but I can see if they can do it.' Dr Enleigh left the room, presumably in search of a staff member that could assist.

'He might be a while, the X-ray suite is three floors up, two wings across.' Erron picked up a mug of cold coffee and took a sip, wrinkling his nose with disgust. He stared blankly at a large resin plate sign of the medical caduceus hung on the far wall, taking in the details of the wings and the intertwined snakes.

Nikita's phone buzzed and she opened an email notification. 'Oh, perfect, the CCTV from Kensington is ready to collect. I have requested some more from the businesses around the Bonanza club too. Casey was there and might have some information that could be useful.'

'What was Casey doing at a club?' Erron looked puzzled.

'He was on a late-night walk. He said a woman approached him, saying she was being followed by a strange man,' Nikita explained.

Erron set the mug down sharply. 'Did Casey give a description of the bloke?'

'I didn't have time to take a statement from him. But we'll need to speak with him as soon as, really. I've got to go and get this CCTV as a matter of urgency.' Nikita took her gloves off and slung her bag over her shoulder, ready to leave.

'I'll do it. I need to speak to Casey,' Erron said after a pause.

'Oh, thank god,' Nikita exclaimed. 'He doesn't need any bees.' She left before Erron could ask what she meant.

# 12

## *Traitor*

CASEY HAD RECRUITED THE HELP of Ember Songfire, his closest friend from the Fortuna Division, to renovate Erron's room. Less than an hour after he'd called her, she had turned up to the apartment building in Canary Wharf, bouncing with excitement and dragging a bag on wheels full of tools for decorating.

'Thank you for this,' Casey said as he unlocked the door.

'My pleasure!' Ember beamed, the radiance of her cheerful face complementing her bright yellow dungarees. She stood the bag inside the door and pinned her long braids up on top of her head out of the way. 'So, what's first?'

'Well, we need to get the old bed out of here first.' Casey led her through the flat as he spoke, explaining the plan. He had already express-ordered a new bed from an agency store, who promised to recycle the old one. As they worked, Casey broached the subject of the Fortuna murders.

'I knew Willow. She was a good friend,' Ember said wistfully. 'We were meant to get one of those Arcane Ink tattoos together – you know, like the one Jared had the other week?'

'From Elysion?' Casey questioned, vaguely remembering the conversation they'd had in Nightjar previously.

'Yeah, it's got that new artist there. The ink allegedly gives you various boosts. Willow said she went for . . .' Ember furrowed her brow in thought. 'Something like Ares ink? It was supposed to give her more confidence, I think, but I'm staying open-minded about whether they actually work. Either way I wanted some new ink.'

'I can't say I have ever thought about getting a tattoo.' Casey pulled another slat off the bedframe.

'I had a few before I died, but only the really sentimental one stayed when I came back as an agent,' she explained, pulling her sleeve up to reveal a small forget-me-not design around her elbow. 'I had this one done when my best friend passed in college. I vowed never to forget her.'

It was well known that anything that had a significant impact on a person in their mortal life tended to stay on their skin, permanent scars that were etched into the very soul of a person that couldn't be erased.

'It's nice you still have the reminder,' Casey said.

Ember nodded, rolling her sleeve down to carry on dismantling, lost in her own thoughts for a few minutes before Casey spoke again.

'Are there any suspects, do you know?' he probed.

'Emrys hasn't told us much about the deaths, only that it's suspected foul play, and we need to be vigilant.' Ember shifted her weight where she sat on the floor to get more comfortable. 'I knew Leo a fair bit too. He was celebrating the other night with a bunch of the team at Bonanza.'

'What was he celebrating?'

'I don't really remember, but I think it was either his mortal birthday or his Bakeday.'

A lot of agents made a tradition to celebrate their Bakeday, which was when their soul had been fully cold-pressure baked.

'Ah, fair enough.' Casey was one agent that never got behind a Bakeday celebration. He'd started his career in Nemesis Division and many of them didn't like to acknowledge the violence or injustice of their passings. Ember, on the other hand, saw it as a good excuse to raise the roof and throw down some shots.

Just then the doorbell chimed. It was the agency store with the new bed.

Ember stretched and shook out her arms once they had finally assembled it and indulged in numerous triple chocolate cookies to keep their energy up. 'So, what's next?'

Casey stared at the blank wall in the bedroom. He rubbed his chin in thought. 'I hear you're quite the artist,' he answered, a cunning smile forming on the edge of his lips as he explained his idea.

Ember beamed, fetched her bag on wheels and dug out a case of paints and brushes. 'I'll get started, but I think it's high time for a cuppa.'

Casey agreed and went to make them a drink. Searching for a spoon, Casey stumbled on a gift box crudely shoved in the kitchen drawer. Curious, he opened it to see a red-painted pebble heart with the initials 'I C' and 'E G' drawn on in marker pen. A small card was crumpled down the side of the box, and he couldn't help but read it. His hands trembled as he read the words again, over and over.

*Dear Erron, please accept this small gift as an apology for the other day. I really think our friendship is special and could become so much more if we could just go back to talking again. I'm thinking of you always, Izzy xxx*

An overwhelming nausea rose in his gut, and he shoved the gift back in the drawer haphazardly, slightly tearing the card. Heat rushed to his cheeks as he fished out a teaspoon, attempting to slam the drawer shut, despite it having a soft-close mechanism. He watched it slowly mock him, as it decided to close in its own, sensible way, adding to the anger that was welling up in his throat. He let his intrusive thoughts invade the logical side of his brain, playing out any plausible reason that Erron had kept the note and pebble, and every one of them bringing images to the surface of them in bed together. After a moment of excessively stirring both cups of tea, Casey chastised himself for his reaction, knowing deep down the only physical intimacy Izzy had had with Erron was a violent assault. But as much as he rationalised it, it still gnawed at him why Erron would have kept the gift.

Plastering on a smile, he went back to where Ember had already made a start on the mural he'd asked her to paint.

* * *

Instead of returning to the hospital, Nikita had taken the CCTV footage she'd collected to the Eligos, wanting the silence and comfort of the library to help her think. She'd texted Erron, filling him in on her whereabouts for the afternoon.

As the sun hung low, she caught herself staring into the distance. The last rainbows danced across the floor from the crystal-studded window and birds were twittering as they went to roost for the evening. She began to think about her encounter with D-O-A in the haunted pool room on the lower floor. A slight shiver ran down her spine at the memory of the way the ghosts had spoken to her, quickly replaced by curiosity over the whole ordeal.

She was abruptly brought out of her thoughts by the sound of frustrated scrambling at the door and a few muttered curse words before Erron burst into the room.

'I couldn't get the bloody code to work,' he grumbled, noisily scraping a chair over to sit next to Nikita, a lollipop stick wedged in the corner of his mouth.

'Coffee?' she asked.

'Sure. Actually . . . tea?'

Nikita smiled and went to the tea urn, dropping a tea bag in a mug. 'I take it you've signed your contract now?'

Erron held up his shiny new Medusa badge. 'All official.'

Nikita finished making the tea, setting two mugs down as she joined him. 'I've been busy trying to clean up that CCTV from earlier. It's blurry as hell but at least it's in full colour.'

'Did you see the guy?'

'Have a look and see what you think.' Nikita brought up the video on her tablet.

They watched in silence for a few minutes. The camera angle didn't show the alleyway directly, but it covered the exit in the corner of the screen. Twelve minutes in, Erron leant closer, asking Nikita to pause and rewind, the last of the flat lollipop clacking against his teeth.

'I recognise that fella.' He jabbed at the screen, where a blurry figure was sitting at an outside table with distinctive long hair and a paisley bandana. They could just make out a large rucksack by his side, and he seemed to be looking through binoculars into the crowd. 'He followed me over a week ago when I met up with Freya. He was acting strangely.'

'You never mentioned that.' Nikita zoomed in on the man's face. 'What did he do?'

'Nothing really, but he was staring at us. It was like he could see right through our cloaking. But it was definitely him.' Erron tapped the screen a second time for emphasis.

'Could he have been an agent or one of the other agency staff?' Nikita started jotting in her notebook.

'I suppose. He wasn't close enough for me to really tell.'

'And whereabouts was this?'

Erron faltered, his mind going blank. 'I honestly can't remember. Nowhere near the crime scenes. I know that much.'

'OK, if it comes back to you let me know.' Nikita paused the video and printed a screenshot of the man before resuming.

Some time went by. The crowd round the café swelled, and with it, the man disappeared into the throng of people.

'Willow comes around this corner in a few seconds . . . There she is.' Nikita pointed out the vibrant Fortuna agent, happily bobbing along through the cluster of pedestrians. She paused at the entrance of the alley, as if someone had called to her. A bright glare from the sun blocked out the next twenty-three seconds of video, before it settled, showing only the man with the long hair running from the direction of the alley a few minutes later, blood on his clothes and his rucksack thumping against his back as he jogged across the road. Both agents noted the small dark item that fell from his bag and rolled towards the kerb.

'I would say he's definitely our guy,' Nikita confirmed, taking a long sip of her tea.

'Without a doubt. Did you get the CCTV from Bonanza?' Erron asked.

'No, the places I have requested all said it would take a few days, and that's even with my best Apollo charms. Have you spoken to Casey yet?'

Erron focused his attention on his mug and tapped his fingers against its side, nervously. 'No, I haven't had a chance.'

'You've had most of the day. What have you been doing?' She rolled her eyes.

'I assisted Jared with the autopsy on Leo. I've been trying to get as much evidence from the victims as I can before they start growing mushrooms,' he said sharply.

'OK . . .' Nikita let it go. 'At least from this CCTV we can identify the place where the suspect was sitting. It might be a long shot, but whatever fell from his bag may still be lying in the road. It could be a lead if it's still there.'

Erron checked his watch. 'I can swing by there to check the road.'

'That's great. Oh, I picked up a camera today. It's mid-range but user-friendly.' She plonked a box on the table with a camera logo emblazoned across it. 'I've been setting it up so I can head back over to the Raphael Sanctuary and get some decent images.'

Erron pulled out the instructions, unfolding them eight times until they were almost as big as an *A–Z* map of London. 'Yeah, I'm glad you sorted this,' he said, eyes wide at the tiny print.

Nikita pulled the top of the instructions down to lock eyes with Erron. 'Now, about Casey . . . The longer you leave it, the harder it will get.'

'Oh, I know.' Erron ran his fingers through his hair, his expression uncomfortable.

'I meant the harder it will be to break the ice,' Nikita said.

'Of course you did. I knew that.' His cheeks flushed slightly.

'Text him, for god's sake.' She rolled her eyes. 'I'm sure he doesn't bite.' She started packing her bag and paused. 'Unless of course you want him to, then, that's between the both of you and I need not ask.'

Erron turned crimson and abruptly stood up. 'I'll text him; I promise.' He gathered the mugs and hurried out of the room to find the nearest sink where he could rinse them out, knowing full well he wouldn't be able to cleanse the thoughts that had just entered his mind as easily.

Nikita grinned to herself, feeling accomplished, before planning her route back to the hospital. On her way out, she grabbed the printouts of the suspect and bundled them into her bag.

# 13

## *Strange and Beautiful*

Sam had made exceptional sales that morning, his last customers leaving just after 2 p.m., which gave him the chance to close up early and think about his plans for the following week. He had fast become an active and influential member of the Oracles website. For the first time in his life, people really listened to what he had to say. Although his morbid curiosity had left him with blood on his hands and an internal turmoil about whether he was doing the right thing, the validation was addictive and he saw no reason to pull away. He was itching to go out again and find another Firefly.

He logged back into his private messages on the forum. A familiar name was already online.

TruthHunter11: *Have there been any further plans?*
AlphaKingGetYou9: *I've decided to go out hunting again this evening. I will find another one, but this time I want to see what makes them tick. Learn more, y'know? I'm going stir-crazy thinking about all this shit.*
TruthHunter11: *So are you going to collect any more trophies?*

AlphaKingGetYou9: *I will, but I want to observe a bit more first. These trophies, though, they're definitely lucky. The Greens must be like genies or leprechauns or some shit, granting wishes or something. I need to know more. Where they go, where they come from, what their purpose is.*

TruthHunter11: *We know the Greys cause terrible things to happen. Maybe the Greens are the good guys?*

AlphaKingGetYou9: *Maybe, but I have seen them around together, so they must all be working for the same people or gods or whatever this bullshit is.*

TruthHunter11: *Man, I wish I was as brave as you getting this close.*

AlphaKingGetYou9: *We can't all be the hero. But I will share my location with you so you can get involved if you want. We just can't be seen talking. We can't know each other in public, you understand?*

TruthHunter11: *Yeah, I get it. I'll be there if I can.*

*AlphaKingGetYou9 has gone offline.*

Sam signed out of the website and decided to go out into the streets of London and observe any Greens he could find. The cold air carried a bite to it, and he made the effort to wrap up warm, braiding his hair and pulling on a thick maroon beanie hat and matching scarf.

The place where he had seen the most Greens in one area was in Kensington, so he headed to Westferry Station as the afternoon light slipped between the long evening shadows across the pavement.

Alighting at South Kensington just over half an hour later, he noticed a glimmer of vibrant green in the distance. It surrounded a figure heading into a small pasta place, and Sam saw it as the perfect opportunity to watch his newly acquired target.

His stomach cramped with both anxiety and excitement the closer he got. The Green had taken a seat at the back of the cosy restaurant, pulling out a book to read. It was too perfect; he had every chance to watch her for some time without trying to follow her through the city.

He paid for a medium carbonara and took a seat on a table adjacent to her, taking out a book of his own, thinking it was a good way to watch her over the pages. She had a particular glow to her besides the green aura, bright, welcoming eyes and long, unkempt blonde braids. Paint spattered her bright yellow dungarees and smudges of it were brushed on her face and fingertips. Her pasta arrived, accompanied by a frothy milkshake with bright rainbow sprinkles. The smile she gave the waitress was like watching the first crest of dawn break through on a summer day, warm and beautiful to behold. Sam lowered his gaze, glancing over the top of his book every few minutes.

The more he watched her, the more he felt lucky to be in her presence, the sheer positivity she exuded, the gleeful way her eyes sparkled with every turn of a page in her book. To be so happy, with the simplest pleasures in life, was a blessing unlike any other. Sam remembered a time he'd felt that carefree, as a teenager surrounded by snacks watching the Formula 1 with his dad on a Sunday afternoon, his mum singing in the kitchen to Stevie Nicks as she made her famous red velvet cake. Memories of his dad burned behind his eyes, reigniting the rage he felt at losing him to one of the Greys. Watching the young woman, he felt conflicted, knowing she was part of the same mysterious legion as the Greys, but feeling inexplicably drawn to her.

His carbonara arrived, and he picked at it, trying to untangle the mess of feelings in his head along with the spaghetti strands. Ten minutes later, the Green received a phone call, Sam listening intently.

'Hey, Emrys!' She beamed, pressing the phone to her left ear.

Sam could just make out the low tone of a male voice on the other end of the line.

'I mean, sure, I can swap a shift for tonight, but I need to be away by 2 a.m. if that's OK. I'm pretty tired.' Her brow furrowed slightly, and she stirred her drink slowly as she nodded and *mmm-hmmed* to whatever was being asked of her.

'No problem, boss. I'll get there in an hour or so. I just have to nip home first and get changed . . . OK, bye!' She hung up and checked the time on her phone, deciding to read to the end of the chapter before she set off.

'Good book?' Sam asked across the tables, a slight crack in his voice from hesitation.

She looked up at him. 'It's good, similar to a lot of his others but I like the predictability.' She gave Sam a smile similar to the one she'd gifted the waitress. His stomach danced a little.

'Ah, sometimes that's better than too many twists. I couldn't help but overhear you've been called in to work. I bet that's ruined a few plans for this evening.'

She cautiously laughed. 'Well, yeah, but I love my job, so it's no biggie.'

'That's lucky, then. What do you do for a living?'

'Very lucky indeed. I'm a bike messenger. And I really ought to get going.' She made a point of finishing off the last of her pasta before gathering her stuff together to leave.

'Must be important to call you in on a Sunday evening,' Sam queried.

'What can I say, business is booming.' The Green gave him a terse smile.

'Well, it's a shame we couldn't chat more. I didn't catch your name?'

'Ember.'

'It's nice to meet you,' Sam replied.

Once she'd left, Sam waited for a few seconds before vacating his seat, following her at a cautious distance.

He tailed her through the throng of city crowds in Kensington, having no trouble keeping a visual of her with her vibrant green aura, undulating around her like her very own *Aurora Borealis*.

She stopped off for twenty minutes at a maisonette in a side street, and Sam stayed across the road out of sight, watching and waiting. When Ember finally emerged from the doorway, she had changed into a blue sequinned dress hemmed with tassels and a white denim jacket adorned with matching blue flowers. Her sunlight-blonde hair was flowing loose to her waist, a single diamanté hairclip holding it off her face. She looked ready to take a casino by storm or dance the night away at the kind of club that had a membership fee. She certainly wasn't dressed like the average bike messenger. Either way, Sam felt he was in the presence of an ethereal creature, a being so unbelievably sublime that the gods themselves would weep at her loss. She practically skipped to a large building with magnificent stonework and beautiful stained-glass windows, an ironwork fence running around the perimeter.

She was met by another Green, a man in his forties with scruffy spiked hair and the look of a university professor in his tweed suit and bow tie. He handed her what looked to be a selection of cards, and they spoke for a few minutes before three more Greens turned up, two men and another woman.

Sam shuffled a little closer, trying to hear what they were talking about while remaining out of sight in an alcove of the building. The scholarly looking man was referred to as Emrys and appeared to be their boss, potentially more powerful than any of them. He seemed to be giving instructions for the other Greens on an event they were to attend for work, though the rest he missed. Ember's colleagues were all equally radiant, despite their different ages and styles.

Sam had managed to take some photos of the group before four of them climbed into a nearby black cab, leaving Emrys behind. He was excited to share the images on the Oracles forum, thinking it might prove that he was the closest to finding out the truth so far, and knowing two of their names was an extra bonus, as it might even be possible to find records of them somewhere online.

Once the cab had disappeared out of view, Sam retraced his steps to the little maisonette that Ember seemed to call home, taking a moment to see if there was any other activity through the yellow-framed windows.

No lights were on, and the house seemed quiet. Sam went up the front steps and peered through the letterbox before trying the door, just on the off chance that Ember had forgotten to lock it. The door had a little give, it was old and creaky, but it was definitely bolted. Sam hopped down the steps and went into the narrow alley that ran beside the house, finding a back entrance into the building and a narrow window.

That door was also locked, but with some encouragement, the window prised open, giving just enough space for someone to squeeze through.

Sam had a small frame, and managed to wriggle through with little difficulty, landing hands first into a bathtub and pulling himself free of the window ledge.

The tiny bathroom was Victorian blue tile, with updated fittings, and an array of soaps and shampoos were littered around the cramped storage spaces. Sam snapped a few photos, curious that the Greens must obviously still indulge in bubble baths and have a need to wash their ethereal glowing hair, along with any other normal bathroom habits.

He crept into the hall, ever alert for any sound that would signify someone else was home, but the house was quiet, filled with a calming scent of lavender incense and cheerful pictures of flowers all over the walls.

He explored every inch of the house, finding a compact kitchen with normal, human food stacked in the cupboards, a cosy living room filled with plants and bright artwork, sixties wallpaper and mismatched, retro furniture. Upstairs was a single bedroom with a small double bed squeezed in between the window and a desk, the purple polka-dot bedding obviously slept in, and an assortment of books and journals scattered on the top of the desk. Behind the door was an eclectic selection of frames on the wall, each of them containing grainy black and white photos that seemed to have been taken by an old camera. Sam peered closer, noticing one striking image of Ember, smiling outside a busy theatre on Palace Pier in Brighton. He was confused, having visited the pier with his parents as a child. The theatre had long been removed and replaced by an amusement arcade, which indicated that either he was looking at an older relative of Ember, or she didn't age.

He took a few more photos of the room and flicked through some of the journals, deciding to put one in his bag from a bundle that didn't look obvious, with the view to read it later on. He wasn't at all surprised to find the oldest journal was dated January of 1961. All of them carried the same rounded cursive, the same bubbly, insightful entries about Ember's day, who she'd met, where she'd been, what food she'd had.

Sam checked the time on his phone. He'd been reading the journals for nearly half an hour and was conscious he needed to leave. Getting out of the narrow window was harder than getting in, as there was a much higher drop. He decided to wriggle out feet first to avoid breaking his wrists on the pavement. Carefully, he closed the window behind him and made his way back to his quiet little shop.

* * *

Erron had been scouring the streets around the alleyway where Willow had been murdered, looking for the unidentified item that had fallen from the suspect's bag. The dark didn't help, especially as he had no clear idea what he was looking for. Momentarily defeated, he decided to wait for the rush-hour traffic to ease, and phone Casey instead. His stomach churned as he found the number on his phone, his mind rehearsing what he might say, but it didn't make it any easier to press the call button. In his hesitation, he searched around in his pockets for another flat lolly but came up empty.

'Oh, fuck it,' he muttered to himself and went on a short diversion to the nearest off-licence, buying a cheap pack of cigarettes and a lighter.

Walking back to the alleyway, his hands shook as he lit the first cigarette he'd had in weeks. The first lungful of acrid smoke both soothed and disgusted him, but he vowed he was just doing it for temporary relief, not wanting to fall back into his previous addiction. He coughed harshly after the second draw, his lungs rejecting the imposition. Despite how his throat burned, he leant back against the wall and closed his eyes, enjoying the wave of nicotine as it entered his system.

Ten minutes later, he exhaled the last of the smoke and opened his phone again, not allowing himself to hesitate before pressing the call button.

'Case,' he said quietly when he heard the voice on the other end. 'It's me.'

'Erron,' Casey replied, reserved and steady. 'What can I do for you?'

Erron closed his eyes, forgetting everything he'd rehearsed. 'I guess it would be easier to speak in person maybe. I'm working on the Fortuna agent murders. I need your help with it, if you can.'

'Go on,' Casey answered, tight-lipped.

'Nikita mentioned you might have seen a possible suspect while out clubbing. I have a photo from CCTV I want you to look at, to see if it's a match. We'll need a statement from you about anything you saw, anyone you spoke to, that kind of thing.'

'I wasn't clubbing. But sure, I will do what I can to help.'

Erron breathed a silent sigh of relief. 'I really appreciate that.'

'You know where to find me. Let me know when you're about.'

'OK great, yes, thank you.' Erron's heart skipped. 'Casey, I—'

Casey hung up.

'—miss you,' Erron whispered down the empty line.

He stared at the blank screen of his phone for a moment, not entirely sure if the interaction had gone better or worse than expected – and he was no closer to understanding Nikita's comment about bees.

He slipped the phone back in his pocket and pulled out another cigarette, telling himself it would be his last as he lit it.

The traffic was easing, so he took his chance to have a closer look along the road, ducking in and out between cars and crouching down near all the drains to shine his phone light into the darkness. As drivers angrily beeped their horns at him, he spotted a grubby dark object wedged in the grate of a drain. Precariously pulling it free by one corner, he found it to be a mini notebook, no larger than a matchbox and curled up like a Pringle. Not wanting to damage or contaminate it further, he bundled it into a clear evidence bag and stuffed it into his inside pocket. He carried on looking until it became apparent he'd covered every inch of the streets in a hundred-foot radius from the scene.

Heading back to Nikita's, he got a call from Theodore Roscoe, informing him they needed him back at Hades for a shift in the morning. Hiding his frustration, he agreed before continuing on.

An hour later, he reached Nikita's apartment block and snuck another cigarette before going inside, craving the comfort of his old habit and kicking himself for giving in a third time in a row.

Nikita was already home, cooking a batch of cheesy pasta bake and garlic bread, the Fortuna boss, Emrys helping her set out plates. Steam from the hob was swirling around the downlights and upbeat music was playing from a speaker in the kitchen, the table filled with a chaos of crockery and condiments, the smell of garlic and herbs heavy in the air. It was the perfect picture of a warm, welcoming home.

'Ah, sorry, am I intruding?' Erron subtly backed up against the door.

'No, not at all.' Emrys gestured that he'd set out three places at the kitchen table. He whisked past Nikita to fetch some glasses, pausing on his way back to plant a series of small kisses on the back of her neck. She giggled and pushed him away playfully.

'How'd you get on in Kensington?' Nikita looked over at Erron.

He pulled the evidence bag from his inside pocket and smiled. 'I found this. It looks like what we saw on the CCTV.'

Nikita rushed over and examined the bag, turning it over several times. 'It's promising. We can examine this later after dinner. Oh, did you speak to—'

'Yes, I rang Casey,' he cut in. 'I'm going to set up a meeting with him to discuss the suspect description.'

'How romantic,' Nikita teased.

'I'm trying.' He looked defeated.

She softened and went to hug him. 'I know, hang in there.' She pulled away and wrinkled her nose. 'You smell of smoke. I thought you quit?'

He rubbed the back of his neck and gave her a sheepish smile.

'Dinner's served,' Emrys chirped, gesturing for them to both sit down.

Over pasta, Erron started to relax, enjoying the light-hearted conversation, as all of them had agreed not to talk about murders, the apocalypse or Marmite for one evening. They shared a particularly awful bottle of wine and played a game of cards after dinner before Emrys stretched, yawning. 'Well, it's late. I better get back to the moon.'

'You can stay over if you want.' Nikita gave him a pleading look.

'I would, Rocket, but I need to get some sleep tonight.' He winked at her and kissed the back of her hand. 'Besides, you have this other man hanging around your apartment and I'm burning with jealousy.'

Nikita laughed. 'You've nothing to worry about there.'

'Oh, I don't know, he's quite the heartbreaker.' Emrys shook his head in mock defeat. 'I wouldn't expect you to choose a scruffy art teacher over a guy that looks like that ... what's-his-name ... Irish actor with dark hair, always looks a bit worried.'

'That narrows it down,' Nikita said with a laugh.

'I am right here, you know,' Erron pointed out.

Nikita rolled her eyes at both of them. 'Emrys, I only have eyes for you. Trust me on that.'

'She means it. Besides I'm no heart-throb.' Erron scratched his head.

'Oh, you do tick the boxes, Grover. Not to inflate your ego,' Nikita admitted. 'But I prefer my men blond, artistic and in charge of a whole afterlife division.'

'Emrys, I'll be out of her hair in a couple of days and you two lovebirds can go back to your sickly sweet displays of absolute infatuation in no time.' Erron decided at that point to give them space to say goodbye, retreating to the sofa.

'I can't wait to have you to myself again.' Emrys brushed Nikita's hair gently from her face.

'I look forward to it. Now get home and stay safe.' She wrapped her arms around him and kissed him goodbye. 'There's a killer on the streets.'

'Yes, my darling. Let's hope he's not an astronaut too.'

When the door clicked closed behind him, Erron came back to the table and carried the plates to the sink. 'I hope I haven't put a spanner in the works with you and Emrys by being here?' he asked. 'I'm pretty good at damaging relationships lately.'

'Don't be daft. You're my guest and I can go to Elysion if I want alone time with Emrys. He's only teasing. A small, healthy dose of jealousy, nothing more.' Nikita walked up behind him and rubbed his back as he started to wash the dishes.

As soothing as the gesture was meant to be, Erron flinched in pain at her touch.

'Oh god, sorry, I forgot.' She withdrew her hand instantly.

'It's OK, it's just still a little sore. I've been trying to ease off the morphine.' His wing-removal surgery was taking its time to heal, particularly with the raw scar tissue from the runes that had been carved down his spine by Izzy. Dr Enleigh had assured him it was on the mend, but parts of his back still felt worse than eating ice cream with sensitive teeth. It didn't help that his Hades wings had now begun to form.

'When do you get your new wings?' she asked, picking up a tea towel to dry the dishes.

'Oh, they are growing; I can feel it like toothache. I expect they will start to break through in a few days. It's different to your first set obviously.'

'Yeah, I didn't realise I had to be given the right supplements to start mine off. I've got my appointment next week for the preliminary bit, so I won't be far behind you.' Nikita was itching to get her wings, if only to avoid so much travel on the Underground.

'You'll love it when they're here but make the most of being able to easily lie in the bath while you can, they take some getting used to.'

'Noted, my fellow flightless bird.' She playfully nudged him. His solemn face broke into a grin, and he flicked dishwater back at her.

'At least we're not geese,' he retorted.

'True, that might be worse than having a Reaper haunting your kitchen,' she teased as they both put away the last of the dishes.

'Speaking of which, I've got to do a Hades shift tomorrow,' he stated.

'Yeah, I think I ought to head into Apollo too and see whether I'm needed. Should we take a look at that notebook now?'

Erron agreed and they went back to the table. He pulled a bundle of forensic gloves from his pocket and carefully opened the evidence bag. The little book was significantly water damaged so opening the pages was a delicate affair, but they were able to peel a few apart and make out some of the scribbled notes, blurred in places where the rain had bled the ink. Nikita fetched her new camera and took photos of each page as Erron turned them.

'What does that look like to you?' She stopped him at the back page, where a bundle of letters and numbers were under a single word: *Oracles*.

'I don't know. I think it will be easier to make out when we can zoom in on the pictures.'

'It could be some kind of password maybe,' Nikita mused. 'Or an order number, something like that.'

'Maybe,' Erron conceded.

'I'll get these photos loaded on my laptop before bed and see if we can zoom in on any of this.'

'Great, but do you mind if I turn in?' Erron yawned. 'I'm so tired and it takes about seven hundred buses to get to Highgate from here.'

'You go ahead.' She smiled.

* * *

Over in the little shop in Pennyfields, Sam was wide awake, still buzzing from his spontaneous encounter with Ember, and seeing the ins and outs of her tiny home. He'd gone straight onto the forum, uploading a sample few of the photos he'd taken, keeping others just for himself. He was keenly watching the results of a set of auctions, all pieces of the last Green that had been uploaded for sale.

It was approaching eleven in the evening and Leo Romano's feet were in an air-tight bag at the bottom of a dirty standing freezer, the ragged cuts at the ankles turned purple and frost-bitten. They were the main listing and proving very popular. Twenty-eight ice-cube trays were stacked on the shelf above, all containing frozen cubes of the sparkly Fortuna blood that had been collected from the night of his murder. Each item had been meticulously photographed and listed for sale.

Sam had watched the bids pile in through the evening. The auction was being held over a cloaked website that could only be accessed by invitation – to anyone else, it came up as a site for the newly launched DFS sale. Eleven people from the

Oracles forum had been pursuing the feet, the bids climbing to a lofty £4,520, the description speculating that the body parts could provide a boost of godlike powers to whomever possessed them. Sam didn't actually know if the feet had any impressive powers, but it was a good selling point.

The frozen blood cubes were doing well, averaging over £250 each, and marketed as a drinkable elixir for an ultimate boost of fortune. After two initial buyers with good standing on the Oracles forum had testified to their potent use, the value of them had skyrocketed. It seemed the demand would soon outstrip the supply once bidding had ended in the early hours of Monday morning.

Despite the lively and enthusiastic bidding on the trophies from the second Green, Sam still harboured a very uneasy feeling about the whole affair. It was his thirst for knowledge that was keeping him so entrenched in the Oracles community.

His attention was drawn back to the picture of the Greens he'd posted. The one he'd chosen didn't fully show Ember's face, as he wasn't ready to share her with anyone else just yet. Comments had been flooding in, some curious, some sceptical, but most downright disturbing in nature. The one thing Sam couldn't ignore was the unfiltered hatred that the bulk of the people displayed towards the Fireflies, another online echo chamber of blind rage and shared vision. He'd had that same anger, fuelled by the shared experiences of the others, but over time and since meeting Ember it had simmered into his quest for discovery.

By 1 a.m., Sam was barely able to stay awake, despite the online buzz. He gave in to his tiredness and collapsed on his bed, only just finding the strength to shake his trainers off before dragging the wool blanket over himself.

# 14

## *Hold the Line*

CASEY WAS SLUMPED IN HIS armchair, lost in thought and swirling a cocktail umbrella around the top of a double-caramel milkshake. He glanced at his antique carriage clock on the mantelpiece, it had gone midnight. He was exhausted from the day spent in secret at Erron's apartment rearranging and redecorating the open-plan bedroom, but he still wasn't able to sleep.

Having discarded the idea of starting a colony of bees on his rooftop terrace due to the logistics of setting it up, he had frittered away the early part of the evening trying to entertain himself with an impossible jigsaw puzzle of baked beans. He'd given up after spending over three hours on the first twelve pieces, ending up staring at the wall, unable to think of anything other than Izzy's gift in Erron's kitchen drawer. After finding it, he'd questioned everything he thought he knew about the situation between Izzy and Erron, and even Ember's sunny disposition failed to bring him out of his grey cloud towards the end of the day.

Hours seemed to melt away as he went over all the events he'd been through with Erron in recent months, and before long, the streets outside had grown quiet, and his living room had taken on the chill of the night.

Erron's call earlier had landed on the fourth baked bean of his puzzle, and Casey had found it impossible to hide the build-up of resentment that had simmered away in his stomach since Erron had pushed him away a few weeks prior. He'd tried everything in his power to move on, with the buried hope that things would eventually go back to how they were, but his days at Apollo had turned into a lonely blur of monotony since Erron had transferred, especially with Nikita busy investigating the recent murders. Before he knew it, tears were sliding down his cheeks as he gripped the cocktail umbrella, longing for his life before the world nearly ended.

The buzz of his phone startled him, sending what was left of his milkshake across the floor and down the arm of his chair. Cursing, he fetched a bundle of tea towels to mop it up before checking the phone. A couple of texts flashed up, both from Erron in quick succession.

*Case, are you about tomorrow morning? Breakfast at The Ivy, my treat?*
*For the statement, if you can.*

Erron was referring to The Ivy at Canary Wharf, a place they had previously been for pancakes before work as it was a stone's throw from the Apollo Division headquarters. Casey stared at the texts, feeling conflicted. No matter how much he wanted to rebuild everything they had, he couldn't help but feel hurt and betrayed, especially discovering Erron was harbouring gifts from the woman who had supposedly abused him in the most horrific way. His fingers lingered over the phone for some time before he set it aside.

He stood, pacing indecisively, glancing at the phone on the arm of his chair before picking it up once more. His fingers hesitant, he tapped out a reply.

*I can do 8 a.m.*

Casey closed his eyes and pressed the phone to his chin, waiting for a response to come through, hoping it wouldn't. Less than thirty seconds later, it vibrated against his jaw.

*Thank you, I owe you. Goodnight, Case x*

* * *

Half a mile away, in the cold light of the morning, Erron was staring blankly at the mirror in Nikita's bathroom, still wary of any spontaneous twisted shapes of Chaos agents materialising behind his reflection. His eyes were bloodshot, dark rings surrounding them, and his usual messy hair was in need of washing. He had several days of stubble, his chin beginning to itch with the growth. He deeply missed his Apollo glow, where even on his most unkempt days he still looked charming and intentionally rugged. As a Reaper, the face that stared back at him was tired, pale and untidy. It was no wonder that the *Umbra Noctis* turned people's gaze away.

He'd barely slept, having been woken by another violent nightmare and then kept awake by the anxiety of meeting up with Casey. He splashed cold water on his face before turning tentatively to see what he could of his back in the mirror, scanning over the runes; the more the scar tissues settled, the clearer the characters became, crowned by the small nubs of flesh where his wings were beginning to protrude. Only doctors had seen the runes in detail, but part of him wanted to know what they meant. He'd thought about asking Nikita to translate them, but he knew deep down he wasn't ready to know their meaning, no matter how strong his curiosity grew at times. It was a part of himself he wouldn't get back once he knew.

A knock at the bathroom door startled him.

'You OK in there?' Nikita's muffled voice came through the door. 'I just need to grab a bag.'

'Yeah, sorry, hold on.' He pulled a T-shirt haphazardly over his head and opened the door.

She smiled, her expression softening into concern. 'Bad night?'

'A little.'

'I heard you shouting. I was worried.'

'I'm so sorry for disturbing you. I've been waking up like that a lot.' Erron stared at his feet and leant back against the sink.

'It's fine.' Nikita opened her arms and gestured for him to come over.

Hesitantly, he did so, tensing up slightly as she hugged him, but eventually allowing himself to relax into the embrace.

'Any more nightmares, come find me.' Nikita fixed him with a sincere look as she gently let go. 'I don't care what time of night.'

He managed a smile. 'Thank you.'

'Anytime. Now, don't use up all the hot water.' Nikita stepped out of the bathroom and began to close the door.

'We're in the afterlife; we've got good boilers,' Erron answered before turning the lock and running the water. By the time he was showered and dressed, Nikita was multitasking at the kitchen table, eating a bowl of Weetabix and scrolling through the photos of the notebook again on her laptop. She was still in her dressing gown, her hair tumbled around her shoulders, the Apollo radiance working well for her in her sleepy state.

'How do I look?' Erron asked quietly. He'd made a decent effort in styling his hair and trimming his stubble, pairing the look with his usual smart shirt and tie, suit trousers and polished boots.

She appraised him and nodded approvingly. 'Practically dreamy, my Grim Reaper friend.'

'Thanks.' He looked down at himself. 'Not too bad for Death.'

'Not bad at all. Now, go see your man,' she instructed.

* * *

Erron arrived ten minutes early. He paced nervously back and forth, finally crumbling to the temptation of a cigarette to settle his anxiety while he waited for Casey. He barely got through five puffs of smoke before he felt a tap on his shoulder.

'I thought you quit those.' Casey's voice sounded disappointed.

Erron spun around wide-eyed and dropped the cigarette, stamping it out with his boot. 'I did. I mean, I have. I just . . . I had a bad night.'

'OK.' Casey held open the door for him. 'Shall we?'

They sat in awkward silence after ordering their pancakes. Casey slowly sipped at a strawberry milkshake, making little eye contact and occasionally glancing over in the direction of the kitchen.

Erron cleared his throat and pulled out a notebook and pen. 'Nikita tells me there's a chance you might have seen the suspect out at Bonanza.'

'I can't be certain, but I will tell you what I saw.' Casey looked up and folded his arms on the table.

'Do you recognise anyone?' Erron pulled out the photo of the man from the CCTV and four other, generic CCTV images of random people.

'That one.' Casey immediately pointed to the suspect. 'He was the one that followed the woman and was acting very odd.'

'OK, great.' Erron tucked the images back into his notebook and proceeded to ask questions in a methodical way, using his best detective skills to cover all bases with the statement. When their pancakes arrived, they ate in silence, Erron barely getting through half of his. He set his fork down and carried on with his questions.

'So you didn't really know Leo, you just happened to be right outside Bonanza not long before he was found?' he asked. 'You weren't out with him or his friends that night?'

'No, I'm not exactly going to lie about something like that.' Casey furrowed his brow and sat back in his chair. 'Do you think I was out partying, then?'

Erron shook his head. 'No, I don't think you're lying. I am just making sure I have the whole story.'

'It's always good to know the truth of a matter,' Casey replied, his tone sharp.

Erron met his gaze, confused. 'Umm, yeah. Of course.'

'I spoke to Ember, and she said Leo had been out celebrating his Bakeday anyway. Even if I was friends with him, which I'm not, I'm not big on Bakeday celebrations. You of all people should know that,' Casey stated defensively.

'Right, yes, I realise that. So when did you speak with Ember? Did she say anything else?' Erron probed.

'Yesterday actually. We talked a bit about the victims, I don't think there was anything particularly interesting.' Casey rubbed his chin, deep in thought. 'Only about Willow getting a magical tattoo and Leo out celebrating. Ember didn't really offer anything that I would consider groundbreaking.'

'Willow didn't have a tattoo.' Erron was confused. He'd examined her body head to toe and found nothing remotely resembling such a thing.

'Well, I never saw it; you might have to speak to Ember about that.' Casey took a sip of his milkshake and set it back down.

'Have you got her number?'

'Sure.' Casey shared Ember's contact with Erron.

Casey checked the time. 'I'm going to have to get going soon. Despite what Toto say, love actually *is* always on time.'

'I like that song.'

'I know.' Casey had caught Erron singing it many a time in the past, usually when he had been impossibly drunk. 'How else would I have known it?'

'You got me there.' Erron pursed his lips into a half-smile.

Casey returned the smile, but it failed to reach his eyes. He stood up and pulled on his jacket, a grey peacoat to match his trilby. He paused and rested his hands on the back of the chair. 'I know it's a few days away yet, but have you got anything planned for your birthday?'

'I hadn't even thought of it,' Erron answered. His real birthday was twelve days away, and he usually spent it playing chess with Casey at the Sky Pod bar. His Bakeday was twenty-three days after that, and traditionally he'd use it to get blind drunk on the same whisky that had killed him.

'Well, I was working on the assumption you wouldn't want to spend it with me this year, so I brought your card today in case I don't see you.' Casey reached into his inside pocket and pulled out a small envelope, handing it to Erron gingerly. 'Your gift is at your flat already. You'll understand when you see it that I couldn't exactly wrap it, or time it for the day itself. You can see it when you are ready. No rush.' He walked past Erron, giving him a gentle squeeze on his upper arm as he did so, before heading in the direction of the Apollo building.

Erron was left standing with the envelope in his hand, unable to open it, a warm tingle in his arm from Casey's touch. He pushed the envelope into his pocket and hurried to the Tube where he typed a quick text to Ember Songfire.

# 15

## *Bad Habits*

IT WAS NIKITA'S FIRST SOLO assignment and she was busy lining up her shot at a young woman who was sitting on the edge of a fountain in Regent's Park, just as the prospective partner perched himself next to her. She had to complete several solo assignments to be signed off probation, despite the fact most assignments were doubled-crewed. Her hands were clammy with the pressure and her mind kept wandering back to the notebook that potentially belonged to the killer. She fumbled the second arrow, but still managed to hit the man in the kneecap. It was enough to consider the assignment a success, as the couple shared their first kiss.

Her morning gradually got better, and at lunchtime she met up with Casey.

'How was your first morning alone, then?' he asked as they made their way to the nearest coffee shop.

'Pretty good, no misses. All I need now are my wings.'

'That must be soon?'

'I'm going into the Raphael this afternoon for my assessment,' she said, the excitement glowing in her eyes. 'But I have no idea what to expect.'

'It's not too bad. You'll get supplements made of extra stardust injected into your back, to start the process,' he explained. 'You won't know yourself when you've mastered flying.'

'I can't wait. When I was little I always wanted to be able to fly,' she enthused. They took up a bench seat in a cosy tearoom where a kindly older lady took their order. Casey set his hat down on the table and stretched.

'Of course, once you grow your wings, you have to undertake the Flight Test,' he said gravely.

'You're kidding. Is it how to flap your wings at the right altitude or something?'

'Not quite, a bit more like the driving test. There's even a hazard awareness thing now, and a theory test.'

'So ... I need to know my stopping distance in the snow when flying below the cloud layer. Or I need to know how to reverse with a trailer attached to my arse, yeah?' Nikita rolled her eyes. 'People just can't let other people enjoy things, even after death we still have red tape.'

Casey laughed. 'Something like that.'

'So where do I shove the L-plate?'

'Don't ask.'

'Anyway, how was breakfast?' Nikita changed the subject.

Casey was quiet for a moment. 'It was OK. I am finding this tough, though. It's like we're not even friends right now. I don't know what to do.'

'Give it time, do you want me to speak to him? Tell him you how you feel?'

'I don't know. I gave him his birthday card early. I wasn't expecting him to want to spend the day with me, but I get the feeling he doesn't want to even see me outside of this

Medusa task force thing.' Casey exhaled. 'We've always spent his birthday together.'

'What date is it?' Nikita asked.

'Twenty-first.'

Nikita's eyes wandered as she tried to work something out. 'That makes him an Aries . . . yeah, that checks out.'

Casey looked confused. 'So . . . his star sign is responsible for him not wanting to see me?'

Nikita snapped her gaze back to him. 'Oh no, not at all. He's just very much an Aries, in general, you know: fiery, stubborn, all that jazz. Maybe he just doesn't want to celebrate at the moment?' Nikita offered.

Their tea and biscuits arrived on a quaint tray with a silver bowl of sugar cubes. It was followed by a plate of mini sandwiches and two warm croissants.

Casey paused briefly. 'Maybe. The thing is, I found a gift at his house from Izzy. It had a soppy love note with it. Surely he wouldn't want that at his place?'

'Oh, Casey.' Nikita was stumped for words. She didn't want to automatically start making excuses for Erron, but was sure there was an explanation.

'Am I going mad or something? Do you think I should ask him about it? Ember and I have completely redecorated his room as a surprise. I wanted him to have it as a birthday gift, but now I feel like I would be invading his privacy by saying I found the thing from Izzy. But I couldn't sleep all night from thinking about it.' He leant on the table, looking thoroughly conflicted. 'I couldn't even focus on my baked bean puzzle.'

Nikita raised an eyebrow. 'Well, we can't be having that. Where was the gift?'

'It was in the cutlery drawer. I was making tea.'

'It's a reasonable place that you would look without expecting to find anything incriminating. I don't think that's an invasion of privacy,' Nikita reassured him. 'Maybe, when he's seen the effort you have made at his place, then raise it casually. It might be nothing. He might just have thrown it in there with the intention to chuck it out. But you need to raise it if it's bothering you.'

'Yes, it's possibly that,' Casey conceded.

'Maybe he kept it to use as evidence?' Nikita hypothesised, taking a sip of her tea.

The idea hadn't occurred to him, but it seemed like a sensible one. It filled him with a shred of hope.

'Here's a thought, why don't I ask if you can help with the Medusa investigation? It'll give you something to focus on, and you'll have a good reason to be around Erron for a bit, in a professional capacity. It might be what you both need,' she suggested.

Casey's smile broadened at the idea. He'd been secretly hoping he might be brought into the fold. Nikita filled him in on the investigation so far as they finished their lunch, reassuring him she'd do what she could to get him involved in the team.

Casey checked his watch. 'We better get over to that thing ... what was it again? There were a lot of assignment cards?'

'It's an orgy, Casey. We've got to shoot thirteen arrows at an orgy.' Nikita fixed him with a knowing look.

'Oh, I mean, those aren't exactly common.' He raised his eyebrows and took a final sip of his tea. 'And on a Monday afternoon? Seems a bit odd.'

'Well, maybe it's so people can pretend they're at the office. What day of the week do you normally go to orgies?' Nikita folded her arms and leant back, an inquisitive look on her face.

Casey put his teacup down, his jaw falling open. 'I don't even know how you can insinuate such a thing, young lady!' He shook his head, shocked, before putting his trilby on. 'I can't even get one man to love me, let alone a room full of them.' A wry grin formed on his lips.

'Oh, he loves you all right. It just might be a while before you get him naked,' Nikita replied.

'I'm fine with that. It's more romantic to wait anyway.' Casey opened the door for Nikita and followed her into the street.

* * *

Across the city, Erron's workday wasn't nearly as intriguing. He was on Hospital Watch, where a Ghoster would linger around the city hospital wards to collect a few souls that cropped up for assignment that day. Sometimes there were enough to keep them in one hospital, other times they'd do the rounds of several. That morning he and Roscoe had been sent to Whittington NHS Hospital to release a soul destined to join the agency, among others. Erron dawdled from ward to ward with a stale cup of coffee, busying himself reading the drab leaflets pinned to corkboards in the halls. He was dressed in surgical scrubs and carrying a fake clipboard under his arm, on the off chance he needed to jump into character, but dressing up for assignments felt empty and dull without Casey, almost pointless. His feet ached, and the growing pains from his wings compounded the general gloom of his morning. He vaguely paid attention to a bold poster on why to stop smoking, though all it did was make him crave another forbidden nicotine hit.

Roscoe sat idly in one of the chairs in the waiting room behind the ER, opting to blend in more by wearing a fake arm sling, using his free hand to read a newspaper. It was an easy shift, owing to most patients having a name chart and a cause of death that gave away, in most cases, which department they'd be found in.

Dr Enleigh turned up in the oncology department just as Erron rounded the corner.

'Hey, you're my Reaper I take it?' Dr Enleigh asked.

'Depends who for?'

'I'm collecting a soul for cold pressure baking: Nemesis Division recruit, name of Logan Weatherly, room four.'

Erron held up his card. 'That's the one. Four minutes, no family with him. Hey, while you're here, that first Fortuna agent, Willow, you didn't see a tattoo on her, did you?'

'No, I can't say I did. The other guy had one though. Any reason?'

'No reason.' Erron vaguely remembered seeing a faded tattoo on Leo's right arm but made a mental note to take another look at it.

A tall nurse exited room four and turned his attention to an elderly patient in the hallway.

'Showtime.' Dr Enleigh smiled, nodding for Erron to follow.

Logan was barely conscious, tubes and wires carefully laid out across his body as machines bleeped and clicked. He was in his forties, an unhealthy grey tinge to his skin and a rasping, sickly air escaping from his lips.

Erron leant over and gently touched the man's forehead, feeling his body relax underneath him and hearing the man's final thoughts in his head. He drew out his assignment card and jotted them down – nothing profound, just a mere observation: *This pillow is too crinkly.*

'Well, I best get this guy back to Dr Carroway.' Dr Enleigh placed his hands over the man's chest and drew out a glowing, glittering golden sphere the size of a football, then gently placed it in a Tesco Bag for Life.

Erron raised his eyebrow. 'Nothing says classy travel to the afterlife like a supermarket carrier bag.'

'Ah yeah, I think it used to be more of a ceremony, but they had to streamline these things, so I hear.' Dr Enleigh whistled as he left the room, leaving Erron to wonder if his soul ever got bundled into a bag like a radioactive iceberg lettuce.

His phone brought him out of his thoughts as it vibrated in his pocket. It was a reply from Ember, who was happy to meet with him that afternoon to answer his questions. He suggested they meet at the Raphael Sanctuary after his shift ended, in the hope she might be willing to view Willow's body and point out where the tattoo allegedly was.

* * *

'You look like you need a stiff drink,' Nikita remarked as she and Casey left the location of the orgy.

'Uh, no, I don't need to see anything else that's stiff for one day, thank you.' Casey looked shell-shocked.

'You'd change your mind if Erron was here.'

Casey threw her a scolding look. 'That's wholly inappropriate, young lady.'

'Hey, it's the truth,' she scoffed.

Casey blushed. 'Enough of that.'

Nikita grinned mischievously. 'Well, I thought it was a positive experience myself. You don't get to see that sort of thing every day.'

'For good reason! Besides, how can the Fates really say all those people fell in love today? I know it was only a brief infatuation arrow but still ... *all* of them?' Casey practically jogged to the perimeter gate.

'Maybe they're destined to take their casual sex to a professional, competitive sex level. And the whole gang needs to be perfectly in sync and in love to do so.' Nikita kept a straight face.

'Seriously? That stuff has gone professional?'

'Oh yes, there's talk of it becoming part of the Olympics.'

Casey took a moment then gave her a withering look. 'You almost had me fooled there.'

Nikita checked the time. 'As fun as this is, I need to start making my way over for my wing assessment.' She couldn't contain her excitement.

'Of course. I would offer to come with you, but I need to hand in our assignments and see if there's anything left to do this afternoon, as I doubt you'll be feeling like coming back to the office.'

'That's OK. I guess I will see you in a couple of days? I am off on Medusa duty tomorrow. I'll make sure to ask if you can join up.'

'Ah, I forgot you were doing that. No problem.' Casey slumped a little, disappointed he would be working alone again.

Nikita picked up on his slight change of tone. 'Hey, it's not for long. Besides, you'll hopefully be joining us soon.'

'Yeah, that will be nice. You best get going.' He smiled and waved her off.

* * *

Forty minutes later, Nikita sat nervously in a plastic chair outside Dr Carroway's lab. He called her in, the same deadpan look he always wore, his face never ageing past his peak midlife misery.

'Wings, right? Apollo, Hades, Kentucky-fried, Red Bull – which ones you in for?' Dr Carroway asked, his tone never inflecting with any kind of enthusiasm.

'Apollo Division, though I could go for the fried ones,' Nikita joked.

'Sadly, they aren't easy to fly with; the breadcrumbs leave a trail.' Dr Carroway prepared a tray of syringes, checking for bubbles in each shimmering liquid within. 'It's all very well until the pigeons follow you everywhere.'

'I'll stick with the Apollo ones.'

'Good choice, please remove your top and lie face down on the bed.'

Dr Carroway pulled a privacy screen around her while she undressed and returned when she was face down on the cold leather gurney, her stomach turning after seeing the size of all the needles.

* * *

The process was as uncomfortable as she imagined it would be, and Dr Carroway sighed scornfully each time she jumped involuntarily from the injections. Once he'd finished, he pushed himself away on his rolling chair to the computer and updated Nikita's medical notes on the system.

'Right, you will start to feel very lethargic over the next day or so, so no extreme sports, cable car rides or climbing through air vents to save a building from terrorists, that kind of thing.

Also, take ibuprofen for the pain and inflammation, and try not to sleep on your back,' Dr Carroway reeled off.

'Is that so I don't squash the wings?'

'No, it's so you don't snore.' He rolled his eyes. 'You'll need a check-up in a few weeks to ensure everything is developing as it should.'

'Thank you, is ibuprofen going to cut it?'

Dr Carroway audibly huffed. 'It's normally sufficient. But I also recommend getting yourself something called a sound-wave cocktail at the Good Vibrations bar in the neon district in Elysion. Personally, I'd go for the green one, if I was so inclined.'

'And they are . . . ?' Nikita asked.

'Drinks that play music inside you through cosmic sound-waves. Actually really good for pain, but don't get the blue one, my god, it's a mix of wartime music and whale song, and neither one is all that uplifting. You might be relaxed but you'll be ready to fall on a bayonet after two of them.'

'Noted,' Nikita replied, wide-eyed.

She left the hospital feeling more than a bit sore, the lethargy beginning to set in before she reached her apartment. Her arms felt like lead weights as she fumbled for the lift button. By the time she reached her living room, she only had the strength to drape herself over the sofa.

When Erron got to her place after his shift, he found her fast asleep, limbs haphazardly splayed across the cushions and her head almost on the floor. He knelt down and tried to gently move her head back up on the seat, but she woke up with a start.

'Oh god, I didn't even hear you come in!' She scrunched up her face, her mouth dry and eyes crusted from sleep.

'Your wing appointment, right?' He grinned mischievously. 'I felt like I had been hit by a train when I first grew out my wings. But you shouldn't sleep on your back.'

'I know, I know, it makes me snore.' She rolled her eyes.

'No, you'll squash your new wing nubs. They'll grow pretty quickly this week.' Erron was more than aware of how fast they grew, as his already had three small feathers each and still ached. Nikita was in for a few weeks of growing pains.

'It feels like toothache in my back,' she winced.

'Take a hot bath – it helps. Once they get their feathers you'll have to stick to showers for a bit until you've learnt to look after them properly.' He shrugged off his overcoat and went to hang it on the back of a chair, then headed into the kitchen to rummage around in the cupboards. 'No painkillers?' he asked, coming up empty.

Nikita forced herself to sit up. 'No, I haven't needed them since dying. No migraines, no bastard periods, it's been bliss. But I forgot to get some on the way home.'

'I've got some of the good stuff, hold on.' He went to the bedroom and emerged with his prescription pack of tiny tablets.

She looked up at him, laughing at the absurdity of a Grim Reaper handing her pain medication. 'Thank you.' She took one of the tablets. 'Any further forward with the investigation?'

Erron pulled up a kitchen chair and sat down back-to-front on it, folding his arms over the backrest. 'So, Casey identified the suspect from the CCTV as being present outside Bonanza. We have a notebook that may or may not be the killer's with a code of some type. We do have one solid link between the victims: both had a tattoo, which have completely disappeared since they were murdered.'

Nikita sat for a minute with the information before speaking. 'Interesting. Disappearing tattoos . . .'

'Ember Songfire was able to confirm that Willow got hers done on Elysion, so it makes sense we ask the tattoo place if they also served Leo. It's a very tentative link, but we should cover all bases.'

'It could just be a coincidence, but we can check it out. Tomorrow though.' Nikita stretched her uncomfortable shoulders. 'I'm taking your advice and going to lie in the bath for an exceedingly long time.'

'Stay there, I'll run it for you.'

'You're contracted as my in-house dishwasher, not a total servant.'

'That may be so, but I'm also your friend and care about you. Besides, I'm sure if I've mastered running the sink I can progress to a bath.'

'You're a sweetheart, Grover.' Nikita couldn't help but smile.

'Don't go telling everyone.'

'I wouldn't dare. Did you make amends with Casey this morning?'

Erron rummaged in his pocket and pulled out an envelope. 'He was very blunt over breakfast, but he did give me an early birthday card. I think I've really pushed him away. He said he left a gift at my place. I'll have to find time to go there.' There was a long silence as he stared at the envelope.

'You both need to clear the air,' Nikita stated. 'Open the damn card.'

Erron sighed and did as he was told. He couldn't help but smile at it. It was a personalised one of a sulking photo of Erron sitting across the chess table at the Sky Pod Bar having lost a game to Casey. The caption underneath said: 'A Knight to Remember!' Inside, Casey had written brief but sweet words, clearly trying not to come across as suffocating.

Nikita took the card and read it. 'Erron, explain how you feel, tell him why you are pushing him away. He will understand, I promise. But you can't keep him at arm's length without an explanation. It's torturing him.'

'Yeah. I know.' He hung his head. 'I know.'

'I get it, you aren't good at being vulnerable around Casey. But you need to learn how.'

Erron stared blankly at the floor.

'At the end of the day, it's up to you, I just want the best for you. Do you want me to come with you to your flat to see what the gift is?'

'I don't know yet. I will see how I feel.' He sighed and rested his hands on his head.

'OK, let me know if you do.' She sat up slowly, easing through the pain in her back. 'Now, are you running that bath or not?'

Erron stood, taking a dramatic bow with a wry grin on his face. 'Her ladyship desires the finest tub of hot water, and she shall have it.'

'I could get used to this.'

'I'm not helping you get in though,' Erron said as he walked to the bathroom.

'Spoilsport!' Nikita called after him.

When she could hear the water running, she eyed up the Poltergeist Podcast headphones that were on the table, wondering if all liminal zones, including her flat, were haunted by the ghosts of lost souls. Her bathwater was a lot less creepy than the Eligos pool, and if D-O-A was right about the ghosts, they might just want to chat.

Twenty minutes later, Nikita was soaking in the bath, having found the strength to climb in on her own, and was lazily twiddling the dials on her headphones.

Over the noise of swirling bathwater, she jumped a little when a crackling voice came through. As her heart settled, she realised it was the sound of Erron putting on the TV in the other room.

*Wolf.*

The word was eerily clear, and a voice that was neither feminine nor masculine. It had a gentle cadence, though seemed to be filtered through subtle layers of static. Instinctively, Nikita's eyes snapped open and she went to cover herself in case someone was in the room.

*Not looking*. The ghostly voice echoed in her headphones. *Can only see energy.*

'Where are you?' Nikita asked quietly, her eyes searching the room.

*Everywhere and nowhere, cosmic web. Stuck*, it replied, the voice fuzzing and grating in the headphones. *Beware, Reaper next door*. The voice sounded wary.

'He's just watching TV.'

*Lazy Reaper.*

'How long have you been hanging around?'

*No idea. No clocks here.*

'Can I help you with something?'

*Helping you. Bad energy in the web. Danger.*

'Who has the bad energy?'

*The blood thief.*

'What's his name?' Nikita sat up, gripping the side of the bath, the breath catching in her throat.

A sharp knock on the bathroom door startled her and she ripped off the headphones, accidentally dropping them in the water. 'You OK in there?' Erron asked through the door. 'You sounded like you were talking to yourself.'

'Sorry, yes, I'm fine.' Nikita scrabbled for the headphones, realising with dismay that they were waterlogged and completely useless.

'I'm thinking of making pasta,' Erron said. 'You want some?'

'Is it safe?' Nikita teased. Erron wasn't exactly known for his culinary skills.

'Harsh. But not entirely unfair. I'll put a pan on.'

When his footsteps had disappeared, Nikita shook out the headphones, annoyed at herself that she'd already ruined them. 'Bollocks,' she cursed, pulling herself out of the bath, wishing she had been able to finish her conversation with the unseen entity. Wrapping a towel around herself, she wondered whether the senior Ghoster, D-O-A, would give her a crash course in communicating with lost souls without the use of any fandangled Elysion tech.

She remembered what he'd told her about the liminal ghosts: they were harmless, but their messages had suddenly gained some clarity. It was entirely possible the one in her bathroom was just trying to delay its boredom by making up some fictional danger in the cosmic web. But it had called it the blood thief, a scary coincidence considering Leo Romano had been drained of his blood.

# 16

## *Whataya Want from Me*

EARLY THE NEXT MORNING, ERRON stood outside his apartment door, a nervous energy coursing through his veins. His fingers were damp with sweat, holding the key, and it took him a few minutes to settle the churning in his stomach at what he might see. The longer he'd spent away from his flat, the more unsettling it felt for him to return, but he knew he had to get over the hurdle sooner rather than later.

Finally, he unlocked the door and stepped inside, where he was immediately met with the distinct smell of fresh paint and clean laundry.

Tentatively, he looked around the open-plan space. It wasn't long before his eyes were drawn to where his bed usually was. Except it looked nothing like how he'd left it. The furniture had been rearranged and there was a modern, floating-style bed on the floor, underlit with soft LEDs. On the wall behind it was the most striking mural of the comic book character Ghost Rider, on his flaming motorcycle, with a backdrop of a deep purple night sky. It had been one of Erron's favourite comics and he had raved about it when the first film was made. He'd talked Casey's ear off after leaving the cinema about all the special effects and backstory, bringing it up in conversation as many times as he could before Casey would roll his eyes and artfully change the subject.

Erron stood, absorbing every detail of his new room, tears silently rolling down his cheeks. He wiped them away with the back of his hand and cautiously went to rest on his new bed. The bedding was brand new, a muted charcoal colour and still starchy to the touch. Lying on top of the duvet, he felt like he was in another place, miles away from his pain, all the sadness and anger melting into the soft mattress and disappearing through the floor.

He glanced over to his giant fish tank; the fish were being fed by an automatic timed dispenser and were merrily swimming away, as if nothing had changed. He'd missed watching their illuminated shapes while lying in the dark of his room at night. He'd missed the view from his window, his daft googly-eyed Roomba, Roscoe, and, more than anything, he missed who he was before Izobella Cain.

No matter the distance between them, Casey was still there in the background, showing his love in every possible way he could, and Erron was avoiding him for no good reason. He pulled himself together and sat up, swinging his feet to the floor. He was due to meet Nikita at the Medusa office at 9 a.m. so decided to make himself a coffee using his own mug and kettle.

The anxiety slaked off him like water the more he relaxed in his home comforts, until he opened the drawer for a teaspoon and was jolted back to harsh reality when he saw the gift from Izzy. Worse than that, it had been thrown back in haphazardly, the note slightly torn, not where he'd originally put it. He instantly knew Casey had seen it, and finally understood his coldness the previous morning.

Erron threw the gift in the bin and decided against the coffee. He picked up his phone and dialled Casey without hesitation, determined to make amends.

'Hi,' Casey answered, still a little curt.

'Hey, Case.' Erron choked up. 'Umm, are you busy later?' His voice wavered.

The line was silent for a moment. 'Are you OK?' Casey's tone was suddenly filled with the deep concern and warmth that Erron was so desperate to hear.

'Case, I—' Erron's voice cracked. 'I really need to see you.'

'What's happened?' Casey asked, worried.

Erron regained his composure, calming his breath and pressing the phone hard against his ear. 'Please, if you have time later, can we just meet up?'

'Of course. Let me take you to dinner, somewhere quiet. What time?' Casey asked, keeping his tone gentle.

'Seven p.m.?'

'I'll send a cab. What address will you be at?'

'I'll be at Nikita's. Case, the bedroom—' Erron began to say.

'Tell me over dinner whether you like it or not. It will be easier face to face,' Casey cut in. 'I look forward to seeing you.'

'You too. I'll see you later.'

Erron held the phone against his heart for some time, a surge of relief filling the silence. He had nine or so hours to think of what to say to Casey, in between trying to solve two murders.

* * *

At the Eligos Library, Nikita had given up searching for D-O-A as he wasn't haunting any of his usual reading spots that morning. Her questions about the liminal ghosts would have to wait. She still felt like she'd been hit by a truck after her wing supplement injections and had taken another of Erron's painkillers just to function. Osato and Emrys had joined her in the Medusa room, hoping for a rundown of the investigation so far.

'I've arranged a memorial for Willow and Leo,' Emrys stated. He was clad in a cheerful lilac jumper and olive tone corduroy trousers, paired with a green bow tie. Nikita thought he looked adorable; Osato wasn't so sure.

'So what happens to them, seeing as they weren't correctly reaped and didn't retire from the agency?' Nikita asked.

Osato leant against the window, wearing a sleek white knit dress and a wide black leather belt. Nikita had never seen her in any state other than perfectly elegant. 'We've missed the window for Hades to be able to complete the Ferryman's Touch, so they'll have to be cremated the standard way.'

'But after that they get an early retirement to paradise, yeah?' Nikita queried.

'Sadly not. Agents that die in service don't go anywhere. Don't you remember what happened to Kendra? The last energy of their souls returns to its source, the stars. You only get to retire into peaceful eternity if you physically travel there in your current form; after all, you are just a solid soul. There's a process for that, but you have to be conscious for it to work.' Osato cast her eyes out the window, watching a light spring mizzle soak the glass and dampen the fresh greenery outside.

'Oh, that's awful, that's like, actually dying then,' Nikita reflected. 'Or at least, what I used to think dying was.' She had never asked what had happened to the former traitorous Apollo Division boss, Kendra, and no one had really explained the process at the time. Suddenly, the investigation seemed to weigh a lot heavier, knowing that the victims didn't get a glimpse of the paradise they deserved.

'We're having the ceremony this afternoon at Fortuna HQ, but all divisions are welcome. You should have got an email from Freya this morning,' Emrys explained.

'I haven't seen anything.' Nikita pulled out her work mobile to check. 'But I'd like to be there.'

'It will be nice to have your support,' Osato stated. 'It starts at three o'clock.'

Nikita took it as a good opportunity to ask Osato whether Casey could join the Medusa team.

The Nemesis boss considered the request. 'I'll speak to Freya this morning about it. See how much time she can allow for another abstraction. He can join, but it will be down to her how frequently he gets released for duty.'

Just then, Erron turned up, not expecting to see the division bosses in the room.

'What did I miss?' Erron checked his watch, noting he was fifteen minutes late.

'Agent Grover, we've been talking about the memorial for the two victims. Nikita has also appraised us of your progress so far. She tells me you plan to visit a place called Arcane Ink this morning?' Osato asked. 'What's the connection?'

Erron pulled out a chair for himself and sat down. 'Very little other than they both had a tattoo recently and both have disappeared off their skin. Arcane Ink is apparently promoting magical tattoos. It's not much to go on but might answer some questions.'

'Don't waste too much time there if it's a dead end,' Osato said firmly. 'Find out what you can. Your badges authorise you to make your enquiries with reasonable force if necessary.'

Erron questioned what constituted reasonable force.

'I think a power of entry would be suitable. And I think we need to establish an ability for Medusa agents to detain people for questioning.' Osato rubbed her forehead, realising the magnitude of setting up an internal investigation team. The agency didn't have any particular set of laws that differentiated from mortal ones. Most of the agents operated well within the basic working guidelines, and recruits were usually only selected from people who had a (mostly) law-abiding history. Prior to the murders, the Nemesis Division was sufficient in keeping the agency in line for all major or minor misconduct issues.

'We do have an image of a possible suspect.' Nikita produced the printouts and handed them to Osato. 'We haven't any solid evidence that he's an agent, but working on the assumption he can clearly identify Fortuna agents, it's a strong suggestion he works internally in some capacity.'

Osato nodded, studying the blurry face in the printed image. 'I don't recognise him, but he might not be from this district. He might even have changed to a back-office role, so wouldn't have any obvious division identifiers.' Osato was conscious that not all agency staff were on the front line. Many worked in various other roles, from assignment clerks to agency shop owners. 'I'll make a start on trying to identify him through staff records but don't hold your breath, it's a slow process. Without a name or division, we can't easily search him on the personnel files. Not to mention if he's retired, his file will be buried in an archive somewhere. I'll speak with all the senior agents, including those in neighbouring districts. You'll have to give me a few days.'

'I think the biggest questions is how the killer has got past the Fortuna Diaboli.' Emrys wore an expression of deep concern. 'And how much more the luck scales might drop if this continues.'

'I'm sure the Medusa team will figure it out. I've got to head back. I'll make a start circulating these.' Osato held up the CCTV printouts.

Once she'd gone, Nikita confessed to Emrys how she'd ruined the headphones he'd bought her by dropping them in the bath.

He laughed. 'Don't worry about it, Rocket. I'm more upset you're trying to have a bath with lost souls. What next, dinner with goblins? A romantic beach walk with a vampire? I can't compete with that.'

She shook her head before breaking into a laugh. 'You need to up your game then, don't you?' Her phone buzzed with an incoming email, and she opened it, waiting for a file to download.

'Perfect, the shop adjacent to Bonanza has provided an eight-hour-long CCTV attachment. Erron, were you able to narrow down an approximate time of death?' Nikita asked.

'The blind card gave a time of 4.52 a.m., Roscoe and I arrived just before 6 a.m., owing to the fact it wasn't originally our reap,' Erron explained. 'I would search the CCTV between 4 a.m. and 5.45 a.m.'

'Great, we can look through that once we have got back from Elysion.' Nikita stood up, ready to leave.

'I'll get back to work, then.' Emrys also stood, taking Nikita's hand and kissing the back of it with a subtle bow.

She blushed and smiled broadly. 'We'll get dinner tomorrow?' she asked him.

'Anything you wish, for the brightest star catches the pizza.' Emrys winked at her and turned to leave.

'Sure, OK.' She had no comeback for that one.

* * *

The entrance to Arcane Ink was more obscure than one of Emrys's phrases. It took Erron and Nikita the best part of two hours to find it, and only through asking around in popular hotspots did they finally succeed. The shopfront was just a doorway at the rear of a takeaway bar that specialised in deep-fried Weetabix with various unusual toppings. Erron made a face of disgust at the one covered in baked beans.

A small painted sign hung above the door and the lights inside were off. Nikita knocked politely, hoping someone lived onsite. Five minutes went by before Erron stepped up and hammered on the door with his fist.

A petite woman with silky dark hair and several piercings eventually answered, her face confrontational. 'We are closed until noon!' she snapped.

Erron stuck his foot over the threshold and leant on the door frame. 'We're investigating a double murder and need to ask some question to the owner of this shop. Would that be you?' His tone was firm.

'Murders? What do you mean? There are no murders in the afterlife,' she retorted in a self-assured way.

'Are you the owner of this shop?' Erron pressed.

'Yes, I am. And who exactly are you?' She folded her paint-brush-thin arms and scowled.

'Agents Wolf and Grover of Medusa Division,' Erron answered bluntly, showing her his Medusa badge. 'Do any other staff work here?'

'What the fuck is Medusa Division?'

'Like we said, we are investigating the murder of two agents, please let us in, we just need to ask a few questions,' Nikita interjected, playing the good cop and offering the woman a terse smile.

'Come back after opening time,' the woman spat, grabbing the door and trying to slam it. Erron pushed his arm against the door, swinging it open with force.

'Let's not do this the hard way.' He guided her inside to a swivel chair and sat her down. 'What's your name?'

She eyed them both warily, trying to gauge which division they were from. 'You, you're a Ghoster, I can tell,' she said coldly, her narrow eyes fixed on Erron. 'Arrogant pricks, the lot of them.'

'Very observant.' Erron pulled a chair from the waiting area and sat down facing her. 'I bet you used to be Nemesis.' He tapped a pen to his lips and tipped his head to one side. 'Early retirement, I take it? Or moonlighting?'

She huffed. 'Retired with full service actually, but I didn't fancy going to Arcadia just yet, unfinished business and all that . . . Arlana Malloy.'

'Nice to meet you, Arlana,' Nikita said, carefully leaning on the glass counter filled with various jewellery for piercings. 'We believe both victims had a connection to this shop.'

Erron pulled out photos of Willow and Leo. 'Do you recognise either of these people?'

Arlana reluctantly studied the images. 'No.'

'Both of them are believed to have had a so-called magical tattoo that you do here,' Erron continued.

Arlana furrowed her brow. 'There are three artists here with their own clients, only one of them started doing those gimmick tattoos a few months back. I don't get involved in his accounting; he uses the back room and just pays me rent. He's none of my business.'

'What's his name?' Erron leant forward and rested his elbows on his thighs.

'He is just known as Djinn.' Arlana remained cagey, leaning back and pouting. 'You'll have to make an appointment to see him.'

'What days does he work?' Nikita asked.

'He comes and goes as he pleases; his waiting list is months long. You'll have to contact him on this number, text only.' Arlana pulled a business card from a bag that was hung up just within her reach.

Erron took it and studied it. The card gave nothing away. It was a black rectangle, a single number typed in red font. 'How about you call me when this Djinn guy next turns up?' Erron scribbled his phone number down on a scrap of paper and handed it to her.

'I can't guarantee I will remember.'

'Arlana, you were a Nemesis agent, right?' Nikita asked.

'A long time ago.'

'So wouldn't you naturally want to see justice for the victims of these murders?' Nikita asked softly, her eyes fixed on the woman's. She was trying to exude her normal Apollo Flush, but she was feeling sluggish from the wing growth and seemed to be having limited impact on the tattoo shop owner.

Arlana didn't blink, her face remained empty of emotion. 'I used to care, very much so. But there are so many evil people out there, it's just easier to shut off to it. I'm enjoying my retirement away from them all. The evil ones don't make it to the afterlife. It's good up here, people are kind. I can walk the streets without a care in the world.'

Nikita sighed. 'I understand. But for those of us still down on earth, still wading through the detritus of humanity, will you please at least call us when Djinn turns up? We have reason to suspect the killer is an agent, retired or active, which means the streets up here aren't as safe as you'd like.'

Arlana wrapped her arms around herself.

'Can you show us to his studio?' Erron asked.

'Sure, then will you leave me alone?' Arlana scoffed.

'For now.'

She led them into a tiny back room with a leather gurney and a small desk covered in tattoo equipment. Behind the door was an elaborate set of robes with a mask, the walls were covered in client photos of beautiful designs, all intricate and ethereal in nature. Among them was a framed art print that stood out, a collage of past and present Formula One cars all from the McLaren team, clearly autographed by several drivers.

'This Djinn a racing fan?' Nikita asked, pointing at the art print.

Arlana shrugged.

'And these robes, does he wear these for tattooing in?' Nikita continued. She took photos as she went around the room, focusing on the strange garments hanging up.

'It's all part of his performance. He likes his air of mystery,' Arlana replied, nonchalant. 'No one has seen his face.'

A light spilled across the floor from a glass-fronted mini fridge glowing underneath the desk, filled with strange vials of shimmering liquid.

'What's in the fridge? Those inks?' Erron asked, going over and peering through the glass door.

'Not our inks, they're his specialist ones.' Arlana shifted uncomfortably on her feet.

Erron opened the fridge and brought out a handful of small vials. They all had a similar glow with slight differences in colour. They were marked up with separate names with a subheading in brackets: *Ares* (Andromeda), *Asteria* (Lyra), *Achilles* (Ophiuchus), *Aphrodite* (Corvus) and *Artemis* (Orion). 'Nikita, what do you make of these?' He handed her two of the vials.

Her blood ran cold when she read the names, and she subtly gestured for them to leave. 'Arlana, we'll be off now, but call us when Djinn comes back.'

'Sure,' Arlana answered, her voice lacking commitment.

Back out into the streets of Elysion, Erron stopped in an alley between a fantasy photography booth and a lunar plant shop. They were a few hundred feet from The Last Woolworths, which had gained a cult following since they'd disappeared in the UK.

'So what are these then? You seem to recognise them.' Erron pulled out a total of five vials that he'd managed to swipe, each with a different name.

'These names are very familiar,' she said in a hushed tone. 'I want to test them at the Raphael ASAP.'

# 17

## *Hold On*

Dr Enleigh was in the makeshift morgue when they arrived. The cold greeted them like a slap in the face and the smell of bleach hung in the air. He was cleaning down the two gurneys the victims had been on, their bodies completely gone.

'Where are they?!' Nikita exclaimed in a panic.

The young doctor spun around, startled. 'I signed their bodies over to be cremated early this morning. There's a ceremony being arranged for their ashes to be spread. Forensically, there's nothing more we could have got from them.'

'Fuck,' Erron spat. 'Does Osato know about this?'

'I was the one who spoke to her. She was happy to have them released,' Dr Enleigh explained, gesturing for them to calm down. 'There's nothing else you could have gathered, realistically.'

'Did you get the X-rays completed, at least?' Erron asked.

'Yeah, it took me hours to sort that the other day, but the images are in the files.' Dr Enleigh nodded to where two steel clipboards sat on an instrument trolley.

Nikita picked them up and slid the images onto a backlit viewer. 'I'm no doctor but they don't look right.' She tilted her head, studying the images.

'They didn't suggest anything overly abnormal, in my opinion. Slightly distended, but probably from fighting the garrotte,' Dr Enleigh stated.

'Well, thank you for getting the images anyhow. Can we still use this room for a bit? We have a few more things to go through,' Nikita asked.

'Knock yourselves out.' He checked the clock on the wall. 'I'm in surgery shortly.' Dr Enleigh excused himself.

Nikita immediately sought out a fridge and took the vials from Erron's coat pocket before he had a chance to react. She sealed them inside a plain envelope and stuffed them to the back of the fridge.

'Until I have run the tests on these, I think it's best we don't disclose what we found at Arcane Ink to anyone else,' she said quietly, making sure the hallway outside was empty.

'OK, care to explain?' Erron looked confused.

Just then, Nikita's mobile trilled with a landline number. She answered, pressing the phone to her ear and leaning on one of the empty gurneys.

'Hi, Agent Wolf. It's Freya.'

Nikita was momentarily concerned why her boss was calling her, but she returned the greeting nonetheless.

'I've just got off the phone from Osato about Casey helping out with your team. Normally, I wouldn't be able to spare him, but between you and me, I think it might help him to have a few hours out of the office while I sort a temporary crewmate for him,' Freya explained quietly.

'We'd be glad to have him.' Nikita couldn't hide her excited expression.

'I'll send him over. He's going to the Fortuna memorial later so he may as well stay with you today.'

'We're at the Raphael Sanctuary. Tell him we're in the temporary morgue; someone ought to give him directions.' Nikita said her goodbyes and ended the call.

'Who are we having?' Erron asked, his expression inquisitive.

'Oh, just a temporary Medusa agent.'

'Oh, OK.'

'We've got a bit of time before he can get here. It's a good opportunity to go through that CCTV,' she suggested. 'But first we need to text Djinn and request an appointment.'

'Sure, but not in here. It's so cold parts of me are inverted.' Erron rubbed his hands together to keep his fingers from turning blue.

'Well, we don't want that now, do we.' Nikita laughed and led him out of the morgue.

They found a small staff break room which was unoccupied, and Nikita rummaged in her bag for her laptop. Before switching it on, she popped another of Erron's prescription painkillers and tried to stretch out the growing pains in her shoulder blades.

'I'll be joining you in a morphine hit.' Erron took one of the tablets, holding it under his tongue as he tapped out a message to the elusive tattoo artist.

Nikita had loaded up the laptop and found the CCTV, fast-forwarding it to the time Erron had suggested.

They watched in silence for some time. The footage showed only a small section of the alley behind Bonanza, not quite the view they were hoping for.

The timer read 4.41 a.m. when two figures turned the corner into the alley, clearly laughing and falling about, inebriated. One looked strikingly like Leo from his photos. The other was wearing a hooded top and kept his face down.

'That's them.' Nikita paused the video and zoomed in. The frame was grainy, and it didn't help that the second figure was conscious of not being seen on camera. He was wearing jeans with the hoody, nothing distinctive. Nikita pressed play again.

At 4.52 a.m. there was bright flash of light across the camera as though a flare had been set off, dying down quickly. Nikita rewound and watched it again in slow motion, the light building from no particular source and depleting in moments.

'What was that?' Erron asked, transfixed on the screen.

'I don't know. It could be camera interference, or maybe a security light somewhere close by?' Nikita suggested.

'It looked much brighter than that.'

They continued watching for another hour, seeing nothing more until the time that the first Reaper had turned up on scene.

Casey crept quietly into the room and leant in between Nikita and Erron as they focused on the screen.

'So what are we looking for here, then?' he asked, making both of them jump.

'Bloody hell, Casey!' Nikita spun round, clutching her throat in fright.

Erron's face was a vision of shock, until it morphed into a wide smile.

'I came bearing gifts.' Casey set down a tray of takeaway coffees in front of them.

'Now, that's an entrance.' Nikita took one of the cups and gleefully sipped at it.

Erron gently pushed a chair out so Casey could sit next to him. Casey perched on the edge of it, keen to get involved.

Nikita rewound the CCTV when Casey had told her what time he was near the nightclub. They watched the screen quietly, Nikita noticing Erron's cautious glances at Casey, the subtle way he chewed on his lower lip, clearly lost in his own thoughts.

Casey was oblivious, his face fixed on the screen, his coffee cup poised in both hands. 'There, that's me!' he said animatedly as the image of him walked into the corner of the frame, slightly blurry and speaking to an unknown woman.

'She was being followed,' Casey affirmed. 'The man was back here.' He traced his finger across the screen to the edge of the alleyway, where after a few minutes the shape of the long-haired man appeared.

Nikita paused it when they had the clearest image of him. 'It looks like he must have put the hoody on later, but before the murder.' The long-haired man was dressed in a deep red and black chequered shirt and jeans. They could just make out the straps of a rucksack on his shoulders. 'I bet he had a change of clothes in that bag.'

'Hmm. Maybe he did, so he could easily dispose of it once it was covered in blood,' Erron suggested. 'It's definitely the same bloke though, the one that followed me to the park and was seen on CCTV at the scene of Willow's death.'

'Casey, you used to be a doctor, right?' Nikita asked rhetorically. 'It wouldn't hurt for a second expert to check the medical reports.'

'Sure, but isn't this place full of experts?' He raised an eyebrow.

'It is, but if you're joining the team you need to see all the evidence,' Nikita replied, gesturing for them to follow her as she stood.

Casey grinned, picking up his coffee and following her. Erron shuffled behind, feeling particularly washed out in the radiance of Casey's Apollo glow.

* * *

Back in the morgue, Nikita opened up the files of evidence and flicked on the light for the X-ray viewer. She clipped up the images and invited Casey to go through everything they'd gathered so far.

'What do you make of it all, then?' Nikita asked.

'You know I was a doctor before X-rays were even invented, right?' Casey reminded them.

'I'll take it into consideration, just see what you think.' Nikita shrugged.

Casey studied the images for some time. 'It looks like the hyoid bone is fractured in both victims. Neck distension, there was a lot of force here. I don't suppose I can see the bodies?'

'Unfortunately not. Jared ... Dr Enleigh ... sent them for cremation,' Nikita said bitterly. 'But we took plenty of photos.'

Casey flipped to the back of the files to view the printed images. Despite the gruesome injuries, he pored over the pictures. 'I'd put money on the victims both being hanged. The way the line goes up towards the nape of the neck, the wire was pulled up from above. I would say some type of steel cable, thin enough to cut into the skin like this, but heavy duty enough to hold the weight of the bodies.' He flicked back and forth through pictures of Leo and Willow. 'Both of them have the same injuries. Willow has conjunctival petechiae, haemorrhaging in the eyes from hypoxia. Very common in fatal strangulation like this.'

Nikita glanced over at Erron. He was completely immersed in watching Casey, his eyes following every movement of Casey's hands and visually tracing the outline of his mouth as he spoke. Erron's face was soft with the glow of adoration, his usual hard-edged anger at the world replaced with the wide-eyed wonder of a kitten seeing its first Christmas tree. Nikita felt the smile well up on her lips and warm her heart in the cold room.

'So the victims weren't just garrotted, then?' Nikita asked.

'No, let me demonstrate . . . carefully.' Casey scanned around the room and picked up a stethoscope. 'May I?' He gestured for Erron to turn around.

'Sure,' Erron replied instinctively, having been so immersed in daydreaming, he hadn't heard a word he'd said.

Casey stood himself behind Erron and gently placed the long section of the stethoscope around his neck.

'Oh, jeez,' Erron muttered, blood rushing to his face, and not from the mock strangulation. 'I thought you wanted to check my heartbeat.'

'Someone's not being paying attention,' Casey chided playfully. 'So, if I was just strangling the victim you'd see these force lines.' Casey pulled the rubber tubing just enough to make light horizontal indents around Erron's neck. Nikita nodded. 'But for a hanging, there needs to be an upward force, and the lines go up at this angle.' He adjusted the tubing by holding it up behind Erron's head, using his height difference as a major advantage.

'So this guy has got to be pretty strong. Or really tall,' Nikita stated.

'Something like that.' Casey loosened the stethoscope tube and ruffled Erron's hair with one hand. 'Thanks for your contribution.' He smiled warmly.

Erron rubbed his neck, pretending to be gravely injured. 'Anytime.' He feigned a raspy voice. 'Though I might not survive another brutal attack like that.'

'No, because Casey's actually the main suspect in this investigation.' Nikita played along. 'He only spared you as I was a witness.'

'Oh, definitely,' Casey agreed. 'I just snapped one day and decided to collect severed feet.'

'It's because I wouldn't let you get any bees.' Nikita shook her head in mock sorrow.

'Exactly,' Casey said, trying not to laugh. 'You've no idea what that does to a man.'

Erron shook his head and smiled. 'There's only one person here taking souls and it's definitely not the guy whose idea of a stiff drink is a double caramel milkshake.'

'Harsh . . . but true.' Nikita laughed. She glanced at the clock on the wall. 'I think we ought to make a move soon to get to the service. I'm going to nip to the loo, back in a minute.'

With Nikita out of the room, an awkward silence fell.

'Case . . .' Erron spoke up, his whole body tensed as he held the distance between them. 'Are we still on for tonight?'

Casey's face softened. 'Of course.'

* * *

Though the memorial service for Willow and Leo was short notice, nothing about the preparations seemed rushed. Osato had organised a team of her Nemesis agents to help set up the ceremony in the large social hall at the Fortuna HQ, its vast ceilings and ornate stonework reminiscent of a cathedral. Like every room in the building, beautiful round windows of stained glass cast colourful light across the flagstone floors, creating unique images in the shape of butterflies and birds.

Rows of fold-out chairs were beginning to fill with sombre guests from all divisions, their voices kept low between the echoing walls. At the front of the hall, a low stage sat, upon which two large images of Willow and Leo stood in frames, a garland of flowers draped beneath them. Hundreds of unlit candles stood in rows down the sides of the hall and soft melodies floated on the air from a speaker system Emrys had set up.

Casey took up a seat in a half-empty row and Nikita made a point of making sure Erron sat between them.

'Have you seen the buffet?' Casey whispered, trying to make conversation.

'No, it's not my main priority at a funeral.' Nikita rolled her eyes and smiled.

Erron's stomach growled at the mention of food. It had been a long time since his breakfast of a cup of tea and sneaky cigarette.

Casey pulled a folded serviette from his jacket pocket and handed it to Erron. 'I swiped these for us while you were reading the order of service,' he said quietly.

Erron peeled the serviette open and found three jam tarts. 'You never cease to amaze me, Case,' he whispered back.

A whistle of a microphone interrupted them, and the room fell into a deep hush. Emrys had taken the stage, having put a long black jacket on over his lilac jumper and swapped the green bow tie for a black one. Somehow, he'd made the ensemble look right. His soft voice filled the room as he welcomed everyone, carrying through the cavernous hall as the silence fell like autumn leaves.

'I wrote this poem, for our fallen colleagues, and though they may never find paradise in our afterlife, may they find peace.' Emrys shuffled his notes, unfolding a crumpled piece of paper, before reading off the verses in a slow, poignant manner.

*The stars among us.*
*Shadows, in a land of light,*
*They left without a word,*
*Like whispers in the dead of night,*
*Voices no longer heard.*
*Lost to us, through immorality,*
*Unfading, bitter scars,*
*Though denied their immortality,*
*Rest in peace, among the stars.*

Soft murmurs undulated through the crowd, punctuated by the occasional sniff of tearful Fortuna agents, friends of the victims. Emrys invited a list of speakers to share their memories and speeches before guests were asked to light a memorial candle on their way to the wake. The ashes were due to be scattered on Elysion later that evening, across the Lake of Eternity, the closest they could get to Arcadia.

Throughout the speeches, Erron's right knee had twitched up and down, a subconscious result of pent-up anxiety. He pushed his hands into his coat pockets and tried to remain as still as possible, despite his back aching. His Hades wings had grown big enough to almost unfold, but the dull pain reminded him they still had a long way to go before they reached full size.

Without a look or a word, Casey lightly placed a hand on Erron's knee, and though Erron's initial instinct was to recoil from the touch, he felt a soothing calm wash over him, the tenseness in his leg dissipating slowly. He soon realised he was feeling the intentional relaxing influence of the Apollo Flush, something he still wasn't used to being on the receiving end of. His heart ached with withdrawal when Casey eventually moved his hand as the service came to a close. He wanted nothing more than to keep it there, but could only acknowledge Casey's gesture with a weak but grateful smile.

The buffet room was fairly crowded as the ceremony hall emptied, so the agents naturally spilled out into the courtyard at the front of the building for some fresh air. Erron took the opportunity to check his phone, but there was still no reply from Djinn. He sent a follow-up message to the tattooist.

* * *

Perched on a wall across the road, Sam Rivera watched them all through binoculars, having spent all his spare time lingering around where he last saw Ember, hoping to get another glimpse of her. He had read her stolen journal front to back, though found nothing that disclosed exactly what she was, other than the photo of her in Brighton which strongly suggested she was much older than she appeared.

His efforts were not in vain, and after three hours, he saw her outside, her usual radiance dimmed somewhat, but her beauty still without compare. She was standing with several other Fireflies, some that he recognised. Sam observed them all for some time, the sheer array of colourful auras intermingling for what seemed to be a funeral of sorts. They had been laying flowers at the entrance of the building, and many of them had looked teary-eyed, comforting one another. He entertained the thought that maybe they were in mourning for the murdered Fireflies, indicating that they might hold similar ceremonies in the way humans would.

He lowered the binoculars and pulled a camera from his rucksack to take several shots, focusing mostly on Ember.

Slowly, the crowd of Fireflies left the building and went their own separate ways. The light in the sky was starting to dip into the early stages of a spring sunset. Sam didn't wait around to be seen and cautiously climbed down from the wall, before making his way to the nearest Tube station.

Back in his room beneath the shop, he scrolled through the images, zooming in on their faces, trying to distinguish anything about them that confirmed his suspicion that they weren't human at all. Though the auras didn't show up on the photos, Sam could tell them apart. The Greens and the Golds had a youthful glow, no matter their age: soft skin, bright eyes, shiny hair; their body language was friendly, warm and engaging. The Greys had a distinct sullenness about them. The last group were the Reds, noticeably mostly from oppressed groups and overwhelmingly women, all of them carrying an air of carefully contained rage.

He scrolled back to Ember, his heart bursting every time he saw her face, the gold of her hair, the kindness in her eyes. A creeping darkness within him overtook his thoughts, convincing him his new-found admiration of her was no more than a spell, some witchcraft that the Fireflies could cast. His mind strayed into a deep well of self-pity, indulging in the idea that she'd enraptured him through dark magic and nothing good could come of it. After staring at the wall for over an hour lost in his thoughts, he came to wonder how much her feet would sell for on the Oracles website.

# 18

## *Train Wreck*

LESS THAN AN HOUR AFTER the service, Ember Songfire was sitting in the waiting room at Arcane Ink, thinking how she owed it to Willow to go ahead with the tattoo, planning to commemorate her late friend in the design. She'd left the wake early, feeling overwhelmed by the whole ordeal and wanting to escape the sea of sadness that swirled through the halls of the Fortuna Division HQ. Dr Enleigh had joined her so she had some company and support. She was browsing a book of designs by the elusive artist named Djinn, one catching her eye of a shooting star surrounded by intricate aurora-coloured swirls.

'That would be a lovely tribute, as she's with the stars now,' Dr Enleigh said when she showed the sketch to him.

'I think so,' Ember agreed.

The tattoo shop was busy, with other artists behind screens and the distinctive buzz of needles going.

Dr Enleigh checked his phone, his face creasing with annoyance. 'I'm sorry, Ember. I've just had a message that I'm needed at work to cover someone. I'm going to have to go. Will you be OK on your own?' he asked.

'Sure, no problem,' Ember said with a hint of her usual bright smile.

Dr Enleigh turned to leave, but paused, seemingly wrestling with his thoughts briefly. He spun back round, a slight sheen of sweat on his forehead. 'Say, Ember, I was wondering ... is there any chance you'd like to go for dinner with me sometime this week?'

'Oh.' She seemed startled. 'Like ... a date?'

'Yeah, something like that.' He scratched the back of his neck.

She looked uncomfortable but smiled. 'That's very sweet of you, but maybe just as friends?'

He sighed. 'Never mind,' he replied curtly and left the shop.

Ember settled back into her seat, unbothered by his response. She'd had enough trouble with men in her mortal life. Being young in the sixties was a time for rebellion, festivals and road trips, and she'd had her fair share of flaky or unambitious boyfriends taking advantage of her. Jared seemed like a nice guy, but there was no man that could compete with the joy of being free.

Nearly half an hour later, the door to the back room opened and a man dressed in elaborate black and red futuristic robes glided into the waiting area. His face was almost completely covered by a black mask with silver embroidery around the edges. Other clients and artists looked towards him with quiet awe, a hush filling the room.

Silently, he pointed at Ember and gestured for her to follow. She obeyed, excitedly settling in the tattoo chair in the tiny room. Djinn worked quickly, prepping the skin on her ankle and loading the ink cups with a specialist ink from the fridge.

'Oh, did I say I wanted the Ares ink? The one that's supposed to make you more confident?'

Djinn nodded slowly and proceeded to load the needle.

Two hours later, Ember had a spring in her step when she returned to London, feeling particularly excited to show everyone her exclusive new artwork. It was only that evening when she felt a little off, putting it down to having a long day and a dodgy slice of pie at the buffet.

* * *

It was 6.27 p.m. and Erron was back at Nikita's flat; his stomach was doing backflips as he hastily got ready for dinner with Casey.

He'd barely had time to shower after leaving the Fortuna wake and had been agonising over what to wear with his black jeans out of the limited options he had at Nikita's place. He haphazardly buttoned up a plain white shirt in front of the mirror, his fingers fumbling the fastenings as he tried to wedge his feet into his boots at the same time. Once he was dressed, he nervously paced in the open-plan living space, twiddling with his agency silver ear cuff and regularly checking his appearance in the mirror. He craved a smoke but refused to let himself down by giving in again.

'You're making *me* nervous,' Nikita commented as she watched him go back and forth.

'I can't help it. I've spent the most part of the last few decades with him, so I don't even know why I'm so tense.' Erron shook out his hands.

'You had the safety net of just being friends. Everything changes the moment you say those three little words to someone.' Nikita was slowly putting together the stuff she needed for an evening at the Eligos. 'I take it it's been a while since your last boyfriend?'

'I was mortal, put it that way, and it was a girlfriend,' Erron replied, his voice barely masking the panic. 'Casey was ... unexpected.'

'Ohhh.' Nikita raised her eyebrows. 'I didn't realise. I don't blame you for being anxious. But you'll be fine, just talk things through.'

As seven o'clock approached, his racing heart almost stopped when his phone went off in his pocket. It was Casey, informing him that his cab was outside, and he would see him at the restaurant.

'Wish me luck,' Erron said, his voice strained.

'You won't need it.' Nikita waved him out the door.

The taxi driver seemed unnerved by him, choosing not to make small talk with the Ghoster.

'We're here,' the driver finally said, pulling up outside a cosy Italian restaurant on the outskirts of Soho. 'A Dr Hart has already paid for the fare so you're free to go.'

Erron's heart leapt as he saw Casey outside, wearing a smart blue shirt and black trousers, his hair tied back in a low ponytail.

Erron approached him, hands shaking, despite having seen him only a couple of hours before. He shoved his hands in his pockets and looked at the floor.

'Hey, I hope this place will do.' Casey instantly made him feel at ease as he guided him into the restaurant.

'I wasn't expecting anything fancy,' Erron replied as they were seated in a quiet corner booth, a flickering candle between them.

After ten minutes they ordered, the awkwardness hanging heavy in the air.

'So, I first wanted to say I love my early birthday gift,' Erron finally said, sitting on his hands to stop himself fidgeting with nerves. 'How did you manage all that?'

'I had help from a very talented Ember.' Casey was calm, folding his arms on the table, the candlelight glimmering in his eyes.

'It's amazing, genuinely.' Erron's right leg bounced uncontrollably, and his palms were cold with a nervous sweat.

Their drinks arrived and Casey toyed with the idea of exuding just enough Apollo Flush to relax Erron but was conscious that it might be considered an unwanted intrusion. Instead, he kept the topics of conversation neutral and his tone mellow. After discussing work, the memorial service and how nice the restaurant was, Erron couldn't beat around the bush much longer and took a decisive breath.

'When you were at my flat, Case,' he started, the words drying in his throat. 'When you were there, I think you saw something that may have made you think differently of me.'

Casey leant back, his expression imperceptible. He didn't respond.

'It was something from Izzy,' Erron said quietly.

Casey nodded slowly.

'I wasn't keeping it on purpose. I threw it in that drawer without a thought, and every time I wanted to get rid of it, I couldn't bear to even look at it. There was nothing I was hanging on to for any other reason.' Erron lowered his head.

Casey's face softened and he leant back on the table. 'I admit I have been struggling to understand what's going through your mind lately.' He absent-mindedly fiddled with the strap of his watch. 'When I saw that, I'm ashamed to say I assumed the worst. That things might not have been how you first told me. I'm sorry for that, but it's been tough not knowing where I am with you.'

A long silence hung between them.

Erron finally met Casey's gaze, not wanting to hide anymore. 'Casey,' he said quietly. 'Izzy forced herself on me. I was drugged. I had no control over my body. I don't even remember most of it.'

Casey couldn't help but picture the photos from the trial, the overwhelming evidence of the assault and how it had been framed to show Erron as a willing participant. Originally, he never knew what to believe, but deep down didn't think Erron would have been party to anything that had gone on. Though the doubts had resurfaced when he'd found the pebble. Hearing Erron say the words out loud, seeing his pained expression and the sincerity in his eyes, there wasn't a shred of doubt left in his mind. He wanted to reach across the table and take Erron's hands, to comfort him in some way, but he knew he was at a pivotal moment where Erron just needed to be heard.

'I feel nothing but hatred and disgust towards her. Most of the time, I feel nothing at all, complete numbness. When I do feel it, all I want to do is crawl out of my skin and disappear. I can't escape it, she killed part of me that day, and I can't seem to find my way back to who I was.' Erron's voice shook with both despair and rage.

'It'll take time,' Casey said softly.

'How long though? How long will it be before the nightmares stop? Before I can look at myself naked and not feel ashamed? How long will it be before I want to be touched? What kind of relationship could I offer you if I can't even let you touch me?' His voice cracked, just as their stone-baked pizzas arrived.

Casey used the pause to collect his thoughts. He wanted to say exactly the right words and not push Erron even further away.

Erron stared at the pizza, his appetite all but gone.

'I don't have to touch you just to love you,' Casey said softly.

'You say that, but I can't make you go however long without anything physical. I just don't think I can—' he ran his fingers through his hair '—you know.'

'It's OK. I'm not worried about any of that. I will never abandon you just because you feel like you should be doing things you aren't ready for,' Casey said gently.

There was a long silence before Erron leant forward, his voice almost a whisper. 'The thing is, I *do* want you. You have no idea how much I want you. To know you in every possible way. And if you feel that way about me, who am I to deny you that? I can't give you what you want, at least not right now.'

Casey shook his head slowly. 'Be honest with me, Erron. Do you think I'm just after some wild fling full of carnal desire and no substance?'

Erron rubbed his forehead, a tense smile on his lips. 'You don't seem like a wild carnal desire kind of person. It's more wild croissant desire.'

Casey laughed. 'Well, I might be using the croissants to cover up my reputation as a raging sex god, you just don't know.'

'You went redder than a double-decker near the kinky clothes in Camden when we went shopping there last. I can't imagine that was a clever ruse, Case.'

'Point well made.' Casey smiled shyly, his voice taking on more sincerity. 'But what I'm getting at is that I have felt this way about you for over forty years, looking at you from the safe bubble of our friendship, enjoying every platonic moment we had together. You may never heal from what happened with Izzy, and do you know what? I will understand. I don't need you to take me to bed to prove you're worth loving.'

Erron tilted his head, his lips pursed as he fought the wave of emotion welling up behind his eyes. He opened his mouth to speak but closed it again when he couldn't think what to say.

'Remember when we were in Bedford, standing on the butterfly bridge?' Casey continued. 'You put your hand on mine, an act of friendship at one of our lowest points. But I've hung on to that all this time, and I'll wait another forty years for you to just hold my hand. Gladly. Your presence alone sustains me through the darkness.'

A tear slid down Erron's cheek. He tentatively reached across the table, extending his shaking fingers. With the lightest touch, Casey rested his hand over Erron's and gave him a look of tenderness.

'How about we reset the clock, to when we were just friends. No expectations. Everything and anything at your pace,' Casey whispered, gently withdrawing his hand and noticing Erron's body relax slightly. 'Take your time. We have forever.'

Erron nodded reluctantly.

'Now eat your pizza, or else you're paying,' Casey joked, despite the lump of sadness that settled in his chest.

Erron picked up a slice, his heart still pounding, and his stomach tied up in knots, but a huge weight had lifted from his shoulders. It would be a long time to repair all the damage Izzy had caused, but he wanted nothing more than to try and rebuild everything he'd lost.

'It's good pizza,' he admitted after the first bite.

'We'll have to come here again soon. Not to mention we haven't played chess in so long.' Casey tilted his head and smiled warmly. 'How's that sound?'

'Yeah. I'd like that.' Erron smiled.

# 19

## *Devils Don't Fly*

AFTER ERRON HAD LEFT FOR his date with Casey, Nikita hadn't taken long to get her stuff together for an evening at the library. She'd been there less than half an hour before a familiar shape graced the doorway, making his way to the Classics section and returning a book to the middle shelf.

Undeterred by his suffocating aura of death, Nikita practically skipped up to D-O-A, taking him by surprise when she greeted him with a cheerful hello.

'Sorry to make you jump.' Nikita grimaced slightly. 'I need your help with something, if you have a few minutes?'

His cold blue eyes rested on her face, searching for any indication of the usual discomfort people felt in his presence. She smiled back at him, hopeful, almost *happy* to see him. 'And what might that be?'

'I spoke to a lost soul when I was in the bath, but I dropped my headphones before they could tell me about the danger I was in.'

'Ah yes, they've been nattering about danger and foreboding.' D-O-A shook his head. 'It's entirely possible they're just reliving their deaths.'

Nikita lowered her voice to a whisper. 'See, I thought it might just be some spooky nonsense, but then it mentioned a blood thief, bad energy in the web. One of our victims had his blood stolen, surely that's not a wild coincidence?'

D-O-A looked briefly pensive. 'Did it say any more about this bad energy?'

'Not much.' Nikita shifted the weight of her bag on her shoulder and folded her arms.

'Hmm. Well, I dare say we won't know any more unless we ask.'

'Can you teach me how to hear them without the headphones? Because it was the bathroom ghost that told me about the danger. I don't expect you to sit in the bath with me, obviously.'

'They're not in your bathroom; they're just connected to all liminal zones, the cosmic web. Whoever you heard in the bath will also be here. You don't need the headphones if you've got good reception, or so I've found recently.' D-O-A scratched his chin before gesturing for Nikita to follow him to the other side of the library, where the staircase led down to the pool room. His floor-length black coat flowed behind him like a trail of shadows, cutting through the candlelight of the ground floor, framed by immense black wings that loosely trailed across the polished mosaic, centuries of memories tied up the weight of his feathers.

Nikita followed silently, only her footsteps echoing on the stone steps descending into the pool room. It was empty, the cool air filled with the swirling steam from the warm water, performing its ghostly ballet with the echoes in the vaulted ceiling.

D-O-A spoke calmly as he removed his polished black shoes. 'If you want to hear the souls connected to the cosmic web, being submerged in water will speed up your education.'

He shrugged off his long coat and neatly draped it over a lounge chair.

'Sorry, what?' Nikita asked, confused when he climbed into the pool wearing his black shirt and trousers. 'As in, fully submerged?'

'You'll soon dry off,' he commented, gesturing for her to follow suit. 'Like I said, water is the most powerful medium.'

Questioning her afterlife choices, she kicked off her trainers and set her bag aside before clumsily jumping in. Warm water engulfed her in its soothing embrace, weighing down her clothes.

'It's easier for a Reaper to hear the dead when there isn't a thinning of the veil. But now they've gotten really noisy, I'm almost getting full sentences,' D-O-A explained. 'All you need to do is try to clear your mind.'

Nikita found the task of clearing her mind nearly impossible on any given occasion, as it teemed with more trains of thought than the platforms at Paddington Station. She inhaled deeply, closing her eyes to encourage some internal calmness.

'Tell us about the danger in the web,' D-O-A asked nobody in particular, his voice echoing off the ceilings.

Nikita watched him tilt his head and narrow his eyes, clearly picking up on some kind of response.

'Do you trust me?' the Ghoster asked, holding his hands out to her.

'Absolutely not.' Nikita let out a nervous chuckle and cautiously took his hands.

His skin was as cold as the grave, though his touch was unexpectedly gentle. 'Understandable. Take a deep breath.'

'What?' Nikita managed to fill two-thirds of a lungful of air before the Reaper pulled her under the water.

They sank slowly, resting on the bottom of the pool at the deep end, D-O-A keeping his eyes steadily on hers. He released one hand and tapped his ear, indicating for her to listen. Within seconds, she could hear a mass of swirling voices, rippling and bounding through the water, a medley of watery emotions expressed in distant words.

The voices began to settle, as a dominant one came forward.

*Oliver-Alliott*, it warbled, the water distorting the tone with its gentle motion. *Wolf.*

Nikita's eyes stung with the chlorine, but she dared not close them. She could almost pick out shadowy shapes in the corners of the pool, swirling and dancing in the depths.

*Danger in the web*, it said urgently. *The blood thief has disciples. Deep. Deep and dark.*

Thirty seconds turned into forty-five, and Nikita's lungs were beginning to burn. She considered herself a good swimmer, much less a breath-holder. D-O-A gripped her hands tighter, his face showing no signs of needing to resurface. Tiny air bubbles escaped his tight-lipped expression, his white hair swirling in the water like an exotic sea anemone.

*Not disciples. Another word.*

The voice fell quiet, and others began to mutter in the depths.

Sixty-seven seconds ticked by. Nikita was doing everything she could not to panic, her eyes scanning the surface of the water several feet above her head.

A second voice chimed in, higher pitched. *Not disciples, Gunther. Oracles.*

Nikita's eyes widened at the mention of the word, and the familiarity of the name.

*Find the oracles. In the deep. Danger in the deep dark.*

The first voice piped up once more with urgency. *Onions. Oracles on dark onions.*

The voices began to swarm around them, all muttering and vying for the spotlight, their words blending and washing into one another.

A minute and a half had gone by, and Nikita had reached her limit. Her chest was screaming to take a breath, and the panic began to grip her. She pulled away from the Reaper and started to fight her way to the surface, darkness crawling into the corners of her vision and a ringing filtering its way into her ears. The weight of her wet clothes pulled at her limbs, and before she breached the surface, the warm taste of pool water filled her nose and mouth, finding its way into her throat. Instinctively, she tried to cough, only taking on more water, the light fading completely and her limbs dropping like weights.

Ghostly voices milled into her ringing ears and a painful sensation of intermittent pressure on her chest brought her into a semi-state of consciousness. She was brought back to stark reality when she felt the outline of a mouth pressed against hers, forcing air into her lungs. She violently spluttered, coughing up water on the cold tile. Strong hands rolled her onto her side and rubbed her back as she expelled the last of the water from her burning throat.

For a few long moments she inhaled glorious oxygen; vibrant colour and sound returning to the room as her glazed senses slowly came to.

'I owe you an apology,' D-O-A said, his voice still muffled as the clarity was returning to Nikita's hearing. 'I don't make a habit of killing anyone who's not on a card.'

Nikita gradually sat up, pushing her wet hair from her face. 'What happened?' she spluttered as searing pain in her chest caught the air in her lungs.

'You tried to breathe underwater. Forgive me, I had to do CPR.' D-O-A was knelt beside her, his usual unreadable expression full of concern.

If she wasn't in so much pain, she might have laughed at the idea of a Reaper saving her life.

'I think you cracked my ribs,' she rasped, the sharpness in her chest making her wince.

'A little.' D-O-A got up and fetched his coat, returning to drape it over her shoulders. 'We should get you checked out.'

'Did the ghosts say anything else?' Nikita ignored his comment, but wrapped the coat tighter around herself, shivering.

'I was too busy dragging you out of the pool to finish the conversation.'

'Sorry about that.'

* * *

Three hours later, Nikita was sat on her sofa, a blanket draped over her and a thick textbook in her hand covering the mysteries of the cosmic web. Her chest still ached and her throat was raw, but she was incredibly glad to be back home with only bruised ribs. D-O-A had stayed with her the whole time at the hospital. He hadn't spoken much but had shown a rare glimpse of warmth and humanity in the way he fussed about her welfare.

It was gone eleven o'clock when Erron turned up, seeming in good spirits as he kicked off his boots by the door.

'Good dinner?' she asked, bookmarking her page.

He unfastened his cufflinks, slumping down on the sofa next to her. 'It was and it wasn't, I guess,' he answered.

'Do you want to talk about it?' Nikita pried, trying to cover her burning curiosity with a casual tone.

Erron loosened his collar and leant back on the sofa. 'He suggested we start over, rebuild our friendship first. I've got a lot of things I need to work through before . . .' He trailed off.

'Before you're ready for anything more. I get it.' Nikita nodded. 'Don't rush it, it'll happen.'

'Yeah.' Erron gave her a faded smile. 'I hope so. Anyway, how was your evening?'

'Well, I drowned in the pool listening to ghosts at the Eligos and spent two hours in the hospital with Darren Oliver-Alliott getting checked over. Aside from that, I've got two possible lines of enquiry.'

Erron's face morphed between shock and confusion. 'Sorry, start again, you drowned?'

'I was listening to ghosts in the pool. It's a long story.' She waved her hand dismissively.

'It seems like an important one.' Erron's eyes widened.

Nikita relented and told him all about what led her into that situation and the messages she'd received from the ghosts.

'Oracles …' Erron chewed his lip in thought. 'That relates to the word we found in the suspect's notebook. Seems like too much of a coincidence to me.'

'They described the oracles as disciples. The suspect must be the blood thief,' Nikita reasoned.

'If the ghosts see energy of all agents, they must know where to find this killer, or as it turns out, any followers he might have.' Erron leant his head back in exasperation. 'This just keeps getting more complicated.'

'Well, if you can hold your breath longer than me, please do go and ask for some clarity, but they take so long arguing with each other it's pretty gruelling. I don't fancy doing that again in a hurry.'

'We'll park that for a moment, then. Can't say my lung capacity is all that great,' Erron conceded.

'Maybe if you stop bloody smoking.' Nikita raised an eyebrow at him. 'Anyway, instead, I started looking into the names linked to the vials we found at the tattoo shop. I wanted to check if they correlated to what I thought they might.'

'Hit me with it. What did you find?'

'These subheadings, Corvus, Andromeda, Lyra and Orion correspond to the sources of stardust used in the reanimation of new agency recruits. This last one, Ophiuchus, however, is not one I have heard of before. Now, these main names of Greek deities might just be gimmicky names for the inks, to give them some implication of power, but when I get to the Raphael tomorrow I will run the samples to test if they have anything in them that links them to agency blood.'

Erron's face went ashen. 'Not this blood magic stuff again?' he asked, his voice barely a whisper.

'No, I don't think so. None of the vials looked like blood. Maybe plasma, but it could just be some kind of sourced ingredients that's used in reanimation. It could just mean nothing, of course.' She patted his shoulder.

'I know Apollo blood is Corvus, and Hades is Orion stardust. I heard enough about that in the trial,' Erron said numbly. 'But I don't know how they relate to the other names on the labels.'

'I don't think they do really. I looked through a fair bit of Greek mythology and they don't have a huge amount linking them. The one that is sticking out like a sore thumb is the Achilles ink. I get that Achilles was this amazing warrior, but he's more associated with his heel, the main point of weakness.' Nikita tapped the edge of the textbook against her lips, deep in thought.

'Maybe it's for tattoos to overcome weakness,' Erron suggested.

'Maybe. We'll test them in the morning. But right now, I'm too tired to think about anything more. I can't move for pain. My ribs hurt from the CPR, my wing nubs ache and my lungs feel like I inhaled fire.'

'You need to rest. Take the bed tonight, Nikita. It's my turn on the sofa.'

'I would but I can't face getting up.'

'Right, you leave me no choice.' Erron stood up and took the book out of Nikita's hands before scooping her up in her blanket and carrying her down the hall.

'I was not expecting that,' Nikita remarked. 'That's quite a deadlift.'

'I'm stronger than I look.' Erron grinned as he set her down on the edge of the bed.

'I'm starting to think Ghosters are significantly more caring than people make out,' Nikita teased.

'Yeah, well, they haven't beaten it out of me yet.' Erron set down a half-empty pack of his morphine tablets on the bedside table for her. 'Get some sleep.'

'Thank you. You'll need this.' Nikita handed him her sofa blanket.

Erron closed the bedroom door and wandered back into the living room, not quite ready to sleep. He decided to have a look at the suspect's notebook to take his mind off the dinner with Casey. Carefully peeling apart the pages one by one, he found the tiniest line of handwriting in faint pencil. It read *Oracles forum* with a jumbled web address with the domain name *.onion*.

Erron wrote down the information more clearly on a scrap of paper before continuing the careful page turning. After half an hour, he gave up, having found nothing more than bundles of monetary amounts jotted down in a long list. He put the delicate notebook back in the evidence bag and made up his bed for the night on the sofa. Having forgotten to grab a T-shirt from the bedroom beforehand, he stripped off to his boxers and carefully hung up his best shirt and jeans over the kitchen chair.

With the lights off, he lay in the dark, going over his earlier conversation with Casey in his head, his mind occasionally drifting back to the memory of their kiss on Casey's rooftop terrace in the rainstorm, the night Erron had confessed his feelings to his best friend. He could still remember how it felt to have Casey's hair between his fingers, the cold rain running down their faces, the taste of his lips. The memory was harshly interrupted by a vivid flashback of Izzy, a mixed-up disjointed montage of sensations of her body, the way her teeth found his flesh, the overpowering smell of blood and sweat. He pressed his hand over his mouth, dampening the involuntary agonised cry that escaped his lungs. Shaking away the intrusive images, he stared blankly at the ceiling for what seemed like an eternity before the plane of sleep finally accepted his boarding pass.

* * *

Not far away in the little shop in Pennyfields, Sam was back on the Oracles forum, which was lit up with demands for more of the magical blood auctions. The supply had sold out within days and there were buyers from all over reporting that they'd had at least one day of incredibly good fortune from consuming or injecting the blood. The new owner of Leo's feet had been relatively quiet on the discussion boards, not letting on too much about the effects of their new acquisition. Sam was overwhelmed with curiosity about the types of luck people had experienced, but he was more keen to know whether the feet had brought greater fortune than the blood.

He had the username of the person that had bought the feet but was hesitant to ask directly if they were happy with their purchase. He imagined that if they weren't, it would have been a hot topic of discussion by now. The forum was swamped with some very questionable characters of whom even Sam was wary, and he didn't like to speak too freely among them in case they were being monitored. His hands idled over the keyboard, as he wondered if he should join the conversation, but thought better of it. With all the stock gone, it was only a matter of time before fresh blood was in high demand, and for the prices it was selling for, it would become a very lucrative enterprise.

Sam had been regularly checking the news, both on TV and online, and there was no mention of the murders. It was not unheard of for serious crime to go under the radar in London, but for something as gruesome and sensational as these, he would have thought there'd be some mention, some witness coming forward to sell their story to the media. It solidified his belief that the Fireflies were above humanity in some way and would have covered up the deaths to protect their identities. The alleyway in Kensington had been clear the night he'd gone back to check if the woman's body was still there, so someone had discovered it and someone had moved it. He'd been meticulous in checking the news daily and was confident that no one was publicly looking to solve the crime, which only deepened the mystery of the Fireflies' true nature.

# 20

## *Treat You Better*

HEAVY RAIN OVER LONDON HAMMERED against the lounge window, rousing Erron from his fitful night's sleep just before dawn the next morning. He peered through the blinds at the grey light, stretching out his aches and pains.

The sound of a key in the apartment lock startled him, and when the door was carefully opened, he was even more shocked to see the Fortuna boss creeping into the apartment clasping an elaborate bouquet of flowers and a box of chocolates.

Emrys didn't immediately spot Erron in the dark but visibly leapt in alarm when he locked eyes with the Reaper stood at the window in nothing but his underwear.

'Sorry, I thought you'd gone back to your own place.' Emrys gathered his thoughts and stood awkwardly by the kitchen table. He couldn't help but notice the long angry scar on Erron's stomach from where he'd been stabbed and made a conscious effort not to stare at it.

'Uh, yes, sorry I should have been . . . I needed the company, that's all. I slept on the sofa.' Erron was feeling increasingly exposed and was looking around for something with which to cover himself.

Just then the light went on as Nikita had come to investigate the hushed voices.

'Holy shit!' she exclaimed. 'Emrys, you scared me! Erron, put some clothes on, will you? You're making me look bad.'

'Sorry, it was meant to be a surprise.' Emrys held up the gifts apologetically. 'I was just going to leave them on your table, so you had something nice to wake up to, after your incident in the pool. I would have sat with you in the hospital if you had only told me when you were there.'

'I didn't want to worry you,' Nikita soothed. 'Honestly, I'm fine, but thank you.'

'I can't help but worry.' Emrys fixed her with a sad expression.

Nikita took him aside, Erron disappearing to get dressed in another room.

'I hope I have really got the wrong idea here,' Emrys said quietly.

Nikita wrapped her arms around his neck. 'You really have. You should know by now I am absolutely not his type.'

'Of course, I know, I just, sometimes these things aren't always that clear cut.' He tilted his head.

'Trust me on this, I'm all yours,' Nikita said softly.

He looked down at her oversized pyjamas printed with cartoon weather symbols. 'I mean, he might be *really* into the Met Office.' He gestured at her attire and laughed.

'I guess. It's a very common kink,' Nikita replied drily. 'I'll have to be careful not to tease him with my seductive storm clouds.'

'You better not.' He scooped her up into a tight hug, her legs wrapping around his waist. 'You're *my* Met Office. And I am feeling a warm front moving in from the south.'

She giggled mischievously and kissed him for long enough that he had to set her down halfway through.

'Thank you for the slightly creepy romantic intruder tactic, certainly a new one on me,' she said, grinning.

'Yes ... well ... I better go, I was only meant to be here a moment. I certainly wasn't expecting to run into your secret lover cavorting around in his undergarments. How scandalous.' He winked at her.

'I'll ask him to be more discreet in future.' Nikita laughed and herded him towards the door.

She closed it just as Erron reappeared, fully dressed. 'Sorry about that.'

'No need to apologise. It's me that's in the way.' Erron headed over to the kitchen counter and filled up the kettle.

'You're not in the way,' Nikita said sternly.

'So, what's the plan today? You said about testing these plasma thingamajigs?' Erron set out two mugs and dropped a spoon of instant coffee in each. 'Sugar?'

'Two, please. Yes, we'll head over to Raphael, I think.'

'OK. How are you feeling this morning?' Erron paused after putting three sugars in his own drink, then added two more for good measure.

'A bit better now. Did you sleep?'

'At some point.' Erron tipped a sixth spoon of sugar into his coffee, hoping it might miraculously get rid of the wing ache and nicotine cravings in one hit. 'Oh, before I forget, I looked through the notebook again last night and wrote this down.'

He fetched an ink-riddled bit of paper, handing it to her before going back to stir the coffees.

Nikita studied it. 'I guess that might explain the onion thing the ghost mentioned. Is that an agency thing?'

'Not that I'm aware of.'

'We'll have to figure it out, then.' Nikita took a grateful sip of the coffee she was handed.

* * *

The pre-dawn rain became lighter as the sun rose behind thick grey clouds. The Raphael Sanctuary was its usual quiet self, with only a handful of patients that had been admitted overnight for minor injuries or planned procedures.

The morgue had been brought back up to normal room temperature, as it was no longer needed to refrigerate any bodies. They were both glad of the ability to work in the room without worrying if their eyeballs would freeze over part-way through the day.

Nikita locked the door before removing the Arcane Ink vials from the fridge. She rolled a tall metal stool over to a microscope and prepared some slides.

'Right, I am going to take a normal blood sample and compare it to the ink with the Corvus subheading,' she explained, wheeling herself to a nearby set of drawers and searching for anything she could use.

Erron looked on as she found a sterile needle pack and used it to prick her finger, massaging the area so three droplets fell onto a slide.

She peered into the lens of the microscope, turning the dial until it focused on the blood sample. Her expression turned to fascination as she watched the tiny flecks of stardust shimmer and burn on the surface of her red blood cells, as if they were painted with a sheen of fire and gold.

'Wow, no wonder I have such a radiant glow!' she whispered excitedly, gesturing for Erron to take a look.

'I guess you're going to be asking to look at mine now.' Erron grimaced.

She already had a clean needle in hand. 'You survived being impaled by a demonic sword, I'm sure you can handle a tiny prick.'

Erron raised an eyebrow and stifled a smirk. 'Bit personal, Nikita.'

She blushed and pushed him playfully. 'Shut up, you know what I meant.' He held out his hand, palm up, while she unboxed the needle.

Under the microscope, no flecks of gold swam over the surface of Erron's cells, instead a silvery-grey smoke swirled through the blood, still twinkling slightly, but with the fire of a cold, dying star surrounded by a shadowy nebula.

'I guess that explains why I look like my smoking habit finally caught up with me.' He sighed, wheeling himself away from the microscope.

'Hush, you look fine. All Ghosters have that dark and brooding look.' She didn't like to say that although he still had his alluring good looks, he'd definitely lost the movie-star glow he had as a Cupid.

'Hmm,' he grumbled.

'Anyway, let's check out these inks.' She used a dropper to draw out a small volume of the vial labelled '*Aphrodite – (Corvus)*' and placed it onto a slide.

There was silence as she viewed the sample, her facial expressions covering a range of internal emotions.

'Well . . . ?' Erron asked impatiently.

She sat back and gestured to the microscope, where he rolled his seat over to take a look. Similar to her blood, the ink sample swam with a living film of gold, sparkling and burning in the clear liquid.

Silently, Nikita prepared a slide of the vial labelled '*Orion – (Artemis)*' before switching them on the plate. They both observed the familiar Hades silvery liquid smoke swirling around the empty fluid.

They tested all of the inks, coming to the conclusion the greenish glitter belonged to Fortuna, the ink that glowed like crackling lava belonged to Nemesis and the fifth unknown sample had a clear, iridescent luminosity.

'So, what does this tell us?' Erron asked.

'I'm no expert, but I would say these inks are derived from agency plasma; either that or they are actually just the raw stardust in a liquid suspension that is used in reanimation.' Nikita rubbed her temples. 'Either way, I highly doubt they are meant to be used in a back-alley tattoo shop on the moon.'

Erron was quiet for some time before he spoke. 'Should we get Dr Enleigh in here to run these samples?'

'Actually, I think we need to keep this to ourselves for now. We have to be open to the possibility that if these are substances that originate from the reanimation department, someone might be taking them off site without permission.'

Erron admitted he hadn't thought of that. 'We need to find out if anyone can obtain these, or if they are restricted, which I'd imagine they are.'

'Going on the agency regulations around blood mixing, I'd say they are restricted,' Nikita theorised. 'Of course, we could always test if they have a reaction.'

'You mean, inject the ink?' Erron was taken aback. 'What about the *Umbra Amictus* effect or whatever it was called, seeing as it nearly ended the world?'

'Precisely that. Because of what Kendra and Izzy did, we already know the outcome of the Apollo and Hades blood mix. The difference is we're in a controlled environment here, and neither of us want to kill mortals to take over the world.' Nikita began to roll up her sleeve.

Erron grabbed her arm. 'You're serious about this?'

'What's the worst thing that can happen? If anything goes wrong we're in a hospital,' Nikita said pragmatically. 'I'm not going to cause another apocalypse, I promise.'

Erron reluctantly released her arm. 'OK, but let me do this. I don't want anything happening to you.' Erron hastily unbuttoned his shirt cuff to expose his arm. 'Give me the Apollo one.'

* * *

Freya Carthage had collared Casey the moment he'd turned up for work on Wednesday morning, to mentor a new transferee.

'His name is Warren Larkin, he's already waiting for you. I'm sure you'll get on like a house on fire,' Freya explained.

Casey was hoping to be released for Medusa duties, but was happy to meet Warren, who was perched in front of his desk. He was a tall, thin man, with a handsome and studious look to him, brown hair swept in a side parting and just a smattering of freckles. He looked up with a broad smile when Casey approached him and stood to shake his hand with enthusiasm.

'Honoured to meet you, sir, I have heard just so much about you. I took the liberty of fetching us both a coffee,' he said, his perfect Queen's English making Casey's well-spoken tone sound closer to Erron's Cockney accent.

'Why, thank you.' Casey invited him to sit back down as he took his own seat opposite. 'I assume you know the drill; it's just a case of finding where everything is here?'

'I toured the building before you arrived, so I'm just keen to get out and about.'

'Wonderful. Well, the assignment process here is pretty straightforward.' Casey took a long sip of his coffee and savoured its warmth.

'Oh yes, I have already collected our assignments for the day, and I've had a good look through the files for each person.'

Casey almost spat out his coffee. He collected himself and leant forward on his desk. 'I'm sorry, what? You've already read the files?'

'Yes, sorry, is there a problem?' Warren looked struck with concern. 'That was our policy in my district.'

'None whatsoever.' Casey was pleasantly surprised.

'Anyway, I brought you these, as a thank you for agreeing to take me under your literal wing.' Warren picked up a small pink box from beside his chair and handed it to Casey. Delicate silver lettering on the box spelled out the name of an upmarket bakery several streets away. 'I thought we could enjoy them while en route to umm ... Wellington Arch. I have got the directions ready, sir.'

Casey peered inside the box: twelve perfectly formed miniature profiteroles sat atop a gold plastic tray. 'Well, I could get used to this.' He gave Warren a warm smile. 'And no need to get directions, I've got a fair grasp on where most places are.'

'Of course, of course!' Warren blustered. 'Forgive me, I forgot you've got quite the impressive service. You must know London like the back of your hand.'

'Mostly, but you'll be amazed how much changes over time. When is the first assignment?' Casey was keen to start on the profiteroles, regardless of the fact he'd not long had breakfast.

'We can get going shortly. I cannot wait to hear all your stories from over the years.' Warren's enthusiasm was infectious. 'But if it's OK, I've ordered us a taxi. I just had my trousers dry-cleaned and don't particularly enjoy the underground system here.'

'Oh, that's absolutely fine.' Casey grinned, popping a profiterole in his mouth shortly after.

During the journey, Casey learnt some of Warren's history as he enthused about how he was so glad to be an Apollo agent, having previously spent his mortal life working with computer coding and general IT. They kept their voices quiet, so the driver wasn't able to eavesdrop easily over the rough diesel engine. Warren had graduated with a master's in computer science from Oxford University in the early 2000s, spending eight years in a swish tech company before drowning in a rowing accident just before his thirty-eighth birthday. He'd been on an exceptional salary and had an eye for expensive fashion, priding himself on his style and success prior to his death. 'You know what's the best part about this afterlife?' Warren said, his hands clasped neatly on his lap. 'I will never change now, and my best clothes will always suit me just right.'

'That is a huge bonus.' Casey reflected briefly on how he was able to wear his favourite suits for decades, without being plagued with middle-aged spread, especially with his penchant for sweet treats.

* * *

Erron was poised for the injection, slightly apprehensive on what it might do to him.

Nikita drew 5 ml of ink from the Aphrodite vial in a syringe. 'You sure about this?' She fixed him with an unblinking expression.

He presented his bare arm and nodded. 'Like you said, we're in the right place if it goes wrong.'

A few moments after the injection, Erron didn't turn into shadows as expected, but did report feeling ever so slightly feverish. They waited half an hour, with Nikita taking his temperature every ten minutes, which gradually seemed to increase in tiny increments.

'How are you feeling now?' she asked.

'I'm not sure. Something is definitely happening, I just don't know what yet.' He scratched at his arm and fidgeted in his seat.

Another eleven minutes passed before Nikita sat up, alert. 'Wait, I can see it.' She rolled closer to him and touched his face; it was hot to the touch. 'You've got a sun-kissed glow, like you used to have as a Cupid. Not so obvious, but it's there.'

He began to look uncomfortable. 'Oh god, I think it's like some version of the initial stages of the Apollo Flush.' He closed his eyes tightly.

'Ah, I remember it like it was yesterday.' Nikita laughed, glad her Apollo Flush had settled to the base level without the intense lustful thoughts that came with the first twenty-four hours.

'Yeah. I hope it doesn't last.' Erron's warm glow gradually turned into a deeper shade of crimson.

'I'd say this experiment has been successful. We are definitely dealing with a pure sample of Apollo stardust. It doesn't react with your Hades blood, but it does mimic Apollo abilities. Clearly this tattoo artist has found a way to give his clients a taste of another set of abilities. Or supersize their existing ones, I expect,' Nikita deduced. She picked up a folder and started to fan cool air onto him.

He tugged at his collar, huffing with the uncomfortable sensations of heat running through his body. 'I think I need to isolate until this passes.'

'Ah, am I now your type?' Nikita teased. 'Shall I sit further away?'

'Umm . . .' He wiped the dampness from his brow. 'I mean, don't assume you weren't. But probably best you stay a good distance away, for my sake.'

'Oh, I see.' Nikita raised her eyebrows, taking a moment to process the flippant comment. 'That's just the Flush talking. But don't worry, I was ready to jump on anyone in that Apollo office on my first day, including you and Casey. I'll go get us a can of Sprite each from the vending machine. It should cool you down a bit.' She let herself out of the room, noticing him cover his eyes with his hands to prevent himself watching her leave.

It took four hours before Erron was fully in control of himself. In that time Nikita had gone out to get them a takeaway lunch and after they'd eaten, she'd left again to see if she could sneak her way into the reanimation department undetected.

She'd managed to spot various vials of the cosmic liquid and make a quick getaway before anyone spotted her skulking around in the restricted area. She got back to the morgue to find Erron pressing an ice pack to his forehead.

'That bad, huh? I guess I should be grateful the ice pack isn't on your lap.' Nikita stifled a laugh.

'Not funny.' He glared at her, the rosy glow of his cheeks gradually beginning to pale. 'Did you find anything?'

'Yes, they are baking a soul now, and lo and behold, there are big containers of these so-called inks on the side in there. They're restricted substances. I would hazard a guess and say whoever this Djinn guy is, he's got a friend on the inside here selling him stardust under the counter.'

'That may be so, but it still doesn't really help us with these murders,' Erron replied.

'Unless . . .' Nikita's mind whirred at lightning speed, connecting dots that only she could see. She went back to the fridge and pulled out the Achilles vial. 'Aphrodite is mostly known for being the goddess of love and beauty, yes? So it makes sense that Cupid powers are linked to that. Similarly, Ares, god of war, perfect for Nemesis. Now, what is their innate ability called?'

Erron had to think for a moment. 'Something like the Nemesis Inferno. It's like a subtle heat that makes people feel guilty or justified in their presence, depending on their moral compass, plus it heightens people's anger at injustice.'

'I guess a god of war would have a certain level of rage,' Nikita stated. 'Hades, then, with Artemis. Goddess of the hunt.'

'Ghosters make you feel like you are prey,' Erron realised.

'That's exactly the feeling the *Umbra Noctis* gives off, a hunter in the shadows,' Nikita agreed. 'Makes sense.'

She had to google *Asteria*, finally coming to the conclusion the person that named the inks was making a tentative link with luck and stars, just to keep the names all the same letter.

'So what does all this mean, then?' Erron asked, slightly impatient.

'These goddesses and gods are all just gimmicky brand names for the actual stardust power. But there's this fifth one, Achilles. Known for his weakness, it makes no sense.' She pressed her forefinger to her mouth and paced back and forth, deep in thought.

'What's the other name on the vial, the official medical name?' Erron broke the silence after a minute or two.

'Ophiuchus,' she responded. 'The internet says it's the serpent bearer constellation. I know it's right in front of me, but I just can't see the connection.'

Erron nodded his head towards the wall, gesturing for her to look. At the back of the room where the resin plate image of the caduceus, the symbol of medicine, two snakes around a winged staff, had been staring at them the whole time.

'Archangels,' Nikita mouthed, the pieces clicking into place. 'It's Archangel stardust.'

'They have no discernible powers aside from flight,' Erron added.

'No powers, their Achilles heel,' Nikita muttered. 'Holy shit, I need to test this.'

'Please, for the love of god, test it on me before I do actually need this ice pack in my lap,' Erron pleaded, holding out his arm again.

'I suppose it's not fair to make you suffer, but I'll take that as a compliment.' Nikita suppressed a giggle, setting up a syringe with Achilles ink. 'Hold still.'

Within an hour of him receiving the shot, the Apollo Flush was gone, as was his aura of death. In fact, Nikita thought, Erron looked incredibly, mundanely mortal.

Nikita typed up her findings, sending a detailed email of her notes to Osato and Emrys, instructing them to notify all agents not to undergo any tattoos at Arcane Ink while it was under investigation.

'OK, let's look at the possibilities here,' Erron said. 'Two victims with tattoos that potentially sucked away their Fortuna Diaboli and left them vulnerable. It could be complete coincidence, or … or this suspect knew they were sitting ducks somehow.'

'Let's say it's not a coincidence, that the suspect orchestrated this, that means he must be an agent. You said the tattoos on the victims both faded, right? So, there's potentially only a short window that the killer had to work with. It's just a theory at this stage, but it seems likely the murders were planned to coincide with the tattoos,' Nikita suggested. 'I gave Osato printouts of the suspect yesterday. She said it would take her a few days to get it circulated well enough to come up with any identification. If this guy is an agent, we will find him.'

'We need to get hold of this Djinn fella. Because he's looking incredibly suspicious right now.'

'I take it you've had no response from the number on the business card?' Nikita asked.

'Nothing. I've tried a few times.' Erron shrugged.

'If he's involved, our presence at Arcane Ink likely scared him off. But this does put him up there as our number one suspect at this point. We'll have to go back there and see if we can detain him,' Nikita suggested.

'We won't be able to just blunder in; we ought to run it past Osato first. If we actually catch him we need to figure out where to hold him in custody.'

'Good idea. Best speak to her first.' Nikita checked the time. 'If you do that, we'll grab some food, then if Osato gives the go ahead we'll try and arrest this Djinn guy.'

'Sounds dangerously like a plan.'

# 21

## *Saturn*

THAT AFTERNOON, EMBER SONGFIRE BOBBED along Morton Road in Islington, her cheerful self buttoned into bright red dungarees covered in a sunflower print. She was in a good mood despite the rain being on and off.

Her afternoon was filled with good luck assignments, each fairly close to one another. The first being an elderly lady by the name of Beatrice Mathers at number twenty-three. Ember's ankle was still throbbing from the tattoo, and she was still feeling a little rough from it, but she didn't allow it to dampen her mood any more than her hair in the rain.

A blue BMW drove by at speed, dousing her with the dirty water from a blocked drain. She jumped in shock, not expecting for one minute to be unlucky enough to be drenched by a passing car. She brushed it off as some form of red-light luck that would somehow manifest as beneficial, squeezing the dirty water out of her twin plaits. She approached Mrs Mathers' front door while humming 'Brown Eyed Girl' by Van Morrison.

There was a long pause after the cheerful ding-dong of the bell, Mrs Mathers opening the door a crack and wrapping a knitted shawl tighter around her chest as she eyed the visitor up and down with suspicion.

'Yes?' she said in a croaky voice that hadn't spoken to a living soul in weeks.

'Hi there! I just moved down the road. I have seen you about and wanted to introduce myself. My name is Jenny.'

Still narrow-eyed and holding the door tightly with gnarled fingers, Mrs Mathers glanced up and down the street before replying.

'Why you want to say hello, Jenny?' She had a subtle, yet distinct Jamaican accent, watered down from decades living in cold and dreary England.

Ember spun a lie about wanting to discuss gardening tips and the elderly lady invited her in, charmed by her warm smile.

Ember tripped up the step as she followed, catching herself before she hit the carpet. 'What is with me today?' she muttered to herself.

'My friends call me Bea,' Mrs Mathers said with a toothless smile.

'Well, it's lovely to meet you, Bea.' Ember noticed the clock on the wall. She had about fifteen minutes before she needed to complete her assignment. Bea was meant to have an aptly named Lucky Escape by accidentally pulling out the telephone cable, which would prevent her tripping over it with a heavy pan of potatoes and breaking her neck on the edge of the marble countertop. Luck assignments that were meant to divert death were fairly common and the Fates used them to remind people of the value of their lives.

Ember enjoyed listening to stories of Bea's past and sharing gardening tips as the elderly lady slowly peeled a pile of potatoes, dropping them into a pan of water until it was full.

'Well, I best be going, Bea. It was wonderful to meet you,' Ember excused herself.

She gave Bea a friendly hug and the essential kiss of luck on her left cheek as she left.

Ember ambled along for ten minutes down the road, reflecting on her spate of misfortune, a coldness creeping into her gut. It was then she turned a corner down by a park and bumped into Theodore Roscoe.

'Theo!' Ember beamed.

'Miss Songfire, no less!' he replied, offering her a tight hug. They had known each other for decades and often shared stories of the glory days of festivals and the spiritual liberation of the sixties generation.

'What brings you here?' she asked, after they had exchanged pleasantries.

'A mop-up job of a failed Lucky Escape. Looks like it might have been yours,' he said with a sincere, caring look.

'Not Bea?' Ember's heart sank and a lump formed in her throat. 'But I completed my assignment.'

'Beatrice Mathers? Potato-related neck injury,' he confirmed, looking at his assignment that had not long been populated with the mystical writing that appeared on a blind card. 'I'm late for this one, it was last minute. I'm afraid she's already gone.'

'Yes, that's her. I should have stayed longer, made sure the kiss worked.' Ember shook her head sadly. 'I don't understand. I feel like I have lost all my luck today.'

The senior Reaper pressed the back of his hand to her forehead. 'Why not get yourself to the Raphael and get checked out? You feel very cold.'

'You know, I might just do that.' She sighed. 'I'll have to call in someone to cover my next assignments.'

'Good idea, my sweet.' Roscoe squeezed her shoulder.

'Be good to her. Bea. She is . . . *was* a good lady,' Ember said sadly.

'When have I ever not been the kindest angel of death you could wish for? I will make sure she goes with dignity,' he replied, checking the card as Bea's last thoughts had been recorded. It was the Hades agent's responsibility to check they matched up if they were there in time before the person died. 'You know what, Ember, I'm not supposed to share this, but Bea's last thoughts were of you. "What a sweet young girl, reminds me of my Rosie",' he read out. 'She's lucky enough to have met you.'

Ember smiled weakly and bid him farewell as she headed back to headquarters, phoning a colleague on the way to ask if they would cover her shift.

Back in Kensington, she told Emrys what had happened, and he gave her the same advice to get herself to hospital for tests, in the hope it was nothing more than a blip in the grand scheme of things.

Unbeknownst to Ember, on her way to the hospital, Sam Rivera had begun to follow her, hopping down from his regular perch not far from the Fortuna building.

* * *

After Ember had left his office, Emrys slumped down in his chair, an icy feeling of dread washing over him. He glanced over at the luck scales, convinced the red cosmic ball had dropped a fraction lower.

Shaking his head, he opened an email that had come through from Nikita, detailing their discovery around the tattoo ink at the Raphael Sanctuary, confirming his fear that other agents were vulnerable to losing their luck. He responded, copying in Osato to explain the situation with Ember and how the issue might be escalating.

Emrys picked up his office phone and called Ember, though it went straight to voicemail. He assumed she was still travelling to the hospital, and likely couldn't hear her phone.

An hour passed before he called again, knowing by that time she was likely undergoing assessment at the Raphael, or at the very least would be in the waiting room. But having received no reply to his calls or texts, he grabbed his coat from the back of his chair and headed out to see where she was. He couldn't stand the thought of any harm befalling another one of his agents.

* * *

Osato had given the go-ahead for the arrest attempt at Arcane Ink that afternoon, explaining they would be able to bring the suspect back to the Medusa room for questioning. She'd also suggested that if he wasn't there, then the Medusa team should undertake a stakeout at the location so he couldn't slip through the net, but she'd need to arrange for some cover if that was the case. Erron and Nikita had taken the opportunity to wedge themselves into a tiny booth at a rundown café to grab a hot drink. They quietly discussed their plan of action for the arrest and how they would manage it without any proper equipment.

'Cable ties, then?' Nikita asked.

'Yeah, it's probably the most effective thing aside from handcuffs, which we don't have.' Erron took a long sip of his lukewarm coffee.

'Can't we just get some cuffs from Ann Summers? I mean, we can take the pink fur off to make them look more professional.' Nikita paused, mug in hand.

Erron fixed her with a withering look and shook his head slowly.

'You don't seem on board,' Nikita observed.

'I can't imagine what might go wrong,' he answered sarcastically. 'But no, they aren't exactly made to withstand significant resistance.'

'Sounds like you speak from experience.'

'Don't even go there.'

'I bet I could use my Apollo charms to get a proper set from a police officer,' Nikita mused.

'You probably could, as well as their phone number and bank details, but let's not go down the route of abusing agency privileges.' Erron knew damn well he would have done exactly that if he still had the Apollo Flush, but he didn't want Nikita falling into his bad habits so early in her career.

They finished their drinks, batting ideas back and forth about possible scenarios they might encounter and how they would deal with them, before Erron suggested they make a move to the nearest ice-cream van.

Just as Nikita went to grab her phone, it vibrated off the edge of the table and clattered to the floor, making her jump. She scrambled to answer it. It was Emrys.

'Hey, I got your email. How's Ember now?' Nikita asked before he got a chance to speak.

'I can't find her. She's not here.' He sounded worried and short of breath, as though he'd been running up and down the halls of the hospital.

'Just take a moment, breathe ... What time did she head over? Was there a chance she went home?' Nikita asked, keeping her voice calm and slow.

'She left HQ around 3 ... maybe 3.30 p.m. I came to the Raphael, and no one here has seen her. Reception staff haven't had anyone check in since 2 p.m., most of the wards are empty. I went over to her house and there's no answer, and her phone is just ringing out.' Emrys relayed everything, his mind racing with any detail he could have forgotten, anything Ember might have mentioned.

Nikita's gut told her something was wrong, but she wasn't intending on adding to the panic. 'Let's be methodical here. You know her best. Where else would she likely be?'

He racked his brain. Ember was very much a free spirit and was well known for being easily distracted if something caught her attention, but it was highly unlikely she had wandered off to some indie gig or underground art exhibition when she'd been so distressed. He sighed heavily before answering. 'Honestly, Rocket, I have no idea. She looked extremely worried and under the weather. I feel like she was genuine about going straight to hospital.'

'OK ...' Nikita paused to think. 'I think it's reasonable to assume she might be in trouble. Who does she hang around with most? I've seen her a few times at Nightjar, but we've only just got to know each other.'

'Casey Hart. She's been friends with him for decades, I know that much. I don't really know many others, but she's a social butterfly really, nearly everyone gets on with her.'

'Right, well, I think the priority is to start looking for her. I'll contact Casey. See if you can get any of her close friends from Fortuna out looking as well.'

They said their goodbyes and Nikita immediately called Casey, explaining the situation.

He listened, growing more concerned. 'I can start looking straightaway. I know some places she likes to go. It's not out of character for her to wander off, but I'd rather not assume she's safe. Freya will understand.'

'We'll help you,' Nikita offered.

'I've got my new crewmate here who says he's happy to help too,' Casey explained.

'The more the merrier. We'll meet you shortly.' Nikita arranged a place for them to converge before ending the call.

'Change of plan?' Erron queried.

'Yeah, we'll have to put off our moon visit for a few hours. We need to help find Ember. She's missing.'

* * *

Ember's eyes flickered open slowly. Her nose burned from an overpowering astringent odour in the air, and the sound of fans whirred in the distance. The air around her was bitterly cold, biting at her skin and bringing her round gradually from a dreamless depth of unconsciousness.

Her vision was sluggish to return, but shapes and colours gradually faded in from the darkness. The only illumination she could detect was the soft glow of a fire exit sign and dim green strip lights on the kickboards of what looked like steel kitchen cabinets.

Her body lay at a strange angle: she was on a cold flat surface, partially stood upright, but more distressingly, unable to move. Consciousness flooded back to her with a sudden, desperate panic as she discovered the thick leather straps that belted her securely to a steel gurney. One covered her throat, only allowing her to turn her head a few inches to either side. From her restricted field of vision, she could just see a dull grey tiled floor, metal storage racks on the walls and a kitchen trolley with various tubs of equipment; nothing was clear enough to see any detail. The room seemed small and grubby, a thin film of abandonment over every surface. There were no windows or natural light, and she could only see a few inches of what seemed to be a heavy fire door.

Cold sweat formed on her skin like dew on a blade of grass, her mouth felt dry and her arm was stinging. Peering down, she could see a cannula in her arm, attached to a thin tube which ran behind her to an unknown piece of equipment. For a brief moment, she wondered if she was in hospital and had woken up in the middle of treatment, her heart rate slowing long enough to consider the possibility. Yes, she thought, she had been heading to the hospital, but her last memory before waking up was that she'd just got to the entrance gates but she could recall nothing past that.

She waited for what seemed to be an eternity, thinking any moment a doctor would come in, a cleaner, a nurse. Anyone that might be able to help her or answer her questions. Hours ticked by as she wriggled in vain against her restraints, realising that she was no closer to getting free.

Once her eyes had fully adjusted to the dark, she was able to pick out details that had evaded her earlier. The tubs of equipment on the trolley included a saw, some clamps and a bundle of polythene bags, a tall stack of ice-cube trays and a bag of tubing. Confused, she wondered if she was in a commercial kitchen or some kind of butcher's shop; either way her fear began to rise again.

Eventually, the sound of footsteps echoed outside the room, and she cried out, her voice hoarse but seemingly muted by foam soundproofing on the walls. There was a pause outside before she could hear the sliding of heavy bolts. Ember's heart swelled with relief, until the footsteps sauntered over, seemingly unfazed by her pleas for help. The person didn't speak and she couldn't turn her head far enough to see them in the gloom. After some sounds of rustling, a dirty rag was used to gag her. She struggled, the strap around her neck rubbing her skin raw with her thrashing, the cloth compressing her tongue and filling her mouth with a rancid taste. Tears spilled down her cheeks as deep terror set in. The hands that had gagged her were a man's, young in appearance with the distinct smell of coal tar soap. He worked silently, preparing some type of fluid which he injected into the tube in her arm.

Within seconds, darkness overwhelmed her, and her head lolled forward as she slipped into a deep sleep once more.

* * *

Nikita, Erron and Emrys were gathered on the pavement outside Notting Hill Gate Tube station talking quietly while waiting for Casey to arrive. Emrys had already sent out several Fortuna agents to check anywhere they felt Ember might be lurking.

Erron spotted a grey trilby bob through the crowds, his heart surging briefly before plummeting at the sight of the tall handsome stranger that accompanied him.

Warren Larkin eagerly shook all their hands with a perfect smile before stepping aside for Casey to hand them all pages of a notebook.

'These are the addresses of all Ember's favourite places in this area,' Casey explained. 'I dismissed any that would be closed by now, and I've already checked at her flat again with no answer. There's also a picture of her for each of you, to ask around if any agency staff in these places have seen her, obviously the mortal-run places won't remember her with our cloaking.'

'I am very confident that with such a wonderful band of people we will find her in no time.' Warren pressed his hands together, his tone full of sincerity. He failed to notice the unimpressed expression Erron threw his way.

'The Fortuna HQ is around an hour-and-a-half walk from the Raphael,' Emrys stated. 'But Ember would have more than likely used the Tube.' He checked his watch. 'She's been gone around three or four hours now. She could be anywhere.'

'I know, but she'll more than likely gravitate to a place of comfort if she's not feeling great; somewhere familiar, that is, *if* she's wandered off,' Casey replied. 'I know it's not long since she left, but I think it's important we rule these places out early on.'

Nikita agreed and asked who was going where.

'I'll stick with Mr Hart. He's been the best guide around the city so far,' Warren said quickly, glancing over warmly at Casey.

'Fine. Nikita, Emrys, would you both head over to Maggie's club in Fulham Road? Erron, do you want to come with us over to the Tabernacle, then we can work through the list and meet in the middle?' Casey suggested.

Erron looked Warren up and down, his stomach turning at how close he leant into Casey, the way his eyes seemed to sparkle with the enthusiasm of a puppy going for his first walk. 'Actually, Case, we'll cover more ground if I go to another location alone.'

Casey pursed his lips in a tight smile. 'I guess that makes sense. Can you head towards Westfield shopping centre then? Ember likes the Nando's there.'

'Sure.' Erron loosely folded his arms.

'We'll reconvene here at, say, eleven?'

Everyone agreed, Nikita and Emrys making their way to their first location while Erron lingered just long enough to see the smug look on Warren's face as he guided Casey back into the crowd, his hand pressed gently on the small of his back. Feeling dejected, Erron buttoned his coat and headed inside the station.

* * *

It had gone midnight before Nikita and Emrys got back to her flat. Between the five of them, they'd covered a total of twelve locations in and around Kensington, with no luck, and no other agents reporting a sighting.

At one forty-five, both Nikita and Emrys were woken by the buzzing of her phone with a text from Casey.

'He's had no luck.' Nikita slumped, disappointed by the news.

'She's been missing around nine or ten hours now. The other victims were killed almost straightaway . . . Do you think we're overreacting?' Emrys ran his fingers through his hair.

'I think it's a good idea to be cautious. You tracked her phone, didn't you? Where did it last show activity?'

'It pinged to the Fortuna HQ. When I got back to work I found that she left it on her desk, along with her coat. She often forgets things. I didn't think to check on my way to the hospital.' Emrys shook his head. He fumbled around for his phone and updated Osato with the situation over text.

'OK, that doesn't help us much, but it explains why she isn't answering her calls or texts. There's a possibility she went to crash at a friend's house and will turn up to work tomorrow to a ton of missed calls,' Nikita reasoned.

'You're probably right.' Emrys rubbed his tired eyes. 'Sorry I fell asleep.'

A key rattled in the door before Erron stepped quietly into the room, expecting the place to be in darkness. 'Oh, you're both still up.'

'I take it you had no luck either?' Nikita asked.

'No, a couple of the agency-run places recognised the photo of her, but both said they hadn't seen her in days.' Erron pulled up a kitchen chair and slumped down.

'There's not much else we can do tonight,' Nikita conceded. 'Come on, mister, let's get to bed so Erron can have the sofa back.' She stood up and pulled at Emrys's sleeve, leading him down the hall.

Once they were enveloped by the duvet, Emrys drifted off in five minutes flat, exhausted from the stress of the day. Nikita lay next to him in the dark, gazing at the soft glow of city lights cast across his sleeping form. She lightly stroked his hair, the blond and grey strands shining silver in the dim light, the rhythmic rise and fall of his chest so peaceful in the silence of the room. There was so much kindness written in the lines on his face. She felt so safe, so utterly comfortable in his presence.

She realised a lifetime of chasing and begging and trying to prove her worth to someone was never the romance she needed. No matter the passion, the arguments, the ferocity of emotions she'd had before, nothing compared to what she had in front of her at that moment. An uncomplicated, gentle, selfless man that made daft jokes and brought her flowers before dawn.

She pictured her afterlife with him, comparing it to her mortal life. She saw no familiar screaming matches, broken vases or days of silent treatment. She saw no need to go through his phone to see what half-naked women or list of exes he was following on social media, or who he was messaging behind her back.

She placed her hand on his chest, caressing his skin, loving every imperfection of his body, adoring every facet of his soul. To her, he was nothing less than perfect.

He stirred slightly, a small smile forming on his lips, his hand finding hers and pulling her into a close hug. Though she dozed on his chest, her mind was still fighting sleep to solve the puzzles of the case, going over and over the comments made by the ghosts in the pool. It crossed her mind whether she ought to ask them for more guidance, though she wasn't yet ready to get back underwater.

She eventually surrendered to unconsciousness around 4 a.m., hoping that by sunrise Ember would be found safe and well.

# 22

## *In the Stars*

EMBER COULDN'T BEAR THE COLD. She didn't know how long she'd been asleep, but all her fears flooded back to her the moment she awoke again, still strapped to the gurney, her mouth filled with the vile cloth, her tongue as dry as plasterboard and her head pounding.

The room was still dull, some of the equipment had been moved and other things had been brought into her field of vision: packaging boxes, tape, empty jars and tubs. There was an unfamiliar glow coming from behind the gurney and a faint whirring of a machine, but nothing she could see or identify.

She was more concerned that her other arm had been hooked up to another tube and a controlled stream of blood was being collected into an IV-style bag hanging on a stand near her head. Sensations were coming back to her numb body like the crackling of a radio being tuned. Gradually, a dull pain in her ankle ramped up to a searing agony. She tugged against her restraints to look down and from the angle she was held at, it appeared that her right foot was missing, the stump of her ankle swathed in bandages, dried blood staining the sunflower print on the leg of her dungarees. A guttural scream lurched from her throat, muffled by the rag but no less animalistic.

The pain swelled until she drifted in and out of consciousness, trying desperately not to let the nausea overtake her, aware that if she was sick, she would choke to death. Tears silently streamed down her cheeks, dripping off her chin onto the dull grey tile.

The creak of mattress springs startled her. There was someone behind her and she heard their footsteps quietly approach. She whimpered, desperate for the pain to stop, the anticipation of the unknown terrifying her.

'You're quite popular.' A man's voice, purposefully disguised. She vaguely recognised it, but couldn't place it in her state of dizziness and nausea. 'You're almost sold out. I knew from the moment I saw you that you'd be a prize acquisition.'

Ember prayed her luck would return, that it would help her wriggle free, that the gurney straps would weaken just enough for her to slip her hands out, that by some miracle she could escape.

'It was almost a shame to take your foot. You're such a divine creature, a goddess almost. You were perfection. But unfortunately, I need the parts of you up for grabs.' He walked away again, and she heard the tapping of keys on a keyboard. 'Auction is almost over. Don't worry though, I'll keep you alive another day or two. I need you to stay fresh.'

The gag muffled her heart-wrenching screams of despair as she wrestled against her restraints, the last shred of hope evaporating into the dank air.

* * *

The auction, indeed, had proved more popular than the others. Bids had flooded in from all over the country, along with dark requests to see images and videos of the captured Green. Such requests had been denied, as it was far from the aim of the whole undertaking.

Sam couldn't believe the figures on the bidding screen, almost double what the previous Green had generated, and with more parts for people to choose from, the buyers were clamouring for possession of the rare and mysterious articles.

The glow of his computer screen in the dark basement was gradually making his eyes itch. He checked the time; it was approaching 7 a.m. He mumbled out loud that it must be Thursday, reminding himself that he needed to open the shop early for a customer that had booked an oracle card reading at 8 a.m.

He checked his messages on the forum before logging off. He had more than usual, his inbox overflowing with disturbed requests and conversations about the Green. He'd had conflicting feelings about her being auctioned and had already mourned the fact he'd never know her how he wanted to, but the Oracle cause was far greater than any affection he had for her, and it was inevitable that her life would be ended. He accepted that the sooner she was gone, the sooner he could move past his interest in her.

He left the basement room in darkness as he ascended the stairs to open up the shop.

His customer was early, a short, squat man with a handful of long hair combed over a balding head. He wore a Metallica T-shirt and was fidgeting in his seat as Sam settled across from him at the small card-reading table in the corner of the shop, and began shuffling a deck of cards.

He turned over cards one by one, giving an enthusiastic but vague meaning to each, occasionally watching the range of expressions that played across the man's face with each new bit of so-called wisdom.

It struck Sam as too much of a coincidence that he'd gone from reading oracle cards to joining a secret organisation called the Oracles, almost as though the universe was giving him glaring signs of his life's purpose. It might not be the path his parents would have wanted him to follow, but if Sam's work with the Oracles uncovered some truths about the spiritual world, it would be a historical breakthrough.

* * *

Casey was running on less than five hours' sleep as he pressed the bell for Ember's flat once more, hoping that she would answer and have some fantastical or daft explanation for where she'd been. The urgency of the bell rattled around the hallway but stirred no one within. Warren had once again joined him, eager to help in whatever way he could.

Casey had kept Nikita updated with the additional places he'd searched through the night, and she'd responded first thing to say she would meet him at Ember's flat.

It had just gone 8 a.m. and Casey was on a late shift that afternoon, so had time in the morning to continue his search despite his exhaustion. He was worried about her. As unreliable as she was known to be, his mind kept straying back to the horrific murders of the two Fortuna agents. She'd been missing for roughly sixteen hours, which could easily be explained away if she'd gone to stay with a friend, but he wasn't convinced. Nikita turned the corner and gave him and Warren a tense smile, her Cupid glow faded from lack of sleep and the gnawing pain of her growing wings.

'No luck?' she asked.

Casey shook his head, reaching for the bell one last time.

'Emrys has gone back to the office to see if she turns up for her scheduled shift. She's due in at 9 a.m., but if there's no sign of her he's going to head over to the hospital again.' Nikita checked the time on her phone.

'I'm out of ideas of where else to look, to be honest.' Casey hugged his chest, the cool air finding its way under the thin jumper he was wearing.

'The upside is that Hades have confirmed her name hasn't come up. So, she's alive somewhere.'

'That's some good news at least,' Warren added.

'If she doesn't show up, we might have to consider the worst-case scenario and focus our efforts on identifying this killer. If he's got her hidden away somewhere, we need to find him ASAP,' Nikita stated.

'What can we do to help?' Casey asked, starting to feel exasperated about the whole ordeal.

'It would be good to have you come with us to Elysion to see if we can detain this tattoo artist, but first I want to go back to the hospital to cover all bases.'

With no sign of life from Ember's flat, Nikita suggested they make a head start at the Raphael Sanctuary and wait for Emrys to call.

By the time they had got there, he had confirmed Ember was still missing and he planned to head back to the hospital to speak with the staff.

'Let's take a look around while we wait for Emrys to get here,' Nikita suggested. 'She might be on a ward, and they messed up the records when booking her in.'

Casey could tell Nikita was trying desperately to stay positive, but both of them had the sinking sensation that their chances of finding her alive were getting slimmer.

'Where's Erron? Is he meeting us here?' Casey asked.

'He's made a head start to Elysion to scope out a possible suspect. We will join him shortly,' Nikita explained.

'And what if you don't find the suspect?' Warren queried. 'Is there a plan B?'

Nikita sighed. 'We have another tentative lead, but it's just some random ghost ramblings about the deep dark danger, the cosmic web and something about a blood thief being on onions.'

'Do you think they mean the dark web?' Warren asked. 'Onion is a domain name on the dark web.'

'Really?' Nikita felt a spark of hope in her chest as she fished around in her bag for her notes. 'How do you know that? Do you think ghosts would know that?'

'I used to work in IT.' Warren shrugged. 'You know what they say about ghosts in the machine, maybe they are actually flitting around in cyberspace?'

Nikita passed him the note Erron had made about the Oracles. 'Does that look like anything you might find on the dark web?'

Warren glanced at the note and nodded. 'I could probably find a way into this website if I had enough time.'

'Could you do that today?'

'I'll give it my best shot. But I've got to be at the Apollo office later on, so if I don't crack it this morning I'll get into it as soon as I can after work.'

'Thank you so much.' Nikita squeezed her hands together with relief.

Warren smiled graciously and reassured her he would make a start on it the moment he got to his laptop, leaving them with the note in his hand.

'Who's the suspect?' Casey asked.

'Some mysterious tattoo artist that's been dabbling with restricted stardust in the inks to make agents lose their abilities,' Nikita explained.

Casey stopped in his tracks, his Apollo glow fading as the blood drained from his face. 'Ember mentioned that she'd booked in for a tattoo on Elysion.'

Nikita's eyes widened at the news. 'Case, we better call Erron. That confirms Ember is highly likely to be the third target. We weren't sure if she'd had a tattoo but now it's our strongest link.'

She had her phone in her hand before he could reply. The call went to answerphone. She tried twice more without a response. 'He must be on his way up there.'

'Wait, if you think the killer is linked to the tattoo shop and he blunders in there on his own asking questions, he might be putting himself in serious danger,' Casey said, his voice panicked.

'He's not going into the shop until we get there; he went on ahead to watch from a distance. Besides, he didn't leave that long ago, he's probably just going through the vortex. We'll have a quick scan around the wards then head straight to the moon,' Nikita reasoned.

'OK, let's get going then.' Casey upped the pace, heading for a set of swing doors with an overhead sign for Cosmic Cardiology.

They bobbed their heads in every ward they could access on each floor of the hospital, working their way up as they went.

They discovered they were able to exert a little Apollo influence over any of the staff that challenged them, giving acceptable enough excuses for being in restricted areas to be allowed a brief visit.

'We're really not supposed to use the Flush on Archangels, or any other agents, for that matter,' Casey muttered as they left the X-ray department, having given a false story about carrying out PAT testing on all the light bulbs.

'Since when do we follow the rules, Case?' Nikita nudged him and gave him a conspiratorial grin. 'We didn't save the world by doing things by the book, did we?'

'No, you're right,' he agreed, knowing full well he'd used his Apollo abilities outside the boundaries of the rules more often than he could count. But always on the proviso that it was with good intentions, unlike Erron who had always enjoyed blagging a free cocktail at Nightjar with some exceptional levels of charm.

They reached the last ward on the top floor without any sign of Ember. They hadn't seen many patients, the hospital itself was nowhere near as large as a standard city hospital but was very well equipped for any eventuality. Despite that fact, it had taken them over half an hour to check all the relevant departments.

They paused by a stairwell next to a large board with department names listed. Nikita studied each line to check if they had missed anything while Casey pulled out his phone.

He dialled Erron's number, pacing back and forward as it rang out. After a second attempt he left a voicemail, asking that Erron call them back the moment he got the message.

'He probably forgot to charge his phone. You know what he's like,' Nikita reasoned, trying to remain optimistic.

'Yeah, let's hope that's the case.' Casey stared at the screen on his phone, visibly frustrated.

'He won't do anything stupid.'

'This is Erron we're talking about.' Casey sighed and swept the loose strands of hair off his face. 'I don't want him getting hurt.'

Nikita squeezed his arm reassuringly. 'He won't. Look, there's a lower-ground floor here that says Occupational Therapy. We'll just have a quick look in there and then head to the nearest ice-cream van?'

'OK, yes, of course.'

At the bottom of the stairs they came to two sets of doors that led into the Occupational Therapy unit. The overhead lighting flickered on, controlled by a motion sensor, illuminating a long hallway with one ward, a row of chairs in the hall and two closed doors marked up as 'Storage'.

The ward was empty and looked as though its function was to house faulty or unused equipment. The beds were stripped bare and only the dim emergency lighting buzzed overhead.

'Nikita! Casey! What are you two doing down here?' A chirpy voice startled them from behind.

They both spun around to face the Archangel, Dr Jared Enleigh, who was carrying a box of supplies. Nikita let out a long breath, steadying herself from the jump scare.

'Oh, we were looking for Ember. She's gone missing,' she explained. 'No chance you've seen her at all?'

'Not since the day of the memorial service. How long has she been missing?' he asked, his brow furrowing with concern.

'Since around 4 p.m. yesterday. She never turned up to work this morning,' Casey replied.

'I hope nothing bad has happened to her. But why on earth do you think you'll find her down here of all places?' Dr Enleigh started to walk towards the disused ward.

'We know she was heading here and yet no one saw her arrive,' Nikita said. 'We're just trying to cover all bases, but it doesn't look like this hall leads anywhere useful.'

'No, this unit has been moved off-site to a small clinic. We've been using the rooms as storage until it's due to be refurbished,' Dr Enleigh explained, setting the box down on the nearest trolley inside the ward.

'What's kept in those storage rooms?' Nikita asked, her curiosity unable to contain itself.

'Nothing exciting, old shelving units, one of the X-ray machines that broke a couple of months ago, bags of shredded paper, that sort of stuff. Certainly no patients.'

'Ah right,' Nikita muttered, disappointed.

'I wouldn't go rummaging around in those rooms, there might be some hazardous bits and pieces in there. Shall I show you back to reception?' The young doctor started to herd them gently back the way they had come.

'Can you keep an eye out for Ember, ask around some of the staff?' Casey asked as they wandered back.

'Of course. I hope she turns up safe and sound.' Dr Enleigh opened the door for them.

'Jared, is there any CCTV of outside the hospital?' Nikita asked.

'Not that I know of.'

'That's odd.' She raised an eyebrow.

'It's out of my hands. Look, I better be going, I am scheduled for a surgery in twenty minutes. I'll let you know if I hear anything about Ember.' Dr Enleigh excused himself and left them at the doors on the ground floor.

Emrys met them as they approached the reception desk. The worry over Ember had dulled his usual lucky shine and highlighted the fine lines on his concerned expression.

'Emrys, we've checked all around the wards but there's no sign of her. We've got a solid lead with the suspect on Elysion, though, so we're heading up there next,' Nikita explained. 'Are you able to come with us?'

Casey was anxiously stepping from foot to foot, keen to get to Elysion to establish Erron's whereabouts.

'I can't; I have a mountain of things to get done today, the Fates keeping piling it on, but first I wanted to speak to some of the staff here,' Emrys explained. He unfolded a stack of printouts of Ember's staff photo that he'd pulled from his inside coat pocket. 'I'll ask them to put these up everywhere too, see if it jogs any memories.'

'OK, I'll catch up with you later.' Nikita kissed him on the cheek and whispered, 'Miss you already,' in his ear before turning towards the exit.

'Same,' he said quietly, watching her and Casey leave.

# 23

## *Life Is a Lemon and I Want My Money Back*

ERRON WAS LATE GETTING TO Elysion as the ice-cream van that was usually in a car park on Trafalgar Way was undergoing some maintenance. The Mr Whippy machine was leaking, and ice cream was travelling in a sticky trail all the way to the moon, leaving an unwanted puddle in the celestial energy pool at the other end. It was well known that parts of the Milky Way were actually formed from the residue left behind from so many lunar journeys leaving a trail of ice cream, where the machines hadn't been so high-tech in the early years of agency portals. Thankfully, incidents of dairy-based malfunctions were few and far between in the modern age. Prior to ice-cream vans it was milk floats, before that portals were positioned in outhouses, which created a very different issue if there was an unfortunate leak.

It was gone 10 a.m. before the repairs were completed and Erron made a conscious effort not to fall into the melted ice cream once he safely landed in Elysion. Once there, he struggled to remember the way to Arcane Ink and wandered a few streets before he managed to get his bearings. The memory of the place with beans-on-Weetabix surfaced involuntarily in his mind to remind him where the tattoo parlour was located.

Although he'd agreed with Nikita that he wouldn't go in without her, he was confident he could ask a few questions of the owner without incident to save some time. The parlour was still closed, but that didn't deter him from banging on the door.

The shopkeeper, Arlana, was just as unhelpful as the first time he'd spoken to her.

'Why do you keep showing your arrogant face here, Agent Fuckwit?' she squawked at him, her petite nose wrinkled with anger.

Erron composed himself, counting to ten in his head. 'You know, you could make this a lot easier by just telling me what I need to know.'

Arlana folded her arms defiantly. 'Ask me your stupid questions, then.'

'Firstly, is Djinn here?'

'No artist is here, because we're not bloody open yet!'

Erron dug out a photo of Ember Songfire and held it out to her. 'OK, have you seen this woman at all?'

Arlana gave in and studied the photo. 'She was here Tuesday. One of Djinn's clients,' she snapped.

'You never called to say he was in. We had an agreement.' Erron tried to temper the anger in his voice.

'I have more important tasks to do than remember such things.' Arlana leant against the door frame and twiddled with a silver hoop in her ear lobe.

Erron took a deep breath in. Just as he was about to respond, the distinct aura of sunshine and croissants appeared next to him.

'Could have answered your phone,' Casey scolded him.

'I didn't hear it ringing.' Erron checked his phone and gave Casey an apologetic look after seeing the myriad of missed calls and messages.

'Arlana.' Nikita stepped forward from behind Casey. 'We heard you say that Djinn was here Tuesday. Mind if we look around his studio again if he's not here?' Before Arlana could answer, Nikita had pushed past her and was striding through the shop.

'Hey! You can't just barge your way in here!' Arlana spat, spinning round to chase after her.

Erron grabbed the back of Arlana's T-shirt, pulling her against the door frame. 'Actually, she can. And if you obstruct our investigation again we'll have to put you under arrest. This agent, Ember, well, she's going to die if you don't help us, and her blood will be on your hands.'

The petite shopkeeper maintained an expression of sheer rage, though shrank away from him and lingered by the door as Erron and Casey joined Nikita.

'If he turns up we need to make sure Arlana doesn't warn him,' Erron stated.

'I'll go and sit with her,' Casey volunteered.

'Let us know if anyone turns up.'

Nikita donned a pair of black latex gloves, wasting no time in rooting through everything in the room, going as far as taking down the collage of McLaren Formula 1 cars and checking every inch of the frame. Erron followed suit, starting on the opposite side of the wall.

They could hear Arlana protesting in the next room. 'This is illegal, they can't do this.'

Casey was using his gentle charm to pacify her, explaining how important Ember was to him and eventually getting her to understand the gravity of the situation.

Forty-five minutes went by in near silence. Erron searched methodically, his inner detective harking back to process and order, his dextrous hands finding every possible hiding place for anything that might link Djinn to the murders. Nikita was less organised, a whirlwind of scattered papers, a frantic determination to uncover some vital piece of the puzzle.

She rifled through a thick sketchbook of artwork on the side, when Erron popped his arm up from under the desk. In his hand was a yellow Post-it.

'This was on the floor.'

In scruffy handwriting, Ember's name and mobile number was scrawled on the note.

'Coincidence? Or something much deeper?' Erron asked.

'It could just be her details when she booked her appointment.'

'It's possible, I suppose. We need to find out the identity of this artist,' he said, then called out into the main shop. 'Case, can you bring Arlana back in here?'

Casey did as he was told and escorted the shopkeeper in, seemingly far more passive and content than usual.

'We need to know Djinn's full name and address,' Erron demanded.

'Good luck, no one knows that,' Arlana said, her voice subdued.

'You can't employ someone on Elysion without at least having a record of their identity.' Erron crossed his arms.

'I told you idiots before, I don't employ him; he rents the studio. He doesn't show his face, he doesn't speak. I don't ask questions of people paying me rent. His portfolio was enough to convince me that he would attract business,' Arlana explained.

'Why do I think you're lying, Arlana?' Nikita snapped. 'You're protecting this guy, aren't you?'

'Of course not!'

'Where do you keep the records of all your rent payments?' Nikita demanded.

'I'll show you.' Arlana gestured for them to follow. 'Then you'll know I'm not lying.'

She led them to her office. Despite the shambolic way she appeared to run the business, her record-keeping was top-notch. Every invoice, document and purchase order were catalogued and filed in neat blue folders along the wall. She pulled out the file for studio rentals and handed Erron a thin manila folder.

Inside, a very brief rental agreement was signed by the name Djinn, personal details were all blank, but the record of rental was completed with weekly payments made via anonymous nova transfer.

'You didn't think for a minute that this was strange? No given identity, hidden payments?' Erron asked.

'No, his whole aesthetic is mystery. Aside from his art, it's what makes people clamour for an appointment. He's very serious about his privacy.' Arlana snatched the file back. 'He makes the payments with a burner cuff, and I don't care to ask where it's from.'

'Great. So we're chasing Lunar Banksy, then.' Nikita rolled her eyes, growing ever more frustrated by the constant obstacles. 'What exactly is a burner cuff?'

Erron explained that surplus ear cuffs for nova payments were stored in the recruitment headquarters, and before they were assigned to an employee, they would be linked to an empty nova account with no name. If an agent got their hands on one, they could transfer their wages to the blank cuff and trade without being identified. It was against agency policy, but it wasn't unheard of. A handful of them had gone missing in the late seventies and were being used by a group of retired agents that called themselves the Moonlight Mafia. They were known for buying and selling pirated VHS tapes behind a casino in downtown Elysion, before cable TV ruined their whole enterprise. Erron failed to mention he had an entire case of the pirated VHS tapes tucked away in a cupboard in the hope that they might come back into fashion the same way vinyl music did.

'So somehow he's got one of these accounts and, what, we can't trace it at all?' Nikita huffed in frustration.

'It's all encrypted and automated and could take weeks to get someone to find anything useful with the data.' Erron seemed equally disheartened.

'When is Djinn next due in?' Casey cut in, keen to have some input.

Arlana threw her arms up in defeat. 'I don't know! You've asked me that a million times already! He doesn't share his client list with me, and nor do I expect him to, none of the artists share those details. He's like the wind, you never know when he'll turn up or how long he'll stay.'

'Did he have any electronics here? A computer, tablet, anything like that?' Nikita asked.

'Not that I am aware of. Look, I understand. I will call you if he turns up. I don't want an innocent party getting hurt or killed.' Arlana was sincere, and her irritable attitude had all but faded.

'Thanks. Right, gentlemen, I think we should finish up our search here,' Nikita stated. 'Arlana, we won't bother you again until you call.'

They left Arlana in the office and returned to Djinn's studio. Nikita found a small bin bag and started emptying the fridge of magical tattoo ink inside before doing one more cursory search around the small room.

'We should set up across the street and watch this place,' Nikita whispered. 'Catch him if and when he turns up.'

'Agreed, but we'll need to let Osato know, and get some supplies first. It could be days before he turns up again, especially if he knows we've been sniffing around here.' Erron scratched his head. 'Not to mention we'll need access to a nearby building with a good view.'

'I vote for a stakeout at the beans-on-Weetabix place,' Nikita suggested.

Casey made a face of disgust.

'I'm concerned this might be a damp squib. We're playing with Ember's life here; whatever we decide to do, we're running on limited time,' Erron reasoned. 'We have to make the right call where we focus our efforts.'

'I know, I am painfully aware of that. I'm hoping Warren cracks this Oracles website to see where it fits in the puzzle. But our strongest link right now is this Djinn bloke. If you have better suggestions, I'll gladly hear them.' Nikita rested her hands on her hips. 'If I have to drown myself again to get some more information from the ghosts, then so be it.'

'Let's nip back, get enough stuff together to camp out for a few days here then find a place nearby to wait for Djinn to turn up,' Erron said diplomatically, well aware their options were limited. 'I'll call Osato and get her to find cover for us.'

They started to head back to the portal through the vibrant streets of Elysion.

'Anyone fancy a cake? I'm starving,' Erron asked as they passed a particularly inviting bakery apparently renowned for its popping candy doughnuts.

Casey checked his watch. 'I'm going to have to get to work soon.' He sounded dejected. 'I start at 1 p.m. today.'

Erron's jaw dropped. 'You always have time for cake.'

'Obviously,' Casey agreed. 'But I'll have to make it quick. I can't abandon Warren.'

'Ah yes, *Warren*,' Erron grumbled, leading them into the bakery. The indulgent aroma of fresh doughnuts and buttercream icing enveloped them like a warm hug.

'He's a nice person, Erron, if you'd care to get to know him. He reads the files.' Casey didn't need to browse the menu; he went for the triple caramel rocky-road cupcake he'd had a few times before.

Erron pulled a mocking face behind Casey's back. It was childish, but made him feel better. Nikita jabbed him with an elbow and a pointed look.

'At least can you see if Warren had any luck with the thing on the dark web?' Nikita asked.

'I'll let you know what he says,' Casey replied.

Nikita braved the doughnut named The Firing Squad with its hefty layer of explosive popping candy atop a chilli-chocolate icing and neon-red dough.

'You're feeling feisty.' Erron raised an eyebrow as the assistant handed her the treat worthy of Wile E. Coyote.

She grinned widely. It was just what she needed after so little sleep.

Erron chose a lemon muffin and paid with his agency ear cuff for all three.

They had a ten-minute walk back to the return portals, just enough time to talk and eat before going their separate ways.

Nikita took her first bite of the neon menace, the intense crackling immediately drowning out anything else she could hear, her ears ringing as though a hundred untuned radios were transmitting directly inside her brain. Despite the heat of the chilli and the explosive topping, the doughnut was delectable.

'How long is this Warren guy going to be working with you, then? Is it just until Nikita gets back?' Erron quizzed.

'Freya didn't speculate, but if Nikita's tied up for some time we might just find her a different crewmate when she gets back. Warren is thinking of moving to London so it could become permanent,' Casey answered, polishing off the last speck of his cupcake. They stopped outside the return portal zone. 'He seemed really happy at our office.'

Erron hovered awkwardly, wanting nothing more than to fling his arms around Casey, tell him not to go, that he needed him, and he couldn't stand the fact that Warren was leaving such a good impression on him. Instead, he scratched the back of his head and bit his tongue.

'Eh?' Nikita answered, having barely heard the conversation over the sound of her doughnut. 'Did you say you're replacing me?'

'Nothing's set in stone yet.' Casey shrugged, hoping against hope that Erron might step closer, offering a friendly goodbye hug or reach for his hand, but there was no indication he would.

'Right, I'll speak to you later, I best get going.' He waved and stepped reluctantly into the portal.

'That doesn't sound encouraging. I didn't even know I might be replaced. I haven't even fully grown my wings yet,' Nikita sulked, simultaneously flexing her shoulders to feel the tiny wings in their entirety.

'Well, you replaced me easily enough,' Erron reasoned.

'You chose to leave.' Nikita took a tiny nibble of her doughnut, so she could still follow the conversation.

'Good point.'

'Do you think I'll end up with another crewmate? I hardly know anyone else,' Nikita said, trying to hide her level of concern.

'I can't see it happening, once we crack this case you can go back and kick out that usurper, Nutkin,' Erron replied.

'Larkin.'

'Whatever.'

* * *

Ember had lost all concept of time. She was being kept in a state of semi-consciousness, she felt weak, listless and excruciatingly hungry. Her exhausted body longed for a warm bed, a hot drink and as much Cadbury Dairy Milk as she could manage. The only blessing was she had numbed herself to the pain, focusing deep within herself for the positive resolve that usually carried her through everything.

She'd been blindfolded, the filthy gag had been replaced with strong tape, but she was thankful to be able to move her tongue more freely – a small upside, but an upside, nonetheless. She'd spent any time she was lucid working away at her restraints, desperate for her luck to return and give her some miraculous escape.

The man had been in and out of the room, rarely speaking. He handled her with coldness and precision, and only when necessary. She gave up her muffled pleas long ago and focused her mind on getting free by her own volition while he was out of the room. Hope flooded through her as one of her wrists finally slipped from its restraint.

Frantic, though her arm felt as heavy as lead, she fumbled around to find the buckle around her throat, dragging, pulling and ripping it open in any way she could until the belt gave way. Her head free, she inhaled deeply, the effort making her dizzy, but she was determined to get out.

She pulled off the blindfold and the tape, finding the room in complete darkness, her eyes taking ages to adjust enough to see the outlines of anything around her. She winced as she tore the cannula tubes from her arms, caring not for the mess they made on her skin.

Relentlessly, she fought her other wrist free, the weight of her body lunging forward on the strangely angled gurney. She cried out as she felt the ankle belts give way under the sudden force, twisting her legs as she slammed to the cold floor. Suppressing the urge to scream and cry from the pain, she paused, holding her breath in the darkness, hoping her captor hadn't heard anything.

The memory of her missing foot rushed back to her. She couldn't stand, her knees were on fire from the contorted impact, so she crawled. Inch by inch, she scraped and slithered across the tile, her mental resolve pushing down the pain the closer she got to freedom. Eventually, she reached the door, pulling herself up to a sitting position, her eyes adjusting slightly to the sliver of dim light coming in from under the door. She leant her weight against it, feeling it judder slightly on its hinges, but not open freely. Her hand felt along the edge of the door and upwards, seeking out the handle and finding a cold metal lever with her outstretched fingertips. A surge of hope welled up in her as she strained to reach high enough to pull down on the handle.

Cold sweat trickled down her back as she wiggled the handle, almost managing to unlatch the door, just as she heard footsteps approaching. Panicked, she shuffled as fast as she could under what looked like a small metal bed in the darkness. She pulled herself into a tight ball, checking around to make sure none of her was sticking out from the frame overhead.

The door swung open and heavy boots entered, their owner seemingly struggling with something heavy. He backed into the room, dragging a large and unwieldy object. Ember pressed her hand over her mouth trying to control her breathing, her heart slamming against her ribs.

'What the fuck?' the man hissed as he got far enough into the room to shut the door behind him, noticing the gurney was empty. The heavy shape he'd been carrying was dropped abruptly in a heap on the floor with a dull thud.

Ember could just pick out that her captor was fumbling for the light switch, but as he flicked it on the bulb crackled and blew, plunging the room back into darkness.

'Where the hell is my torch?' The man cursed under his breath and began blindly searching around the worktops and cupboards, clearly frantic.

Ember crushed herself as close the back wall as she could, catching her hair in the metal of the underside of the bed and doing her best to withhold a pained squeak. She considered crawling to the door but knew she didn't stand a chance of outrunning the man when she was couldn't even walk. Her only hope was to make herself as small as possible, and as a last resort, fight with anything she could. With one hand, she silently felt around her environment, hoping to find something to use as a weapon.

Her fingers fell on the plastic of a pen that was wedged behind the bed along with a dirty notebook. It wasn't much, but it was better than nothing.

A dull glow illuminated the room. Her captor had found a small torch with fading batteries and was frantically swinging it around the room to check for signs of where Ember had gone. As he did so, Ember briefly saw the shape of the heavy object her captor had dragged into the room. It was a body. She only saw its legs before the light moved away from it, but it was wearing brown suede boots. She had no idea if the person was alive or dead but couldn't hear any movement.

The captor crouched down to look at the tiny spots of blood that had been flicked on the floor when Ember had torn out the cannulas in her arms. The trail had quickly stopped, and the man rushed to the door, swinging it open and disappearing outside.

Ember allowed herself to exhale slowly and quietly in the gloom.

She waited, poised, the pen gripped tightly in her sweating palm, ready to jab at anyone who looked under the bed, her keen ears listening out for the sound of the footsteps returning. She fought the temptation to crawl out of her hiding spot to see if the body on the floor was alive and could be woken, but her instinct told her it was a bad idea.

* * *

Warren was eagerly awaiting Casey, who turned up half an hour late, which really wasn't like him. He apologised to his new crewmate and asked if he had picked up the assignments already.

'Oh, of course, sir. Take your time, we have an hour before the first one.' Warren slid over two files. 'I take it there's been no news about your missing friend?'

'No, unfortunately not,' Casey replied quietly, glancing up from the files and only just noticing that Warren had seemingly taken up residence at Erron's empty desk. He'd cleaned it and arranged his own accoutrements in a neat and tidy way.

'Is something wrong, Mr Hart?' Warren asked.

'Uh, no, sorry. Did Freya say you could take that desk?'

'No, but she did say to take up an empty one. This one was empty.'

'I see. No problem.' Casey hid the fact that it was definitely a problem. He plastered on a smile and busied himself reading the files.

'Mr Hart, I know this is a little unconventional, but I was wondering if you might join me for dinner one night? I thought you might know some good restaurants around the city, and I'd love to hear more of your stories.' Warren perched on the edge of the chair, his hands clasped in his lap and a hopeful look on his face. 'My treat, of course.'

'I . . . well . . . I can definitely check my diary,' Casey answered cautiously. 'But there's a lot going on at the moment with Ember missing and these murders.'

'Of course, I should have waited to ask. My apologies.'

'It's quite all right,' Casey reassured him, his stomach fluttering slightly with the notion of being asked out for dinner, though he quickly suppressed the sensation. 'Have you had any luck with that website?'

'I haven't got as far with it as I would like but I will take another look after work today.' Warren smiled a wide, charming smile with his perfect teeth and boyish freckles. It was easy to see that he was the perfect candidate for Apollo, with his effortless natural charm and sophisticated style, which no doubt would have had people falling over themselves for him even before he'd joined the afterlife.

'I'll let Nikita know,' Casey replied, the eye contact between them lingering for a moment before he pulled out his phone and sent off a quick text.

* * *

Across the city, Nikita and Erron had just finished packing any necessities they might need for an extended stakeout, having to scout around some shops in Central London for a decent pair of binoculars and a Dictaphone for evidence gathering.

'Do you mind?' Erron held up a pack of cigarettes outside their last stop. 'I'm climbing the walls.'

'Go for it, I won't tell.' Nikita checked her messages and saw that Casey had updated her. 'No luck with the website yet. This Djinn character better be who we're looking for.'

Erron cursed as he tried to light a cigarette, his hands trembling, the flame of his lighter repeatedly going out. 'Let's hope,' he murmured, finally getting it to light.

'Where's the nearest ice-cream van?'

'I'll check the app.' Erron exhaled a cloud of smoke and unlocked his phone.

'There's an app? I didn't know that!'

'Uh, yeah, how else would we keep track of them? It should be installed on your phone – Delivermoon.'

Nikita looked up at him with incredulity. 'Really?'

'Yes, really. Anyway, the nearest one is in Covent Garden, eleven minutes' walk from here.' Erron zoomed in on the screen to show her.

'Best get going, then.' Nikita led the way, determined to beat the estimated walk time on the map. Her legs were already tired and her miniature wings were still throbbing with growing pains, but she forged on, determined not to give in until Ember was safe.

# 24

## *9 Crimes*

At 4 p.m., Nikita and Erron had just arrived in the backstreets of Elysion, staying out of sight of Arcane Ink until they could find the perfect stakeout position. Osato had informed them that their reinforcements would likely arrive around 9 p.m., letting one of them get a few hours' sleep, then after that they would rotate between themselves for five hours at a time, always leaving two people awake and watching. Erron had volunteered to do the first long stint, fully accustomed to insomnia and willing to keep himself alert with a family-sized bag of gummy bears and two litres of Tizer.

He had led them to an interactive city map embedded in the brass-lined wall of an Elysion clothing shop. It was a bit out of their way but was better than wandering around outside the tattoo parlour drawing attention to themselves as they searched for an observation point. Artfully, he zoomed in on the district covering Arcane Ink and furrowed his brow as he considered their best options.

'It looks like there's no official second exit to Arcane Ink, so this is our only scope for a good view of the main door.'

He drew an invisible circle around three buildings that would have some kind of vantage point. 'I'm more concerned about this alley though, I think the only way we're going to see the whole thing is by camping out in this end building here.' He pointed at a small triangular building and pinched the screen to zoom in further.

'Wigs of Kettering, huh.' Nikita made a confused face. 'Next to a place called The Forgotten Coat. Who names these places?'

'Fuck knows. Let's go check out some wigs.' Erron shifted his rucksack into a more comfortable position on his shoulder.

'I think we need to get some food on the way. I can't stare out of a window for hours on end without at least something greasy to eat,' Nikita suggested.

Half an hour later they were stood at the side door of the wig shop with two bags of takeaway from a strange food stand that put anything you ordered inside a giant Yorkshire pudding, whether you wanted one or not.

A petite sixty-something-looking woman with an apple figure opened the door, a small bell tinkling as she did so. She wore a pastel pink dress with an abundance of ruffles, and a ginger curly hairstyle neatly framed her face. She had a smile that was simultaneously welcoming but unnerving, as though she was a mannequin come to life.

'You folks here for a fitting?' she asked in an overly cheerful tone with the right amount of falseness to put Nikita in a state of caution.

'Um, no, but we have an unusual request,' Erron said, peering around the woman into the shop, where hundreds of wigs were displayed, all of them short, ginger and curly. 'We're working on behalf of Nemesis Division investigating a serious crime and need to observe the street in this location for some time. We'd like to know if you'd allow us access to your upper-floor window?'

'Well, of course!' She bustled them inside with enthusiasm, her smile finally reaching her eyes. 'How exciting! A real investigation.'

'We may be here for some time, days ev—' Erron started to say but was quickly cut off.

'My name's Gertie, and the upper floor is just my storeroom. Make yourselves comfortable, agents … ?'

'Nikita Wolf, and this is Erron Grover.' Nikita held out her hand for Gertie to shake. Instead, the shop owner looked at it curiously.

'Interesting little shop you have here,' Erron jumped in. 'I guess this season has a particular style to it.' He nodded towards the rows and rows of identical wigs.

'Oh, well, it's not so much about the style,' Gertie explained. 'These are Hive-Mind Wigs. Whoever is wearing them at the same time can read and share thoughts with each other. They work up to a range of two miles. Imported all the way from my factory in Kettering.'

Nikita was too confused to ask any follow-up questions. She was already convinced Gertie was some kind of android creating mind-control wigs in the Northampton town for a nefarious purpose that would one day become clear. At any moment she half expected a soldier from the future to appear to convince her to bring down the curly ginger version of Skynet.

'Impressive …' Erron was starting to sound uncomfortable himself. 'So, what are their main purpose?'

'Oh, whatever people want really. Some like to use them for relationship therapy. It's a very easy way to communicate thoughts and feelings without the barriers of conversation.' Gertie seemed very confident in her product. 'But most people use them like a hands-free walkie-talkie of sorts.'

Nikita struggled to picture herself sat next to Emrys telepathically discussing relationship problems while both looking like extras on *The Golden Girls*.

'Well, we best get set up.' Nikita nudged Erron towards the stairwell. 'Thank you, Gertie, for your hospitality.'

'Anytime!' Gertie herded them upstairs before returning to her shopfront.

Nikita and Erron looked around the odd-shaped stockroom. Two rocking chairs sat against the back wall among boxes and boxes of ginger wigs. A half-bay window jutted out from the angular wall, giving them an excellent view of the entrance to Arcane Ink, and around twenty feet of the alley that led away from it in the other direction. Gertie had said there was a small room adjacent with a kettle and sofa that they were welcome to use, but there didn't appear to be any toilet facilities. Nikita perched on the wide windowsill and pulled the pair of binoculars from her bag.

'Oh, these are actually so comfy.' Erron was already leaning back in one of the rocking chairs, moving it in a steady motion, his head draped over the back of the headrest.

'Get your arse over here, will you? We've got a killer to catch,' Nikita hissed.

'OK, OK,' Erron huffed, pulling himself back to his feet and wandering over. 'We've got about five hours before someone will get here to give you a break. Let's eat, shall we?'

She agreed, taking out a soggy paper bag from the takeaway order and tentatively trying her lasagne wrapped in a giant Yorkshire pudding. Erron regretted ordering curry, thinking it might arrive in a tub instead of the egg-and-flour monstrosity. As much as he loved some of the cafés and restaurants on the moon, some places took artistic licence too far when it came to strange food combinations.

* * *

Casey had kept himself busy and distracted in an attempt to push aside the concern over Ember's disappearance. He knew he was powerless to help and was desperately hoping to hear good news at any given moment, even though the worry churned away in his gut. Warren was doing his best to keep Casey's mood afloat, but there were only so many profiteroles that could be eaten before the dopamine switched to nausea.

Part-way through their shift, Freya Carthage walked over to join them, explaining that Casey was needed for a Medusa shift and would be given double pay for overtime if he agreed.

He glanced at Warren then back at Freya. 'How long am I needed for?'

'It could just be this evening, or over the course of a few days. It's some kind of stakeout. I'll need to know your answer now if possible.'

'What about Warren?' Casey asked, a look of guilt and concern spreading across his face. 'Will he be able to help?'

'I'm afraid not, but I'll rejig the rota until you're back. Warren, you're OK with that, aren't you?' Freya asked.

'Of course, yes.' Warren masked his disappointment.

'Casey, you'll have to text Erron or Nikita to find out their location,' Freya said before retreating back into her office.

Once she'd gone, Casey sent a quick message to Nikita.

'Sounds exciting, Mr Hart.' Warren rubbed his hands together with glee. 'A stakeout, like they do in the movies. I hear they've started calling this killer the Butterfly Catcher.'

'Have they now?' Casey was confused.

'Word got around pretty quick that Fortuna agents were being murdered. Owing to their butterfly wings, it seemed like an obvious nickname, I suppose,' Warren said quietly.

Casey was unimpressed. 'It amazes me how quickly people turn serious things into gossip.'

'Oh, I didn't mean to be insensitive.'

Casey waved it off. 'I know, I'm just worried about Ember.'

'I understand. I'll get working on that website as soon as.' Warren pulled out a business card with gold printed font. 'Here's my personal contact number, and I am staying at the agency hotel in Park Square, should you need me.'

'Thank you. We'll arrange dinner soon, if you like,' Casey suggested.

'I'd love to, sir.'

* * *

Ember had been crouched under the bed for less than half an hour before the man had stormed back in the room, the glow of the torch sweeping left and right before being clicked off, throwing the room back into darkness. Ember listened intently to every sound the man was making, but he'd fallen almost silent. By the time she picked up on the creeping of his soft-soled shoes, the dim torch was switched back on, pointing directly in her face.

'There you are,' he sneered, a touch of glee in his voice.

Blinded by the sudden light, Ember panicked. She felt his hands grabbing at her hair, attempting to drag her out like a cornered animal. She fought hard, biting, scratching and jabbing the pen into his arm and hands as hard as she could. She pivoted her body to kick out with her remaining foot, catching him square on the nose. He grunted and stumbled back, but recovered quickly, grabbing the bandaged stump of her other ankle and yanking it hard.

Ember screamed, the searing pain rushing up her leg like hot irons being forced through her bones. The man grabbed her other leg and dragged her out from under the bed, the torch clattering to the floor.

The last thing she saw was the skittering shadow of a spider escaping the light before a heavy hand knocked her out cold.

* * *

When Casey climbed to the top of the stairs at the triangular shop called Wigs of Kettering, he was faced with an image he never imagined he'd see in his lifetime.

Erron and Nikita were both sitting in rocking chairs staring out of the window, slowly eating a large bag of gummy bears, wearing the same bizarre ginger wigs that lined the shelves downstairs. They both rocked gently in time and were in complete silence. Nikita had her laptop open but didn't seem to be clicking on anything.

'Am I interrupting something important? Like a cult ritual, perhaps? Or do the wigs need to feed on colourful sugar bears to keep them from stealing souls?' Casey asked, one eyebrow raised.

Erron spun around and snatched the wig off his head, his face reddening. His eyes briefly lit up when he realised Casey was their backup for the evening.

Nikita turned her head to face him with a wide smile. 'Hey, Casey, so glad you made it.'

It was late and he was tired after such a long day, but seeing Erron had given him a surge of energy. 'So, when do I join the wig cult?'

'We were just testing out these things as the woman downstairs said they allow you to read minds,' Erron blustered. 'We were playing a game of trying to think of the same shape at the same time . . . a bit like rock, paper, scissors without the actions.'

'They really do work, though, it's so weird! Try one on and tell me what I'm thinking about.' Nikita grabbed Erron's wig and threw it to Casey.

Curiosity got the better of him and he pulled it over his long sandy hair.

Immediately, he was assaulted with images, sounds and a chaos of thoughts which gradually became clearer as Nikita focused.

'You're . . . you're thinking of a sunset beach with palm trees and roller-skaters going down the coast, looks like the eighties by the clothing,' Casey marvelled.

'I was! I was thinking of a scene from a film.' Nikita grinned. 'I can see what you're thinking too. There's a lot about your day with, what's his name, Warren?'

'It crossed my mind, yes.' He noticed the very subtle change of expression on Erron's face and pulled the wig from his head. 'Only work stuff, obviously. I only just clocked off; it's bound to be on my mind.'

'Of course, totally professional,' Nikita added.

'Anyway, I am here to let one of you have a break, so I'll be needing one of those rocking chairs.' Casey was looking forward to a sit down after his long shift.

'That'll be me.' Nikita sprang up from the chair and made her way to the door. 'I'm going to the loo at the Weetabix café then planning to crash on the sofa for a few hours. Play nice, fellas.'

They waved her off and Casey settled down in the rocking chair next to Erron, a slightly strained atmosphere still between them as Nikita wasn't there to act as an emotional buffer.

Erron broke the silence by offering Casey a gummy bear.

'How have you been?' Casey asked quietly.

Erron exhaled slowly. 'So-so. How about you?'

'Trying to focus on work, hoping Ember will turn up safe.' Casey drummed his fingers on his knees, while trying to keep his eyes on the tattoo parlour.

'I hope she will too.' Erron stared out the window, deep in thought. 'So, this new guy then, how's he compare to your old crewmate?'

Casey had almost been anticipating the question. He didn't think it was a good idea to say how well they had got on, or how much they had in common. The last thing he wanted was to alienate Erron as he was coming to terms with all the changes they'd both undergone. 'Warren's pretty easy to work with. But the other guy I used to work with, well, he really did have something special,' Casey answered light-heartedly.

'Yeah, he did. Then he threw it away.' Erron let out a dramatic sigh.

'No, he didn't. You know that.'

Nikita had returned from her short walk to the Weetabix café. She went into the back room with the kettle and softly closed the door, not wanting to interrupt them.

'I have so many regrets,' Erron said quietly.

'Let's not focus on what's gone wrong.' Casey smiled. 'How's it going at Hades?'

'I've hardly been there, but I'm working with Roscoe. Not my Roomba, the Reaper,' Erron clarified, having named his trundling vacuum after the Reaper some years ago.

'You know, had you not made that clear I would have assumed you'd drawn the short straw there with a mentor. He's one above Henry the Hoover,' Casey mocked.

'That would totally suck.'

'I've heard that's generally the case.' Casey paused before laughing loudly.

'I bet Warren doesn't set you up with such wonderful jokes.' Erron looked smug.

'No, but he does know where to get the best profiteroles.'

'Suck-up.' Erron rolled his eyes.

'No, that's your crewmate. You know, the Roomba guy.'

Erron couldn't help but smile, admitting he walked right into that one. He ate another handful of gummy bears and rocked back in the chair, feeling more relaxed.

They talked over the murders, Casey filling Erron in on the nickname the Butterfly Catcher, and all the information they had to date.

'So, the guy I saw at Bonanza, that could be this man called Djinn. I take it we can't locate him on employee records?' Casey asked.

'Osato and her team are working on it, but it's near impossible with only a grainy CCTV picture to go on. She reckons he might not be a UK agent, apparently no one recognises him.' Erron rocked the chair forward and shuffled it slightly for a better angle.

'Hence why sitting here in a mind-control wig shop watching an alleyway is currently our best bet at finding the killer.' Casey slumped back in his chair, his hand on the armrest brushing against Erron's. His stomach backflipped at the unexpected contact, and the fact that Erron didn't immediately withdraw his hand.

Erron cleared his throat, looking intently out the window but keeping his little finger still lightly touching Casey's hand. 'With any luck he will turn up and we can go in there, detain him and hopefully find out if he's got Ember, and if so, where she is.'

Ever so gently, Casey lifted his own little finger and rested it over Erron's protectively.

'I hope we find her,' he said, keeping his voice measured despite the butterfly dance taking place in his heart.

'Yeah,' Erron agreed, sliding the rest of his hand under Casey's palm while feeling the beat of his cosmic satsuma racing against his ribs. It crossed his mind that he needed to take his own comfort break at the Weetabix café, but in that moment he would rather suffer a ruptured bladder than move his hand, especially when Casey had interlinked his fingers over the top of his.

They sat in silence for some time, both watching the tattoo parlour, on high alert every time a person went in or out of the door. None of them distinctly resembled the suspect. An hour passed, and Casey had pulled their entwined hands across to rest on his thigh, a relaxed gesture, and Erron hadn't objected.

'Are you OK?' Casey asked, as Erron had begun fidgeting in his chair.

'Yeah, I just . . .' Erron grimaced. 'I regret drinking nearly two litres of Tizer and now I really gotta go.'

Casey laughed and released his hand. 'Why didn't you say earlier?'

'I didn't want to ruin the moment,' Erron answered sheepishly.

Casey smiled softly, his eyes filled with an inner warmth. 'There's always another moment. Now go before you . . . go.' He shooed him out of the room with a hurried gesture.

Erron hadn't the patience that Nikita had to walk down the street, instead he snuck into an alley behind the wig shop and relieved himself behind a bin before he burst. Feeling much better, he decided to walk to the nearest late-night café to wash his hands and grab a coffee.

When he got back to the wig shop, Casey was busy texting someone, a warm smile on his lips. He looked up abruptly when he noticed Erron enter the room and tucked his phone back into his pocket.

'Something interesting?' Erron asked, trying to remain nonchalant as he took up his seat once more.

'Oh, no, not really. Warren was just telling me about a thing that happened on his way back from work.' Casey stared off out the window but settled his hand back on the armrest.

'Oh, right.' Erron glanced down at Casey's hand but kept his own in the pockets of his jeans.

It was gone 2 a.m. when Nikita emerged from the small room at the back, stretching out her aches and pains from the cramped sofa snooze. Erron was perched on the edge of his rocking chair, eyes fixed on the tattoo studio, while Casey had succumbed to exhaustion and was snoring softly on the chair beside him.

'I warn you now, that sofa isn't wing-nub friendly.' Nikita grimaced. 'How much longer will my back hurt this bad?'

'At least until they're mostly grown.' Erron could distinctly feel the same dull aching, which he'd managed to ignore for the duration of the evening. 'I'd never want to cut them off again, that's for sure. I forgot how torturous the growing pains were.'

'I'm never chopping mine off either. I take it there's been nothing happening over the road?' Nikita asked quietly.

'Nope, they're still open though. They seem to get busier the later it gets,' Erron answered, not taking his eyes away from the window. His right leg twitched up and down and he had a handful of gummy bears that he was picking off one by one.

'You OK? You seem a little off.'

'I'm fine. Just tired,' Erron lied.

'You're bound to be. I guess moon-time works differently up here with the opening hours of some of these businesses. How long's he been out for?' Nikita nodded towards the napping Cupid.

'About an hour.'

'You want to get some sleep, Erron?' Nikita asked, concerned.

'Should we let him catch up first?' Erron glanced towards Casey, who was still fast asleep, his head lolled to one side.

'I can manage this stakeout solo. Go get yourself a few hours. I'll let Casey sleep.'

'You sure?'

'I'm sure.'

Erron eased himself off the chair, wincing slightly as he realised just how long he'd sat in the same position, the edge of the chair digging into the back of his thighs.

Just as Nikita was about to take his seat, movement outside caught her eye.

'Wait, what's that?' She leant on the windowsill and pressed her face to the glass.

Erron joined her, just as a shadowy figure emerged from the alley, dressed head to toe in elaborate futuristic robes in red and black with silver embroidery. The figure was wearing a hood and matching mask and seemed to be quickly approaching the door to the tattoo shop. A handful of queuing customers started to gather around him excitedly as though he was an A-lister on the red carpet.

'Do you think that could be him?' Erron asked.

'It has to be! Those robes were behind the door in his studio!' Nikita exclaimed in a hushed tone. 'We need to get down there.' She threw her jacket on and started stuffing a handful of the mind-control wigs into her bag, claiming they might come in handy, and Gertie wasn't likely to miss a few.

Erron moved towards the door. 'Do we wake Sleeping Beauty?'

Nikita wasted no time in rocking Casey's chair hard and startling him awake. 'On your feet, Hart, we've got our target.'

'Holy fu—fridge magnet!' Casey almost fell off the chair as he was jolted into stark consciousness. He clambered to his feet to follow them, taking a quick look out the window just in time to see Djinn disappear into Arcane Ink.

The three of them bolted down the stairs, Erron in the lead, racing across the street and skidding to a halt at the door of the tattoo parlour. He threw the door open, fumbling for his Medusa badge in his jeans pocket.

'Stop, stay where you are!' he bellowed, raising the badge at the robed man twenty feet away. Nikita and Casey almost collided with Erron as they entered the shop, just as Djinn bolted for a storeroom at the back of the room, pushing a customer over to get past.

The tattooist disappeared in a flurry of sweeping fabric, closing the door behind him, the crashing of glass ringing out in his wake.

'That doesn't go anywhere, does it?' Casey asked.

Erron and Nikita were already jogging to the storeroom. 'I hope not,' Erron shouted.

Djinn was gone.

He'd broken a thick pane of mirrored glass on a locked door that separated Arcane Ink from the kitchen at the Weetabix café and pushed his way through. A ragged swatch of fabric had caught on the glass and a trail of blood revealed where he'd clearly caught his arm.

Erron was the first to climb through, rousing a scream from a waiter carrying a heavily loaded tray of beans-on-Weetabix dishes, which went crashing to the tiled floor. Nikita narrowly avoided sliding over in the mess and warned Casey before he stepped right in it.

'Oi!' the manager yelled after them as they followed the drips of blood smeared across the floor and leading out into the street.

Erron caught sight of Djinn pelting down the pathways, robes flowing and feet bounding along the pavement aided by the lower gravity. Within Elysion, it wasn't as slow and graceful as the rest of the moon's surface as the city's gravity was engineered to be closer to Earth's, but there was a definite advantage of being able to take immense strides. Erron took chase, soon realising Djinn was heading towards the nearest portals. Nikita and Casey almost caught up, breathing heavily and unprepared for just how fast Erron was running. He launched himself over a short wall, gaining on Djinn by a fraction.

The tattooist seemed to all but disappear into the crowd outside a popular night-time spot called the Palace of the Moon, where it was commonplace for attendees to wear elaborate costumes and dance in a ballroom filled with champagne-flavoured bubbles and sparkling orbs of pure moonlight. Erron pushed his way forcefully through the throng of agents in their sequinned suits and ball gowns, only to find a bundle of ditched robes next to a glittering fountain on the lawn.

'Erron!' Nikita called through the crowd, trying to locate him.

She saw his arm wave them over before he took off again after spotting a shape in the distance running from behind a full-size Cinderella carriage prop.

'My god, it's like trying to keep up with Tom Cruise in any of the films he's always running in,' Nikita huffed, her lungs burning.

'Tell me about it.' Casey was already covered in a sheen of sweat and his hair was sticking to his neck. 'He's certainly *Mission: Impossible* at times,' he muttered under his breath.

'At least you've got long legs,' Nikita grumbled as they fell out the other side of the cluster of partygoers, picking up the pace once more. 'I don't even think the lack of gravity is helping me much.'

They finally caught up with Erron, who was hunched over, leaning his hands on his knees and gulping air. 'He jumped through a portal. I just don't know which one,' he said through laboured breaths.

They were by an International Portal Wall, where several portals led to major cities across the globe.

'Fuck!' Erron screamed, gripping his hair in frustration, the sweat running down his back and chest. He kicked at a rock and sent it skittering through the portal to New York. 'I nearly had him. I was this close!' He gestured an inch with his fingers.

'You did your best,' Nikita commiserated.

'It was not bloody good enough!' He sank to the ground and leant against a wall, exhausted.

'Why didn't he fly?' Nikita asked.

'I'm guessing he wouldn't want us to see what division he was in. Plus, he got far better cover on the ground.' Erron shook his head.

'Not to mention flying here is a bit trickier. Lack of updraughts, it can be really exhausting,' Casey added.

'Ah, I didn't know that,' Nikita said, dismayed.

'I guess there's no point staking out the tattoo place now,' Casey finally said after the dust had settled.

'No, he won't be coming back if he knows it's being watched.' Erron sighed.

Nikita and Casey slumped down next to him.

'Maybe we head back and try and get a half-decent sample of the blood he left at the scene?' Nikita suggested.

'We can try. Though it might not be any good; agents don't carry DNA in their blood like mortals. But it will show which division he belongs to,' Erron explained.

'Well, it's a start,' Casey agreed.

By the time they had got back to the Weetabix café, there seemed to be no trace of the blood. One of the employees looked up at them, confused and gripping the handle of a mop, as they frantically searched the route of the chase back to the broken glass between the two businesses.

'Where's the blood?' Erron spun around, trying to spot any tiny fleck of crimson on any of the tiles or door frames.

'I've cleaned it all up. It was putting people off their Weetabix,' the employee interjected.

'And the beans weren't?' Erron hissed, pushing past to get back out into the street. He crouched down, looking around for any specks, but found none on the cobbled path.

Nikita had gone to the dividing door between the kitchen and Arcane Ink. Casey and Erron joined her shortly after.

'There's some dried blood on this piece of cloth Djinn snagged on the glass,' Nikita said, having nabbed a pair of Weetabix tongs to examine the fabric closer.

'We'll have to take it back to the lab at the Raphael and see if we can find anything on it.' Erron searched his pockets, realising he had nothing that would resemble an evidence bag.

'Here.' Casey held out a clean sandwich bag from a stack of them in the kitchen.

'Cheers.' Erron broke into a genuine smile and held the bag open for Nikita to bundle the cloth into.

Casey's phone pinged with an incoming text, and he pulled it from his pocket. An involuntary smile flashed across his lips as he saw it was another message from Warren.

'I've just got to make a quick call. It's Warren.' Casey gestured to his phone and stepped aside.

'Sir, I've located the website, but there's a bit of process to get into it. I need to jump through some hoops to be able to view the content,' Warren explained.

'Good work, when do you think you'll get in?'

'Could be a few hours, maybe a day or so, I will keep you posted. I think someone from the inside needs to approve me opening an account on there before I can progress.'

'Thank you for the update. Keep in touch, won't you?' Casey said softly.

'Of course, Mr Hart.'

'Thank you, I'll update the others.' Casey put his phone away, catching a slightly disheartened expression on Erron's face before he looked away.

# 25

## *Ain't No Sunshine*

THE RAPHAEL SANCTUARY WAS ALMOST silent in the early hours of the morning as the Medusa team prepared to test the blood sample they'd found. The atmosphere was heavy with their joint fatigue, and Casey was trying to keep himself alert by splashing cold water on his face from the sink. Nikita was focusing on the small print of an instruction booklet regarding a blood-testing kit they had in the inventory. She glanced up, seeing Erron hunched over by a microscope, his head resting on his arm.

'Erron, you really need some rest. You've not had a break.'

'I just need a coffee.' He sat up and rubbed his eyes. 'What do the instructions say?'

'Well, that depends on whether the blood has dried or not.' Nikita picked up the sandwich bag with the cloth scrap in. 'We can either scrape it or swab it.'

'Right. Look, I'm not going to be able to sleep. Why don't you both go and rest up for a bit? I'll run this sample,' Erron volunteered, opening his hand for the instructions.

'You really ought to be the one resting,' Nikita insisted, passing him the leaflet.

'I won't be able to switch off. Honestly, I'd rather get going on this.' Erron made a point of stretching and shaking out his arms, forcing himself to be more alert.

'I'll get you a coffee in that case. I know how stubborn you are.' Casey walked past, ruffling Erron's hair as he did so.

'Told you he was an Aries.' Nikita gave Casey a wry grin.

'I'm what now?' Erron turned to face them, pushing the hair out of his face.

'Nothing to worry about,' Nikita replied. 'I'll be in the waiting room across the hall. Wake me up as soon as you have an idea of what division we're dealing with.'

Erron was carefully scraping some of the dried blood off the cloth when Casey set a hot vending-machine coffee down beside him.

'You absolutely sure you don't want to take a nap?' Casey sat on the chair next to him and wheeled it close.

Erron set the scalpel down and managed a tired grin. Without thought, he reached over and tucked a loose section of Casey's hair back over his ear, his fingers lingering briefly. 'I'll be fine.'

'OK.' Casey's eyes softened, his Apollo radiance adding a warm glow to his sleepy smile.

Erron opened his mouth to speak, but Casey's phone trilled with an incoming text. 'You best check that, it might be important,' Erron said quietly as Casey's hand reached for the phone.

Erron leant closer, hoping to see who the text was from, when Casey shoved the phone back in his pocket. 'It's nothing groundbreaking,' he said, slightly flustered.

'You like him, don't you?' Erron asked quietly, looking back at the cloth sample.

'Who?'

'Warren.' Erron robotically scraped at the blood on the fabric, his voice empty of emotion.

'What makes you say that?' Casey wheeled back slightly on the chair, blushing, the unopened text from Warren burning in his pocket.

Erron took a moment to form the words on his tongue without any malice. 'He's good for you, Case. Even I can see that, and I've barely seen him.'

'Don't say that.' Casey's voice cracked. 'I don't want anything from him.'

Erron glanced up, his eyes tired and red. 'I wouldn't blame you, if you changed your mind.'

Casey's gaze fell to the floor, a heavy sense of guilt washing over him. 'There's only one man I want. I just hope you know that.' He reached over to rest his hand on top of Erron's.

'Right, OK. Well, I best get back to this, time is against us.' Erron withdrew his hand and carried on with the testing kit.

Casey reluctantly rose from the chair. 'If you need me I will be here in a heartbeat.'

Erron nodded and watched Casey leave before returning his focus to the blood sample, a wave of numbness moving over him.

It took him longer than he would've liked to scrape enough of the sample to use the test kit, eventually showing no definitive result of any kind. He had to repeat the process several times before he came to the conclusion that either the kit was faulty or it wouldn't work on agency blood. Time had crawled by, but the clock hands reached 6 a.m. when he finally gave in, unsure what else he could do.

A heavy presence filled the room behind him and the quality of the light dramatically dimmed.

'Grover,' a quiet, ominous voice said.

Erron spun round to see the senior Reaper, D-O-A, looming in the doorway, his ice-blue eyes piercing through the gloom of his shadowy aura. Erron looked expectantly at him, assuming he was being called back into Hades Division.

'Grover,' he repeated, his tone solemn. 'Ember's name came up.'

D-O-A stepped into the room and gently set down a card in front of him. Erron stared at the ink, a heavy weight sinking to the pit of his stomach.

'Oh shit,' he whispered.

* * *

Casey woke up when a firm hand squeezed his shoulder. The fluorescent light of the staff lounge hurt his eyes as he blinked them open. He'd been stretched out on a bench seat, Nikita across the room on another. Erron stood sombrely in front of him, his expression saying enough.

'Case, I've got some bad news.'

Casey sat up, tucking his messy hair behind his ears, a lump forming in his throat. They sat in silence for a moment before he spoke. 'It's Ember, isn't it?'

Erron hung his head and nodded. 'Her name came up on a blind card, ten minutes ago.'

Casey closed his eyes and drew in a long, slow breath. He rested his elbows on his knees and lowered his head into his hands.

'I'm so sorry,' Erron said quietly.

'Where did they find her?' Casey finally asked, his eyes stinging with the tears he was holding back.

'She's in the emergency room, according to the card. She died here at the hospital.'

'Is there a chance they could save her?' Casey looked up, hopeful. 'I mean, they must be working on her, right?'

'I don't know. D-O-A said I was assigned as her Reaper due to my involvement in the case, and because we won't be using the Ferryman's Touch,' Erron explained gently. 'I can tell you more once I have been over there, if you like.'

'I want to see her.' Casey stood up and wiped his eyes on his sleeve, taking a moment to compose himself. 'Let me come with you.'

'OK.' Erron stood, noticing in the corner of his eye that Nikita had woken up on the other side of the room. He turned to her with a pained expression.

'You guys go on ahead,' she said softly. 'I'll be here when you get back.' She sat up once they'd left the room, making the decision to give her friends time alone to process the news.

Erron and Casey were met by a young Archangel doctor at the reception of the emergency room. She guided them to the private room where Ember lay on a hospital bed, her cold skin still glowing with the life she'd lived, as if she were sleeping, a golden-haired angel taking some rest on a cloud. D-O-A had taken up quiet residence in the corner of the room, having reassured Erron he was there purely for support.

The doctors had covered her with a sheet, with only her face showing, a blunt trauma wound just above her left eye, the blood matted in her hair.

'How did she get here?' Casey asked.

'One of our surgeons said he found her crawling into the rear yard when he was on his break. He brought her in, but she passed before the emergency team could get to her,' the doctor explained. She looked past Casey at Erron who hung back at the door. 'Are you her assigned Hades agent?'

He stepped forward. 'I am, yes.'

'How did she die?' Casey asked quietly.

'We've not had a chance to fully examine her yet. It's protocol to wait for her assigned Hades agent to be present for anyone that dies on hospital grounds. But her injuries are . . . significant,' the doctor answered. 'But as you're here, we can begin.'

Erron glanced down at Ember's card in his hand. He was too late to hear her last thoughts, though they were scrawled in ink under her name. The breath caught in his throat as he read them once more. *Please let them find me.* Across the city, in the silence of a glass case, the scales of luck had dipped a little further to one side.

Erron walked around the bed to stand near the senior Reaper, hoping for some guidance with a subtle glance in his direction. D-O-A stepped forward and the walls seemed to close in with the weight of his ancient *Umbra Noctis*, the oppressive sense of morbidity enveloping every inch, floor to ceiling, and flickering the lights. Erron's own *Umbra Noctis* was the gentle shade of a willow tree in comparison.

'We're just here for the formalities. You don't need to do anything except write up the assignment as complete,' D-O-A whispered to Erron.

'Right, OK,' Erron replied quietly with a curt nod.

A different doctor joined them at the bedside, a burly man with short black hair and a soft smile.

Ember's body had been meticulously mutilated, and the breath caught in Erron's throat at the first sight of it. The doctor began to run down the injuries they observed.

The colour drained from Casey's face, and he excused himself from the room, choking back the burning grief in his throat. The burly doctor continued with his observations.

'Both feet removed, and efforts made to stem blood flow. Right hand severed with severe bleeding; three fingers removed on the left. Multiple needle marks down the inner arms, appear to be either for fluids or blood being drawn. Sections of skin removed from the upper thighs and arms.' The doctor gently opened Ember's mouth and turned her head side to side, examining around her ears, neck and eyes, all while the lights flickered intermittently. 'All rear molars removed, left ear missing. Large sections of her wings have been removed also, but this appears to have been done at least a day or so ago.'

'Official cause of death?' Erron asked.

'Exsanguination, I would expect.' The doctor pulled the sheet back over her. 'I guess you'll be wanting to take her down to the room you were using as a morgue?' he asked.

'Yes, but first I'd like to speak to the surgeon who found her, see if I can get some details of where she might have come from,' Erron replied. 'My friend outside, he was very close to Ember. Do you mind if we had some time alone with her before we move her?'

'No problem. She was found by Jared Enleigh. He's currently being looked after in the surgeons' lounge on the second floor, he's pretty shaken up,' the doctor explained.

'Ah yeah, I know him, he's on our team. We'll head up there in a while.'

'I'll send your friend in.' The doctor gave Erron a sorrowful smile and left the room.

Casey joined Erron once more, his eyes bloodshot. 'Was it him? This bastard killer?'

Erron nodded, all too familiar with the signature MO of the Butterfly Catcher, the missing body parts creating disturbing imagery that didn't help his already consistent nightmares.

'I need to see again.' Casey wiped his eyes on the back of his shirt cuff.

'I don't think it's a good idea, Case.' Erron reached for Casey's hand and gently squeezed it.

'For Ember's sake, I need to know what she went through. I have to.' Casey exhaled slowly, regaining his composure. 'I can do this, please.'

Erron withdrew his hand and nodded.

Casey had seen his fair share of horrific injuries in the years of being a doctor in his life, but nothing prepared him for what he saw when he pulled the sheet away from Ember's body. He closed his eyes and took in a deep breath, steadying himself by leaning on the rails of the hospital bed. Memories of Ember's cheerful smile and her infectious laugh flashed into his mind, the decades of friendship they'd shared brutally ripped away by an act of unfathomable cruelty. He blinked away tears, forcing himself to look back down at her lifeless form. The dirt and blood that coated her brightly coloured clothes seemed to stain her very spirit, diminishing every last shred of sunshine that once enveloped her.

'Case—' Erron began to say, reaching to lightly touch his arm.

Casey politely waved him away. 'I can do this,' he repeated and pulled on a pair of blue hospital gloves, pushing past his feelings and trying to engage the logical part of his brain.

Methodically and silently, he repeated the examination of her body, closely checking the age of each injury, the level of clotting, the depth, angle and style of the incisions. He handled her with care and diligence, wanting to afford her body the tenderness and dignity that her death did not.

'She went missing Wednesday afternoon. So she's been gone for just under two days,' Casey said, crouching close to her, his keen eyes taking in any relevant details. 'He kept her restrained. There are marks on her neck, upper wrists, ankles – she fought against them. Tape marks around her mouth. These last injuries seem rushed. The final pieces he took, he took quickly.'

'We may never know if she was dumped here or escaped from somewhere nearby. Maybe the killer changed his mind. I just don't understand why he kept her and not the others,' Erron said.

Casey stood straight and hugged his chest. 'By the looks of it, it was to keep her alive longer to harvest more trophies.'

* * *

Nikita was sipping a cup of cold water and waiting for the others to return. She was fighting through the throbbing pain of her growing wings, having struggled to get much sleep at all.

'I've been looking for you.' D-O-A swooped into the waiting room, bringing his usual gloomy aura that rivalled the misery of being stuck on the M25.

'You have?' She met his gaze, surprised to see him there.

'I've been speaking with the ghosts, whilst you've been busy.' He sat down beside her. 'I had hoped they might assist further in your investigation.'

Nikita looked at him expectantly.

'This one that is helping us, Gunther. He was very forceful in his last message. I hadn't even reached out to him.' D-O-A pulled out a slip of paper from his coat pocket and passed it to her. 'He repeated this over and over yesterday evening when I got to the Eligos.'

Nikita cautiously opened the folded paper, taking a moment to process the words that she read.

*He's got another one. More luck for sale. Nine, nine, nine.*

'Does he mean there's another agent been taken?' Nikita read the words a few more times. 'And is that nine as in the number, or does Gunther speak German and is saying "no" over and over?'

'I had hoped you might know. It might just be referring to the emergency number?' The Reaper folded his hands in his lap.

'I better call Emrys and check if any of his team went missing yesterday.' Nikita pulled out her phone, dialling the number for the Fortuna boss. It rang out, and she left a brief voicemail.

She tried a couple more times, having no luck, before scrolling back through their text conversation. She'd been so swept up with the investigation she hadn't noticed that no messages from Emrys had come through since they'd seen each other the previous morning. She could no longer put it down to him just being busy, and turned to the Reaper with a concerned expression.

'Could you possibly try and get more information from this ghost, if you have time? Maybe something less cryptic?'

'Of course.' D-O-A bowed his head slightly and stood to leave, exiting the room just as Erron and Casey returned.

Erron instantly noticed the atmosphere had shifted, and the pallor of Nikita's face. 'What's happened?'

'We've reason to believe the killer has another victim,' Nikita murmured, her mouth dry. 'And I haven't heard from Emrys.'

'Since when?'

'Yesterday morning.' Nikita didn't look up.

Erron glanced at the clock on the wall, it was 8.12 a.m. 'He might only just be heading to work now. I expect he's just been caught up with everything.'

'He texts me "good morning" every day at seven thirty. I've tried calling, it just goes to voicemail.'

Erron reached for his own phone and dialled the number for the office at Fortuna HQ. After a long time, a female voice answered the phone.

'Fortuna Division, Laney Williams speaking,' she said in a professional yet chirpy tone. She was the main assignment clerk at Fortuna.

'Is Mr Taliesin there?' Erron queried.

'No, sorry, he's not here right now. Can I put you through to a senior agent?'

'When was he last in the office?'

'We last had him overseeing assignments yesterday morning around eight thirty. Can I take a message?'

'Uh, yes, actually, can you tell him to give Agent Grover or Wolf a call as soon as he turns up?' Erron asked. 'He'll know who we are.'

When Erron ended the call, there was a heavy silence in the room. All three of them were beyond exhausted, their focus spread as thinly as their collective hope that Emrys was just late to work.

'I'll get us all a coffee. Then we can come up with a plan,' Casey finally said.

'Nikita, we'll find him,' Erron said firmly.

'All of him though?' she said blankly, her stomach a churning mix of terror and panic, manifesting as a mask of complete numbness. 'I don't understand. He wouldn't have got a tattoo. This can't be right, it's got to be a misunderstanding.'

'Then maybe there's hope it's not what it seems.' Erron moved to sit next to her and pulled her into a tight hug. When Casey returned with three cups of the strongest hospital coffee, Nikita was curled with her head in Erron's lap, staring unblinkingly at the wall, her phone gripped tightly in her hand.

'Try and get her to have a drink,' Casey mouthed as he passed Erron two cups of coffee.

Erron nodded in silent agreement. 'One of us needs to speak with Dr Enleigh. He's in the second-floor surgeons' lounge and was the one that found Ember. We need to know everything we can . . . as quickly as we can.'

'I'll go, you stay with Nikita,' Casey volunteered, wrinkling his nose in disgust at the bitter coffee as he left the room.

# 26

## *Lovely*

EMRYS COULDN'T SHAKE THE IMAGES of Ember being dissected out of his head. He was dizzy from his own blood loss and the headache was unbearable. His ears rang from how Ember had screamed, the blood-curdling pleas she made of her torturer, speaking his name, trying to reach him on a human level.

Nothing bothered Emrys more than the persistent silence and darkness of the dank room in which he was held captive. He was breathing through the pain and discomfort of his situation, almost hoping the killer would come back and finish him off before he had to spend another hour strapped to the gurney just waiting to die.

The cannula in his arm was taking blood in a slow *drip-drip-drip* that rivalled a leaking kitchen tap, slow enough that he wouldn't go into shock, but constant enough that he was feeling light-headed and sick. He hadn't eaten in over a day, and his stomach growled in protest, the only music to break the muteness of the room.

He made the conscious effort not to be afraid. He'd died before; he could do it again. Through the stifling plastic of silver tape across his mouth, he hummed a tune to keep his mind occupied and dim the searing pain in his left leg. His mind repeatedly tried to think of everything he was about to lose, but he pushed the thoughts down, knowing that giving into his despair wouldn't help the situation one bit. Instead, he dwelled in the happy moments he'd shared with Nikita, convincing himself that their journey wasn't yet over.

He fought hard with the last ounce of energy he had, rattling every restraint against the gurney and making it roll slightly, but nothing budged. Defeated, he stared up into the darkness, waiting, just waiting. A faint glimmer of hope still hung over him that Nikita would find him. If anyone could track this evil killer down, it would be her. Tenacious, fearless Nikita.

But if he was to die, he would make sure he was the last victim. Flexing his left hand in the restraint, he started the painstaking process of using what he had of a nail on his middle finger to carve the killer's name on his own palm, in the hope that, whenever his body was found, he would still have his hand attached.

* * *

Dr Enleigh sat across from Casey, his knees pressed together and arms hugging his chest. He looked pale and unsettled; his feet jittered on the linoleum. His face and hospital scrubs were smeared with blood.

'She was one of the first to befriend me when I joined the agency.' Jared sniffed, his eyes red and puffy. 'How could someone do this?'

'I know, she was a good friend to me too. You said you were on break and found her, where exactly?' Casey asked, struggling to mask his pain of Ember's death under his usual calming tone.

'By the door that leads into the rear yard, it links to an alley. I think she must have crawled from there, it's the only place she could have come from,' Dr Enleigh answered quietly. 'She was in such a bad way. I have never seen anything like it. I can't imagine what she went through.' His voice caught in his throat, and he shook his head as he spoke, as if to shake the images from his mind.

'Did she say anything? Give any indication who may have hurt her?'

'No, when I found her she was barely moving. I expect her heart gave out shortly after I picked her up. She said nothing comprehensible.'

'Did you try any CPR, or to get her to surgery?' Casey asked.

'I alerted the team on the radio.' Dr Enleigh pulled a small walkie-talkie off his belt and held it up. 'It was about two minutes before anyone got to me. I tried CPR, but it was hopeless. She was already gone, and the emergency team said it would be nearly impossible to get her back.'

Nikita appeared in the doorway of the lounge. Her eyes were vacant, and she spoke in a rushed, quivering tone.

'Jared, can you show us where you found her?'

'Of course.' He rose shakily to his feet and gestured for them to follow.

He led them through the hospital halls and down sets of stairs that led them to the disused hallway they'd stumbled in the morning before.

'This looks familiar,' Casey said. 'Weren't we here yesterday?'

'Yeah, I saw you both here yesterday. I take my break outside in the yard when I need some fresh air,' the doctor explained.

They passed the storage rooms and exited via a fire door into the rear yard, where the morning sun was glowing against a white painted wall. The yard was small, covered in gravel and led into an alley as Dr Enleigh had stated. Casey walked down its length, pushing on any doors he found until he was in a backstreet of terraced houses. When he returned to the yard, Nikita was crouching down in the spot Dr Enleigh said he'd found Ember.

'She died of blood loss, right?' she asked. 'That's what Erron told me.'

'I would have said so, from the state of her,' Dr Enleigh confirmed.

'There's not much blood, considering she probably would have taken some time to crawl along here,' Nikita stated.

'Her wounds were crudely bandaged; a lot of the blood had soaked into those and her clothes.' Jared sat down on the step by the fire door.

'I'm just going to take a few notes, if that's OK,' Nikita said, extracting her trusty notebook. 'Ah shit, I've lost my pen.' She patted around her pockets.

'You can use mine.' Dr Enleigh passed her a colourful ballpoint.

'Thank you.' Nikita jotted down everything he'd said and sketched out a quick drawing of the courtyard. Her hands were jittery, and she struggled to concentrate when her mind kept wandering to Emrys's whereabouts. She absent-mindedly slipped the pen in her pocket and pulled out her phone, taking pictures of the scene before heading down the alley to check the doors that Casey had already looked at.

'I can't see where she would have come from, unless it was one of the terraced houses in the street.' Casey caught up to her.

'Possibly. Or she could have been dropped off here from a car. Maybe the killer had second thoughts and wanted to leave her to get help,' Nikita pondered out loud.

'Our best bet is to check the street for cameras, I suppose. See if there was a car dropping her off or which direction she came from,' Casey suggested.

'Yeah, let's do that.'

'Where's Erron?' Casey asked.

'He said he would move Ember to our morgue,' Nikita answered. She looked up and down the street, seeing if there were any council CCTV systems overhead. It was an older road, with only a stretch of about twenty-five houses, and no immediately visible cameras. 'I think doorbell cameras might be a good place to start. We'll have to knock on doors, see if anyone has seen anything or recorded anything unwittingly.'

Dr Enleigh approached them, having made his way down the alley. 'Is there anything I can do?'

'If you have time, can you help Erron with anything he needs for Ember? The poor guy hasn't slept for over twenty-four hours. He's running on gummy bears,' Nikita asked. 'Get him a Red Bull or something.'

'Maybe a Monster instead, I'm not a fan of Red Bull. I've already got wings.' Dr Enleigh gave her a half-smile and went back down the alley.

Casey could tell that Nikita's sharp and motivated mind seemed to be misfiring as she tried to focus on the task at hand, while an invisible Sword of Damocles hung above the head of the man she loved.

'I'll go left, you go right,' Casey said decisively.

'See you back here soon.' Nikita made a start knocking on the first door she came across.

* * *

Erron had reached the stage of exhaustion where he was beginning to see things that weren't there. He said hello to a person in the lab that turned out to be a coat hanging on a peg, then mistook a pair of Marigold gloves for a rubber duck.

Ember lay on a gurney in the makeshift morgue, just as Willow and Leo had done before her. The room temperature had been cranked as low as possible again, and as it started to form an icy condensation on the windows, it began to wake Erron up a little.

'I've been sent to help you.' Dr Enleigh appeared at the door with an offering of an energy drink.

'Great, thank you.' Erron accepted the can and pulled the ring, taking a several gulps of the caffeinated elixir, hoping it would keep him focused. 'Any idea on how I might get some useful info from a blood sample we got from the suspect?'

'Oh, from experience, agency blood doesn't really give away much. Certainly no DNA profile.'

The kilo of gummy bears in Erron's stomach was reanimating under the influence of the energy drink and starting a nauseating, zombie-bear rave.

He paused, allowing the nausea to settle, before fetching the sandwich bag with the remaining piece of cloth from Djinn. 'This is what we have. I just want to narrow down the division, if anything.'

'Chances are any cosmic energy has long since gone if it's been drying into fabric,' Dr Enleigh stated. 'You OK, bud? You're not looking too hot.'

'Just a bit jittery.' The caffeine was ramping up in Erron's system.

'You're looking a lot worse than most the Reapers I've seen. You want to go and lie down for a bit?' Dr Enleigh folded his arms and fixed Erron with an authoritative look.

'No, I'm fine. Just help me out with this blood sample.'

'OK, best I can suggest is our own version of a catalase test, which just proves the presence of blood. But what it *will* do is confirm if the suspect is definitely an agent or not.' Dr Enleigh rummaged through a cupboard before pulling out a small bottle. 'Human blood reacts to hydrogen peroxide. Agency blood doesn't. It does, however, violently fizz when exposed to concentrated manatee urine.'

'I have so many questions.' Erron pinched his forehead, unable to comprehend how that was even discovered.

'Here we go.' Dr Enleigh used a dropper to add a little of the manatee urine to the fabric sample.

They waited patiently, but no fizzing happened.

'I hate to break it to you, but whoever you chased in Elysion must be mortal. There's no agency blood on this fabric,' Dr Enleigh stated.

'Mortals can't get to Elysion. Can they?'

'You tell me. It's not like the ice-cream vans have a huge amount of security. It's not exactly Border Force, is it?'

'Oh jeez.' Erron didn't even know how to comprehend someone collecting manatee pee, let alone a mortal getting to the Moon through an ice-cream van.

Nikita and Casey turned up conveniently to share what they'd found. Dr Enleigh excused himself, saying he had to get to a scheduled surgery.

'Erron, you look like death,' Casey said.

Erron raised an eyebrow, waiting for the penny to drop.

'I mean, OK, I know you technically *are* death, but you know what I mean,' Casey flustered, eyeing the empty can. 'You look like death on gummy bears and energy drinks. Not a good mix.'

Nikita paced back and forth, a cold sheen of sweat on her brow. 'We've had no luck whatsoever with any witnesses or doorbell cameras that could have shown where Ember came from.' She angrily kicked out at a small bin that got in her way. 'I don't know what to do. I just don't know where to start.'

Erron stepped into her path to try and calm her, catching her arm and pulling her into a hug. He felt her knees give out, and hot tears streamed down her face as she choked for breath through sobs. Casey immediately engulfed both of them with his wings, knowing his Apollo Flush wouldn't work on Nikita, but hoping the warmth and support would help in some small way.

They stood in silence for some time, allowing Nikita time to feel the weight of the situation, and process it in the only way she could. Once she had composed herself, she was guided to a chair.

'Have you found anything helpful?' Casey finally asked Erron, gesturing towards the desk with the cloth sample.

Erron scratched his head and shrugged slightly. 'Jared reckons it came from a mortal. It didn't react to his manatee piss so apparently it's not agency blood,' Erron explained.

'I . . . what?' Nikita was taken aback.

'Don't ask. The haystack just got a whole lot fucking bigger. I'm sorry.'

'So that leaves us with this Oracles website, a grainy CCTV image of the suspect and some dude named Djinn.' Nikita's shoulders slumped, defeated.

'We're not giving up. Have you tried calling Emrys again?' Erron asked.

'Only about sixty times so far between us. It's just a dead line now,' Casey explained.

All three of them glanced at the clock. It was nearing 11 a.m. Emrys was last seen over twenty-five hours ago. Ember had lasted around thirty-nine hours.

Casey's phone rang and all three of them looked on, hopeful. 'It's Warren,' he announced quietly, swiping to answer the call. He spoke briefly to the transferee, his face playing out a range of different emotions before he ended the call.

'Warren's got access to the website. He says it's urgent, we need to see what he's found. He's at his hotel,' Casey explained.

Nikita sprang from her chair, holding on to some hope that the website might be the miracle they needed.

* * *

TruthHunter11: *These auctions are going crazy.*

AlphaKingGetYou9: *I know, it just shows what we're dealing with. It's a shame we can't go public with all this . . . yet.*

TruthHunter11: *What do you mean, go public?*

AlphaKingGetYou9: *Well, once we've got enough proof of all this we can blow it wide open, can't we? Hunt all these fuckers down and expose them for what they are.*

TruthHunter11: *There's so many though. We can't exactly kill them all.*

AlphaKingGetYou9: *Where's your ambition?*

TruthHunter11: *One at a time is tricky enough.*

AlphaKingGetYou9: *Not when there are more Oracle followers to help. There's talk of a meet-up, a scouting mission, if you will.*

TruthHunter11: *Sounds like the start of a revolution.*

AlphaKingGetYou9: *Exactly that, my brother. I appreciate the work you are doing for the resistance.*

TruthHunter11: *Just doing my bit.*

AlphaKingGetYou9: *Got to go, I've got to get back to work.*

*AlphaKingGetYou9 has gone offline.*

Sam stretched as the computer went through its shut-down process. He had to get back up to the shop as his self-allotted lunch break was over. As he waited for customers, he couldn't help but ponder the real ramifications of the Oracles going public. It was all very well discussing it in the safety of the forum, but in reality it could be catastrophic. If the Fireflies were genuinely god-like, or the pawns of greater deities, who knew what power they held as a collective? It was clear the Greys could kill people with a single touch, so they were likely the guard dogs of all the others and could easily wipe out any of the Oracles if they were so inclined.

*But what a way to die, a martyr in a grand revolution*, Sam thought. His name would go down in history, he wouldn't fade into oblivion like so many others. *What a way to die.*

He glanced down at his hands, hands that had been soaked in the glittering blood of demi-gods and sworn into servitude of his new brotherhood of Oracles. He felt powerful, almost god-like himself.

All the information he was learning about the Fireflies, he fed back to his followers, tantalising them with images of the ones he'd identified. There was an absolute frenzy on the forums when it was confirmed that the Greens had wings like a butterfly, and that some of the wing portions would be up for auction.

But nothing beat getting up close and personal to a Firefly, learning about them and finding out the limits of their supposed humanity. He reached over for the journal he'd removed from Ember's house, trailing his fingers lightly over its edges and pressing the book to his nose to absorb the last lingering scent of her room. He wanted nothing more than to go back there, to take in every detail of her life, the last remnants of her existence before pushing her out of his mind once and for all. A jingle of the shop bell brought him out of his thoughts, and he carried the journal up the stairs to greet two customers.

* * *

Nikita and Warren were scrolling through discussion threads on the Oracles forum as Erron and Casey perched on the bed in Warren's plush hotel room.

He had uncovered a whole cult of people that were determined to end the existence of the agents using so-called 'Oracles' that could allegedly pick them out in a crowd by reading their auras. Nikita's mouth was agape as she read the horrific and hateful comments and the sheer volume of users that added their opinions to the mix.

'Can they actually see us, or is it just lucky guessing?' Erron asked, busying himself by taking in the details of Warren's room, trying to get a feel for the unbearably pleasant Apollo agent that had so quickly latched on to Casey. Everything was painstakingly neat, clean and matching, his whole existence seemed to convey some kind of aesthetic, though Erron wasn't well schooled enough to recognise the style. Two heavy vintage trunks with beige leather straps and bright brass buckles were stacked on the ornate wardrobe, the type of suitcases that looked like they had rolled right out of the fifties. Warren's four pairs of polished cap-toe Oxfords were lined up like soldiers near the door, next to a coat stand with two pristine Savile Row jackets carefully draped over wooden hangers. Erron looked down at his scruffy, wrinkled attire, his posture shrinking slightly, suddenly conscious of how dishevelled he looked.

'I don't think this is just guessing.' Nikita spun the laptop around – on it was an image taken from a distance of Fortuna Division HQ, with herself, Casey, Erron, Ember and Emrys outside after the memorial service for Willow and Leo. Each of them had been labelled with a colour, with a tag over Erron's head saying, 'Grey – previously Gold . . . possible mercenary?'

Erron shook his head and couldn't help but laugh with disbelief. 'A mercenary? Will reap for the highest bidder.'

'This is serious, look at these,' Nikita snapped, as she scrolled down to multiple images of Ember.

Erron took a sip of the coffee that Warren had graciously provided him with and was disappointed to find it was delicious. 'How long has this guy been watching us?'

'I don't know, but two of them seem to be very active confirmed Oracles . . . some TruthHunter11 and an AlphaKingGetYou9. Typical names for the chronically online.' She rolled her eyes.

Warren turned to face them. 'It appears the password in the notebook wasn't for this website, but a linked one. I'll show you that shortly.'

'So which one is the killer?' Casey asked. He went to watch over Warren's shoulder, and Erron quickly followed suit.

'Based on the amount of vitriol in a lot of these forum threads, I would say AlphaKingGetYou9 is our guy. He's the one that approved my account and had set up the website in the first place. And then there's this . . .' Warren clicked on another link that took them to a sister site where they saw a bootleg version of the new DFS sale.

'Not the time for a cheap sofa, to be fair,' Erron commented.

Warren shook his head, irritated. 'Give me a minute.' He clicked into the menu and found a tab for private auctions, entering the password that had been written in the suspect's notebook. All user information was anonymous, and each separate link required the same password entry to view. He opened the tab for the closed auctions, revealing a file full of images of Willow and Leo after their deaths.

'Jesus,' Erron whispered. 'They're selling bits of them.'

Casey went pale and almost dropped his mug.

'They've been auctioning them as good luck trinkets. They know the power of Fortuna blood,' Nikita said in quiet horror.

The sales were in the hundreds of thousands.

'With that kind of profit, this will never end. It's only a matter of time before they figure out what the rest of us do, and how to market us.' Nikita leant back in her chair, sickened. 'And we were on the money with the name. That Alpha bastard is running the auctions, he's the only named member on here listing the goods.'

'I need you to steel yourself for this,' Warren said, his tone full of trepidation. He navigated back to the original website and entered a thread called *Count Your Lucky Stars.* The most recent entry flashed up in bold letters with bright, eye-catching graphics.

> *EXCLUSIVE AUCTION ANNOUNCED! Our Firefly-Hunter has secured the most prized Green, a senior demi-god of pure fortune. Confirmed as the head of the Green organisation! Premium members can access the auction link at 06.00 Saturday. Sign up now for your chance to own a piece of the most powerful luck on earth!*

A blurry photo of Emrys was next to the announcement. There was a £100 registration fee just to have the privilege of joining the auction.

Nikita knocked over her coffee in a rush to the bathroom to throw up. When there was nothing left inside her, she knelt on the cold floor, staring numbly at the wall. She felt strong arms lift her to her feet and hold her in support.

'We'll find him,' Erron said reassuringly. He picked up a luxury monogrammed flannel from beside the sink and ran it under the warm tap, passing it to Nikita so she could clean her face. 'Don't give up hope yet.'

Erron guided Nikita back to the bedroom once she was ready, realising that Warren had disappeared to the downstairs reception to find supplies to clean the spilled coffee off the expensive cream rug.

Casey was sitting in front of the laptop and scrutinising the screen. 'We will find him, Nikita. We need to save all this information somehow.'

'Take screenshots,' Erron said.

'I don't even know how to save a picture in Paint.' Casey looked panicked.

'Give it here.' Erron slid the laptop across in front of him. 'I forgot you are bloody ancient, Casey-Hartosaurus.' His fingers hovered over the keys and went blank as to how to make it take a screen capture.

'You're not all that young yourself, Grover.' Nikita pulled the laptop away from him and took a load of screenshots, forcing herself back into the mindset of the investigation.

'All right, no need for that. I would have figured it out,' Erron grumbled.

'This guy is about to chop up the man I love and I'm not wasting time letting either of you two play technology catch-up.' Nikita clicked through different photos until she found one that stood out.

It was an image of Erron on the phone through the window of what appeared to be a small shop. 'This was taken around the end of February. Erron, do you remember where you were?'

'Fuck knows. I can't remember anything right now, my brain is scrambled.'

'Please try,' Nikita urged.

Erron chewed his lip and scrunched his brow in thought. He looked at the date of the photo again and checked his phone calendar. 'It would have been around me leaving Apollo Division.'

'I ate your share of the pizza,' Casey said wistfully.

Erron's eyes lit up with some clarity. 'It was when that guy followed me. The suspect, the one we saw on the CCTV.'

Erron spoke fast, realising they could be onto the best lead they had yet.

'Right, can you tell me which route you took? We need to find the location of where this picture was taken. You look like you were standing still here. Can you remember anything about the surroundings?' Nikita zoomed in on the images as best as she could. It was grainy, but she could see the outline of a neon sign in the window and a shelf in the foreground with books and crystals.

Erron thought hard. His memory was muddled with all the nights of insomnia and nightmares; he had been in survival mode for so long, details weren't sticking all that well. 'I . . . I don't know.' He cursed in frustration. 'I wish I could get inside my own head and sort my bloody memories out.'

Nikita bit her tongue impatiently before an idea struck her, her eyes lighting up. 'Can I try something?'

'Anything.' Erron rested his head in his hands.

Nikita pulled two ginger curly wigs from her bag and held one out to him. 'I just remembered I swiped these from the wig shop, just in case they came in handy. It's a long shot, but would you let me wander around in your mind instead, see if I can find the memory?'

Erron raised an eyebrow before conceding. 'Fuck it, go on then.' He took the wig and fitted it over his hair as Nikita did the same with the other one.

'Try and clear your mind. As best as you can,' Nikita instructed as the first fuzzy images were coming through. 'This is trial and error at this point.'

'You mean trial and Erron,' Casey joked.

'Same thing.' Erron shrugged with a wry smile.

Casey watched on, fascinated as they fell silent, syncing their brains. He sipped at his coffee, glancing at the door to see when Warren might return.

Nikita gave Erron prompts with her mind, focusing on the image of him outside the shop window. She closed her eyes and sank deeper into his memories, filtering through random images, snippets of conversations. Erron tried his best to focus, taking himself back to February, but exhaustion was fogging his mind, and he could feel Nikita getting lost in the depths of his consciousness, peering into places he tried to avoid.

'What the hell is going on?' Warren entered the room with several cloths and cleaning solutions.

'Shh. They're doing some kind of mind control,' Casey whispered, pressing a finger to his lips.

Warren made a face of sheer perplexion and began quietly cleaning the coffee stain.

*Stop thinking of anything*, Nikita instructed telepathically. *Let me take full control.*

Erron obeyed, emptying his mind as best as he could. Nikita found herself wandering across broken stepping stones along a vast lake in Erron's mind. Images lingered in the mists above the water, spectral projections of memories past. She pushed herself along, mentally hopping across the stones which changed direction randomly, spindly black trees emerging from the gloom distorting certain memories, repressed within their branches. The mist smelled of whisky and cigarette smoke, and the lake churned with eddies of pitch-dark water. A ghostly figure walked among the trees, across the surface of the lake, a twisted, evil grin upon her face and a blade in her hand.

Everywhere Nikita went, Izzy emerged, haunting every corner of Erron's mind.

Instinctively, Nikita reached out and clasped Erron's hand in the hotel room, tightening her fingers around his. The lake began to swirl and fade, becoming a long corridor full of rooms, flickering lights overhead and the indiscriminate sound of voices from various directions. Nikita glanced in some of the rooms, some were warm, cosy images of Casey, smiling in the sunlight, playing chess in the Sky Pod Bar, eating lunch on top of the BT Tower in Fitzrovia. Nikita was surprised to see herself in some of the images: her first day, the chat they had over the ugly teapot in the café, her determined face as she came to their rescue from Elzifur. The crisp, recent images of Ember's mutilated body flashed over the happier memories, jolting Nikita in her seat.

Other rooms were filled with darkness: the spiteful voice of an older woman; the abusive shouting of a man; images of a small boy hiding in a room full of comic books and cuddly toys, his face bruised and tears drying on his face. More images played out like an old movie projector: Erron, no more than twelve years old, defending his older brother from his mother brandishing a belt; the sharp crack of the buckle against his cheek, followed by the hot sting of blood.

Nikita wanted to rush into the room to comfort his inner child, but reminded herself it was just a memory, a distant vision of events long gone.

*Take me to the week when you left Apollo*, Nikita murmured in her mind, realising she might be wandering the vast depths of Erron's mind forever if he had no focus whatsoever. The images melted away, replaced with a montage of different zones: the Apollo office, Freya Carthage, Casey sipping coffee at his desk. Nikita spun around, following the sound of a phone conversation between Erron and Freya, footsteps on pavement, the smell of spring in the air.

*There!* Nikita found herself in a courtyard, a row of shops to her left. She walked his footsteps, a phone was pressed to her ear, Freya's voice on the other end. She glanced to her right. A drab red door, a neon sign. *Path of Destiny*.

Nikita ripped off the wig, her mind somersaulting back into the hotel room.

'Was that it? You found it?' Erron asked, his tone hopeful.

Nikita leant forward and kissed the scar on his cheek. 'You're a lifesaver.'

Erron's face reddened and he scratched the back of his neck as a distraction. Warren looked up from where he was knelt cleaning the carpet. 'What's going on, then?'

'Path of Destiny, look it up. It's where this suspect took the photo of Erron before he followed him to the park,' Nikita said with renewed enthusiasm.

Casey hurriedly searched the location on his phone and found it in under thirty seconds. 'It's in Pennyfields. That's not that far from the Apollo office.'

'Warren, can you stay here and go through as much as possible on this forum to see if there's any link to this suspect and the shop in Pennyfields?' Nikita asked. 'Or anything at all you think could be useful, a real name, a plan of where he might be, anything.'

Warren nodded. 'Absolutely. I'll call as soon as possible if I find anything.'

'Let's go,' Erron declared, standing up and gulping the last of his drink. 'I'll get us a cab.'

Casey plucked the wig off Erron's head as they exited the room.

# 27

## *Eyes Closed*

FORTY MINUTES LATER THEY WERE in Pennyfields, outside a small spiritual shop with a dull red door. Nikita rushed at it, fully intent on breaking it down if it was locked.

'Nikita, wait!' Erron grabbed her arm. 'You've no idea what he's got in that shop. You might be running into a death trap.'

'He's got my Emrys, that's what he's got,' she said defiantly, trying to pull her arm free.

'And we're going in, but we need to be a bit more tactical. Don't forget this bloke knows we're agents. Not to mention he might have just been a customer in this shop when he took the photo.' Erron pulled her away from the view of the window. 'Casey, can you fly up and have a look around the building to check for any other exits or safer points of entry?'

'Sure.' Casey did as instructed, soaring off the ground in a way that made the flightless agents mildly envious. He returned a few moments later, his wings disturbing the dust and debris around their feet.

'Anything?' Erron asked.

'There's another exit towards the back, looks like a fire door. That's all,' Casey confirmed.

'Shit, what was that?' Erron said at the sound of a loud clatter and the slam of a door.

Casey took to the air again, just in time to see Sam running full-speed away from the rear of the shop. 'He's on the run! I'm going after him!'

Erron and Nikita watched powerlessly as Casey soared off into the distance. His first instinct was to take off on foot in pursuit, but Nikita grabbed his shirtsleeve. 'Please, help me find Emrys. He's got to be here.'

'I don't want Casey getting hurt.' Erron's eyes were wide with fear.

'Please,' Nikita pleaded. 'Emrys might be seriously hurt already.'

Erron tensed up with the conflicting urgency of the situation, eventually folding with the look of sheer desperation on Nikita's face. 'OK, we'll have a quick search here.'

Nikita wasted no time in picking up a rock and smashing the glass door of the shop, stepping through the mess she'd made and making her way to the back. Erron tested the door handle and found it unlocked but didn't care to tell her.

Shattered glass crunched under their feet and the overwhelming smell of incense filled their lungs.

'Here!' Nikita waved Erron over.

She was pushing her weight against a heavy wooden door that wouldn't budge.

'Move back.' Erron waited until she was out of the way and kicked the door as hard as he could. It crashed open, revealing a dark stairwell into a basement.

Dank air rose from the darkness, and Nikita felt around for a light switch, finding none. She felt her way down the steps until her fingers touched a switch at the bottom of the stone stairs. The silence in the room was deafening. She knew when she turned on the light she might be assaulted with an image so distressing she'd never recover, but nevertheless she had to know.

The light flickered on, revealing a dirty basement, a metal cot bed, a computer desk and a set of metal drawers overspilling with clothing. No blood, no missing limbs, no Emrys.

'No,' Nikita mouthed, her heart sinking. 'No, no, *no*,' she repeated.

Erron was talking to her, but she couldn't hear what he was saying, she could only stare at the grimy living quarters, fixed in place, unable to comprehend that they'd got it wrong.

'Agent Wolf!' Erron shouted in her ear, bringing her round from her trance. 'We have to keep going. This is our suspect; this is where he lives!' Erron shook her gently, holding a red paisley bandana he'd found on a hook behind the door as proof. 'He must have a secondary location. Nikita, we have to search this room to find anything that might lead us there.'

She slowly turned to face him, taking in his tired, bloodshot eyes, the smell of smoke, his ruffled, unkempt hair, his gruff Cockney accent bringing her back to reality.

'We don't give up now,' he barked. 'Snap out of it, Wolf, and help me search.'

She did as she was told, going into overdrive ransacking the room for any evidence that might lead her to Emrys.

Erron tipped out the desk drawer and rifled through it. It was a collection of oddments, concert tickets, photos, an old camera, an empty wallet and a baseball cap featuring the number 11 and the initials SP on it. He looked through the photos; they were old Polaroids of the suspect and a couple who seemed to be his parents; smiling, happy family photos. It was the same man on the CCTV, right down to the suspect's pale eye.

Nikita came over to look at what he'd found.

'Just old family photos, a few trinkets,' he said, exasperated.

Nikita picked up the hat and turned it over in her hands, deep in thought. Erron had moved onto a paperwork basket on the desk.

'Well, we've got his name,' he announced, holding up a council tax letter. 'Samuel Rivera.'

* * *

Sam had dived underneath a parked van shortly after losing sight of the row of shops, his heart hammering in terror. Four bins obscured his view of the street, but from his position he could wriggle under a gate at the back of a takeaway and hide under their steps in the basement access recess.

He had no idea what other powers the Fireflies had, whether they could track him with heat vision like a police helicopter, but when he saw the Gold flying after him, he took no chances and went for the hiding place under the stairs.

He dared not peek from his hiding place for some time, thinking any person that could fly likely had the eyes of a hawk and could pick him out a mile off.

There he waited, listening to the sound of traffic, on high alert that at any moment the face of the Gold might appear over the side of the steps. In his hand he gripped a small fishing knife, knowing it wasn't the best weapon, but he'd not thought to pick up anything better when he'd bolted from the shop.

It felt like hours of crouching in the tight cavity under the steps, and Sam's knees were complaining at the cramped space. He checked his watch, it was approaching 5.30 p.m. and he estimated he'd only been there around half an hour. The sun was getting low, casting long shadows in the dimly lit recess, the swell of rush-hour traffic drowning out the sound of his shallow breathing. He wriggled to find some comfort in his position, ending up sitting with his knees against his chin, determined to wait it out at least until it was dark enough to slip away into the shadows. Despite his discomfort and fear, he was buzzing at the first sighting of a Gold with genuine wings. These were nothing like the butterfly wings of the Greens and made him wonder if the Golds were akin to angels of some type, owing to their radiance and white feathers. He hoped he would get the chance to spread the news.

He had no idea when it might be safe to return home, if it ever was. He needed a safe place to lie low. He had no real friends in the city, and no extended family he could reach out to for help. Instead, he made a mental list of where he might be able to hide, avoiding the cameras of public spaces or questions of any authorities. He was confident one of the other Oracles would give him a safe place to stay, but he needed somewhere hidden to contact them from.

After some time he thought of a place where he could potentially go, out of public view and where no one would need ID or a bank card from him to let him stay. A place he wanted to be, somewhere warm, comforting and colourful with a life once lived.

* * *

Casey returned to the shop at 5.45 p.m. having searched high and low for the escaped man. The others looked to him, hopeful.

'I have no idea where he went. I'm so sorry.' Casey looked crestfallen. 'He's fast, I know that. And he's definitely the person I saw at Bonanza.'

'I don't expect he'll be back here any time soon,' Erron said before exhaling heavily.

'Well, time's running out,' Nikita said, her voice stressed. She grabbed a bin bag from a box under the counter. 'Bundle anything that might have details of this guy's secondary location in this bag,' she instructed, while making a beeline for the computer, aggressively taking out the cables and shoving the whole thing in the black sack.

Between them, they collected every bit of paperwork right down to the last Post-it note they could find. Nikita went round and took photos of the whole room, lingering once more over the baseball cap. Something about it was awakening her instinct, and she threw it into the bag with the polaroids.

'We best not stay here in case someone reports the damage to the door. We'll head back to mine; it's not far from here.' Nikita heaved the bag over her shoulder before Casey took it off her with a gracious smile.

'Allow me.' He lifted the bag and gestured for them to go ahead of him up the stairs.

As they passed the counter, Casey noticed a brightly coloured journal lying beside the till. He lowered the bag and picked up the book, flicking it open to the first page.

'Case?' Erron paused, looking back as Casey's face fell.

'It's Ember's journal,' Casey murmured, not taking his eyes off the delicate writing on the pages.

Erron went over to look, gently taking the journal out of Casey's hands. He flicked through the pages and a few pieces of paper fluttered to the ground. Casey picked them up, turning them over to find several printed pictures of the inside of Ember's house, as well as close-ups of her face that hadn't been shared on the Oracles forum.

'He's been in her house.' Casey's stomach turned.

'Sick bastard,' Erron muttered.

Back at Nikita's flat, the three of them frantically sifted through all the paperwork, notebooks and pictures they had grabbed when leaving Sam's shop. The kitchen table was a mess of information that Casey was trying hard to keep in a neat pile.

'It looks like he's only had the place for a short while. Both parents deceased, one previous flat-share address.' Nikita slumped in her chair, her heart pounding with stress.

Casey's phone rang with an incoming call from Warren. He put it on loudspeaker. Warren's voice sounded frantic.

'There's a post that's just come up on the system. The user has made it anonymous, but he's requesting assistance at an address in London as he claims to have been hunted out of his shop by three Fireflies. He's after someone to pick him up,' Warren explained hurriedly.

'What's the address?' Nikita asked loudly.

Warren read out the address in full.

'That's Ember's house!' Casey practically leapt out of his seat.

'Message him, tell him you're on the way with safe transport,' Erron demanded, slinging his coat on. 'We'll go grab him.'

'Will do,' Warren confirmed and hung up.

* * *

Sam hunkered down in Ember's colourful bedroom, the lights turned off, only the glow of his mobile phone highlighting his face. He knew it was foolish to sneak back into the small house, but it was the only place he could think of away from prying eyes, on a semi-secluded street. Something had drawn him back there; he hadn't been able to get Ember out of his mind since he'd first laid eyes on her.

A message from a forum user named *UnWarrented* confirmed he was on his way to pick up Sam and take him to a secure location where he could lie low. Relieved, Sam waited, keeping a keen eye out on the street for a car to pull up.

* * *

'I can't believe he had the audacity to come here,' Casey raged as they approached Ember's address.

Erron pulled them aside before they got within sight of the house.

'Right, this time, we'll cover all exits,' Erron instructed, his mind swimming with fatigue, but the cold evening air and sheer adrenaline keeping him as alert as possible. 'I'll go round the back, you two go through the front door.'

'Are there any other ways he could get out of the house?' Nikita asked.

'Not that I can think of,' Casey confirmed, having been to Ember's several times in the past and knowing the layout of the place well enough.

'Stick close to the wall on approach, in case he's watching out the window. Try and take him by surprise if you can,' Erron said. 'We'll get this bastard.'

They followed Erron down the last stretch of the street, keeping out of view and separating ways as Casey and Nikita climbed the front steps. Erron shuffled around the side of the building and waited at the back door.

'Umm, are we ringing the bell?' Nikita asked, realising the front door was locked.

'Worth a try, he's expecting a lift.' Casey gestured for her to press the bell.

Hearing the doorbell, Sam checked the street again. He saw no car; regardless, he skipped down the stairs, pulling his rucksack onto his shoulders, keen to get away from central London.

His face froze in shock when he opened the door to two Golds.

'Hi.' Casey plastered on a fake smile before swinging a heavy punch into Sam's jaw, knocking him backwards into the hall.

Despite the dizzying crunch, Sam was quick to recover, scrambling back on his feet and making for the back door with Casey and Nikita in hot pursuit. Sam crashed into the alley and was met by Erron, who grabbed him by the straps of his rucksack and slammed him against the wall.

Casey and Nikita burst through the door just as Sam head-butted Erron, who momentarily lost his grip as pain seared through his face, blood pouring from split skin on his nose.

Sam pulled out his small pocket knife and slashed wildly at all three of them, catching Casey on the thigh and sinking the blade into Erron's upper arm, creating enough of a distraction to pull away and run again.

'Catch him!' Erron screamed, wiping the blood out of his eyes and taking off behind Sam.

Sam was quick on his feet, leaping over a wall and landing on a street where a pizza-delivery boy was walking up to a house, his moped nearby with the keys in.

Casey cursed as he saw Sam leap onto the moped without a moment's pause, taking off chaotically into traffic.

'The taxi!' Nikita waved her hand emphatically at a cab parked up. The driver was sat in his seat, bobbing his head to music and completely unaware of the three agents sprinting towards his car.

Erron could see Casey was gearing up to charm his way into the cab but knew they didn't have time for that. He ripped the driver's door open and dragged the man out of his chair, apologising in the process as the cabbie landed on the pavement in shock.

'Get in!' Erron shouted to the others as he started the engine.

Casey obeyed and dutifully put on his seat belt as Nikita clambered into the back of the cab, just as Erron slammed his foot on the accelerator. The radio was on loud enough that they could barely hear each other talk.

Erron fumbled for the volume of the radio, trying to turn it down but knocking the plastic cover of the volume control off. He skidded around a right turn, the moped on the horizon, the back end of the cab swinging violently.

They tore down the A1200, dodging other cars at every opportunity.

A hard left onto Ebenezer Street sent Casey slamming against the passenger door.

The cab revved and bounced over the junction crossing Britannia Walk, closing the gap between them and the suspect on the twist-and-go Piaggio.

'Case, can you try and turn the music off?' Erron shouted over the bass while making a one-handed spin of the wheel as they made a sweeping left turn onto Westland Place.

Casey was too busy being thrown around in the cab to have a moment's stillness to sort the radio. 'Just keep driving!' he yelled. Nikita clung to the armrest, still fighting to get her seat belt on. The 50cc moped was no match for the speed of the cab and Erron's crazed driving, and Sam could see the encroaching vehicle breathing down his neck as he veered right on the mini roundabout onto Nile Street. He opened the throttle as far as it would go before spotting an opportunity to get past some bollards on Jasper Walk.

'Hold on!' Erron stretched his arm across Casey's chest and with the heel of his other hand he spun the steering wheel, so the back of the cab wheeled forward, skidding hard into the moped and sending Sam sliding across the rough pavement. The cab spun full circle, crashing hard into a bollard and crumpling the bonnet like a tin can in a press.

The engine of the cab hissed, and a thin trail of smoke escaped the wrecked front end, the ignition stalled and the radio spluttered to silence. Casey's heart was pounding, and he glanced over at Erron, who had momentarily rested his head back on the seat and closed his eyes to catch his breath. Streaks of blood were starting to dry down his face, his left eye darkening to a blueish purple.

Sam was unconscious on the ground beside them, his arm seemingly broken, the moped in a twisted heap against the wall.

'Where did you learn to drive like that?' Casey said in a mix of horror and awe.

Erron lifted his head and grinned through his beat-up face. His heart skipped at how Casey was looking at him, an expression somewhere between amazement and lust. He reached over and brushed Casey's dishevelled hair off his face. 'Not bad, huh?'

Casey gulped and shook his head slowly. He would have killed in that moment to lean across the centre console and kiss Erron.

Nikita pulled herself up from where she was crumpled in the footwell, rubbing her forehead from the impact.

'You OK back there?' Erron rested his arm over the back of Casey's seat and turned to face her.

'Kinda,' she grumbled. 'Shit, Erron, your arm!' She nodded to where Sam's knife was still protruding from his bicep.

'Oh,' Erron muttered just as he went to pull the blade out.

'No! Leave it in!' Casey stopped him. 'Just for now.'

'If you say so . . . Let's see what this guy has to say.' Erron withdrew his hand and reached for the door handle, suddenly aware of the pain. Nikita hopped out to join him.

Casey watched Erron walk around the back of the cab and kneel down by the suspect, checking his vital signs before coming back to the cab's open window.

'He's out cold,' Erron announced, resting his arm on the edge of the window, his face creasing with concern. 'You OK?'

Casey managed a nod. 'Y-yeah, uh, yes.' He wasn't entirely sure if he was ready to get out of the cab and stand up.

'Good, I'm glad you're not hurt.' Erron gave him a worried half-smile, and without thinking, he leant through the window and kissed him, leaving blood on his lip. It was the briefest of moments, but it cemented the decision that Casey would need a few more moments sitting down. He closed his eyes and subtly tasted Erron's blood, a distinct flavour that lingered on his tongue.

Erron had gone back to where Sam lay on the floor, unmoving. He called back over his shoulder. 'Case, can you see if the engine will turn over?'

Casey gathered his senses. He'd never once learnt to drive in all his decades of life, but he had the wherewithal to know how to turn the key, at least. The engine cranked slowly and after a few turns, fired up with an angry squealing of the fan belt.

Erron and Nikita were dragging the unconscious killer to the back of the cab and wrestling him into the back seat. 'He's not an agent, that much is clear: no wings,' Nikita announced.

'How would he have managed to land a job on Elysion?' Casey asked.

'I guess we will find out when he comes round. We're, what, about half an hour from the Eligos?'

'About that.' Nikita took a moment to think before climbing into the back with the suspect.

'We'll need to take him somewhere secure to question him. The Medusa room is the best bet,' Erron added.

'Will we be able to take him inside? I've never taken a mortal into a liminal zone,' Casey pondered out loud.

'I guess we'll find out.' Erron double-checked the back door of the cab was locked and climbed into the driver's seat. 'If we can't take him in, we'll bring him to the nearest division HQ.'

The cab protested with spluttering and crunching noises the whole way, limping to the Hampstead Grove crossroads before squealing its final mechanical lament. They were lucky that they didn't attract the attention of the police, and Erron avoided major routes where possible.

In the back seat of the cab, Sam was gradually waking up and beginning to groan from his injuries.

* * *

The three Medusa agents had dragged Sam unceremoniously up to their assigned team room and sat him on one of the chairs.

Casey fussed over the knife in Erron's arm, fetching a first-aid kit and trying to inspect how deep the blade had gone without disturbing it. 'We'll have to put a bandage around it until we can get it properly removed.'

'I'm not sitting here with a knife sticking out of me, Case.' Erron grabbed the handle of the blade and winced, pulling it out with one swift motion. He set it down on the table and flicked the blood off his hand, spattering the floor.

'Great, now you're bleeding everywhere.' Casey rolled his eyes and pressed a wad of gauze on Erron's arm.

'Like you're not?' Erron nodded to where Sam had cut Casey's thigh.

'It's barely a scratch.' Casey was more upset his suit trousers had been ruined.

'Well, we've got more important things to deal with right now anyway.' Erron gently removed Casey's hand and nodded towards where Sam was coming round from his concussion.

* * *

Sam awoke fully and immediately reacted to intense pain, where his left wrist was clearly broken. Nikita afforded him no sympathy and began questioning him the moment he was capable of forming sentences. His irritation increased the more questions she threw his way, constantly demanding to know where he was and who they were.

Erron straddled a chair backwards, his glaring face within two feet of the suspect's.

'I swear! I swear I haven't killed anyone!' Sam whimpered, his annoyance giving way to desperation.

Nikita fished inside her bag and pulled out printed copies of Sam from the CCTV they'd found. 'That you?' she asked bluntly.

Sam studied the pictures. 'Who are you people?' he murmured again quietly.

'Your worst bloody nightmares if you don't cooperate,' Nikita spat.

There was a long pause before Sam replied, 'Yes, that's me in the pictures. The girl in the alley, I just found her. I didn't know what to do. I ran. I didn't kill her.'

Nikita produced a bundle of printed screenshots from the Oracles forum and slapped them down in front of him. 'You sure about that? Seems like you've been making an absolute mint selling bits of our friends on the dark web.'

'That's not me. I've not sold anything on there.'

'Then who the fuck is it, *Sam*?' Erron screamed in his face.

Sam was taken aback that they knew his name. 'It's some other guy.' He slumped in the chair, defeated.

'So, you're telling me you aren't this AlphaKingGetYou9?' Nikita raised an eyebrow, unconvinced. 'Even though you've been at the scene of two murders and graphic images of those victims from the scenes feature on these auction pages?'

'No! It's not me. He sent me there. He told me to go to those locations, to prove to me what he's talking about is real. I never saw a second body, just the girl.'

'I don't believe you,' Nikita snapped.

'Look, I've talked to him, sure, but he's too much of an extremist. He set the website up. I only joined a little while back. I'm this guy.' Sam pointed at another username from the printouts. 'I haven't killed or sold anyone.'

'You're TruthHunter11?' Nikita's heart sank.

'He's obviously lying.' Erron grabbed Sam by the chin. 'Tell us where the other victim is. The Welsh bloke, where are you hiding him?'

'I swear to you, I'm not hiding anyone.' Sam pulled his face away.

'Case, can you, y'know, use the Flush or something?' Erron turned to face Casey, who was leaning up against the tea-making station.

'Sure.' Casey went to sit next to Sam and exerted his best Apollo influence, asking again where they might find Emrys, in his sweetest and most reassuring tone.

'*I do not know!*' Sam snapped back, clearly unreceptive to the Apollo Flush.

Nikita checked the time on her phone and noticed she had a voicemail blinking on the screen. She stepped aside to listen to it, surprised to hear D-O-A's measured tone. The message had been there for over five hours.

'Gunther, he keeps saying *nine, nine, nine. Not eleven.* Over and over, I've had nothing else of use. I hope you've found some sense in that by now.'

She held her phone to her chest in thought.

'Eleven,' Nikita whispered to herself, suddenly remembering the baseball cap they'd found in Sam's basement. 'Why eleven? Why TruthHunter11?' she asked Sam.

Sam sighed and looked at the floor. 'It's just stupid, really. My favourite Formula One driver's number.'

'Does he drive for McLaren?' Nikita remembered the Formula 1 collage in the Djinn's tattoo studio on Elysion.

'Uh, no, Sergio Pérez. He was once a McLaren driver, but years ago . . .' Sam looked at her like she was clearly stupid, not knowing these important things about racing teams. Her face went pale when she realised Sam could be innocent. 'The other guy likes the current McLaren team. We talked a bit about it in the general chat. A fair bit of rivalry over it. You know, banter. It's how we got talking.'

Nikita looked up the McLaren team on her phone, a driver with the number 9 leaping out at her with stark realisation. *Nine Nine Nine*, Gunther had said. *Not eleven*. Bile rose in her gut as she looked up at the man that had nothing to do with Emrys's capture, he wasn't AlphaKingGetYou9.

'Who is this guy, then? How do I find him?' Nikita's heart was starting to pound in desperate terror again. 'I need to find him. You must know where he is.'

'I don't, I really don't know. Please, can you just get me to a hospital, or let me go?' Sam winced as his arm moved slightly.

'You're not going anywhere until we find our friend,' Casey said bluntly. 'You might not be the killer, but you're complicit in all this.'

'We need a Nemesis agent; the Flush didn't work,' Erron suggested.

The Nemesis Inferno had its uses, most notably getting confessions out of people. Sam hadn't responded to either the Flush or the *Umbra Noctis*, another anomaly to his Oracle powers.

'We're running out of time.' Nikita pressed her hands to her face, her palms slick with cold sweat.

'I'll go downstairs and see if there are any agents in the library,' Casey offered. 'If not, I'll call Osato.' He rushed out of the room and his footsteps could be heard hurrying downstairs.

'You know, I could just start breaking his fingers, it would be quicker,' Erron suggested.

'You dare touch me and I will knock you out,' Sam spat. 'What is all this anyway? Who are these agents? Are you genetically modified or some shit, some super-humans that have powers like in comic books?' Sam winced as pain shot through his wrist. 'Or are you actually gods or angels or something?'

Nikita pulled up a chair next to Erron and sat down. 'Sam, look, if you aren't the killer, then we need your help to find him. It's really important that you tell us everything you know.'

'I'm not telling you shit until you explain who you are and what right you have to keep me here. Are you working for the government? Are you even human?!' Sam raised his voice. 'I know you're some kind of walking bad news.' He pointed at Erron. 'People die when they go near the Greys. People like my father.'

'Your future isn't looking overly bright either right now.' Erron glared at Sam, summoning the best of his Hades darkness until the room felt cold and unwelcoming, but Sam still didn't react.

'Erron, perhaps it's best you go and help Casey for a few minutes.' Nikita lightly touched Erron's forearm and shot him a pleading look.

He silently agreed and stood up. His whole body was aching, exhaustion eating him alive, the knife wound in his arm throbbing intensely. He picked up the bloodied gauze and pressed it to his arm as he left.

Once he was out of the room, Nikita softened her tone, hoping to coax information out of the man by reasoning with him.

'Sam, no one here is out to get you. The work that we do only affects people that need us in their lives. I'm sorry to hear about your dad, but it would have been his time, and we all face that in the end, myself included.'

'So what you're saying is that my dad was meant to be murdered. It was written in the stars or some shit?' Sam answered coldly.

'Something like that. Look, I know this is confusing and painful, but I really need you to help me find the person that is committing these atrocities,' Nikita said gently, internally battling the desire to shake the suspect within an inch of his life, anything to get the information she needed as quickly as possible.

'It wasn't me. I haven't hurt anyone. If anything, the one called Ember was the most beautiful woman I had ever seen, I actually wanted to get to know her. You've no idea how much it broke me when I realised he got her. I went to her house, as it was all I had left of her. I can't seem to get her off my mind.' He seemed genuinely sad as he spoke.

Nikita grasped onto his words. 'Tell me about your interactions with Ember. Where did you meet? What did you really want from her?' Nikita took out a pen from her pocket and her notebook from her bag, poised ready to write down his answers.

Sam recalled every detail from his encounter with Ember at the café, admitting he'd first broken into her house and taken her journal, not to hurt her, but to learn more about her. 'I know it was creepy, but she was like an angel walking among mortals, I couldn't help myself.'

'So you were romantically interested in her? Wouldn't that have upset your Alpha friend here on the forum? Surely there are rules saying you can't date these people you're advocating dissecting?' Nikita reminded herself to tone down the bitterness in her voice.

'I didn't tell anyone. I didn't exactly expect her to be interested in me. It wouldn't have gone anywhere.' Sam shrugged. 'But she was special. I just hoped she might want to spend time with me if she got to know me.'

'But you posted photos of the group of us to the forum, practically painting a target on her back.'

'Look, I'm not perfect, I just wanted to belong to something, y'know? I've been uploading everything I've learnt about you people. All we want is the truth, but Ember was a complication.'

'Such a complication that she ended up in bits on some despicable version of eBay,' Nikita scoffed.

'I liked her, OK? I wouldn't have hurt her. I wouldn't have hurt any of you. Except maybe that prick that ran me over.' Sam glared towards the door as if anticipating Erron's return.

'When did you last see Ember?' Nikita changed the subject.

Sam exhaled slowly. 'Do I get a lawyer or anything?'

'You got something to hide?' Nikita leant back and folded her arms.

'No, I don't. But my answer will make me sound bad.'

'Just tell me. You're currently in a place no one will ever find you, let alone a lawyer. It's therefore a good idea you stay on my good side.'

Sam agonised for a few moments, almost accepting his fate. 'OK, I last saw Ember on Wednesday. I think it was around early afternoon. I followed her, she didn't know I was there. I just wanted to know what she was doing, who she was seeing, that sort of thing.'

'Where did she go?'

'She went to some kind of private hospital. The Raphael Service or something. It had no public access. She went around the back and was met by a man in a doctor's coat. They both went indoors; they seemed to know each other well enough.'

'The Raphael Sanctuary?' Nikita was concerned that Sam could see through the agency camouflage for liminal zones, and what it meant for the agency in the long run.

'That was it.'

'Can you describe the doctor that met her?'

Sam puffed his cheeks out and searched his memory. 'Average height, scruffy red-tone hair and a short patchy beard. I don't remember much else.'

Nikita was fervently writing the description down when her eyes fell on the pen she was holding. She lifted it up and turned it over. There was a McLaren logo on the lid and a number nine below it. She remembered when she'd borrowed it at the hospital to sketch out the scene where Ember had been found. She glanced back at the description she'd written down, hot realisation rising in her gut.

Casey, Erron and Nemesis agent Dion Laszlo entered the room just as she had stood abruptly.

'It's Jared,' she stated, her eyes wide.

'Hold on, what?' Erron asked, confused.

'We have to get to the Raphael.' Nikita slung her bag over her shoulder and stuffed all the evidence in it haphazardly.

'Oh, thank god. Please, my wrist's broken. I desperately need a doctor,' Sam said, relieved.

'Shut up,' Erron snapped. 'You fucking stabbed me.'

'We'll need to bring him. Dion, can you help?' Nikita asked.

'Of course,' Dion replied.

Erron pulled Nikita aside before she went stampeding out of the library. 'We need transport, that cab's had it.'

Nikita fluttered her short, stumpy wings. She'd be flying nowhere and nor would Erron, and Sam was in no fit state for a long walk. 'Shit,' she cursed.

'I have an idea. I've been dying to do this.' Erron found the Delivermoon app on his phone and dialled 99 on the keypad. He was immediately put through to an operator with faint ice-cream van music in the background.

'Fabulance, what's your emergency?' a bland voice answered.

'One broken wrist, one stab wound, no sprinkles,' Erron replied. 'We need transport from the Eligos.'

'A unit's is on its way,' the operator confirmed.

# 28

## *Crossfire*

THE STREETS WERE DARK AND empty as they waited outside the library, when a familiar sound came racing out of the stillness. Blaring cheerful music and pink flashing lights accompanied the squeal of tyres, as an ice-cream van came full tilt around the corner of Admiral's Walk onto Hampstead Grove.

It pulled up in front of them, the giant plastic 99 Flake on the roof wobbling uncontrollably between the strobing fuchsia beacons as it staggered to a halt.

'Incredible,' Nikita mouthed, shaking her head in disbelief. 'I never knew they could do this.'

'And in three minutes flat.' Casey was impressed. 'I haven't called a Fabulance in decades. I haven't even eaten a Fab lolly in ten years.'

'Who's broken, then?' The ice-cream van driver stuck his head out the driver's side window. He was in his fifties, with a solemn face and thick salt-and-pepper hair.

'We're all getting in.' Erron held up his bloodied gauze and nodded to the back of the van.

'Climb aboard,' the driver instructed, making no effort to assist.

The Medusa agents bundled Sam into the back of the ice-cream van, with Dion bringing up the rear. Once the back doors were shut, Erron banged on the bulkhead for the driver to set off. Within seconds, they were pulling away at speed in the direction of the Raphael. It was a snug ride, with Nikita, Sam and Casey having to sit atop the twin chest freezers and Dion clinging to the counter as they careened around corners.

Erron had shuffled into a sitting position, his back against the Mr Whippy machine, his knees pressed tightly against his chest. He was beginning to feel nauseous, his stomach rolling in harmony with his exhaustion, the pain in his arm being drowned out by his screaming nicotine cravings.

They reached the Raphael just before 11 p.m., Nikita bursting from the door of the van, quickly followed by Casey and Erron.

Dion took Sam away for treatment as the others searched the building for Dr Enleigh.

* * *

Emrys was almost blinded by the overhead light coming on. After so many hours of darkness, he squeezed his eyes shut against the glaring brightness. The last time the light had been on was when Ember was being cut to pieces and her killer had needed to replace the bulb to do so.

'Good news, Mr Taliesin. It's nearly all over for you.' Dr Enleigh walked in wearing full surgical scrubs.

Emrys blinked repeatedly as his eyes adjusted. He couldn't speak as thick tape still covered his mouth. It had been replaced since Dr Enleigh had removed some of his back teeth.

In all the time he'd been captive, he was trying to work out how he'd lost every ounce of his luck, as he'd certainly not had any tattoos, not that he could inflate Dr Enleigh's ego by asking.

Dr Enleigh was busy preparing a small table of tools and steel kidney bowls.

'Now, you'll have to forgive me, I haven't sterilised these since Ember's procedures, but I did run them under a cold tap.' Dr Enleigh spoke through the surgical mask he wore, his back to Emrys as he set up the table. 'Not that you're going to care anyhow.'

Emrys could only think of Nikita. He pictured her face, her bright eyes and warm smile. The touch of her hands, the smell of her skin, the taste of her kiss. He cast his eyes away as Dr Enleigh approached him with a syringe, not wanting the approach of his violent end to erase the images of love in his mind.

'You need professional help, young man. Can't you see what you're doing here? This is ludicrous,' Emrys said calmly.

'You shut the fuck up, old man,' Dr Enleigh spat. 'I don't need to listen to your bullshit.'

'This needs to stop, Jared,' Emrys spoke softly, his heart pounding under his calm demeanour. 'Think about what you're doing.'

Dr Enleigh's voice was cold, devoid of emotion. 'You don't understand. A real man takes what he wants, he answers to no one. People like you are stuck in servitude to the system. But not me. By tomorrow night I will have made enough money off your body that I can leave this fucking agency and live it up somewhere amazing. I'll be immortal and minted, and you'll be nothing but a corpse.'

Emrys inhaled slowly through his nose, closing his eyes as he did so. 'The agency will find you. And there are worse things to be than a corpse when they do.'

'You're apparently one of the most powerful men in this agency and yet, here you are, your life nearly ended by a simple cup of tea.' Dr Enleigh raised his eyebrow and snorted.

Emrys remembered the drink Jared had made him. It had tasted fine, but he didn't remember much afterwards.

'I can't stand men like you, no ambition to be anything more in your pathetic lives,' the deranged doctor continued.

'I think you have missed the point of living, if money and power is all you care about,' Emrys replied, his voice steady despite the fear. 'And why Ember? She was the kindest soul you could meet. She had ambition, dreams ... she was full of life.'

'You're kidding me, right? I gave her the opportunity of a lifetime, to be with a real man, and she had the audacity to turn me down! Like she could have done any better. So I showed her exactly what happens to bitches that ignore nice guys like me,' Dr Enleigh spat.

'Nobody deserves to die because they reject you!' Emrys raised his voice, a surge of anger burning through his core. 'Ember was a good soul! She didn't deserve this, none of them did!' Tears prickled in his eyes, and he blinked them away. He took a deep breath and steadied his racing heart. 'The world just doesn't work that way. You don't always get what you want. You talk about respect and yet you don't know the meaning of the word.'

'I am done discussing this!' Dr Enleigh screamed, picking up a scalpel in a rage, sending other tools clattering to the ground. His eyes bulged and his face reddened as he pressed the blade to Emrys's forearm, taking sections of skin away and dropping them into a bowl. Emrys breathed fast and shallow through the pain, trying not to scream, trying to be as strong as Ember had been, keeping his eyes closed and focusing on thoughts of Nikita for as long as he could before he felt the life slipping away from him.

* * *

Nikita could tell she was close; everything was starting to slide into place in her mind. All the time they had been focusing on Sam, the real murderer was enjoying free rein, pretending to be part of their team, sabotaging their efforts any chance he got.

At the reception, a lanky nurse with a pierced eyebrow took one look at Erron's beaten and bloodied face and handed him a clipboard. 'Sign in, please,' he said. 'Name, division and Bakeday – you know the drill.'

Erron slid the clipboard back across the counter. 'I'm not here for treatment. We're looking for a member of staff, it's urgent.'

The nurse looked him up and down. 'You, uh, sure you don't want to get looked at?'

'Jared Enleigh, he's one of your surgeons. Can you tell us where to find him?' Nikita interrupted.

The nurse turned his head away from Erron and tapped something on his computer. 'Dr Enleigh isn't working this evening. Can I take a message?'

Casey leant on the counter and gave his most charming smile. 'This is very urgent. We need Jared's home address and access to his locker if he has one.'

'I appreciate your request, but we can't do that.' The nurse was taken aback.

Erron flipped the top of his Medusa wallet and showed the nurse his badge. 'It wasn't a request. Fetch someone who will have been working with him on his last shift and bring up his home address now.'

The nurse, confused, pressed a buzzer to summon assistance.

A fresh-faced woman in surgical scrubs appeared within minutes. 'Can I help you?' she asked in a firm tone.

'We're from the Medusa Division. We need to speak with one of your team to locate Dr Jared Enleigh as a matter of urgency,' Nikita explained.

'For what purpose?' The surgeon furrowed her brow.

'We have strong evidence to suggest he may be responsible for three murders,' Nikita explained quickly. 'And likely another in a matter of hours.'

The surgeon's eyes widened in shock. 'He was here about an hour or so ago. He did some voluntary overtime to sort some old patient files, as far as I am aware he must have gone home. You can search the hospital and his locker, but I can't legally release his home address details without direct authority from the Archangel Chief Consultant. And that would need to be requested by a division head at least,' the surgeon explained apologetically.

'That's bullshit! Someone's life is at stake here,' Nikita raged.

Casey raised his hand in a pacifying gesture. 'Where was Dr Enleigh sorting the files? Can you at least tell us that whilst we get hold of someone?' he asked, already having his phone out and scrolling for Osato's number.

'There's some storage rooms on the lower-ground floor.'

Casey nodded in appreciation, the phone pressed to his ear and dialling. He was one of the very privileged few to have

Osato's personal mobile number and a better chance of her picking up so close to midnight.

'I'm going to the storerooms,' Nikita announced. 'Erron, can you and Casey sort getting the high-and-mighty chief's say-so for Jared's details and call me once you have his address? I need to see if this bastard has been hiding anything down there that will help us find Emrys.'

'Wait a moment.' Erron caught her wrist to stop her running off. 'We ought to come with you, just in case he's still here. Just let us get Osato on the phone.'

'He's not stupid enough to do anything on hospital grounds. Besides, if I run into him he has no idea we're looking for him. I'll make an excuse and text you.' Nikita was already jogging away.

In a moment of conflict, Erron made the decision to follow her, telling Casey not to go to any address without them.

Casey gave him the thumbs-up as he had just managed to get Osato on the phone and was explaining the urgent situation to her.

Nikita led the way, light-footed on the stairs and covering ground quickly and silently. Erron wasn't quite as graceful as he tried to catch up, his lack of sleep was impairing his balance and spatial awareness somewhat, his left eye swollen enough to affect his vision in the dim emergency lighting. The last flight of stairs was in pitch black, and they looked around for a switch before descending. All they found was another emergency light which pooled in the stairwell and didn't seem to extend into the long hall at the bottom. It was better than nothing, and they pressed on, conscious that time was of the essence and hoping to find a light switch in the hall.

They reached the corridor where they'd last seen Dr Enleigh in the storerooms and Nikita skidded to a halt, her keen ears listening for any telltale sound that there might be anyone skulking in the dark.

Faint footsteps echoed in the gloom, accompanied by the sound of heavy breathing. Nikita gripped Erron's arm as they stood poised in silence.

An overhead light flickered on, illuminating the hall and momentarily blinding them, revealing Dr Enleigh with his hand on a light switch several metres away.

'Nikita?' he said, his voice masking surprise. 'What are you doing back down here?'

'An odd place for surgery, Jared?' Nikita ignored his question and nodded towards his bloodied scrubs. Her heart was in her mouth, knowing full well who the blood must belong to, but doing everything in her power to remain calm.

He looked down at himself then back at the two Medusa agents. His eyes narrowed with realisation as he flicked the light switch off again, immediately disappearing into the darkness.

'Shit!' Nikita hissed, bolting forward, but quickly losing her footing on the steps and tumbling down the last three. She yelped with pain as she hit the floor, twisting her ankle and landing hard on her knee.

She felt hands grab her blindly, helping her to her feet. 'Stay quiet,' Erron whispered. 'He's in one of these rooms. We just need to find that light switch.'

They felt along the walls, moving as fast as they dared, eventually finding the switch Dr Enleigh had pressed, but finding it unresponsive. 'He's cut the power. There's probably a breaker down here and he's turned it off.' Erron was audibly angry.

He rummaged in his pockets for his phone, finding it lifeless. 'Is your phone working?'

Nikita reached for hers. The battery was below 10 per cent, but the screen lit up.

Erron told her to stay put as he checked inside the first room, taking her phone with him. Nikita watched the dull glow of her screen move further into the room as she gripped the door frame, breathing as silently as she could.

The phone light disappeared behind a solid object and Nikita lost all sense of depth perception in the darkness. She wanted to call out to Erron but felt vulnerable giving away her position.

There was a dull thud in the gloom and the sound of an object skidding across the floor. Nikita held her breath, then peered inside the pitch-black room. The glow of her phone screen lay face down on the floor under an office chair.

'Erron?' she whispered, tentatively stepping across the threshold.

There was no answer, and she repeated his name a little louder.

After a long silence, panic seeped into her bones and the palms of her hands grew clammy with sweat. 'Erron!' she yelled into the darkness, waiting for a response and praying Dr Enleigh was just as blind in the dark as she was.

Nikita dropped to the floor and felt her way into the room, shuffling as silently as she could, methodical in her search despite fear pulling at her instincts to flail around in panic. The phone screen had turned off, but she was heading in its direction to see if she could give herself the tiny advantage of its light.

She had to find Dr Enleigh. It was her only chance to get Emrys back. She refused to believe he was dead.

'Erron, where are you?' Nikita's whisper carried through the silence. She'd made her way to a row of scattered chairs. 'Please, please answer me.'

Her desperate hands swept over the dirty floor, the dust and grime clinging to her sweating palms. Like a firefly in the dead of night, her phone lit up, buzzing with an incoming call. It was about eight feet away from her and she scrambled over to it, grabbing it before the call ended. It was Casey.

'Casey!' she exclaimed quietly as she answered.

'Did you find anyth—' His voice crackled at the end of the line before the last of the phone battery gave out.

Nikita screamed internally, slamming the phone to the floor and cracking the screen. She shuffled backwards, remembering that the phone had skidded to the left of a large object, and Erron must have gone behind it. Breathing slowly, she kept as silent as possible. A long minute passed, and she found the edge of a tall cabinet, pulling her body around the side of it as terror gripped her.

Her fingers brushed a lifeless hand on the floor. Instinctively, she recoiled and suppressed a scream, before reaching out to find the hand once more, needing to know who it was.

Crawling forward, her hands tentatively felt a neck and chest, her fingertips brushing over the face, finding rough stubble, a swollen left eye and a mop of scruffy hair. It was definitely Erron.

# 29

## *Bloodshot*

'THANK YOU.' CASEY DIPPED HIS head politely to the nurse who finally relinquished Dr Enleigh's details following the appropriate authority.

He tried redialling Nikita's number, thinking they had been disconnected due to lack of signal. The call went directly to voicemail.

'Uh, Nikita, not sure if you'll get this but you both can head back up. I have the address and I'm being shown Jared's locker. I'll come find you shortly if you're not back in a bit,' he said after the beep.

Casey was handed a key and taken to a locker room in the staff quarters of the hospital. The nurse that accompanied him leant against the door frame and watched as Casey carefully opened Jared's locker, wearing latex gloves as he did so.

A bundle of robes with a matching mask were neatly folded on top of a thick black book, looking identical to those Djinn wore. The inside of the locker was plastered in various stickers of sports teams, cars and topless women. Casey pulled the book out and gently opened the front page. Hundreds of entries of bids, dates and payments were neatly listed against various reference numbers, each with an object listing, such as blood, finger, eyeball.

'Oh my . . .' Casey murmured. He tucked the book under his arm and closed the locker, pocketing the key. 'Can you show me to the stairwell from here? I need to get downstairs.'

The nurse gestured for Casey to follow.

* * *

Nikita clutched Erron's hand, shaking him roughly, trying desperately to wake him. In the darkness she couldn't see or hear any sign of life but had found a seeping patch of blood on the back of his head.

'No, no, no . . .' She leant over and wrapped her arms around him, her silent tears falling into his hair. 'You can't leave me here,' she whispered through sobs.

He didn't respond. She sat up, shaking him by the shoulders one last time before collapsing back against the cabinet in defeat.

She didn't have time to indulge in grief or self-pity; she still had to find Emrys. She gave Erron's hand one last squeeze and climbed to her feet, wiping the tears from her eyes.

A noise in the dark alerted her to the corner of the room. It was someone shifting their weight, the subtle shushing of surgical scrubs. Dr Enleigh was in the dark, waiting for her, enjoying the sound of her despair.

Her internal rage drowned out her fear; she wouldn't let him win. She edged towards the sound, keeping her footsteps silent, her heart rate steady, breathing slowly through pursed lips.

She could smell him. The closer she got, the reek of blood and sweat oozed from the darkness. Another scent suddenly became pungent, the fumes of potent alcohol overwhelming her, just before a glass shattered a few feet to her left. Instinctively, she ducked, shielding her head. Another object sailed past her, shattering into thousands of shards on the floor. Her nose burned with the unknown solvent, just as a bright flash ten feet away caught her off guard.

She caught a glimpse of Dr Enleigh holding a lit match, a crazed and gleeful look in his eyes. It didn't take her long to realise he was planning to set the whole place alight, with both of them inside. With a flick of his wrist, the match tumbled through the air and landed by Nikita's feet, bursting into a hot explosion of blue-tinged flames and sending her flailing backwards.

'Burn in hell, bitch!' he spat as he ducked towards the door, the flames galloping around the room, feeding off the ethanol that he had thrown around. He'd left with several glass bottles, seemingly intent on setting the whole lower floor on fire.

Nikita coughed, pressing her sleeve to her mouth and nose, the fire building as stacks of files and paper towels caught ablaze. Wasting no time, she scanned around the objects closest to her for a weapon, the only useful thing within reach was a long pair of scissors.

She glanced back to where Erron lay, faced with a dilemma: she could either get to him before the fire spread further, but she would lose Dr Enleigh in the process, and with him, Emrys. She screamed with rage, knowing she had to choose the impossible. She ran after Dr Enleigh, the scissors tight in her hand, leaping over the low blue flames of the ethanol as it crawled towards the door.

He was splashing the ethanol around the hall before ducking into another room when Nikita's vision cleared. She ran after him, having no regard for her safety, and threw herself against his knees in a low rugby tackle.

He crumpled, the last bottle of ethanol rolling out of his grasp. His boot found her face and he kicked hard, sending her skidding back on the smooth floor, blood spraying from her nose.

Her vision crackled with the shock, but her adrenaline lifted her out of the pain, and she climbed to her feet, thrusting the scissors into his thigh as he rose from the floor. She had the sense to duck as he swung for her and using her full weight, she wrestled him down again, biting and slapping and punching as furiously as she could, aiming for his eyes and throat like an enraged animal.

Dr Enleigh grabbed her by the neck and slammed her over to the side, quickly jumping up and gathering a fistful of her hair. 'I told you to burn in hell,' he seethed, proceeding to drag her into another room and throwing her against the far wall before kicking her hard in the stomach.

She doubled over, winded. Dr Enleigh rained punches to the sides of her head until she passed out.

The heat of the flames brought her round again, and through blurred vision, she could see Dr Enleigh emptying more bottles of ethanol from a nearby cupboard all around the work surfaces and cabinets. He stacked old files among the puddles and lit another match. Blue flames danced hypnotically in the shadows of the room, drawing her gaze.

He knelt down in front of her, a full bottle in his hand. 'You're no match for me, little girl,' he hissed as he poured the liquid slowly over her.

Nikita's vision clarified just enough to see Erron in the doorway, backlit by the flames, a stethoscope in his hands and pure thunder in his bloodshot eyes.

He lunged forward, wrapping the stethoscope tube around Dr Enleigh's neck, twisting it tight. They fell backwards, the writhing surgeon clawing at his throat, his face turning purple. Erron held fast, teeth clenched in silent fury until Dr Enleigh's body went limp.

The overhead lights flickered on in a blinding parade of luminescence, and with them, the sprinkler system instantly kicked in. With a huge sigh of relief, Erron pushed the Archangel's body off himself and shuffled back to the doorway to lean on the frame. Exhausted, he tilted his face back to feel the cold water running over him, soothing patches of burnt skin on his neck. His agency ear cuff was embedded in his blistered and charred ear, the heat having turned the silver dark. He tried to remove it, but it was welded in place, his scorched fingers struggling to free it.

'Holy shit,' Casey exclaimed as he entered the room, seeing the carnage.

He looked down at Erron and immediately knelt down to check if he was OK.

'I'm fine, Case,' Erron wheezed with a half-smile, thinking Casey looked like an angel in the bright hospital lights, his long hair straggly and wet against his face. 'Check her.' He waved a limp arm towards Nikita.

Casey clasped Erron's face in his hands and kissed the top of his head. 'OK. Stay there.'

'Fucked if I can move right now.' Erron let out a weak laugh.

Nikita was trying to sit up straight, but Casey caught her as she slid to one side.

The reception nurse appeared, his eyes wide at the scene. He pressed a button on his radio, calling for emergency assistance.

'Emrys, I have to find Emrys,' Nikita rasped, her bloodied hands gripping Casey's arms.

'You need medical attention.' Casey tried to keep her still, but she was filled with the same hot determination as before.

Pushing through the pain, she pulled herself to her feet and stumbled into the corridor. The fire had all but died, the hall slick with water.

'I've got Jared's address. We'll find Emrys.' Casey followed her out the room.

'Emrys's here, I know it,' Nikita slurred, clutching her stomach as she staggered to the next room. The doors were locked, and there was no time to find a key.

Casey watched momentarily as she slammed her weight against the door repeatedly before telling her to move out of the way.

With an almighty kick, Casey sent the door crashing inwards, revealing another storeroom, with a gurney in the centre of the floor. Upon it, Emrys lay, or what was left of him.

Nikita stood in horror for a second, her pain fading away at the sight and being replaced by a heaviness in the pit of her stomach. She stumbled to the gurney and reached out to touch Emrys's face.

He was missing his right leg below the knee, which had been tied off with a crude tourniquet, his wings gone, his arms and chest were missing sections of skin and a tray beside the gurney contained four molars. Bloodied tools lay on a trolley beside him; a plastic tub filled with bags of blood sat below the gurney. The sprinklers persisted, beads of water trickling off Emrys's body and pooling underneath him, tainted crimson.

Nikita let out a guttural cry. Casey caught her before she fell, and she rested her head on his chest, completely defeated. 'I was too late,' she whispered, her voice breaking with despair.

'Rocket?' A rasping tone split the silence between her wails.

Nikita turned back to Emrys, seeing he had one eye open, looking right at her.

'You're alive!' she screamed, a menagerie of emotions welling up and tumbling over each other in her gut.

'Just lucky, I guess.' He tried to crack a smile, his voice barely a whisper.

'Can we get some help in here?' Casey shouted through the open door, just as a medical crash team were arriving and sloshing through the flooded halls.

The team immediately set about transferring Emrys to a stretcher to take him upstairs for emergency surgery.

'We'll send another team for you and your friend in the other room,' a medic explained to Nikita. 'Stay put, they won't be long.'

'Will he survive?' Nikita asked quietly, her hand brushing over Emrys's arm as they wheeled him past.

'I can't promise anything,' the medic said sincerely.

The sprinkler system eased, decreasing to a slow drip as the pipes emptied.

Once the emergency team had gone, Casey helped Nikita back to where Erron was leaning against the doorway. He was shakily trying to light a cigarette on the last flickers of a dying fire from a paper bin next to him.

'Bastard,' Erron muttered as the flames died before his cigarette could light.

'Maybe not a good idea.' Nikita took the cigarette out of his hand. She folded herself against him in a tight hug. 'I'm so sorry I couldn't save you. I thought you were gone.'

Erron wrapped one arm around her. 'It's fine, I don't blame you.'

'You saved my life.'

''S'least I could do.' He let go as she pulled away.

They looked over at Dr Enleigh. 'Is he dead?' Casey asked.

'I dunno.' Erron shrugged. 'He felt pretty dead, but he could just be really good at sleeping.'

Casey went to check. 'He's breathing. Unfortunately.'

'Ah well, I'm not perfect,' Erron replied.

'He can face Osato's wrath.' Nikita glared at the unconscious killer. 'Though if I had my way, he wouldn't leave this room alive.'

Casey joined them on the floor, looking over their injuries. 'I can't leave you two for two minutes, can I?' he tried to joke, though worry began to catch in his tone.

Erron lolled his head towards Casey and smiled softly. 'You got here just in time, didn't you?' He opened his hand on his lap.

Casey gripped Erron's hand, lifting it up to kiss it. 'You need to stop getting yourself into these situations.'

'Well, if I didn't, I wouldn't get my knight in shining armour turning up to rescue me, would I?' With his free hand, Erron fished around in his pocket for a flat lollipop and pulled the wrapper off with his teeth. He murmured softly as the sugar hit his palate.

'Haven't you had enough sweets by now?' Nikita asked.

'I haven't slept in nearly three days. I really need this.' He coughed. 'Plus, you won't let me have that.' He pointed at the cigarette she'd confiscated from him.

'You can have one when we're not surrounded by solvent,' Nikita chided.

'Spoilsport,' Erron muttered.

# 30

## *Outrunning Karma*

OSATO M'RAYA TURNED UP AT the Raphael an hour after being notified that the killer had been detained. With both Sam and Jared Enleigh in custody at the hospital, she was keen to iron out the facts with her team. She was more than a little shocked at the state of them, with both Nikita and Erron having suffered significant burns, bruises, cuts and minor smoke inhalation.

As her injuries were being seen to, Nikita gave Osato the rundown of everything she knew about Sam, and how she'd found out Dr Enleigh was behind the murders.

'So, they can see agents, then?' Osato picked up on, her face concerned.

'Yes,' Nikita confirmed, wincing as a laceration on her cheek was treated with antiseptic solution.

'I'll need to speak with this Sam, to get to the bottom of who these Oracles are and what long-term threat they pose to the agency.' Osato was already going through a host of outcomes in her head. After some thought, she sent a message to one of her team to lock down the shop in Pennyfields and ensure all its overheads were covered by the agency for the foreseeable.

Around 3 a.m., the surgical team emerged to inform them that Emrys had pulled through but would need extensive treatment to recover.

Nikita slumped in relief against Casey, grateful tears streaming down her bloodied cheeks. Across the room in a hospital bed, Erron was oblivious to his wounds being treated, passed out from the exhaustion of being awake since Thursday, carried along by the over-consumption of gummy bears.

* * *

Osato M'Raya didn't hang around in bringing Jared Enleigh to trial. Her Medusa agents, led by Nikita, had put together all the evidence in less than a week, and Osato summoned all the relevant people to the Hall of the Fates on Elysion.

The Medusa team stood outside the great hall, taking a moment to gather their thoughts before heading inside.

The outer area was built to emulate a scaled-down version of the Colosseum of Ancient Rome, and though smaller, was no less impressive. The archways were clean, sparkling marble with no sign of ruin. An immaculate circular lawn of lunar moss surrounded the building, glittering pathways of polished stone weaving through it to the various entrance ways along the ground floor. Each path was lit with inset lamps, adding an ethereal glow to the landscaping.

Guarding the lawn were ten giant carved stone effigies of people in a half-circle, nine holding above them one of the planets, the tenth displaying the sun in the centre.

'Last time we were here I never really got a chance to take in the size of this place,' Nikita said with amazement. 'Those statues are massive.'

'Those are meant to be the Fates,' Casey replied.

'Actual size?' Nikita asked, staring up at the twelve-foot-high statues.

'No one knows.'

'If they are that tall it will be nice for Casey to know how I feel standing next to him,' Erron said wryly.

'You're about an inch taller than me, so there's that,' Nikita observed.

'Shall we get this over with?' Casey said quietly, before gesturing towards the main path.

'We best had.' Nikita shifted the weight of her bag on her shoulder and led the way towards the impressive building. 'You going to be OK, Grover?'

Erron hung back slightly as they walked. 'Yeah, it's just ... not my favourite place.' His mind went back to the huge evidence screens showing the graphic images of him, when Izobella Cain had been on trial.

The inside of the hall was equally striking, set out like a gladiatorial arena with rows of tiered public gallery seats under the stars of the Elysion dome. In what would have been the sand of the arena floor, stood a court bench in front of a large circular metal grate, deep set into the glossy marble floor. Large free-standing screens were set up beside the bench, displaying the infamous colourful rolling screensaver from a Windows 95 PC. Two sets of stone seating were situated across from the bench: one set for the jury, the other for those giving evidence.

The seats were starting to fill up as agents from every division and bosses from around the world converged to witness the trial of the Butterfly Catcher. The three Medusa agents stood in the arched halls that ran around the circumference of the main atrium, the echoes of low voices and footsteps drifting along on the warm breeze.

Nikita's stomach turned slightly at the sheer volume of people arriving. All of them would be listening to her present her evidence against Dr Enleigh. 'This all seems a bit much,' she said quietly.

'You'll be fine.' Erron smiled at her. 'If I can do it, you definitely can. This trial wouldn't be happening if it wasn't for you.'

Nikita nodded, grateful. 'I can't imagine the courage you needed when you were last here.'

'I just focused on getting my words right so it could be over. That's all you have to do,' Erron said.

Casey gently touched Nikita's arm. 'Do it for Emrys.'

She nodded firmly, just as Osato met them in the hall. She was wearing a very formal red robe that wouldn't have looked out of place in the Roman senate. Her wings blazed behind her, the tips of the longest feathers leaving a trail of dancing embers over the white marble floor.

The Nemesis boss looked them over, glad they had all seen the email requesting they wore smart suits for the occasion. 'You'll need these as you are all taking the stand to give evidence. You know the drill.' She handed them each a black piece of cloth that was somewhere between a cloak and a long shawl, a gold agency pin at the collar bearing all four division symbols. 'We're representing the World Court today.'

Both Nikita and Erron's new wings were almost fully grown, and Nikita was still getting the hang of manoeuvring them when getting dressed or going through narrow doorways. Casey helped her with the court shawl before putting on his own.

Osato handed them each a copy of their own statements. 'We have pre-installed images of your key evidence, and they will be displayed on the screen. Just make sure you follow the numbering system in your statement, so it correlates. Answer any questions truthfully and to the point.'

'Are there solicitors or anything?' Nikita asked.

'No, at this stage this is a formality. Jared Enleigh is guilty, it is just down to the jury to review the evidence and reach one of the sentencing options based on the testimonies given.' Osato lowered her voice and leant closer. 'Between the four of us, I am moving for Obliteration, but a panel needs to decide. It's tradition, the World Court jury are required to reach a unanimous decision.'

An hour later, the trial was underway, and Dr Enleigh was brought in to stand on a caged plinth next to the witness box. He was dressed in a ceremonial grey robe and shackled to the plinth, his expression vacant.

Osato sat in the judge's seat, flanked by two other Nemesis senior agents, the jury made up of twelve international division leaders. The gallery was deathly silent as Casey was called as the first witness, having spent the least amount of time with Dr Enleigh and the Medusa team, and giving only limited evidence when questioned.

Nikita admired how eloquent he was, his clear but soft voice carrying through the atrium, the way he came across as a deeply honest and sincere witness. His personal statement paying tribute to Ember Songfire stirred more than a few tears among the agents present. Nikita felt a lump in her throat as he recounted his friendship with her, the passion behind his words as he directly addressed Dr Enleigh on the plinth.

'You stole a brightness in my world that can't be replaced.' Casey paused, controlling his emotions and maintaining eye contact with the defendant. 'Ember was a friend to so many, but she was so much more. She was the first warmth of spring, she was life . . . she was joy . . . she was peace. Her spirit will live on in all of us.' Casey's voice caught and he hastily wiped a tear away with the back of his hand.

He tried to read on, but his words couldn't pass the tightness in his throat.

'Thank you, Agent Hart,' Osato said gently. 'You may step down.'

Casey nodded, though anger bubbled up inside him – he screwed up his notes and pointed a finger at Jared. 'You looked us in the eye and said you found her in that courtyard. You said you tried to save her, but you knew, you damn well *knew*, that you'd watched her die! You're a despicable monster!' He raised his voice until it boomed across the area, jabbing his finger in the air emphatically. 'You're a fucking doctor, Jared, and you forgot our sacred fucking oath. *First do no harm!*'

A Nemesis agent gently ushered Casey back to the panel of witnesses once he'd said his piece.

'I'm proud of you,' Erron whispered, resting his hand on Casey's back.

Osato's voiced echoed across the amphitheatre. 'I call to the stand, Apollo Division Agent Nikita Wolf.'

Nikita's cosmic satsuma reset itself briefly as she stood, forcing herself to walk slowly towards the witness stand, to mask her nerves. She took a deep breath and closed her eyes, picturing Emrys how she'd found him in Dr Enleigh's torture chamber.

'Agent Wolf, please introduce yourself and submit your opening statement,' Osato instructed.

Nikita ruffled her notes and steadied her breathing. 'My name is Nikita Wolf, and I am one of the investigators leading this case for the newly formed Medusa Division. The evidence I am about to provide will support the finding of guilt against the defendant, Jared Enleigh.' Her pulse slowed, and the confidence started to swell within her as she looked around at the faces of the crowd. Each of them listening intently to her voice. She glanced over at her friends on the witness benches. Erron gave a subtle yet encouraging thumbs-up.

'I will begin with forensic evidence gained from the first two victims, Willow Madison and Leo Romano. Both had unusually extended neck bones and damage suggesting they were garrotted from above, using their body weight against them.' Nikita turned to the bench and requested the first slide, showing the X-rays taken from the victims. 'When compared to the CCTV footage of both crime scenes, there is a distinctive glare around the time of death. Taking into consideration the position of the sun at the time of day Willow was killed, and the streetlighting at the second location, it can be surmised that the flash of light is actually the wings of an Archangel, lifting his victim off the floor sharply with the garrotte.'

Murmurs swelled among the crowd as both segments of footage were shown, slowed down for the distinctive glare that flashed up just outside of direct sight.

'Moving on to the method of removing the victims' Fortuna powers.' Nikita requested an evidence bag of the inks from the tattoo studio be handed to the jury. 'Jared had discovered that Archangel plasma, the synthetic stardust given to reignite the blood of Archangels, had a cancelling effect on the powers of all other agents for a temporary period of time. He abused his position in the hospital to obtain this plasma and had started working for a tattoo business here on Elysion, under the alias Djinn, using these compounds in the tattoos of his victims. We believe he discovered the effects of this accidentally and used this to his advantage, though the defendant has made no comment to this respect.'

The jurors were passing the inks around in an evidence bag, inspecting the names on the labels.

'We also know, in the case of Fortuna Division head, Emrys Taliesin, Jared spiked a cup of tea with a heavy dose of this plasma, and it was found to have the same effect.' Nikita could feel the anger rising in her, unable to erase the image of Emrys lying helpless on the gurney in a pool of blood. She went through the details of how they had established the effects of the plasma in a controlled setting, and their investigation over where it was sourced and how Jared had accessed it so readily.

'Jared's motive comes down to two things,' Nikita said clearly. 'He was angry at the agency for denying him a role that gave him the same powers as his victims, and his jealousy festered, manifesting with the murders of agents who he felt deserved to die due to their privilege. As can be seen in the pages of this journal found by Agent Hart in Jared's locker at the Raphael Sanctuary.' Nikita requested the slideshow of the journal, with several pages of text where Jared had rambled about his manifesto for ending the lives of agents he envied. 'What's more disturbing is this entry, detailing how he planned the murder of Ember Songfire based on her rejection of his request for a date.' The slide skipped ahead to an entry of the journal in frantic writing, angry words splattered across two pages, and the plans to end Ember's life spelled out clearly. 'For the apparent crime of saying no, Agent Songfire paid the ultimate price. An all-too-common occurrence in the mortal world, but not here. It begs the question, how a monster like Jared Enleigh made it into the agency at all. But allegedly, the Fates can't dictate our destiny after death, or who people might become,' Nikita said firmly.

'His secondary motivator was money. The Medusa team have calculated that Jared made in excess of a hundred and eleven thousand pounds selling trophies of his victims on a dark website of devout followers who believed him to be what they referred to as an Oracle, a mortal that could identify agents by their aura. We are currently investigating the extent of this forum and are attempting to recover the items that have been sold.'

Nikita turned some pages in her notes, conscious of the silence in the amphitheatre, all eyes fixed on her. 'Jared has shown the development of a serial killer right from the start. His disturbing manifesto, taking a position of trust, his victim selection becoming more specific and personal. With Willow and Leo, he had to work fast, as the moment they died, a blind card with Hades Division was generated, giving him very little time to take his souvenirs,' Nikita went on to explain. 'So, he changed his method when he needed to keep his victims alive for longer. By this point, the money he was making encouraged him to harvest more trophies. Given the opportunity, he may never have stopped. Choosing a convenient place within the hospital to hide his victims, it made for a perfect ruse, allowing him to come up with a plausible excuse for them to be there at the point of death.'

Photo slides of the hospital storage rooms were shown, right down to the last spatters of blood among the charred files and sprinkler-soaked floors.

Nikita had moved on to explaining how they'd tracked him down, up until the point of reaching the hospital, before she rested her case.

'Thank you, Agent Wolf. As our lead investigator for the Medusa Division, we'll open the floor to our jury for questioning,' Osato said, nodding towards the expert jury.

'Did she just say Nikita was the lead investigator?' Erron sat forward, his face crumpled into a frown.

Casey stifled a laugh. 'I'm sure they meant *one of* the lead investigators. Obviously, they haven't heard your evidence yet and marvelled at your brilliance.'

Erron shot him a disgruntled look. 'You absolute spanner.'

Nikita was handling the questioning incredibly well. She knew her stuff and had brushed up on her notes prior to the trial. When the jury was satisfied, she was asked to step down.

'Hades Division Agent Erron Christopher Grover, please approach the stand,' Osato called out, but Erron was too busy swapping quiet insults with Casey.

Osato cleared her throat, looking less than amused. 'Grover!' She raised her voice just enough that Erron jumped in his seat. 'Are you joining us today?' she asked, impatiently nodding towards the witness stand.

Erron stood apologetically and brushed down his court shawl, before sheepishly walking across the arena. He introduced himself, and presented his own opening statement, corroborating a lot of Nikita's evidence before explaining the elements of the investigation he was responsible for. Casey didn't want to admit it, but he hung on Erron's every word. Not because he was exceptionally professional, or overly eloquent, but because it was Erron, and his soft, Cupid heart melted every time he heard his voice.

Dr Enleigh's expression remained blank during the evidence, until Osato called one last witness.

'Our final word of this trial will be from Fortuna Division Head Emrys Taliesin.' Osato looked over her shoulder towards the outer corridors of the arena.

Nikita sat upright, having no idea Emrys was even well enough to go through the Elysion portals, let alone attend the trial. She'd only seen him at the hospital a matter of hours beforehand.

A nurse from the Raphael Sanctuary was slowly wheeling Emrys across the floor of the arena towards the witness stand. He was still visibly suffering, his amputated leg and multitude of bandaged wounds were loosely covered with a court shawl, but underneath he still wore a hospital gown.

The nurse parked the wheelchair next to the witness stand and stepped away. Emrys folded his hands together in his lap and looked up at Dr Enleigh, forcing himself to make eye contact with his tormentor.

Dr Enleigh's face flashed with a deep anger, before it settled to a simmering hatred as he glared back at Emrys.

'I only have two questions for you, Agent Taliesin,' Osato said gently. 'Is the defendant the man who caused you these severe injuries?'

Emrys didn't look away from Dr Enleigh when he answered, clearly and bluntly, 'Yes.'

'And as his surviving victim, what is the outcome you seek today?' Osato asked, poised for his answer.

There was a gravid pause in the air, as Emrys formed what he wanted to say. 'I'm not a vengeful man. A few days ago, I would have said I want Jared to be sent for judgement in the Oblivion Fields.' He glanced around at the jury and the seats of witnesses. 'But that was before I had to witness Ember's last moments.'

Emrys fixed his gaze back on Jared, watching his jaw flex with anger, his soulless eyes filled with perverse glee at what he'd done.

'Obliteration,' Emrys said firmly. 'May he feel the pain he inflicted on others, for eternity.'

* * *

The court was adjourned for a couple of hours while the sentence was agreed upon by the jurors and Nemesis panel of agents.

When everyone had returned and taken their seats, hushed mutterings circulated as Dr Enleigh was brought back in.

Erron, Casey, Nikita and Emrys had opted to grab some sub-par filter coffee at the closest café, which specialised in chargrilled goose and was aptly named To Grill a Mockingbird. They'd sat in silence for some time on a bench nearby, barely drinking their caffeine fix, all of them lost in their own thoughts about the trial. They returned just in time as Osato settled in her seat once more. Her voiced commanded attention, as she introduced the final verdict.

'We, the jury, have found Jared Enleigh guilty on all counts of murder and attempted murder in the first degree and have reached a verdict on the outcome of this trial. There has been a unanimous decision that the defendant will face Obliteration,' Osato stated loudly.

Dr Enleigh's eyes widened in horror, his mouth agape. Voices in the public galleries rose in debate, many of them not having existed long enough to ever see a sentence of Obliteration passed.

Nikita gripped Emrys's hand firmly and gave him a thin smile.

'Open the grate,' Osato boomed, calling forth two of her team to the circular vault-sized hole in the arena floor.

Nikita leant across to Erron and whispered, 'Are they actually obliterating him right now, like, this minute?'

'You're asking me like I know? Ask Casey, he's been here thousands of years, I've no idea how this works.' Erron shrugged and whispered to Casey next to him, 'Case, are they obliterating him now?'

'I guess so. I mean, I've never seen this done either. And I'm not thousands of years old, thanks.' Casey folded his arms and frowned.

The Nemesis agents unlocked the circular grate using two golden keys turned simultaneously. Low groaning sounds rumbled through the floor of the arena as the bars of the grate receded in different directions, revealing a solid door with a round central plate with three holes punched into it.

Osato rose from her seat and lifted from under the judge's bench a striking gold trident. She stepped down and approached the doorway, the trident giving her the air of an ancient goddess, her court robes flowing behind her.

She ordered her staff to bring Dr Enleigh to the doorway. He fought against them, throwing his weight to wriggle free, but was unable to escape the firm grip of their hands. He shouted, begged, cried and kicked out, all in vain.

'Please, I'm sorry, please, not this!' Dr Enleigh wailed, dragging his legs and crying so hard that his nose ran incessantly, snot streaking down his face and mingling with his tears. 'This is madness, you can't do this, you bitch!' he spat at Osato.

Osato raised one eyebrow, her lips pursed with internal rage. The embers in her wings ignited, sparking and curdling in her shadowy feathers. 'On his knees,' she instructed tensely.

Dr Enleigh was pushed down facing the door. Osato drove the trident down between his glowing Archangel wings, severing them with sharp blades which were hidden between the prongs. The wings tumbled to the floor to the sound of Jared screaming, blood cascading down the back of his robes. Unaffected by his pleas and cries of agony, Osato walked around him and pressed the prongs of the trident into the holes on the door, using it to turn the metal plate clockwise.

The door slowly rolled back, revealing a lightless void, with deep, ominous inhuman howls echoing in the darkness. The depth appeared infinite, and an overwhelming smell of decay and blood emanated from it.

Casey shuffled slightly closer to Erron, his stomach turning at the thought that not long ago, they both could have ended up being Obliterated for crimes they didn't commit. Erron looked at him with an unspoken understanding, feeling a little uncomfortable himself about watching the process.

'Any final comment, Jared?' Osato asked.

'Don't do this, just don't do this,' he murmured through snivels.

'It has already been done,' Osato replied before addressing the entire amphitheatre. 'Today we witness the first Obliteration in several hundred years. The accused, Jared Enleigh, has been stripped of his wings and that of his status as an agent. He faces the ultimate penalty for his crimes. Let those here bear witness to the consequences of the highest of indictable offences and may this never be repeated.'

Two court staff emerged from opposite outer corridors of the building, each wearing a large drum and beginning a slow beat as they converged into the centre of the arena. The hushed voices in the crowd died down as the low drumbeats increased in tempo and volume.

Dr Enleigh was pulled to his feet and his shackles were removed just as the drumming reached a crescendo, and Osato used the trident to forcefully thrust him into the void, the drums instantly falling quiet. His screams tore through the silence, echoing deeper into the abyss, until they faded into gurgling howls. His body was being eaten alive by the darkness, billions of carnivorous atoms crawling into his cells and shredding them to pieces, a process that would simultaneously break him down into cosmic molecules but keep him conscious for an unknown length of time, bound to the darkness and suffering until all he became was an agonised wail, doomed to repeat his torture for eternity.

Erron shrank down in his seat hearing the screams, closing his eyes and trying not to imagine it being Casey's cries in the dark.

The court fell eerily silent for some time, until the Obliteration portal was closed once more, the swell of conversation in the gallery breaking the tension in the arena.

'What time is the memorial for Ember?' Nikita asked quietly.

Erron checked his watch. 'I think it's at six p.m. Is that right, Case?'

'Yeah, we'll head over after this.' Casey was staring blankly across the arena, his mind elsewhere. 'It's being held at the Lake of Eternity. But I think she would have preferred her ashes to be spread over Dunstable Downs, if you ask me.'

'Where's that?' Nikita asked.

'It's near where she grew up.' Casey cleared his throat quietly. 'She once said to me that running across Dunstable Downs flying a kite was the closest feeling she had to heaven.' He squeezed his eyes shut in a futile attempt to hold in the emotion.

'Then let's do that for her,' Nikita suggested. She turned to Emrys, who had been busy listening to Osato wrap up the trial. 'Emrys, can Casey take Ember's ashes to Downstable Duns?'

'Dunstable Downs,' Casey corrected with a smile.

'What he said,' Nikita continued.

'Of course, you knew her best.' Emrys leant over and nodded at Casey. 'We'll hold the ceremony at the lake, but you can take her ashes to wherever you feel they will be at rest.'

'We'll have to attach them to a kite,' Erron added.

'Perfect.' Casey sat back, a sad smile on his face, relieved he would be giving Ember back to earth where she belonged.

# 31

## *Last Man Standing*

ERRON LAY AWAKE ON NIKITA'S sofa until the early hours of Saturday morning. He'd tried to sleep, but his mind was too busy with everything that had gone on, his impending return to Hades, and normality, on Monday morning.

At half past six, he relented and got up, softly padding to the kitchen in the hope of making a cup of tea without disturbing Nikita. He'd underestimated how persistently loud the kettle was, however, and found himself trying to suffocate it in a headlock with a tea towel to keep it from roaring.

'Two sugars, please.' Nikita appeared in her dressing gown, her hair a peacock tail of straggles that perfectly crowned her tired and bruised face. She wandered over to the kitchen area and leant on the counter as Erron handed her a freshly poured tea. His Hades wings had fully grown in, and their glossy black feathers refracted the golden light of sunrise with a prismatic sheen. The worst burns on the side of his neck were healing, leaving only some scarring on one ear and a few patches of singed hair that was slowly growing back.

'Sorry to wake you.' He poured himself a cup and stirred in several spoons of sugar.

'You didn't. I couldn't sleep either, lying on a pair of wings takes some getting used to.' Nikita held the mug poised under her chin. 'It's Saturday, isn't it?'

'It is indeed.'

Nikita glanced at the calendar on her wall. 'Oh.' Her face paled. 'Happy birthday! I'm so sorry I forgot.'

Erron looked around at the calendar as well. 'Ha, me too. Time flies when you're chasing killers.'

'Well, leave it with me. I'll make sure we mark the occasion.' Nikita took a sip of her tea, feeling the soothing warmth of it work its way into her system.

'You know what I'd like? Just a nice, quiet drink at Nightjar. No murders, no mind-control wigs, no geese, just . . . something normal.' Erron dunked a rich tea biscuit into his mug and cursed as half of it disintegrated, sinking to the bottom of the drink.

'Consider it done.' Nikita couldn't help but focus on the oldest scar on his cheek, knowing full well how he got it from her wander-around in his memories.

'I was thinking, I might go back to my place later. To actually try and sleep the night,' he said quietly, concentrating hard on fishing the soggy clumps of biscuit out of his tea with a spoon.

'You sure you're ready for that?' Nikita set her mug down.

'Nope,' he admitted. 'But I have to at least try.'

'How about we have a sleepover at yours, then, after Nightjar? And if you can't sleep we can stay up watching rubbish zombie films and work our way through a whole caterpillar cake until we both pass out from sugar overload?' She nudged him gently.

Erron laughed and glanced up from his tea. 'I love caterpillar cake.'

'Who doesn't? Get dressed and we'll go and choose one. My favourite is Cuthbert.'

'Don't let M&S hear you say that,' Erron teased.

Later that evening, Erron had bagged a corner table at Nightjar with a bench seat against the wall. Nikita shuffled in next to him and Casey perched on the wooden stool opposite. They were on their first drinks, going over the events of the case.

'You never said what your eureka moment was, Wolf.' Erron leant forward with both elbows on the table, a small tumbler of Kraken rum in one hand.

'It was the pen. Jared lent me it when we were sketching out the place he claimed he found Ember. It was a Formula 1 pen, but it was covered in the McLaren livery. The guy we arrested, Sam, was a Perez fan. Djinn had a collage of McLaren cars in the tattoo parlour. After connecting the dots it all started to make sense. Besides, I had a little help from a few cryptic ghosts. One, I strongly believe, might have been Gunther Hoffmann,' Nikita explained, sipping on the last dregs of a tall pineapple cocktail.

'What, Gunther Hoffmann, as in, our ballsed-up gold assignment Gunther Hoffmann?' Erron suddenly recalled the disturbing dream he'd had under anaesthetic during his wing removal. 'He was trying to tell me about the danger.' Gunther had been a prominent scientist, dead set on saving the world before he'd been caught up in the murderous dealings of Izzy and Kendra to unravel fate.

'Poor guy is still trying to help the world even after being murdered. Maybe he was really in your dream.' Casey shook his head sadly.

'Well, if the ghosts have been given a voice following the Great Goosening, then you never know, they might be a huge asset in future investigations,' Nikita reasoned.

'I'm not even going to think about future investigations.' Erron rolled his eyes. 'I am done with all the weird things in the cosmic web for a few days. I just want to get my afterlife back to normal again.'

'Well, just in case, I'm going to practise talking to them without drowning,' Nikita replied, grinning. 'Though I'm curious what else has changed since the near-apocalypse, especially if the ghosts are now making sense and mirrors everywhere have portal potential.'

'Curiosity killed the cat,' Erron grumbled. 'I'd rather put it all behind us now.'

'Well, here's to the first successful Medusa case.' Casey raised his milkshake – strawberry and kiwi, with white chocolate curls – for them to join him in a toast. 'But more importantly, the birthday of my closest friend in the whole aforementioned weird and wonderful cosmic web.'

Erron's smile was tinged with sadness as he raised his drink.

Nikita clinked her empty glass on theirs. 'I'm going up for another drink. You boys want anything?'

They both looked down at their almost-full glasses and shook their heads. She disappeared off to the bar, to wait in the queue that was at least eight people deep.

Casey seized the opportunity to swap seats and sit next to Erron on the bench. 'Good thing we didn't get Obliterated, eh?' He smiled warmly, stirring his milkshake with a neon green cocktail umbrella.

'Yeah, now I've seen it, I don't fancy it much.' Erron emptied his glass in three gulps, trying to wash away the sounds of Jared's screaming.

'It made me realise how close I got to losing you.' Casey stared at the mini umbrella, his eyebrows furrowing.

'Maybe it wouldn't have been a bad thing. You likely wouldn't have been Obliterated; you could have found someone that wasn't such a broken mess,' Erron said.

'Like who?' Casey's voice turned agitated, already sensing the answer.

'I dunno, someone like Warren Larkin. He could give you what I can't. I can't compete with a man like him, with all his charm and money and fancy clothes.' Erron swirled the empty glass around in his hand, watching the last drop of rum circle the bottom. He regretted saying it the moment it left his lips.

Casey rested his hand on top of Erron's, pushing the glass back down on the table firmly. 'Are you kidding me? Is that what you think of me? That I'd just be fine with that because you reckon I've got a backup plan? Do you really think me that shallow, that all I care about is money and fancy clothes?'

Erron met Casey's gaze, it was laced with hurt and disappointment. 'No, I ... I just mean—'

Nikita got back to the table, empty-handed, interrupting the conversation. 'I gave up at the bar I wasn't getting any further forward.' She slumped onto the wooden stool, deciding against mentioning the seat switch, when she picked up on the sudden change of atmosphere.

'Well, if it's OK with you both I am going to head home. I think everything's caught up with me.' Casey stood to leave.

'Oh,' Nikita said. 'You haven't even finished your weird milkshake?'

Casey gave her a terse smile and slid the drink over to her. 'You can finish it if you like. I'm shattered. I just need to get home.'

Nikita glanced between the two men. Erron was avoiding eye contact, and clearly something had been said between them. Casey put his favourite trilby on and was making his way through the crowd to the door when Nikita turned back to Erron.

He sat quiet as Nikita took a sip of the milkshake with a paper straw. 'What's that about, then?'

'Oh, I fucked up.' Erron rested his head in his hands.

'What's new, Grover.' She folded her arms. 'Well? Aren't you going to follow him, then?'

'Should I?'

'Get out of here. I'll see you later for caterpillar cake.' She shooed him away before settling in to finish the milkshake on her own. 'This is pretty good actually,' she muttered to herself, enjoying the odd combination of flavours.

* * *

Outside, Erron caught up with Casey two doors down from the bar.

'I don't think that of you, Case,' he said, exasperated. 'I just don't want you to feel stuck with me when I can't give you everything.'

Casey paused, staring at the floor.

Erron tugged at Casey's sleeve, pulling him round to face him. 'I say stupid shit, you know that. I'm sorry. I'm always bloody sorry. Don't you know how much this is eating me up inside, that you could do better and I'm just giving you the bare minimum right now? It breaks my heart that I'm your closest friend and nothing more, and I've only got myself to blame for that. I feel like I am stringing you along.'

Casey grabbed Erron's coat by the lapels and pushed him up against the wall, his face pinched in frustration. 'We talked about this! When are you going to realise that there's no one out there I want more than you? And before you say it, I know we're just friends, who occasionally on the spur of the moment might accidentally hold hands in a wig shop or kiss after a car chase. I've never asked more of you, and yes, I am still willing to wait, for however long it takes for you to be comfortable to be more than that. Even if you never are, I love you, Erron, for fuck's sake.'

Erron felt Casey's grip on his coat loosen. He lowered himself off his tiptoes and exhaled slowly. Casey's face softened and he tucked his hair behind his ears.

'Just because you think you're broken doesn't mean I believe you're less valuable,' Casey said quietly. 'You're my best friend. Regardless of whether I can kiss you or not.'

A moment of silence hung between them.

'You can.' Erron's voice was barely a trembling whisper. 'If you like.'

Casey leant one hand on the wall behind Erron and lifted his trilby off before leaning into the kiss.

Erron closed his eyes, his hands finding Casey's hips and pulling him closer, focusing on the sweet taste of strawberry-kiwi-chocolate milkshake on Casey's tongue, desperately trying to block out the internal voice that screamed at him to stop.

# Epilogue

ACROSS THE STREET, AS THE skies darkened over Shoreditch, a grizzled-face man with a crew cut was standing with a camera in one hand, a walkie-talkie in the other, blending into the shadows with his dark-green anorak and navy face mask. His left eye was white, blinded since birth; beside him sat a faithful German shepherd dog, one ear up, listening intently.

'I've got eyes on a Firefly Hotspot here. The place is lit up like a Christmas tree,' he hissed down the radio. 'It's called Nightjar.'

A crackling voice on the other end replied after a pause. 'Do we move in on the target location?'

The man in the anorak mentally tallied up the number of auras he could see before pressing the button on his radio. 'Not tonight. Add it to the list though. There's Greys here.'

'Received.'

The man tucked the radio in his pocket and raised the camera, snapping pictures of every person with a colourful aura hanging around the main door.

'Game over, Fireflies,' he muttered to himself against the repeated click of his camera shutter. 'Let there be no mercy for you.'

# Acknowledgements

Building on my acknowledgements from *Acts of Cupidity*, I want to reiterate my ultimate gratitude to everyone who has made this sequel possible. My fabulous and patient editor, Kelly, who I shall continually frustrate by using the word 'whilst' as often as I can get away with, and I also wish to note that I replaced the stolen Terry's Chocolate Orange in April 2025 as promised. Rianna, for stepping in on the editing for the final flourishes, and for letting me keep 'whilst' as well. Eleanor, the amazingly wonderful human being who has arranged numerous events for me to attend where very few people have even heard of me, but I feel incredibly important attending, I still owe you a goose. Nisha and Tamara, who have done all the clever publicity things behind the scenes, I will do my best to stop making garishly amateur videos on Instagram, but I can't promise anything.

Of course I absolutely need to mention my agent, Gyamfia, again, who is a sparkling diamond of a person, with more charisma and flair than I could ever hope to possess, and who continues to demand that I keep receipts for all my expenses despite the moral dilemma it has on my people-pleasing personality. She is just the best person, and I definitely encountered a Fortuna agent to land such high-end representation. I promise never to make you open gifts in front of me again if you let me take the FlixBus to London for my next event.

My next mention is the fantastic readers and supporters I have picked up from *Acts of Cupidity*, my Goose Crew, particularly Nabz, my first ever ARC reader who introduced me to the joy of the Croydon trams and started a craze of badly sewn geese. Aroosa, my fellow Verstappen fan, who is just the most delightful being and has shown me so much support overlaid with Checo stickers, you are simply lovely. Elisa, the most epic graphic designer and wholesome cheerleader of my daft books, I can't thank you enough for all the work you've put in to gift me a little more spotlight online. Sam, with your star-studded gravelly voiced witch impressions and first dibs on Emrys, you've been an amazing friend all round. To anyone I have not mentioned by name, who has read and loved my book, and taken the time to reach out, thank you eternally for your kind words, encouragement and willingness to come on this journey with me. For future readers, I have utmost appreciation for you choosing to read my books among the bazillion great stories out there, please don't be afraid to reach out to tell me your thoughts, unless you hate the book, then I'm perfectly OK with not knowing.

Special mention to Anca, you've taught me the joy of a Jar of Moles, and we will set up our Bee Cult when the world falls down. Never forget to Loogabarooga. You are the first to claim D-O-A, and he shall for ever be yours.

To the real Gertie the wig, with a lore spanning over twenty years with my best friends Jaime and Sarah, may your soul harvesting in Kettering be bountiful and your desire for power never cease.

Thank you to my sister, Emma (Ermin), who continues to glow in this dark world, you are truly a Casey Hart amongst the shadows, forever optimistic and never too far from a good loaf of bread. I hope in the afterlife, your soul will ride the waves of wild seas as mine chases fireflies on the shores, meeting every so often to talk over hot croissants at a café on the moon. There's so much magic in this world, and you're the fairy dust that makes it sparkle. To my brother, Paul, who promised to make a film with one faceless character who will always be in the background reading *Acts of Cupidity*, I won't forget this promise and will continue to pester you about it. Your beard is unruly but I am glad to be your sibling.

I must mention Noodle, for being my constant supporter, for all the low points and for sharing the highs, I need your encouragement to keep going, when the tides feel against me. As with all my family who have got behind me on this, thank you.

To Salem Saberhagen, my soul cat, and Shadow, the poor ancient spaniel that staggers around my house, I will never be ready for the day you go into the afterlife, but you better be waiting for me over there. Edit, you damn well left me before the copy-edit of this book, and my soul is broken, but I will see you again someday, you beautiful, perfect, daft dog.

And lastly, it wouldn't be right not to acknowledge some of my favourite things: Cuthbert the caterpillar cake, you did not deserve that court case; Terry's Chocolate Orange, I am your biggest fan but you never reply to me on social media. I understand as I am strange, but please can we be friends.

# *Fortune Favours the Grave* Chapter Playlist

As always, I would like to thank the music artists who have helped keep me sane through the endless edits and nights of writer's block. Your passion and lyrics paint the world with deeper meaning, bringing life to the scenes that play out in my head. I also got to see Nickelback live since my first book, and your songs resurrected my inner teenager, with more life than any reanimation chamber could. I thank you for being a small part of my emo angst all those years ago, though I neglected to name any chapters of this one after your songs.

Chapter 1 – Gold – *Imagine Dragons*
Chapter 2 – Hell on Me – *Johnny Huynh*
Chapter 3 – Nothing Breaks Like a Heart – *Damiano David*
Chapter 4 – Bulletproof – *Nate Smith*
Chapter 5 – Over the Rainbow – *Iz Kamakawiwoʻole*
Chapter 6 – My Immortal – *Evanescence*
Chapter 7 – Resurrect Me – *Skrizzly Adams*
Chapter 8 – Slow Hands – *Niall Horan*
Chapter 9 – Leave Out All the Rest – *Linkin Park*

Chapter 10 – Leave a Light On (Talk Away the Dark) – *Papa Roach*
Chapter 11 – It Is What It Is – *Abe Parker*
Chapter 12 – Traitor – *Livingston*
Chapter 13 – Strange and Beautiful – *Aqualung*
Chapter 14 – Hold the Line – *Toto*
Chapter 15 – Bad Habits – *Ed Sheeran*
Chapter 16 – Whataya Want from Me – *Adam Lambert*
Chapter 17 – Hold On – *Chord Overstreet*
Chapter 18 – Train Wreck – *James Arthur*
Chapter 19 – Devils Don't Fly – *Natalia Kills*
Chapter 20 – Treat You Better – *Shawn Mendes*
Chapter 21 – Saturn – *Sleeping At Last*
Chapter 22 – In the Stars – *Benson Boone*
Chapter 23 – Life Is a Lemon and I Want My Money Back – *Meatloaf*
Chapter 24 – 9 Crimes – *Damien Rice*
Chapter 25 – Ain't No Sunshine – *Bill Withers*
Chapter 26 – Lovely – *Billie Eilish*
Chapter 27 – Eyes Closed – *Imagine Dragons*
Chapter 28 – Crossfire – *Stephen*
Chapter 29 – Bloodshot – *Sam Tinnesz*
Chapter 30 – Outrunning Karma – *Alec Benjamin*
Chapter 31 – Last Man Standing – *Livingston*

**Keep reading for an exclusive first look at the next book in the Afterlife Agency Series**

***Karma Before the Storm***

**Coming soon**

# 1

## *Horns*

THE LEVELS OF EREBUS, KNOWN more commonly as Hell, were separated into three.

Level one was known as Diet Hell, named as it was believed to be the healthier, lower calorie version of damnation, with its own lava spa and weekly book club meetings which punctuated the discomfort and occasional light torture that was part of the package. Mandatory consumption of mint-choc-chip ice cream was a daily feature, and residents were forced to wear socks where one toe would always poke out of a carefully crafted hole for maximum discomfort. Populated by those on a light sentence, it housed mostly fraudsters, thieves and people who regularly demanded to speak to the manager.

Level two was just known as The Middle, closer to a realistic version of perdition, with its boiling sludge pits and compulsory, never-ending courses in parallel parking. It was mainly occupied by more serious offenders, murderers, arsonists, micromanagers and people who microwaved their cups of tea.

Level three was known as The Deep. The only place in the known cosmos where even mint-choc-chip ice cream wouldn't venture, housing the most vile souls for eternity. It was the realm of greedy billionaires, sex offenders, serial killers and fascists, many of whom fell into multiple categories.

Lounging in a dingy cell in vastness of The Middle, a teen girl had finished her eighteen-hour shift making thousands of googly eyes in the googly-eye factory, ready to be shipped out to the mortal realm. Due to her age she was only eligible for certain tortures, despite her crimes befitting a stint in The Deep, and most of her tasks centred around the craft zone of The Middle. She was exhausted and would only be afforded a two-hour sleep before her next assignment, which could range from anything between hand-cutting specks of glitter all day or making resin paperweights filled with dog turds from local hell hounds. The monotony and lack of rest were the most impactful elements of the craft zone, and after several months, its residents were reduced to empty vessels, attending their cubicles with a robotic inefficiency, eventually spiralling into a mental decline, where they were shipped off into another zone for reconditioning.

The girl turned her hands over and over in the gloom of her basic room. Her nails were chewed to ragged nubs, her skin filthy from no access to clean water, fingers dry and cracked from endless work. Hallways filled with Lego bricks gave residents constant foot sores, and her skin itched with the single item of clothing she was allotted: a coarse potato sack. The cell was no more than a crevice of rock, her bed a flat slate, warmed by the underfloor heating generated by the brimstone and fires of The Deep.

She'd spent her shift speaking quietly with another resident, Jeff. He was halfway through a hundred-year sentence and had been sent down to The Middle from Diet Hell, for the crime of clipping his toenails over the carpet in the lobby of the Erebus lava spa.

He'd told her of an interesting rumour: that there had been an energy shift in the cosmic web and the security of the interconnected realms was no longer as strong as it had been for aeons. Allegedly, Jeff had explained, an agent of Chaos had accidently made their way from the Chaos realm into The Deep by finding a newly opened portal.

No one had ever voluntarily made their way down to The Deep. It was a one-way street from which no one ever returned. But the prospect of escaping through a weakened portal was a tempting possibility.

'Lights on!' a scratchy voice announced in the halls outside the cells. It was one of the Hellkeeps, skeletal creatures with withered, pale skin, empty eye sockets and jaws of tiny, shark-like teeth. They shambled around the dark vastness of Hell wearing nothing but the ashes of Erebus and carrying their signature weapon, an iron morning star with a handle made of bone. On Tuesdays, however, they often switched this to a flail, just to be exuberant.

Bright, piercing overhead lights came on above the slate beds of the cells, leaving no space for shadows anywhere in the crevices. Inmates would be expected to sleep during lights-on time, as this was a special form of torture that could only be appreciated after several shifts in the craft zone.

The girl lay back on the uneven slate, closing her eyes to the overbearing glare of whiteness from above, silently plotting her way into The Deep. The unearthly scream of an iron whistle tore through the halls exactly two hours after the lights had gone on, signalling the start of a new shift. Jeff was on the same rota as the girl, and he shuffled into the new torture along with several hundred others, all dressed in matching potato sacks.

The craft for the day was assembling felt pom-poms by hand, fibre by fibre. They had a quota to fill, and the girl settled herself in a cubicle next to Jeff, so they could continue their discussions.

'So this new portal ... whereabouts is it?' the girl asked quietly.

'I wouldn't know. I've no intention of serving any time down there.' Jeff scratched at a welt on his head. He was almost as thin and pale as the Hellkeeps, though a scraggly brown beard and watery blue eyes still gave him a small element of humanity. His accent was hard to place, and the filth that clung to his skin highlighted the many age lines that crawled across his gaunt face.

'Do you think it's a genuine rumour? Don't portals need to be opened with blood to work?' the girl asked, throwing a furtive glance over at the nearest Hellkeep, who was too busy texting on an old Nokia 3310 to notice them talking. She watched its long bony fingers rhythmically tapping away at the keys, knowing full well it hadn't needed to charge the phone since 2001.

'Yeah, and we're all full of cosmic blood down here, it's how they keep us alive, immortal and suffering.' Jeff rolled his eyes. 'I overheard one of the Hellkeeps talking about evicting Chaos demons that have been sneaking through these last few weeks to steal some of the inmates of The Deep and taking them back to their realm as a snack.'

The girl's interest piqued. 'Is that so?'

'Straight from the zombie's mouth.' Jeff nodded towards the texting skeleton.

Chaos demons, entities that transcended the entire history of time, existed in their own realm, where their sole purpose was to cause acts of turmoil in the mortal realm. They couldn't access it in their true form, but had the agency to influence certain things, especially printers, which were one of their favourite methods of creating unnecessary stress each time they refused to print or jammed at a key moment. They desperately wanted to unravel the neatly stitched threads of the Fates and bring about chaos to every corner of the universe. They had almost succeeded several weeks prior, resulting in the weakening of the veil between all realms and the near sacrifice of two agents of the Fates.

'This sounds much more than a rumour then,' the girl whispered.

'Clearly there's a portal that's been opened between Erebus and the Chaos realm, but either way, I have no interest in trying to find it.' Jeff cursed under his breath as the pom-pom dropped a few carefully placed fibres.

'I'd give it a shot.'

Jeff looked up, his eyes wide. 'For what?'

'To get home.' The girl went back to her work as the Hellkeep finished his text conversation and glared across at them. 'I know for a fact the Chaos realm has portals that connect to the mortal realm, unlike here.'

'Madness. You might get stuck in The Deep,' Jeff muttered, dropping his gaze back to the desk covered in tiny green fibres. 'Plus, you're technically dead, you can't just go back to the land of the living.'

'There's only one way to find out. And Chaos can't be much worse than here, if I only get that far.' The girl was all too aware of how things worked in the afterlife. She'd had first-hand knowledge of all the places souls might end up, especially in service to the Fates, as she'd once been an agent herself.

'Why don't you just earn your way back up, like me?' Jeff reasoned quietly.

'I've got hundreds of years of this shit.' The girl looked down at her pale hands, the half-finished pom-pom silently mocking her between her thumb and forefinger.

'Suit yourself. But you go down to The Deep, you're never coming back up,' Jeff said.

'Talking is forbidden!' A rasping voice behind them made them both jump. The Hellkeep grabbed Jeff by the collar with one hand and dragged him away, the other hand gripping the handle of a swinging flail.

'Must be Tuesday,' the girl observed. She never saw Jeff again.

* * *

It was seven shifts later when she finally decided to investigate the rumour of the portals, having overheard more mutterings of panic in the underbelly of The Deep, due to so many of the residents going missing. Convinced they were either escaping through portals or being dragged to the Chaos realm, the girl had waited for the opportunity to slip out of her cell and find her way into the terrifying depths of Erebus, all with the hope she might make it home. Over the course of the week during lights-on time, she'd chipped away at a chunk of obsidian from the crystal-bead-making room, eventually forming a small, crudely shaped but razor-sharp dagger.

Her chance came when the whistle signalled the start of a new shift, and cell bars were opened for residents to shuffle down the halls of craggy red rock to their next extended session of menial torture. She knew there was a section of the wall where a small-framed person could just squeeze in between two outcrops of rock when the Hellkeeps weren't looking, and as she approached it, she slipped out of the edge of the human herd and pushed herself as far as she could into the crevice, exhaling every ounce of air in her lungs, to disappear from view. She'd used some thread from the sewing room to stitch a loop into her sack outfit, using it to hold the dagger safe from view and in easy reach.

The rhythmic pained shuffling of bare feet on the Lego brick floor continued for several minutes as the girl took shallow breaths, the edges of the rock jutting into her skin and snagging on the potato sack. The last Hellkeep bringing up the rear of the herd passed by, eventually leaving the dimly lit halls in silence.

With considerable effort, the girl scraped and wriggled her way back out of the crevice, staying as quiet as she could when leaving the craft zone. The Middle was made up of a labyrinth of halls and tunnels, different zones and endless rocky cells housing all manner of the damned. Those that refused to work, or were no longer able to, were condemned to languish in the rooms of fear, where a torment tailored from their most personal phobias took place, on repeat, until such a time they were deemed fit for release. The screams carried from these rooms echoed for miles, rooms filled with scuttling spiders, writhing snakes, teetering cliffs or the endless sound of someone chewing noisily. She passed zones of fast fashion, novelty Christmas gifts and single-use plastic before she reached any indication of the direction to The Deep. Jeff had mentioned that the only way to find the entrance was to follow the smell; the closer you got, the worse it became.

A distinct pungency was beginning to infiltrate the usual chargrilled ashy scent of The Middle, lingering in the direction of an unlit, narrow hall behind a glass booth set into the rock. A sign above the booth read THE DEEP – ADMISSIONS AND PROCESSING, behind the glass sat a large humanoid-looking creature, with no eye sockets in the usual place and a bony crown that protruded from its pale skull. Each point of the crown carried a singular, blinking eye of red, which matched the bloodstained nails on its long, angular fingers.

The girl had no intention of being seen by any official, let alone the ghastly creation that seemed to be checking a list on a clipboard, its red eyes moving in opposite directions as it read different lines at the same time. Settling onto her stomach, the girl shimmied her way over the coarse ground, which gave way to polished, igneous rock the further it got into the narrow lightless hall. She wriggled past the booth, using the smooth downward surface to glide along slowly in her sack suit, like a child going down a helter-skelter on a coir mat.

The dark intensified as the walls closed in, and the overpowering stench of hot dogshit was filling the heavy air, washing over the girl in warm currents from an unknown source. The tunnel got steeper, accelerating her into a fast slide, until she could no longer slow herself using her limbs. Panic rose in her gut as the speed increased, faster and faster, until she was almost pointing face down into the unknown. The rock underneath grew slimy, with claggy lumps of matter that were quickly coating her body. She gagged with the smell, unable to see the substance beneath her – she was moving too fast to have any hope of identifying it.

Without warning, she was launched into nothingness, a stomach-lurching descent into a hot, swirling lake of lumpy hellhound excrement. She went under by force, feeling the nausea rise in her throat as she clawed through the sickening gunk to find air, finally breaking free with a retching gasp. Flickers of light illuminated the cave she found herself in, sconces on the walls each holding a flaming torch, throwing dancing shadows around the black rock.

The cave seemed to have no exit, but as her eyes adjusted, she saw the tiniest break in the wall, a hole that might fail to tempt the hardiest cave explorers with its promise of adventure. Above her, the ledge from where she'd dropped was a staggering thirty feet in the air, with no way to climb back up. Reluctant, but determined, she began the slow and disgusting process of swimming her way through the porridge of shit until she reached the far side, pursing her lips tightly and trying hard to breathe only when necessary.

She examined the gap in the rock, trailing her hands all the way around it, reasoning with herself that it must be passable, for the residents of The Deep to reach their destination. Her stomach curdled as she took the decisive step to climb in head first, feeling her way into the pitch-black space, her arms outstretched, pulling herself into the slight, downward decline. The rock was not as smooth as the slide tunnel, but had the same igneous quality, rippled and cooled in an organic, meandering way.

She kept her breathing as slow and steady as she could, claustrophobia creeping in as the passage narrowed, squeezing and contorting her body at every opportunity, pushing her into shapes that crushed and scraped her, with no light to follow and no hint of an end. She wondered if that was what the inmates in The Deep were condemned to, worming their way through an endless Tartarus of crushing cave tunnels, with no end in sight and no possible way to turn back.

Hours passed, hours of fighting for every inch of space in the suffocating darkness. Heat rose from further down the tunnel, acrid sulphur burning her nose and stealing the air from her pressured lungs. The tunnel tightened, a vice where every movement was a coordinated endeavour of every muscle, calculated and minuscule as her progress slowed to an almost stop. She gasped and clawed for air, tears tracking lines on the dried filth on her face, her skin raw with the effort.

Just as she was about to give up, the smallest glimmer of light appeared at the end of the tunnel. It rolled and cavorted the way a wildfire would crackle across open land. Fire. Hellfire.

She pushed on through, a hundred more metres of crushing agony until the heat of the flames singed her hair and smoke filled her lungs. To exit the tunnel, she had to wriggle through a blazing hoop. With no way to turn back, she pulled the sacking up over her nose and mouth and pushed forward, screaming through the burns as she heaved her way out, the fire licking her skin and catching the sacking ablaze as she dropped into another pit filled with lemon juice. It found its way into every scrape, burn and cut on her body, piercing her with a thousand zesty knives, but cleansing her of the grime and detritus of her journey.

Crying in pain, she fought her way out of the pit, pulling herself free in a room carved out of solidified lava, where a clerk sat at a desk made of black marble, accented with gold leaf and topped with a lamp forged from a human skull. Piles of coals littered the floor, some aglow with fire, others cooling in a red, ashen hue. Behind the clerk was a low turnstile of brass which led onto a platform of dark concrete, with grubby white tiles lining a train tunnel that led deeper into the gloom.

The desk clerk appeared ethereal, ageless, with white hair swept back in a ponytail, a sharp jawline, dark eyebrows and exceptional dress sense. A brass plaque on the desk announced him as Kevin.

'You got your ID?' Kevin asked, raising an eyebrow. 'You seem a little too young to be down here.' His tone was delicate, well-spoken and a touch playful.

'Since when do souls have ID?' the girl replied, still crouched at the side of the lemon juice pool and taking deep breaths of the slightly cleaner air.

'Your branding. You should have got that at the entrance desk.' Kevin nodded towards her wrist, and she instinctively tucked her arms behind her back.

'Um, they forgot that bit.'

Kevin rolled his eyes dramatically before lifting a heavy binder from a drawer and dropping it with a *thud* onto the desk. 'We'll have to find your record manually then. So, what'll it be? Delight me with the nature of your most evil transgressions.' He flicked through a few pages and pulled a small pair of gold-framed glasses from the pocket of his superbly tailored blazer, setting them on the bridge of his nose. 'Name first, crime second.'

'Actually, do you mind if I just take a look around before we do the formalities?' the girl asked, pulling herself to stand.

'Impossible. The only way out of this room is on the train, and I need to know your stop.' Kevin glanced over the top of the gold frames and gestured towards a charcoal-coloured map on the wall.

The girl stepped closer to the map and looked at the route of the Helltrain. Its stops were categorised by crimes, and the track seemed to go in a constant loop, with a timetable of completing the circuit every hour. A tiny outline of an orange glowing train moved around the map in real time, showing it approaching them within a matter of minutes.

'Umm. I'll be in the serial killer zone then,' she murmured.

'How many victims?' Kevin moved his gaze back down at the pages.

'Almost two.'

Kevin glanced back up, furrowing the skin on his near-perfect brow. 'Almost isn't enough. What's your name?'

As he spoke, the distant squeal and roar of a train barrelling through the depths of Hell grew closer.

'Hurry up now, or I'm stuck with you for another hour if you miss the train.' Kevin's voice took on a subtle tone of annoyance.

Past the turnstile, a snort of flames and ash suffocated the tunnel, and the Helltrain pulled up. Its iron frame dripped with scorching embers, huge spoked wheels hissed on the tracks as the whistle of a thousand screaming souls announced its arrival. Lanterns that bubbled and burst with neon green flames marked every carriage, the glass of the windows melted and oozed down the crusted grey doors. No driver sat up front; at least, none that could be seen. The carriages were all empty, awaiting the new arrivals that had crawled their way through the bowels of hell, eager to take them to their eternal damnation.

'Name, please! Make it snappy!' Kevin barked as he checked the train was still stationary.

The whistle squealed once more, a high-pitched wailing of lost voices, as the wheels started to turn. Bellows of steam poured from beneath the belly of the train, and the flames grappled at the walls of its confinement.

'It's, umm . . .' The girl eyed the platform, decisively launching herself towards the turnstile and vaulting over it before Kevin could stand.

She grabbed the rusted handle of one carriage door, yelping in pain at the immediate searing of her flesh, but nonetheless flung it open and leapt in, just as the train accelerated away into the aether.

Inside the carriage, the floors were nothing but iron bars, a grill pan for the damned, painfully hot to the touch and precarious to walk on. The girl's feet sizzled as she hopped back and forth, trying desperately to reach one of the charred wooden seats. The jolt of the track sent her crashing into one, and she clung to the crumbling armrest to steady herself. The seats were warm, much like sitting in a plastic chair on a hot summer's day, her sweat clinging to the bubbled varnish, but far more comfortable than any of the iron surroundings.

The Helltrain screamed onward, lighting the tunnels with its fire and brimstone, careening around corners, its wheels lifting off the tracks and slamming back down on the straights. The girl tried to remember the different stops, strategically planning the safest option for her to alight. She settled on the Billionaire Zone, where she assumed malice and greed ran amok, and the punishments would be befitting of the crime.